Iris Costello is the pseudonym of bestselling author Nuala Ellwood. She has a BA Hons degree in Sociology from Durham University and a Master's in Creative Writing from York St John University, where she is a visiting lecturer. She is the author of eight highly acclaimed novels, the most recent of which was *The Story Collector*. *The Paris Bookshop Secret* is her ninth book.

THE PARIS
BOOKSHOP
SECRET

IRIS COSTELLO

PENGUIN BOOKS

PENGUIN BOOKS

UK | USA | Canada | Ireland | Australia
India | New Zealand | South Africa

Penguin Books is part of the Penguin Random House group of companies
whose addresses can be found at global.penguinrandomhouse.com

Penguin Random House UK,
One Embassy Gardens, 8 Viaduct Gardens, London SW11 7BW

penguin.co.uk

Penguin
Random House
UK

First published 2025
002

Set in 12.5/14.75 pt Garamond MT
Typeset by Falcon Oast Graphic Art Ltd
Printed and bound in Great Britain by Clays Ltd, Elcograf S.p.A.

The authorized representative in the EEA is Penguin Random House Ireland,
Morrison Chambers, 32 Nassau Street, Dublin D02 YH68

A CIP catalogue record for this book is available from the British Library

ISBN: 978–1–405–97461–5

Penguin Random House is committed to a sustainable future
for our business, our readers and our planet. This book is made from
Forest Stewardship Council® certified paper.

For Nerina

'I love her, and that's the beginning and end of everything.'

F. Scott Fitzgerald

Prologue

Latin Quarter, Paris

July 1960

The night air was ripe with the scent of blooming jasmine and the smoke of Gitanes cigarettes as William Kenneally made his way down rue de la Bûcherie towards the book-shop. Beside him, his friend's hand fell perilously close to his, so close he could feel the heat seeping from it. Sam was chancing his luck as always, but this time William didn't feel the need to bat him away. In a matter of hours, he would be with her, the girl of his dreams, the love he had spent a life-time searching for, and they would be setting out on a great adventure, perhaps the greatest either of them had ever known. Just thinking of her brought about an incredible sense of goodwill. The way she looked at him with those deep blue eyes, making him feel as though she could see inside his soul, the softness of her arms, the place where William felt safest, the soothing lilt of her voice speaking of distant shores. Perhaps one day he would be able to find the words to write of their great love story. He hoped so. But that was all for the future. Right now he was happy in the knowledge that they would soon be together. Knowing that, he felt little need to remonstrate with Sam and his advances. It didn't matter any more. None of it did.

'Shall I stay over at the bookshop tonight, William?' said Sam with a wink as they reached the corner of the street, the hulking shadow of Notre-Dame looming from across the water.

William smiled and took out a Gitanes from his top pocket.

'I wouldn't recommend it,' he said, placing the cigarette between his lips. 'It's a full house. Looks like I'll be hunkering down on the sofa in Old Smoky alongside that new fella, Allen, the poet, who's taken residence in the big old armchair. And if Paula's to be believed he's a frightful snorer.'

'Don't tell me George has given away your bed again,' laughed Sam. 'I thought you were set for the summer.'

'You know how it is,' said William, patting down his pockets in search of a lighter. 'He always says I can stay but then a pretty little Italian student arrives with a sob story about having to write a thesis on Edith Wharton and no place to stay and it's "sofa for Mr Kenneally". At least until Miss *Age of Innocence* moves on.'

He looked up at Sam, hoping that the story was convincing enough. He had promised Blythe that he wouldn't tell a soul what they had planned. They were just to disappear. No tearful goodbyes, no awkward explanations. They couldn't leave a trace, even with his dearest friends. William felt wretched for lying to Sam, for leaving without saying goodbye, but there was no other choice, it had to be this way.

'Ah, that's too bad,' said Sam, striking a match and leaning in to light William's cigarette. 'Say, we could always go to my place. I've a bottle of bourbon that needs drinking and a new chapbook that could benefit from your expert appraisal. But remember, if old Ma Tournier is still awake, you're my brother, got it?'

'Ah, that sounds grand,' said William, his heart pulsating at the thought of the morning to come, the moment when he would take Blythe's hand and board that train. This was it, the future he had dreamed of. It was so close he could taste it. 'But I've had a week of double shifts at the bar and I'm dog-tired. The sofa is calling my name.'

'Another time then,' said Sam, looking at him in that intense fashion that always made William feel uncomfortable. Did he sense what was going on? thought William, averting his eyes from Sam's gaze. Did he know he was being lied to?

'Another time,' William replied, guilt churning his stomach as he threw his cigarette to the ground and stubbed it with his foot.

What happened next felt like an absinthe dream.

He had bid farewell in the European fashion, a peck on each cheek, but as he went to pull away Sam grabbed his shoulders. Next thing Sam was kissing him passionately on the mouth; the scent of beer and cigarettes almost made William gag, but he was frozen, trapped in his friend's forceful embrace.

Then, suddenly, there was a flash of light. Stunned, Sam staggered backwards, releasing William from his grip. The flash came again, accompanied by a distinctive clicking sound.

William, temporarily blinded by the light, heard Sam mutter an expletive. He blinked but all he could see were white dots dancing before his eyes, all he could hear was the sound of Sam's footsteps clattering across the cobblestones.

'Sam,' he cried, staggering into the middle of the deserted street. 'Don't run away. Come back, will you?'

It was then that he saw the figure, standing on the pavement behind a row of Vespa scooters, holding a camera. Click, click, click. Each one accompanied by a flash of light.

'Hey, stop that,' cried William, charging towards the person. 'You've no right to be taking my picture. Quit it, you hear me?'

The figure lowered the camera and looked directly into William's eyes, and in that moment the young man's blood froze as he realized who it was.

'What . . . what are you doing here?' he stammered. The light from the street lamp illuminated the photographer's face, the haughty expression, the thin-pursed mouth, the ice-cold eyes. 'Why did you take those pictures and . . .'

He let the sentence hang as the perilousness of his situation began to dawn. There was nothing else for it, he would have to run.

'It's too late, William,' the photographer cried after him, menacingly. The voice was one of power and privilege, of money and corruption. 'You can't undo this. You're dead, now, you hear me? Dead.'

PART ONE

I

ALEXIS

Kent

March 2025

'Another false lead,' I sigh as I walk away from the gates. Climbing reluctantly back into my camper van, I cross Lustrum Manor off my list. Fifteen months after embarking on my quest, I am still no closer to solving the mystery of my mother's whereabouts or uncovering the secret of why she left us.

It has been over thirty-six years since that fateful Christmas Day when she climbed into her sunshine-yellow VW camper van and drove away from me and Dad, and yet it is only now – after leaving my own seemingly happy life and setting out on the road in an ancient but dependable camper van that is a near replica of my mother's – that I am finally trying to confront the past. I'd found her diary when clearing out my dad's house after his death. It was in a pile of her keepsakes and had been written during the year she disappeared. Since its discovery, I have become consumed with thoughts of my mother, my sole surviving parent and my only living blood relative. Dad's parents died before I was born. Mum's, in their late forties when they had her, passed away when I was a toddler. A blessing, I suppose, that, unlike me and Dad, they never lived to experience the pain of losing their daughter, the not knowing what became of her. If she's still alive, she'll be turning sixty-four this spring, and yet, in my head, she is still the young woman who left that day. And though I've lived more years without my mother than with her, the diary has helped me connect to her again. I've spent hours poring over its pages, hearing her voice in my head as I desperately search for clues and prep for the next destination. I thought Lustrum Manor had been it but now, as I tuck my dog-eared list of dead ends back into the diary, I resign myself to the fact that I am back at square one.

It was a TV programme that had given me the idea. Two nights ago, parked up in the van, I had curled up to watch one of those family history shows on my iPad. The ones where celebrities investigate their ancestry. I was half watching, my mind drifting to earlier that day and yet another fruitless search. I'd spent the morning tracking down and then meeting a reiki teacher named Kimberly Harper in Andover who I'd found on Instagram and who, with her tie-dyed skirts and posts extolling the virtues of holistic living, appeared to tick every box until I turned up to meet her and found that she had been born and raised in Hampshire and had never left her small village in fifty years. Another dead end, another blow. As the programme played out, I asked myself how long I could carry on with this quest, how many disappointments I could take. But then my attention was caught by something on the screen: the celebrity, a soap star I didn't recognize, was reading through an online census. 'If anything can help me find where my great-grandad was in 1911,' he grinned at the camera, 'it's this.' I spent the rest of the evening signing up to an ancestry site and paying for premium access that would allow me to search my mother's name on the census records. It took me until the early hours of the morning, squinting at the screen with tired eyes, but as the sun rose, I had a date, 21 March 2021, and an address, Lustrum Manor, Kent.

This was it, I told myself, as I hurtled down the motorway the following afternoon. I was finally going to find my mother. Then, after catching up on some sleep in the back of the van on the Sussex/Kent border, I set off early this morning for Lustrum Manor.

When I first arrived, I thought I'd read Google Maps wrong. The location it had directed me to looked like deserted farmland. Only as I drove closer did I see a set of heavy metal gates, a rusted sign hanging from the hinges. Parking the van at the side of the road, I made my way to the gates and saw, to my relief, the name *Lustrum Manor* engraved on the sign in copperplate lettering. To the right of this was an intercom with a buzzer. I pressed it and waited, my stomach fizzing with nerves and anticipation.

'How can I help you?'

The voice, male and rather abrupt, crackled out into the chill air.

'Oh, hi,' I said, my voice catching in my throat, nerves getting the better of me. 'I was wondering if you might be able to help. I'm looking for my mother and I've been informed that she was living here in 2021. Her name is Kimberly. Kimberly Harper?'

There was a long pause on the other side and for a moment I feared the intercom connection had cut out.

'Hello?' I said loudly. 'Are you still there?'

'You must be mistaken,' said the man. 'There's no one of that name living here.'

I opened my mouth to reply but was met with a sharp buzzing noise, signalling that the man had ended the call. With a heavy heart, I returned to the van and picked up my mother's diary.

According to this, I have one last lead to follow. I read her final entry dated *Christmas Eve 1988*, the day before she left. *I don't know who I am any more*, she writes, in faded black biro. *Everything I thought was real was just a lie. Maybe if I can find them then I can put myself back together again, fix what is broken inside me. Maybe if I can get away from here, head to my soul's home, then everything will be all right.* The words sting just as much as they did when I first read them. To think that my mother had felt so hopeless, so broken that she would up and leave her husband and child like that, without warning or explanation. But who was she trying to find? And where was the soul's home she was heading for? A physical place? Or – and this is something I really do not want to entertain – somewhere beyond this mortal coil?

These thoughts whirl around my head as I drive away from Lustrum Manor and head for the coast. I'll park the van up by the sea tonight, let the waves soothe me to sleep, then in the morning I will work out what to do next. After all, as I keep reminding myself, I no longer have a busy work schedule to stick to, a nine-to-five job restraining my movement. Like my mother, I am as free as a bird, and I will find her, whatever it takes.

It's a beautifully sunny day and I decide to take the scenic route to the coast, detouring from the motorway and its endless traffic queues. In my old life, I would be chairing the morning meeting right now, anxiety welling up inside me as I nodded my agreement to every request, my lifelong fear of delegation pressing on my shoulders as I punched dates and times into my burgeoning spreadsheet, wiping out evenings and weekends and quality time with my wife, and filling them with urgent edits, Zoom meetings with the New York office, replying to emails from an inbox that never seemed to deplete. Thank God that's all behind me, I think, as I catch a glimpse of myself in the rear-view mirror. My skin, once grey from the daily interminable Tube journeys, face pressed against strangers' sweaty backs, is now clear and glowing, my eyes that developed heavy bags from squinting at a screen for twelve hours a day are now twinkling and bright. And though I spend my days driving a battered old camper van I have not succumbed to slobbing it in hoodies and joggers, preferring to stick to my favourite classic vintage attire which today includes a pair of Chanel cigarette pants, black vintage Miu Miu pumps and my beloved red Bella Freud 1970 sweater. When I set off on this journey, I truly thought that I was broken. But bit by bit I am putting myself back together again and a huge part of that is the search to find my mother. I should have done this a long time ago instead of burying my pain in work.

I realize now that, much as I loved it, my high-flying job as senior editor of a big five publishing house took so much out of me, not least the ability to read for pleasure, though I am hoping to remedy this. I glance at the book on the passenger seat beside me and smile. I'd found my old *Time Traveller's Journey* paperbacks in my childhood bedroom when I cleared out the house, and they have stayed with me all through this trip. One day, when the fog clears, I will be able to read them again and feel the magic ripple through me just as it did all those years ago. Written by the literary megastar of the eighties Maeve O'Malley, each instalment of the series took the young reader on a whirlwind tour of a particular period of history in Paris, from the court of Louis the Sun King to the bloody days of the Revolution and the headiness of the Belle Époque. Those stories had not only ignited my love of reading when I discovered them as an abandoned seven-year-old, they had also taken me away from the real world with all its confusion and sadness and transported me to a time and place where anything was possible. When I saw *The Time Traveller's Journey to Belle Époque Paris*, starring the bold and glamorous historical sleuth Darcy Diamond – the woman I wanted to be when I grew up – while sitting in my dad's cleared-out house that day almost forty years later, it felt as though Maeve O'Malley and her fantastical story was soothing my sadness all over again. I remember the look on my mother's face when I opened it that Christmas morning, the happiness in her eyes as I whooped with delight, though as far as I was concerned it was Santa and not my parents who had left the book in my stocking. 'It has a funny picture inside,' I said, opening the book to show my mother the strange but beautiful black-and-white stamp on the title page. 'That's because it came from a special bookshop,' she told me. 'One that only Santa Claus knows about. Perhaps one day you will get to go there yourself.' I remember so little about that day, pain and grief serving to block out most of it, yet that exchange with my mother, the sadness in her voice as she told me about the bookshop, has stayed with me all these years, seared on my heart, a scar that won't heal.

Suddenly, my phone starts buzzing in the holder next to me. I glance at the name on the screen. Tara. My stomach flutters with a mix of excitement and trepidation. I go to answer it, then stop myself. One step at a time, Alexis. But I make a silent promise to call her once I'm at the coast, happily chilled with a glass of wine in my hand as the sun sets. I think back to our honeymoon in Venice, sitting on the terrace of our hotel, a glorious seventeenth-century palazzo, wrapped in each other's arms as we watched the sun go down, Tara's beautiful face glowing in the golden light.

'I want us to always be together at sunset,' she'd whispered, as the day faded into night. 'Does that sound silly?'

'No,' I'd replied. 'It sounds perfect. And I promise you, darling, whether in person or not, however long we have left on this earth, I will make sure we're always together at sundown.'

But I didn't keep the promise. A ripple of sadness passes through me as I think of all those sunsets we have missed this past year, and I vow that I will make it up to her.

Dumping the call, I turn my attention back to the road but am startled to see a figure standing right in the middle of it. I stamp on the brakes, praying that they don't fail, my heart lurching inside my chest. Thankfully, the ancient brakes still have life in them, and I grind to a screeching halt just inches from the person, who is standing frozen to the spot.

With trembling hands, I manage to switch off the engine and jump out of the van.

'I could have killed you,' I cry, staggering towards the person who, I now see, is an elderly woman. 'Why are you standing in the road like this?'

The woman, who has long, straggly white hair, is barefoot and dressed in a rather grubby white towelling robe. She trembles as I take her arm and guide her to the van.

'Come and sit down for a moment,' I tell her, my nerves subsiding as I open the passenger door and attempt to guide her into the front seat. 'Catch your breath. You must have had an awful shock.'

She looks up at me, her face etched with confusion, and mutters something under her breath.

'I'm sorry, I didn't catch that,' I say, leaning closer to her as a lorry rushes by. 'What did you say?'

'I said I have to find him,' she whispers, in a voice that is oddly familiar. 'I have to find William.'

2

ALEXIS

When I finally get the woman settled in the van, throwing my Maeve O'Malley book and my mother's diary onto the dashboard, her agitation seems to dissipate, and she sits in silence, gripping the seat belt to her chest.

'Now, if you tell me where you live, I can drive you home,' I say, starting up the engine which sounds alarmingly croaky. We appear to be just outside a village called Haughton. 'It must be near here.'

I turn to the woman. She is staring straight ahead. If I couldn't see her chest rising and falling, I would think she were dead. Her skin is pale and paper thin, her lank, shoulder-length white hair looks like it hasn't been washed in weeks, and her dressing gown is stained and grubby. A sour smell emanates from her, like spoiled milk.

'Can you at least tell me your name?' I ask gently. 'That would be really helpful.'

The woman turns to me, opens her mouth to speak, then stops. Her face looks stricken.

'I . . . I'm ever so sorry,' she says, her strikingly blue eyes welling up. 'But my mind's gone blank. I . . . I need a drink.'

She puts a hand to her forehead and closes her eyes, her breath shallow and laboured.

'Here,' I say, reaching into the back of the van where I keep a crate of bottled water. I grab one, screw open the lid and hand it to her. 'Have this. Sip it slowly.'

She takes the bottle with trembling hands and as I watch her drink I am again struck by how familiar she seems. I have seen her before, I'm sure of it, though I have no idea where or when.

'Thank you,' she says, when she has finished. 'I needed that. But I . . . I still don't know where I am. I . . . I'm sorry.'

'You don't have to apologize,' I say, placing the lid back on the bottle. 'Speaking as someone who's the wrong side of forty I know all about brain fog.'

I let out an awkward laugh, but she doesn't respond.

'Listen, how about we drive into the village,' I say, aware of the time and the fact that I had wanted to get to the coast to watch the sunset and return Tara's call. 'See if that triggers your memory. If you spot your house just shout, OK?'

The woman nods her head, then closes her eyes. After a few moments she starts to snore gently. I put my foot down and head into the village. There is a central square with empty flower beds and a flagpole. The tatty Union Jack on top flutters limply in the breeze. Around the square sit various rather down-at-heel shops including a butcher's, a wool shop, and a large, double-fronted chemist with an old-fashioned red apothecary bottle in the window. It's like stepping inside my 1980s childhood in suburban Newcastle upon Tyne. No wonder this old lady is lost.

'Do you recognize anything?' I say, as we drive slowly past the shops. 'Anything familiar?'

'It's the village,' she whispers, breathlessly. 'But . . . what are we doing here?'

Up ahead I see a Sainsbury's Local. There's a woman in an orange tabard standing outside smoking a cigarette. Perhaps she knows who this lady is. I pull up outside and wind my window down.

'Excuse me?' I call out.

The woman looks up in alarm and throws her cigarette to the ground, then places her hand to her chest.

'Sorry,' she says, as she approaches the window. 'I thought you were my boss. She gets ever so prickly about us taking ciggy breaks. Crikey, look at that lovely old camper van. We don't see many of those round here. Are you lost?'

'Well, one of us is,' I say, gesturing to the old woman who is still gripping the seat belt for dear life.

'I found her standing in the middle of the road just outside the village,' I say, turning back to the shop assistant. 'I've tried asking her name but she's very confused. I don't suppose you . . .'

'Oh, that's Mrs Hardy,' says the woman, raising her eyebrows in surprise. 'She's . . . well, she's not been herself lately. She lives up at the old manor house. It's about five minutes' drive north of the village, up the steep hill. You can't miss it.'

The woman, who introduces herself as Linda, gives me directions and as I take note, I realize that the place she's describing is Lustrum Manor, where I had stopped earlier. Mrs Hardy must have been walking for over half an hour by the time I found her.

Thanking Linda, I drive out of the village, back up along the hilly road we came in on. As we reach Lustrum Manor I see that the gates, which had been closed when I spoke to the man on the intercom, are wide open. Pulling through them and up the tree-lined drive, I see what is hidden behind those high imposing gates and let out a gasp.

'My goodness, Mrs Hardy,' I say, as the van bumps over the heavily gravelled driveway. 'What an amazing home you have.'

Beside me the old lady wakes from snoozing, looks up, then sighs forlornly.

The house, if you can call it that, is a medieval moated manor with black timbers, mullioned windows and, to my delight, a drawbridge.

'We'll have to park up here and walk the rest of the way. Can you manage?' I ask, switching off the engine before undoing Mrs Hardy's seat belt. 'This hulking van will never get over that bridge.'

I jump out, my feet sinking into the gravel, and go round to the passenger side, but as I try to get Mrs Hardy down from the van, she grips the dashboard, shaking her head violently.

'It's OK, Mrs Hardy, you're home now,' I say gently. 'Let's get you inside into the warm. I bet you're gasping for a nice cup of tea.'

But the old woman will not budge. Defeated, I close the door and make my way towards the grand entrance to the manor.

What is this place? I wonder to myself, as I cross the wooden drawbridge and gaze down into the green, chalky water that looms up from the moat below. It's like something from a Grimm's fairy tale.

'Can I help you?'

A man has emerged from the back of the house and is striding towards me across the cobbled courtyard. He looks to be in his mid- to late sixties. With his salt-and-pepper beard, side-parted, neatly cut hair, creased moss-green cords and tweed jacket he reminds me of the older dons I encountered at Oxford, those who seemed to have been pickled in aspic circa 1940 and remained unchanged for ever more. I recognize the plummy voice I heard over the intercom less than an hour ago.

'Oh,' he snaps. 'I remember your face from the entrance camera. As I told you before, you're in the wrong place. Now, if you don't mind, I'd like you to leave. This is private property.'

'Hi, yes, it's me again,' I say, feeling rather awkward. 'Alexis Harper? Look, I've not come to bother you, it's just that I have Mrs Hardy in my van. I found her wandering down the road outside the village.'

'Good grief,' he says, rushing towards me, his previous hostility giving way to concern. 'We've been worried sick. Is she all right? She wasn't hurt, was she?'

'Thankfully not,' I say, as we hurry across the draw-bridge. 'Though she does seem very confused. She was asking for you, I think. I'm assuming you're William.'

He stops and looks at me, his expression pained.

'Are you sure that's what she said?'

'Yes,' I reply tentatively. 'She was very clear.'

'Oh, dear God, not again. I thought we'd got beyond all that,' he whispers to himself. 'I'm her husband, Professor Hardy.'

'Her husband?' I say, somewhat taken aback. Despite his rather fusty appearance he is a good deal younger than the hunched old lady in my van. 'I . . . I didn't realize.'

'Yes,' he says, his face etched with worry. 'I'd only turned my back to make her a cup of tea and then . . . then I couldn't find her. Ms Harper, I'm so very sorry you've had to come all the way back here.'

When we reach the van Mrs Hardy is sitting motionless, staring straight ahead.

'My darling,' cries the man, pulling the door open. 'Thank God you're safe.'

Then, with the gentlest of touches, he lifts his wife out of the van.

'We were so worried,' he says, removing his jacket and placing it over her shoulders. 'If you needed anything from the village you only had to ask. Come on now, let's get you inside. I've a big pot of soup bubbling on the range. Leek and potato, your favourite.'

He goes to guide her towards the manor, but she halts and turns to me with a fraught expression.

'You'll come too,' she says, her eyes boring into me. It is more of a command than a question.

'Oh, I imagine we've inconvenienced Ms Harper enough today,' says Professor Hardy. 'I *am* sorry I couldn't help with your search, my dear. Would you like a cup of tea before you go? It's the least we can do after all your help.'

'That's very kind,' I say, glancing at my watch. 'But I'll have to get going. I'm on my way to the coast and want to get there before dark.'

'Of course,' says the man, with a weary smile. 'I'm so sorry if my wife has delayed you.'

I look again at the woman and a memory comes to me with a start. A hand grasping mine, a pair of dazzling blue eyes looking up at me, a soothing voice whispering, 'Well done, my dear.' I can't place the memory or quite match it with the bedraggled woman standing in front of me. But as I look at her and she stares back at me with those strange, intense eyes something compels me to stay.

'On second thoughts, Professor Hardy, a quick cup of tea would be great.'

'Oh, marvellous,' says the man, putting his arm round his wife's shoulders and leading her towards the draw-bridge. 'We'll take tea in the orangery. It's this way. And please, do call me Jasper. May I call you Alexis?'

I nod and he leads us across the bridge before taking a right turn through a black-timbered archway.

'This is the gate tower,' he says, his voice echoing against the ancient walls. 'It's where the knights would enter back in the Middle Ages.'

'You're telling me this house is as old as that?' I say, as we enter another courtyard which is surrounded on every side by tiny, mullioned windows. I sense movement behind one of them and look up just in time to see a shadow pass across the glass. Unnerved, I run to catch up with the Hardys who are waiting on the threshold of a huge oak doorway.

'In answer to your question,' says Jasper, 'the oldest part of the house dates back to 1290, so, yes, it is as old as that.'

While Jasper fumbles with the door latch, my imagin-ation carries me away and I see knights clad in heavy armour riding in through the gateway in the early-morning mist, weary from battle.

A shiver ripples through me. There is something unfath-omably strange about this place that I can't quite articulate. It is a feeling more than anything else, a sensation of stale air, of time literally standing still. Perhaps it is the same in all old houses though, I think to myself, as Jasper opens the door and I follow them both inside.

'My goodness,' I exclaim, as we enter a magnificent stone-floored hallway, its walls adorned with faded tapestries depicting hunting scenes and jousting knights. A wood fire blazes in a vast fireplace and the air smells of smoke and beeswax. 'What an incredible place to live.'

'We're both big history buffs, my wife and I,' explains Jasper. 'Aren't we, dear?'

Beside him, Mrs Hardy lets out a faint sigh and pulls her husband's jacket more tightly around her. She looks exhausted.

'Come on, my love. We'll soon have you settled,' says Jasper, gripping her hand. 'This is the great hall, Alexis. The oldest section of the house. Back in the day, this would have played host to magnificent feasts and celebrations. I sometimes think I can hear laughter and lute music when I'm walking through here late at night, though of course it's just my mind playing tricks.'

'That's understandable,' I say, as I narrowly avoid colliding with a taxidermized wild boar, its mouth wide open, razor-sharp teeth bared. 'I feel like I've fallen through time.'

But he doesn't hear me. He is already leading his wife down the long, narrow corridor that leads out from the great hall. Though it is still daytime outside, this part of the house is dark, save for the sickly yellow glow of the oil lamps that are mounted here and there along the panelled walls. I wonder at the effort to light them all. It is beginning to feel rather claustrophobic, so I am relieved when we reach the end of the corridor and step into glorious light.

'This second entrance hall connects us to the newer part

of the house,' says Jasper, glancing at me over his shoulder. 'Built by the Lustrums in 1750. The orangery is just off here.'

I gaze upwards as we cross the hall. Sunlight pours in from the domed glass ceiling, illuminating the chequered floor tiles, the highly polished mahogany staircase, and the elaborate silver-framed mirror that fills an entire wall. It is truly spectacular.

'Here we are,' says Jasper, opening an ornately carved wooden door. 'Do go through.'

The orangery is far less elaborate than the other spaces, more homely. With its glass ceiling and doors opening out onto the courtyard, it feels light, airy and fresh, and for the first time since I arrived here, I allow myself to breathe out. There are two sunken, floral-patterned sofas, faded by the sun, and either side of the glass doors, two beautiful wing armchairs in plush crimson velvet. It reminds me of my own home, the one I left behind. My chest tightens as I recall those lazy Sunday afternoons in our more modern conservatory. Tara stretched out on the sofa while I sat beside her with the *Sunday Times* laid out across my lap, marking off that week's bestselling books with my trusty red pen. But that was another life, I think to myself, blinking away the memory as Jasper closes the door behind us with a thud.

'Now, my darling,' he says to Mrs Hardy, leading her to the chair by the window. 'Let's get you comfortable.'

As I watch him tenderly tucking a thick herringbone knitted blanket around her before kissing her forehead, I think to myself how lucky they are, to have made it to that age and still be devoted to one another. I think of Tara that final, bitter day last January, the look of bewilderment etched across her face. It was the same expression my father had when we stood watching my mother's camper van pull out of the drive, never to be seen again. I had promised myself I would never be like my mother, never inflict pain on another human being in that way and yet here I am repeating that history. I'd told Tara I'd only be gone a month or so but it has already been over a year.

'Now, do make yourself comfortable, Alexis,' says Jasper, his soft voice replacing the harsh one inside my head. I look up and see that he is gesturing to the armchair opposite Mrs Hardy. 'I'll go and put the kettle on. Oh, sorry, I didn't ask – how do you like your tea?'

I am about to answer when a woman appears in the doorway. She seems only a little older than me and is wearing a red polo-neck jumper under a belted camel coat. Her blonde hair is tied back in a tight bun which gives her attractive face a rather startled, stretched expression.

'The wanderer returns,' she says, stepping into the room. 'Where have you been this time, Mrs Hardy?'

'Cordelia, there you are,' says Jasper, rushing to the woman's side. 'She didn't get far, thank goodness. This is Alexis. She found her on the road and brought her back. Alexis, this is Cordelia, our housekeeper and all-round superwoman.'

'Well, I don't know about superwoman, but I'm definitely kept on my toes here,' she says with a laugh. 'Nice to meet you, Alexis. And thank you for helping her. That was very kind of you.'

'It was the least I could do,' I say, glancing at Mrs Hardy who is sitting rigid in the chair, her eyes fixed on the floor.

'It's a busy road. God knows what might have happened if I hadn't seen her.'

'I was just about to make tea, Cordelia,' says Jasper wearily. 'Will you join us?'

'I'd love to but I'm due at the chemist for my afternoon shift. I'm going to need you to sign these too,' she says, passing Jasper what looks like a pile of prescriptions. 'For the pills. Mrs Hardy's going to need them to get through the night.'

'Yes, yes, of course,' says Jasper anxiously. 'I'll do it immediately.'

'And don't you think we should get her to bed after all that walking?' says Cordelia, lowering her voice. 'She'll be stiff as a board if she stays in that chair.'

'Oh, gosh, yes,' says Jasper, flustered. 'What was I thinking.'

'Listen, I'd better be going after all,' I say, getting up from the armchair. 'Leave you to get Mrs Hardy settled.'

'Are you sure, dear?' says Jasper, turning to me. 'I was about to make tea.'

'I'm sure,' I say, hooking my bag across my chest. 'I'm just glad to have got your wife safely back home.'

'And for that I am eternally grateful,' he says. 'Are you able to make your own way back across the courtyard?'

'Of course,' I say. 'It was nice to meet you all.'

'You too, Alexis,' he says, as he ushers me to the door. 'Safe travels.'

'Goodbye, Mrs Hardy,' I say, turning back.

The old lady lifts her head and smiles.

'Goodbye, dear,' she says. 'And mind you don't scuff those beautiful shoes on the gravel. I must say, it's been nice to have a bit of glamour about the place, if only for a short time.'

'Come now,' says Cordelia, frowning at Mrs Hardy's slight. 'Let's get you upstairs.'

As I make my way out into the courtyard, I reflect on what has just happened, still half wondering if it was all a dream. I had felt such a strange connection to Mrs Hardy, like I had known her all my life. Anyway, back to business, I tell myself, as I climb into the van and put the keys in the ignition. An hour's drive to the coast. More than enough time before the sun sets.

But as I try to turn the engine on, nothing happens. I wait and do it again, praying for the familiar bluster as my old van splutters into life, but there is nothing. I try a third time, then a fourth, before finally acknowledging with a sickening dread that, for the first time in fifteen months, I am going nowhere.

3

ALEXIS

'How much?' I ask the man in the oily blue overalls. 'Just tell me how much?'

I am standing in the forecourt of Dawson's Motor Repair Workshop in Haughton village, waiting for Ken, the mechanic, to deliver his prognosis. Though if his strained expression is anything to go by it is not good news.

'To fix it?'

'Yes, to fix it.'

'In my experience,' he says, with a sigh, 'you'd get more from scrapping it.'

'Scrapping is not an option,' I say, folding my arms across my chest. 'This is a vintage gem. There must be some other way.'

'Well, we can do the work, love,' says the man, his tone softening. 'But it's going to come in at around three grand for the engine and gearbox repairs, and that's before we deal with the issue of the rust and water damage.'

'Three grand?' I cry, a lump settling in my throat. 'That's . . . that's impossible.'

For the old me, £3,000 would have been nothing. It was a new handbag or a long weekend in Rome, paid and sorted with a flick of my Amex card. But now things are different. When I left my job I was given three months' worth of salary and untaken holiday pay. But, setting out on this quest to find my mother, I have had to factor in petrol, food, campsite fees as well as paying my share of the mortgage and, not wanting to ask Tara for help, what was left of my money soon dried up. Unable to face returning to the publishing industry after what I did, I have had no option but to take on menial, practical work, living hand to mouth while I focus on finding my mother. It hasn't been ideal, but I could do it because I knew, whatever happened, I had a roof over my head. Never, in this fifteen months of what some would think of as madness, have I factored in the possibility of losing my van, the indomitable old brute that had already seen out four decades by the time I bought him. I think of my mother driving me to school in her identical camper van when I was a kid, blasting out her favourite band, Fleetwood Mac, from the open windows. But it's my late dad's voice I hear in my head, as I stand watching Ken tot up the repairs on his computer. 'You're forty-four years old, Alexis. Aren't you a bit old for all this now? I get it. You were burnt out but you've made your point. Time to face up to what happened and get back to the real world.'

Impossible, I think to myself, as the man prints off the estimate and hands it to me. Even if I wanted to, I cannot go back now. It's too late.

'Do whatever needs to be done,' I say, folding the slip and putting it in the back pocket of my jeans. 'I'll get the money. Just fix my van, I beg you.'

'I'll need you to pay a deposit before we start work on it,' he says, his eyes narrowing.

'A deposit?'

'Standard practice,' he says sternly. 'This work will have

28

to be scheduled in and will likely take at least a week or two to complete. We'll have parts to order from overseas and that, to be honest, could take even longer. Though I may have a few replacement ones to hand, I'll have a look.'

'A week or two? But this van is my home, I . . . Look, how much is the deposit?'

'Five hundred plus VAT.'

'Give me a sec,' I say, pulling out my phone and taking it to the sparsely furnished reception area. Sitting down, I log into my online bank account. The balance is £750. Shit. I try to gather my thoughts. If I pay this deposit, I'll be left with around a hundred quid plus whatever loose change I have in my various pockets and no van. No home. One hundred pounds might get me a couple of nights in a hostel but then what? Ken said the work could take up to two weeks, maybe longer. I think back to a few hours earlier when I had been merrily coasting along towards Lustrum Manor, Fleetwood Mac's 'Gypsy' blaring out, my head consumed with the possibility of finding my mother. Now all I seem to have found is trouble.

'Well then, what will it be?' says Ken, coming over to where I am sitting.

I look up at him, terror and panic pulsing in my chest. What to do?

'I'm only asking as we're closing in ten minutes,' he says, gesturing to the classroom-style clock on the wall above the vending machine. It is almost four o'clock. I should have been well on my way to the coast by now.

'I'll pay the deposit,' I say, gulping down my fear. 'But, please, can you promise me you'll get him fixed quickly? Like I said, he's not just a van. He's my home. My family.'

I whisper this last bit to myself as Ken strides over to the counter and bashes numbers into the till.

'Cash or card?' he says, not looking up as I join him.

Call them, a voice inside my head screams at me. Just swallow your pride and call Scion, beg and plead for your job back, and stop this nonsense once and for all. But then I think back to October 2023, the breakdown that led to the big mistake, the one that cost me my job. I remember what preceded it: the night terrors, the incessant crying, the anxiety that gripped me day after interminable day. I can't go back to that. I'll find a way to get the rest of the money. There is always a way.

'Card,' I say, pulling out my wallet.

'Whenever you're ready,' says Ken, gesturing to the card reader. 'Check the amount and tap here.'

I do what he says and as the receipt slowly curls out of the slot I feel my insides turn to slush while the reality of my situation starts to sink in.

'Right, Alexis . . .' I whisper to myself, as Ken lets me grab some clothes, toiletries and paperwork from the van before showing me out. 'Think!'

'All sorted?' Jasper's face is full of concern as I climb into the passenger seat of his battered old Jaguar. When my van wouldn't start, I had run back over the drawbridge, hammered on the door of Lustrum Manor and begged Jasper to tow me to the nearest garage. He had looked at me as though I had just asked him to man a rocket ship to space. Luckily, Cordelia had a tow rope and between the three of us we managed to get the van attached to Jasper's car. While Cordelia headed to the chemist, leaving Mrs Hardy asleep in bed, Jasper drove me to his local repair shop, the van hulking heavily in our wake. He'd already very kindly offered me a bed for the night while the van was fixed.

'It's not good news, I'm afraid,' I say, trying my best not to cry and make a fool of myself in front of this complete, though well-meaning, stranger. 'In fact, it's an absolute bloody shitshow.'

As the tears I've been desperately trying to hold back start to flow, I tell Jasper the whole story, the extent of the damage, the fact that the van is my only home, the dire state of my bank balance, and how I must now conjure up £3,000 from somewhere.

'Oh dear,' says Jasper, taking a packet of tissues from the glove compartment and handing them to me. 'That's rotten luck.'

'The whole point of the van was to streamline my life,' I say, dabbing my eyes. 'To get away from all the stress, try to find my mother, and now it seems I'm back where I started.'

'I can empathize with you on that one,' he says, sighing deeply. 'Though, in my case, it's going to take more than a camper van to solve the problem.'

He turns to me and smiles sadly.

'My wife is not well,' he says, his voice cracking. 'It's becoming increasingly clear. I'd put it down to fatigue at first but she's just becoming more and more erratic. Today's events confirmed it for me. Something is wrong with her.'

'Oh, Jasper, I'm so sorry,' I say, recalling Mrs Hardy's agitated state when I first encountered her. 'That must be worrying for you.'

'More than you can ever imagine,' he replies. 'The cruelty

of it all is that my wife had a remarkable mind. To see her in this state is just heartbreaking. But I'm her husband. On our wedding day, I vowed to love and to cherish her and that's what I will do. To the end.'

'I can't begin to imagine how that must feel,' I say, my stomach knotting as I remember my own vows. How easily I had broken them. 'Though it sounds like the two of you have an unshakeable bond.'

'We do,' says Jasper, sadly. 'But the stark fact is it's bloody hard. Particularly trying to juggle caring for her and my work. Not to mention looking after the manor. I suppose I should be retiring at my age, but I have no choice but to keep at it. Granted, as an academic specializing in military history I'm not exactly working down a coal mine, but I do have deadlines to meet, papers to mark and a book to finish. Bringing in specialist carers would be rather tricky on my professor's salary. We have Cordelia to help with the running of the house, but she's only part-time. She has to work three days a week at the chemist to make ends meet. So you see, the buck rather stops with me.'

I nod my head sympathetically, feeling for Jasper and his plight.

'I really appreciate you putting me up for the night, what with everything going on. I'll figure something out and be on my way first thing tomorrow.'

I turn and look out the window. The March sky is already darkening as we return to Lustrum Manor. Beside me, Jasper starts talking about the messy first draft he is working on and how he is dreading having to edit it.

And then it hits me. The solution to my problem.

4

ALEXIS

I am just unpacking the meagre contents of my rucksack in the tiny, beamed bedroom I have been allocated for the night at the far end of the east wing, when I feel a presence behind me. I turn and see Mrs Hardy standing in the doorway. Her white hair hangs limply round her shoulders, her skin has a sickly yellow pallor, and she has swapped the dressing gown for an equally grubby-looking brown linen dress that hangs from her thin frame like a loose sack.

'Hello there,' I say, self-consciously removing a pile of underwear from the rucksack. 'I hope you don't mind but I'm going to stay here tonight. My van broke down and I had to leave it at Dawson's garage.'

'Poor you,' she says, closing the door behind her. 'Your lovely van. I do hope they can get it fixed. I'm sure they will. Ken's a very capable chap. You know it's strange, but your face is so familiar.'

She comes over to the ottoman, puts my clothes to one side, and sits down.

'Where might I have seen you before?' she says, her eyes narrowing as she sizes me up.

'Well, you saw me this afternoon, Mrs Hardy,' I say cautiously. 'I was the lady who brought you home.'

'I know you were!' she snaps, shaking her head. 'I'm not

an imbecile. I mean before today. We've met before, I'm sure of it.'

I am about to respond when Jasper pops his head round the door.

'Ah, darling, you're up,' he says, smiling at Mrs Hardy. 'I've been looking all over for you. Supper is ready. I've made shepherd's pie and there's enough to feed an army. I hope you're hungry, Alexis.'

He glances at me, then his face falls.

'Oh, you're not veggie, are you?' he says, alarmed. 'I forgot to ask, though I'm sure there'll be something in the fridge we can rustle up. Cordelia got the big shop at Waitrose yesterday so there's plenty in.'

'Jasper, do stop fussing,' says Mrs Hardy, getting to her feet. 'And may I ask why we need Cordelia to go shopping for us when you know I am quite capable of walking to the village and choosing my own food.'

'Cordelia is our housekeeper, darling,' says Jasper, with a sigh. 'Grocery shopping is part of her remit. Besides, you've always found grocery shopping an awful bore.'

'True,' says Mrs Hardy, her lips pursing. 'But that is beside the point. I will not have you and Cordelia treating me like an invalid.'

'Shepherd's pie sounds great, Jasper,' I say, keen to avert a couple's spat. 'Let me come and help set the table.'

He smiles at me, the relief palpable in his face.

'Thank you, Alexis,' he says. 'I'll lead the way.'

The dining room is located in the heart of the west wing, the second-oldest part of the house, and is suitably grand. One wall, painted a deep green, is dominated by a vast charcoal drawing depicting a lone figure sitting outside a café, the words *Deux Magots* etched in spidery handwriting on the awning above her head. It makes me think of my old life, the long lunches with French clients, the sense of wonder as I signed deals in the very spot where Hemingway and Fitzgerald and Stein once sat to write their novels, the absolute joy I garnered from pursuing the career of my dreams.

'Do take a seat, Alexis,' says Jasper, gesturing to the linen-draped dining table. 'And help yourself to the pie. We don't stand on ceremony in this house.'

Mrs Hardy is already seated at the top of the table, her pale face glowing in the soft candlelight. She regards me curiously as she sips water from a glass goblet.

'There are peas in the tureen and gravy in the boat,' says Jasper, taking a bottle of red wine from the sideboard. 'Some claret?'

'Oh, thank you,' I reply. 'Just a little.'

I watch as he pours the wine, then serves Mrs Hardy her pie and peas. By the time he takes his place at the other end of the table, his face is red and flustered.

'Right, dig in,' he says, tucking a napkin into the neck of his sweater. 'Good health.'

As we eat, with me sitting between the Hardys like an overgrown child, I feel Mrs Hardy's eyes upon me. Jasper fills in the silences, sharing village gossip and telling me about the history of the house, how it was used as a base during the Civil War when Oliver Cromwell himself was said to have stayed the night.

'Perhaps dining in this very room,' he says excitedly, taking a bread roll from the basket and mopping up the meaty gravy from his plate. 'Imagine.'

'I don't know why anybody would be impressed by that,' says Mrs Hardy, placing her cutlery down, her food barely touched. 'Cromwell was a brute, a monstrous man. How he treated the Irish was nothing short of genocide. Don't you agree, Alexis?'

'I'm afraid I don't know very much about him,' I say, my cheeks flushing from the wine and the intensity of Mrs Hardy's gaze.

'Who's for pudding?' says Jasper, getting to his feet suddenly. 'There's some crumble left over from last night. I could warm it up with a bit of custard.'

'From Cromwell to custard,' says Mrs Hardy, shaking her head. 'What a segue.'

'Nothing for me, thank you,' I say, suddenly feeling seven years old again, sitting at my parents' table, waiting for it all to blow up. 'That pie was delicious but so filling.'

Jasper smiles politely as he takes my plate though his left eye is twitching. Mrs Hardy watches him as he stacks the dishes on the sideboard and refills her goblet with water from the glass jug.

'Perhaps I can help you,' I say, mustering up the courage to suggest my only plan for getting my van back.

Jasper turns quizzically to me.

'With your work,' I continue. 'You mentioned in the car earlier you have a first draft that needs honing. Well, I have a solid background in editing and administration. If you need an assistant to lighten the load for a few weeks until Mrs Hardy gets back on her feet?'

He looks at me for a moment, his eyes narrowed, as though weighing me up.

'I have excellent references and am fully DBS checked,' I

reassure him. 'But I completely understand if you'd rather not. After all, you've only just met me and . . .'

Jasper remains momentarily stunned and I worry I've offended him in some way.

'That's a wonderful idea,' interjects Mrs Hardy, brightening. 'You've been trying to finish that darn book for ages, darling, haven't you? And of course I know what a burden I've been.' She looks at her husband encouragingly.

'Well, I can't see why not,' Jasper relents. 'We'd have to discuss the logistics, of course, draw up a contract. For my peace of mind and yours, you understand.'

'Absolutely,' I say, relief flooding through me.

'Well then, Ms Harper,' he says, extending his hand. 'If you're quite sure, I think we have ourselves a deal. Shall we meet in my study at nine tomorrow morning to . . . to discuss the itinerary?'

'Yes,' I say brightly, keen to use the early start as an excuse to leave the table and head to bed. 'That would be great. I'm looking forward to it.'

'I'm glad,' says Jasper, draining his glass of wine. 'Oh, here's Cordelia. My dear, you look exhausted. Long day?'

I look up as the housekeeper enters, clutching a paper bag with the name of the village pharmacy printed on it in bright green lettering.

'Something like that,' she says, sighing heavily. 'I managed to get the prescription though, which is great.'

'I've told you I don't need it,' says Mrs Hardy, flashing a cold stare at Cordelia. 'This morning was just a blip. I was . . . I was just overstimulated, that's all.'

'Darling, please,' says Jasper, his cheeks flushing. 'The only reason you're calm and lucid right now is because of

37

your tablets. You know fine well that today's meltdown was because you skipped your dose.'

'Do you know what it's like to be treated like a baby, Alexis?' says Mrs Hardy, her voice ice cold. 'I am of perfectly sound mind and yet still these two insist on talking to me like an imbecile. In my own home.'

'I'm sorry,' says Cordelia, placing the bag onto the table. 'But I haven't the energy for this. I've had the day from hell, and I need to get some sleep.'

'Yes, of course,' says Jasper, taking a box from the bag and popping out two pills. 'You head up to bed. I'll come and make sure the oil lamps are lit up there. Now, my dear, take these and make sure you drink plenty of water with them.'

He hands Mrs Hardy the tablets before accompanying Cordelia out of the room.

'I'm so sorry,' I hear him mutter to her as he closes the door behind him. 'I know how exhausting this is for you.'

'I'm not ill,' says Mrs Hardy, shaking her head as she regards the pills in her palm. 'I'm just old. Old people get forgetful, don't they?'

She looks up at me and for the first time this evening she seems fragile. Gone is the bravado she had displayed to Jasper and Cordelia and in its place is a scared little girl. But then her expression changes, her eyes brighten, and she smiles mischievously. With the pills still in her hands, she gets up from the table and throws them into the fire.

'You see,' she says, turning to me and shrugging. 'Old people get forgetful.'

And with that, she sweeps out of the room, closing the door behind her.

I am still thinking of that moment, the look on Mrs Hardy's face when she leapt up from the table, as I lie in bed hours later. What am I doing in this house, with these people I barely know, one of whom is clearly unwell? I suddenly feel desperately alone. Taking my phone from the side I click on Tara's number. Agonizingly, it goes straight to voicemail. 'Hey, it's me,' I say, trying to curb my emotions. 'Sorry I missed your call earlier. You'll never believe where I've ended up. Give me a bell when you can . . . I miss you.' Ringing off, I turn on my side and wrap my arms around the soft pillow, imagining that it is Tara. I close my eyes and feel the warmth of her naked body next to mine, her distinctive scent of orange blossom, sugar and freshly laundered cotton sheets, the ease with which we fitted together.

I am just falling down a rabbit hole of heady memories when the door opens, and a figure enters the room. My hands trembling, I switch on the bedside lamp.

'Don't scream, it's only me.'

Mrs Hardy is standing at the foot of the bed, clutching a large Moleskine notebook. Her hair is matted to her face, and she is wearing the grubby white dressing gown from earlier tied tightly at the waist. Her eyes have a manic look about them and I am wondering if she is in the grip of another episode like the one I witnessed this afternoon.

'Mrs Hardy, you gave me a fright,' I say, blinking blearily into the light. 'Is everything OK?'

'Everything is fine,' she says exuberantly. 'And, yes, you can help me. Now, pop this on and follow me.'

She picks up my Bella Freud sweater from the ottoman and hands it to me.

'Follow you where?' I say, scrambling out of the bed. 'It's the middle of the night.'

'I know, dear,' she says, as I pull my sweater over my white cotton pyjamas. 'The best time for it. Nice and peaceful. Come on, now.'

'Where are we going?' I ask, as we stumble into the darkened corridor.

'We're going somewhere only very few people are granted access to,' she says, turning to me with a grin. 'We've got a very important task ahead of us.'

'We have?'

'Yes,' she says, taking my arm and leaning her head onto my shoulder. 'You see, my dear, you are going to help me find William.'

5

ALEXIS

There are moments in life when you cross from one state of being to another, when you know that nothing will ever be the same again, and this was one of them. For in the time it took for Mrs Hardy to lead me down the stairs, across the west wing of Lustrum Manor to a vast mezzanine and into the room we are standing in now, whatever assumptions I had harboured about this fragile old lady had been completely blown apart. Mrs Hardy had smiled at me as she opened the door and, when we stepped inside, I saw my whole life flash in front of me.

'You'll have to excuse the clutter, dear,' she had said, as she strode into the room, oblivious to my shock. 'But then I've always worked best in chaos. Oh, there you are, Daphne. I wondered where you'd got to.'

A sleek tabby cat looked up at us from the window seat, blinking drowsily into the light.

'She's my little darling,' said Mrs Hardy, rushing over to the cat. 'Rescued from the streets of Hampstead when she was a kitten and named after Daphne du Maurier, one of my heroes.'

Now, while she fusses over Daphne, I stand motionless, taking in every little detail, still not quite able to believe what I am seeing.

The room is filled, floor to ceiling, with bulging book-shelves, and is dominated by a huge desk covered in papers, more books, pots of ink and a beautifully ornate Anglepoise lamp. But it is the framed photo on the wall behind the desk that my eye is fixed on, the image I saw when I walked in the room, that caused my whole body to tremble in disbelief. It is a photo of a woman of around my age, sitting on a sofa with Michael Parkinson, the chat-show host. It is a still from a programme that I had watched dozens of times the year my mother left. I had taped it on our old VHS machine and watched, on a loop, as my idol – the woman whose words had soothed and com-forted me, whose stories had transported me from the fear and sadness of real life into a world of magic and mystery – regaled Parky and the audience with anecdotes from her writing life. The woman is holding a book in her hands as she beams into the camera, its title bursting forth in black and gold lettering: *The Time Traveller's Journey to Belle Époque Paris*. The book I had escaped into time and again in the weeks and months following my mother's disap-pearance and the one I have been carrying around with me this past year. But that woman with her trademark black bobbed hair and red lipstick, her dazzling smile and glam-orous gold dress, couldn't possibly be the one standing in front of me now, the elderly Mrs Hardy with her crooked gait and trembling hands.

'Is everything all right, Alexis?' says Mrs Hardy, leaving the cat and coming over to where I am standing. She places her hand on my arm. 'You look like you've seen a ghost.'

And as I turn and gaze into her face I see, beyond the pasty, wrinkled skin, the shrivelled features, the rheumy eyes, just that. The ghost of what had once been one of the most celebrated and prolific authors of the last forty years.

'You're . . . you're Maeve O'Malley?' I stutter, my eyes filling with tears. 'I can't believe it.'

'Why, I thought you knew,' she replies, with a sweep of her hand as she walks across to sit at her desk, a minimalist, mid-century beauty I would have died for in my old life. 'I saw my book in your van earlier and just assumed you'd recognized me. Surely I haven't changed that much, have I?'

She gestures to the photo above the desk and a look of sadness flashes across her eyes.

'My God, this is just too incredible for words,' I say, desperately trying to keep my excitable inner child at bay. 'I have a million questions. I mean, first of all, where have you been all these years? You were the most acclaimed writer of your generation. You were everywhere and then . . .'

I pause, remembering my professional restraint. Calm down, Alexis, I tell myself, as Maeve shifts uneasily in her seat. Remember who you are. You've dealt with people of Maeve O'Malley's status all your working life and never once lost your cool. And yet, the child inside me knows that was all just a front, a shield I built to protect myself. Now, standing here, let loose in what can only be described as a writerly palace of dreams, I feel a happiness I haven't known in years.

'I'm so sorry,' I say, taking a seat at the other side of Maeve's desk and noticing to my delight a glass display cabinet behind her, filled with first editions of the *Time Traveller* books. 'It's just that, well, you were my favourite author when I was growing up. More than that, really. You were the person who made me fall in love with books and stories, made me want to spend my life surrounded by them.'

'Gosh, what praise,' says Maeve, with a kind smile. 'You know, it still astounds me that anyone reads my books. But I suppose that's the writer's mind for you. We spend the majority of our lives hidden away in our rooms battling with characters who refuse to play ball and plot points that refuse to come unstuck and then, suddenly, as if by magic, it all comes together and someone, somewhere, walks into a bookshop or a library, takes down your book from the shelf and embarks on a journey to a place that thus far only existed in the writer's head. If that isn't magic, then I don't know what is.'

She looks up at me and it's all I can do not to weep for she has just encapsulated my career. I put those books on the shelves, I played a part in that magic and then . . . then I ruined everything.

'You understand, I can see that,' she says, handing me a tissue from the box on the desk.

And as I take it, I notice the ruby ring on her middle finger, an art deco beauty surrounded by diamonds, and I'm transported back to 2017, some eight years ago. That glitzy party, the night I had the world at my feet, or so it seemed. And Maeve up there on the stage, the ring glistening in the spotlights. I'd tried to talk to her, but someone whisked her away. I wonder if she remembers.

'I saw you, years ago,' I say, remembering my award, how proud I felt, the sense of acceptance and belonging before I blew it all with one stupid mistake. 'In London. It felt like you disappeared after that, and you haven't published anything since. What happened?'

'It's good to hear you're familiar with my books,' she says, her back stiffening as she pointedly ignores my question. 'I suppose that can only be a good thing.'

'Forgive me,' I say, rising to my feet. 'I've overstepped the mark. I'd better head back to bed. I have an early start with Jasper tomorrow.'

'Sleep can wait,' says Maeve, her expression softening. 'I told you. We need to find William and that is what we're going to do. Now sit down.'

Like a reprimanded schoolchild, I do as she says, but as I watch her place her spectacles on her nose and open her tattered Moleskine notebook, I feel my heart sink. What had I been thinking, letting my childish excitement cloud the fact that Mrs Hardy – Maeve O'Malley – is not a well woman? Goodness, I had listened to poor Jasper describe his frustration and exhaustion from caring for her, seen the despair on his face. Now, I am going behind his back and might very well be aiding his wife's delusions.

'Mrs Hardy, it's late,' I say, as she flicks through the pages of the notebook, her head darting from side to side like a bird in search of a worm. 'You really should get some rest. Jasper will be worried.'

She lets out a snort and continues to skim the notebook, her forehead furrowing. Is this another episode? I think to myself. Have I done the right thing in letting her bring me in here when really I should have summoned Jasper, told him that she had thrown her medicine in the fire and that she was wandering the house in the middle of the night? And yet she appears to be perfectly lucid, for now at least.

'I was interested to hear you had publishing experience,' she says, looking up from the book. 'Editing, you said?'

'Yes,' I reply, desperate to blurt out, in this hallowed place, just how much editorial experience, but stopping myself. After all, she doesn't seem to remember that night in London and it will be too awkward to try to explain now.

'Now Jasper's non-fiction is one thing,' she continues, her eyes darting back to the notebook. 'But I wonder if you would be confident enough to help me with this.'

She pushes the notebook towards me. The page is covered in almost illegible, spidery handwriting, though I can make out the capitalized words at the top of the page: *FIRST DRAFT*. It can't be, I think to myself, my brain fizzing with an excitement I never thought I'd feel again. Could it? Am I actually holding in my hands the latest work of Maeve O'Malley, the author the world has waited almost a decade to hear from?

'You see, the thing is my eyesight's shot and, to make matters worse, I now find typing impossible,' she says, lifting her curled, gnarled hands. 'Blasted arthritis. And I can't get my head around those Dictaphone contraptions. I always end up pressing the wrong button and finding I've spent an hour talking and the wretched thing wasn't even recording. Which is why, if you don't mind, I would like you to help me compose this.'

Of course I want to say yes but I'm gripped with terror. I told myself I would never return to this world, that my editing days were over. I had offered my services to Jasper out of necessity but to do the same for Maeve O'Malley? On what could be her final opus? Why, that would be putting myself right back into the lion's den.

'I . . . I don't think I'm qualified enough,' I say, my voice trembling with a mix of nerves and adrenaline. 'For something as huge as this.'

'Nonsense,' she says, pulling open a drawer and taking out a rather ancient-looking laptop. 'I could tell within a few minutes of meeting you that you are perfectly equipped for this task. Now here, you fire this up and get yourself settled. I shall stand by the window next to Daphne. I find standing helps jog my memory.'

As she walks across the room, her face fixed with determination, I realize that she is not going to take no for an answer.

'Come on, dear,' she says, watching as I switch on the laptop. 'We don't have long. I really must get this down before . . . before it's too late.'

She shuts the notebook that she has clasped to her chest and drops it on the floor by her feet. I open a fresh Word document, glancing at Maeve as I write the words *FIRST DRAFT* at the top. My palms start to sweat as I wait for her to speak, wait for what could be a mortifying moment, a bunch of jumbled words and thoughts with no coherent form. What do I say to her if that happens? What if I am making things much worse?

But then something happens. She clears her throat, straightens her back, and begins to speak. Gone is the elderly croak and in its place the magical, soothing lilt that beguiled chat-show audiences and cast a spell on countless children at her legendary bookshop appearances.

'Now, darling Alexis,' she says, as the years fall away and the skin prickles on the back of my neck. 'If you're ready, then I shall begin.'

6

BLYTHE

Saint-Germain-des-Prés, Paris

23 April 1960

The April sun, ripe as an apricot, was just dipping in the sky when Blythe Aston-Laine arrived at Les Deux Magots café. 'Springtime in Paris,' she whispered to herself, as she stood for a moment surveying the scene. It was everything she had dreamed it would be. The apple blossom just coming into bud on the trees, the maroon and gold awnings flapping gently in the early-evening breeze, the round white tables and wicker chairs in which her literary heroes had once sat, the heady scent of cigarette smoke and freshly brewed coffee wafting through the air, the animated voices, heads thrown back, hands gesticulating. Men and women deep in discussion, laughing and talking freely as equals. It felt like she had stepped into her own dream. After years of wishing and hoping, now she was here at last.

'Voulez-vous une table, mademoiselle?'

A waiter, dressed in the distinctive French cropped black jacket, starched white shirt and neat bow tie, appeared at her side.

Blythe suddenly felt unexpectedly fearful. She had come

this far, had actually set foot inside her dream world, now she would have to fully engage with it. The waiter was not just a character in one of her stories but real flesh and blood. The Parisian guidebook she had purchased from a kiosk outside the Gard du Nord was nestled in the pocket of her powder-blue trench coat. She had spent the last couple of days memorizing the useful French phrases it contained such as asking for directions, ordering a drink, and querying the Métro timetable, yet now, just when she needed them most, the words evaporated from her mind like steam from a kettle. Of course, she could retrieve the book and thumb through the pages to find the correct answer to the waiter's question, but that would prove that she was not a young bohemian who had come to write at her regular table but a gauche eighteen-year-old American tourist who had got lost en route to the Louvre and somehow ended up here, a place she didn't belong.

With an air of discretion unique to the Parisian, the waiter gestured to an empty table on the very edge of the terrace. Nodding her head, Blythe followed him to what she imagined regular patrons would consider the Siberia of Les Deux Magots. Once she was seated, the waiter handed her a menu, then left her to peruse the drinks section. Now, if she were going to truly live out her Left Bank fantasy then she would have gone all-out Hemingway and ordered a Pernod, but with her baby face the chances of being served alcohol were minimal. Besides, she did not want to risk being ejected from the place she had spent the last year of her life dreaming about. Turning to the list of hot beverages, she heard her mother's East Coast drawl in her head. *'Coffee. No cream. No sugar.'* 'Well, Mom,' she said to herself with a wicked smile, 'you're not here, are you.' Better still, the decadent drink she was after was one of the few French phrases she could still recall.

She gestured to the waiter, who took her order for 'un chocolat chaud' with a brisk nod of his head before disappearing, like the rabbit inside a conjuror's hand, into the folds of the smoke-filled terrace.

Once he had gone, Blythe gave herself permission to breathe out and felt the tension of the last few minutes dissipate. Yet, as she looked around from her vantage point at the edge of the terrace, at the women with their effortlessly casual cigarette pants, loose shirts and cropped, androgynous haircuts, and at the men with their thick-rimmed glasses, shirtsleeves rolled up to the elbow and tatty old slacks, their cultivated shabbiness made her feel as out of place as it is possible to be. Looking to the side, she caught a glimpse of herself in the gleaming window and winced with embarrassment. What had seemed the perfect Parisian look back in Connecticut – black Givenchy knee-length shift dress, tan stockings, kitten heels, hair set and curled within an inch of its life, a spritz of Chanel No5 on her wrists – now seemed hopelessly predictable and out of date.

Still, you're here, she told herself, as she pulled her battered notebook and her favourite fountain pen from her satchel. And that is all that matters. She had planned every last detail of this visit meticulously. From what she would wear – black had just seemed so very Parisian chic – to the hour she would arrive – early evening as the sun was about to set, the magic hour when anything was possible and, according to Hemingway, Paris was at its most beautiful – to where she would sit, what she would order, which pen she would use to jot down her story ideas. Of course, the reality fell short of the fantasy she had created in her head. In that dream version she saw herself sitting in the centre of the terrace, reading from her latest opus while Hemingway, Stein, Joyce and Fitzgerald gathered around her, nodding their approval. Reading her inky scribblings now, all she saw were disjointed sentences, platitudes, dead ends. What had seemed like the germ of a great story when she started planning it back in her New England dorm now appeared to be nothing more than the silly ramblings of a teenage diarist. She had a lot to learn. She was aware of that. But for now, she was just thankful to be in Paris, to sit for a while and absorb its magic. And, with a bit of luck, some of its literary stardust might just rub off on her and transform those scribblings into a masterpiece. She could see that book, in her mind's eye, as real as the table and chairs. A beautiful line drawing of the Paris skyline would adorn the cover, the title looped around it in gold lettering. She felt a frisson of excitement as she imagined it. Her story woven through the pages, her name embossed on the front. She could almost feel it in her hands, a weighty hardback, a book her mother referred to as a doorstopper, the kind that people would be proud to display on their shelves. She could hear the chat that would proliferate at society parties: 'Have you read the latest Blythe Aston-Laine yet? Oh, you really must. It's perfection.'

'Un chocolat chaud, mademoiselle.'

She blinked out of her daydream as the waiter placed the steaming glass cup in front of her. It may not have been Pernod, but the rich velvety chocolate tasted like heaven, and she savoured every indulgent sip as the café began to fill with evening revellers. As the last of the light faded, the terrace was cloaked in a violet hue that gave the faces of the men and women clustered round the tables a purplish tint, like the subjects in a Toulouse-Lautrec painting. Blythe wondered if her parents had noticed yet that she had slipped away.

They had gathered in the bar of the Ritz hotel at five p.m. on the dot for pre-dinner cocktails or, in Blythe's case, a slimline tonic water ordered for her by her mother. While her father sipped bourbon and tried to block out the fact that he was thousands of miles away from his beloved America, her mother had instructed Blythe on what to order for dinner – 'steak and salad, hold the dressing' – and what to wear. 'Your Dior cocktail dress. It's elegant yet conservative. We don't want you attracting the attention of young men. After all, you're spoken for now.'

Looking down at the hefty rock on her wedding finger, Blythe grimaced as she recalled the moment Amory went down on one knee and presented her with what can only be described as the ugliest diamond ring she had ever seen. Though it wasn't just what the ring looked like – imagine a gangster's knuckleduster and you'll get the picture – but how it felt on her finger. It was the perfect size, as Blythe's mother had gleefully passed on her measurements to Amory, yet it felt restrictive, like a noose tightening round a neck. Her strongest instinct was to yank it off and throw it in the Seine, but she couldn't do that because Amory's ring was part of a wider, complex plan in which she was the pawn. Despite her academic excellence and her desire to study literature at Vassar, then move to Paris to become a writer, Blythe's future had been decided from the moment she was born. The only daughter of Connecticut steel magnate Chadwick Aston-Laine, and his socialite wife, Hadley, Blythe had spent her life being moulded into what her mother called 'perfect wife material'. As a woman, she could not inherit her father's staggeringly lucrative business, so she would have to be matched with a suitably wealthy young man who would take over the reins of CAL Steel upon Chadwick's death. The training to become 'perfect wife material' began at age four with ballet, horseback riding and art lessons, then from eleven, attendance at society events and instruction in etiquette, homemaking and how to be a consummate hostess. Some of this was fun. Blythe had loved riding horses and had built a lifelong bond with her pony Major, a beautiful dark bay Arab on whom she competed in gymkhanas and three-day eventing, winning so many trophies her parents had to commission a new cabinet to display them in. And then there was Amory Vaughan, the son of her father's best friend, who had been born just two days after Blythe. Timid and gentle with a hatred of sports and a love of drawing and painting, Amory was like a kid brother to Blythe and was never far from her side as they began to navigate the whirl of social commitments. At that point, aged eleven, Blythe had no idea that these activities were part of a wider scheme to mould her into someone's wife. Her world revolved around her beloved horse and, when she imagined the future, she saw herself sitting astride Major and cantering off across the wide plains of Dakota, two free spirits following the call of the wild. Perhaps sensing this, her parents had shipped her off to boarding school the following fall. When she came back for Thanksgiving, she was devastated to find that Major had been sold and all her riding gear cleared away. 'There'll be no more messing around with horses now, Blythe,' her mother had decreed, as she dragged her disgruntled daughter round joyless clothes stores to find a dress for the country club Christmas ball. 'We thought being part of the horsey set would be good for you, but it only seems to have brought out a wild streak and that just won't do. No, your riding days are over, dear. You're to be a lady now.'

Yet what her parents didn't know was that West Connecticut School for Girls, though a hothouse for socialites, was providing Blythe with something that would change her entire outlook on life. An education. Over the years, she found that she could tolerate the endless homemaking and etiquette lessons and the futile chatter of the other girls because she had found a kindred spirit. Mademoiselle Michelle DuPont had joined the school as English Literature mistress last year, bringing with her a European mindset – she had been born in England to French parents, studied at the Sorbonne, and rubbed shoulders with Simone de Beauvoir – that lit a fuse under Blythe. Through Mademoiselle DuPont she was introduced to Hemingway and Joyce, Stein and Baudelaire, writers whose ideas made her feel as though her head was exploding. Such was her excitement, she made the foolish mistake of telling her parents in her next letter home all about Mademoiselle DuPont and the spark she had ignited. *I finally know what I want to do when I grow up*, she had written to them. *I'm going to go to college and I'm going to be a writer.*

The next time she was home, her parents informed her that she wouldn't be returning to school. A week later, a dinner was held at which the guest of honour was none other than her childhood buddy, Amory Vaughan. The only son of an old East Coast banking family, Amory had been forced to hang up his paintbrush to take his place at the high table of capitalism. He was now Chadwick's new CEO and, according to their parents, 'perfect husband material' for Blythe. Though she railed against it at first, she knew that the deal had been sealed long ago. As far as both sets of parents were concerned, Amory and Blythe's courting and subsequent engagement were a fait accompli. As she had sat beside her giddily excited mother at the engagement dinner in January, listening to her father and Amory discussing her future, she felt the noose growing tighter and tighter. There would be no Vassar, no writing career, no riding off into the sunset. In true Aston-Laine fashion, the deal had been struck and there was no going back.

'Excusez-moi, cette place est-elle occupée?'

Blythe, shaken out of her troubled thoughts, looked up and saw a young man standing by the table with a glass of Pernod in one hand and a battered paperback in the other. He was tall and spindle thin, with pale skin, chestnut hair that fell in messy curls around his forehead, and almond-shaped eyes the colour of Wedgwood china. He wore a threadbare black coat that swamped his slight frame, over a rather crumpled linen Henley shirt and baggy wide-legged wool trousers held up by a pair of bright red braces. She had never seen someone as curiously dressed in all her life and found herself gawping at him, open-mouthed.

He repeated his words, this time gesturing to the chair opposite Blythe. She looked about her. Every table was occupied.

'Oh, you want to sit down,' she said, her cheeks flushing. Her limited French was making her feel conspicuous and foolish. 'Sure, go ahead.'

It was the young man's turn to gawp.

'You're American,' he exclaimed, his taut face softening into a wide smile that exposed a mouthful of rather crooked, yet not unpleasant, teeth. Blythe could just imagine what her mother would say. '*These Europeans. They have no concept of dental hygiene.*'

'William Kenneally,' he said, slipping into the seat opposite her. 'Nice to make your acquaintance.'

'Blythe,' she replied. They shook hands. His fingernails were grubby, but his skin was soft. 'And you're Irish.'

'How could you tell?' he cried, slamming his fist on the table in mock indignation. 'Jesus, here I am trying to pass myself off as a born-and-bred Parisian and still the old country comes creeping out. What's that you're writing?'

Blythe felt her cheeks flush again as he reached across the table, picked up her book and began to flick through it.

'Ah, good old Gertie,' he said, pausing on the inner page where Blythe had copied out a quote from Gertrude Stein in the hope that it would inspire her writing. 'Bloody hell, what a line that is: "Writers have to have two countries, the one where they belong and—"'

'"—the one in which they live really."'

The words sprang from Blythe's lips before she realized it as she grabbed the book back.

'So then,' smiled William, rooting in his pocket, and

taking out a pack of Gitanes. 'You're a writer. Are you at the Sorbonne?'

At first Blythe thought he was teasing her, but his face was earnest as he lit his cigarette and waited for her reply. He thinks I'm a writer, she thought to herself, a rush of delight rippling through her body, he doesn't think I'm an idiot tourist. For a few moments she toyed with the idea of lying, of telling this curious young man a tall tale of a different Blythe, a young woman who had supportive academic parents who nurtured her literary dreams and sent her off to pursue her studies in Paris. It was a story she had written in her head a thousand times, a secret wish for an alternate life. But there was something about William, something so true and honest and open, that stopped her from spinning a yarn.

'No, I'm not at the Sorbonne,' she said, taking another sip of her now tepid hot chocolate. 'I'm just here visiting.'

'Wise woman,' he said, leaning back into his chair and gazing up at the darkening sky. 'I have no time for the students. They all have this air of entitlement even though, for the most part, what they produce is formulaic and dull. I'm with VW on this one, they never stray from the designated path, never head into the forest and find the will-o'-the-wisps. Chuck your textbooks in the Seine, that's what I'd say to them, and go and spend a night in Les Halles. That'd give them something to write about.'

'Who's VW?' asked Blythe, raising her voice to be heard above a violinist who had appeared on the pavement next to them and was launching into a scratchy rendition of 'La Vie en Rose'.

'Virginia Woolf,' replied William, giving a wave to the

waiter. 'She's all right is our V, and *Mrs Dalloway* is a masterpiece, but I prefer her friend Tom Eliot. Bloody hell, if I could write poetry like him, I would die a happy man. By the way, I like your pearls.'

Blythe, aware that she had no idea who Mrs Dalloway was, or Tom Eliot for that matter, suddenly felt awkward.

'Oh, these things,' she said, covering them with her hand. 'They seemed like a good idea when I got dressed but now I . . .'

She paused. She was saying too much.

'But now you what?' said William, staring deep into her eyes.

No one had ever looked at her so directly. Not her father who only looked into the eyes of those he was closing a deal with, not her mother who thought making eye contact signified bad manners, and certainly not Amory who Blythe had found, now they were grown-ups, preferred to look at anything other than his fiancée's face. 'He's just shy, sweetie. Always has been, ever since he was a boy,' her mother had remarked when Blythe mentioned it. 'Still, I think it's adorable that he's such a gentleman. What do you want, some handsy creep leering at you?' But William's gaze wasn't leery and it wasn't sexual – rather it was as though he was looking deep inside her, right into her soul.

'You'll think I'm silly,' she said, as the violin rose to a crescendo, 'but I have had this dream of coming to Paris and sitting in this very café and . . . well . . . feeling I belonged. But when I got here it was all wrong. These pearls, my lack of French, this table out in Siberia.'

'Siberia, that's great,' laughed William. 'I'm going to use

that line. It's good. I like you, Blythe with no surname. You're a wit.'

Just then, he sprang to his feet and gestured to a young man and woman who were leaving a table in the middle of the terrace.

'Hey, Estelle, Sam,' he called. Then, turning to Blythe, he shook his head. 'They're my pals. I didn't know they were here. It was so crowded I must have walked right past them.'

The friends – a tiny, sparrow-like woman with bobbed black hair, a slash of red lipstick and a belted mac, and a man with sandy hair and thick, black-rimmed glasses – looked across and waved.

'Hey, William, coming to the shop?' said the man, an American.

'I'll be there later,' cried William. 'When I've finished my shift at Harry's. This is my friend Blythe, by the way.'

'Bonsoir, Blythe,' said the woman, blowing a kiss.

'Nice to meet you,' said the man, taking the woman's arm.

As they departed, William turned to Blythe and smiled.

'See, now everyone knows your name,' he said, draining his glass. 'Simple.'

And with that William Kenneally tucked his paperback into his pocket and disappeared into the night.

7

ALEXIS

Lustrum Manor

'Ah, Alexis, right on time,' says Jasper, when I arrive at his study door at nine sharp. 'Do come in.'

I follow him into the study which, unlike Maeve's, is a rather sparse and underwhelming room. There is a small, functional black desk set within the bay window. On it is a potted cactus plant, a neat pile of papers, the broadband router, and a black cafetière with two mugs. There is an ancient, frayed and saggy sofa pushed against the far wall, a pair of grey metal filing cabinets standing either side of the fireplace and a small bookcase neatly stacked with thick hardbacks.

'Do take a seat on the sofa,' says Jasper, sweeping his hand through his messy hair. 'And I'll pour us a coffee. How do you take it?'

'White, no sugar, thank you,' I say, sinking into the folds of the sofa. There's a damp, fusty smell about it that reminds me of the wash houses in some of the campsites I've stayed in. The whole room looks like it could do with a good dust. While Jasper pours the coffee, I glance at the spines of the books on the shelf. *The Napoleonic Wars: A New World Order* by Jasper Hardy. *Terror on the Seas: How the Age of Naval Warfare Challenged European Supremacy* by Jasper Hardy and Terence North. *Bonaparte: The Man and the Myth*—

'Here you are, dear,' says Jasper, handing me a steaming mug of coffee. 'I hope I haven't overmilked it.'

'It's perfect,' I say, taking a sip. 'I was just looking at your books. You're an expert on Napoleon? How fascinating.'

'I don't know about expert, but it is something of an obsession,' he says, sitting down at the opposite end of the sofa. 'I was Professor of History at Canterbury University for twenty-five years and though I still teach a couple of classes at the local university just to keep my hand in, my main focus is my books and, in particular, my work in progress, the deadline for which is looming ever closer.'

'What's the new book about?' I ask, feeling that familiar spark of curiosity I'd spent my professional life pursuing.

'It's a study of Charles de Gaulle's military career,' says Jasper. 'Made up of letters he wrote from the Front during the First World War. A rather dry subject for some but to a military history nut like me it's a dream project.'

I must admit, it's not my ideal commission but I try my best to sound interested.

'Gosh,' I exclaim. 'No wonder you and Maeve were drawn to each other, all that French history.'

'Maeve?' he says, frowning. 'Ah, I take it my wife has introduced you to her alter ego.'

He lets out a nervous laugh.

'It's a Maeve O'Malley week then,' he continues, sighing deeply. 'When she starts all that up again, it's usually a sign that things are getting bad.'

I think back to the previous evening, the delight on

Maeve's face as she had dictated the chapter to me, the light in her eyes. She was positively glowing.

'Her alter ego?' I say, confused. 'You mean a pen name?'

'Listen, Alexis,' he says wearily. 'I think we both know that the fragile lady who ran out into the road is not who she once was. The bestselling author thing is a story she likes to tell herself and who am I to argue.'

'So you're telling me that Mrs Hardy is not Maeve O'Malley?' I say, my head spinning. 'That it's all a delusion? But what about the books and the photos?'

He shifts uncomfortably in his seat, before clearing his throat.

'I'm saying that whatever she may have been in the past, she is now a very different person,' he says, clasping his hands together. 'She turned eighty-three in February, Alexis. Novel-writing, well, that's a young person's game.'

I smile politely, suppressing the urge to inform him that some of the greatest writers who ever lived were prolific well into old age.

'Anyway,' says Jasper, adjusting his spectacles. 'Let's focus on the business at hand. I see you've brought your paperwork.'

'Yes, of course, sorry,' I say, handing him the folder containing my DBS check confirmation and references. 'Everything should be in order but do let me know if you need anything else.'

I watch as he flicks through the papers, hoping that he doesn't question why there is nothing solid since the beginning of last year. But to my relief, Jasper seems satisfied by what he sees.

'This all looks fine,' he says, removing his glasses and rubbing his eyes.

'Wonderful,' I say with relief. 'So what would you like me to do today?'

'Well, before we get started on the work,' he says sheepishly, 'there's something I'd like to ask you.'

My heart pounds. Has he recognized something in my documents? Wondered why I left my last job with nothing solid to go on to?

'It's a rather delicate question,' he says, handing me back the papers.

He looks at me gravely. My skin prickles suddenly. What has he noticed? My name? My former employer's name? Put two and two together. Perhaps he heard the story of what happened to me. After all, publishing is such a small world and people talk.

'It's about Mrs Hardy,' he says, his voice cracking. 'You saw how she was at dinner last night. The way she spoke to Cordelia and me. It's exhausting to have to constantly tread on eggshells every minute, coax and practically beg her to take the pills, when the truth is that, at the moment, the medication is what is keeping her right. She'd skipped a dose yesterday morning and look what happened next. If you hadn't been so alert, she could have been knocked down and killed on that road.'

'I'm just glad I was there,' I say, recalling the terrified expression on Maeve's face as I approached her. 'She was in such a state.'

'This is what we've had to deal with these last few months,' says Jasper, shaking his head. 'It's becoming almost too much though there is no alternative. She's scared of hospitals, always has been. I just want her to feel safe. I . . .'

He pauses, his hands trembling. Then, taking a deep breath, he looks at me and smiles sadly.

'Like I said,' he continues. 'My wife is not well. And as you have now found out, she is, or rather was, a very well-known figure. Look, I feel awkward asking this but in light of what I've just seen on your CV, your er . . . your background, I must ask you to keep whatever you witness in this house to yourself. I'm afraid we've been stung before with staff selling their stories to the press but now, with my wife in such a delicate state, it really is imperative that we protect her, preserve her public image. You understand?'

'Gosh, of course,' I say, placing my empty coffee cup on the side. 'I've spent my working life nurturing people like Maeve, guarding their privacy. You have my assurance, Jasper, that whatever I see I will keep firmly to myself.'

'Thank you, Alexis,' he sighs. 'I knew that would be the case but I just had to be sure. For Maeve's sake.'

He stands up abruptly from the sofa and collects the empty cups.

'I'll go and wake her,' he says. 'See how she is this morning She doesn't eat until lunch, but I'll take her a hot chocolate to have with her pills. God help me if I forget that. It's a fancy French brand she insists upon having. Luckily, they stock it in Waitrose, but it costs a fortune.'

'Ah, that reminds me of the character in her new novel,' I say, remembering the glee on Maeve's face as she described the deliciousness of the drink. 'The young American girl, new to Paris, sipping her first hot chocolate.'

He looks at me and suddenly all the colour fades from

his face. He wobbles slightly and for a moment I fear he may keel over.

'Jasper? Are you all right? What is it?'

'Did ... did you say, new novel?' he gasps, looking horrified. 'That's all we need.'

'I really don't think it's anything to worry about,' I say, rather alarmed at this reaction. 'Maeve was in great spirits when she was talking about it. In fact, it will probably do her the world of good to go back to her writing, something that brought her so much success in the past.'

'And I've told you it is all part of the delusion,' he says tersely. 'I know what this is about and I'm afraid it has nothing to do with writing a novel. Did she by any chance ask you to "find" someone?'

'Yes,' I say tentatively.

'Oh, please no,' he says, putting his hand to his forehead. 'Last time this happened, we had to fetch the doctor. He was this close to detaining her under the Mental Health Act. I thought we had it under control, but it looks like she's going again. You see, Alexis, every manic episode we've had to contend with this past year has begun with the mention of a name and that name puts the fear of God into me.'

'William?' I say, seeing a tall, pale Irishman, tilting his cap.

'William,' sighs Jasper, a resigned expression on his face.

'Yes, I thought that was strange at first, too,' I say, recalling the first words Maeve spoke to me on the road out there. 'But there's nothing to worry about. William is just one of the characters in her book.'

Jasper shakes his head.

'Oh, how I wish that were the case,' he says, with a fearful expression.

'Look, Jasper,' I say, trying to take hold of the situation. 'You mentioned an itinerary you'd put together for me, things you want me to work on. How about you give me that to look over while you check on Mrs Hardy, then I'll get started.'

'Of course, yes,' he says, flustered. 'It's . . . it's just here.'

With trembling hands, he takes a plastic folder from the desk and hands it to me.

'Have a read and if you have any questions, we can talk about them when I get back,' he says. 'I won't be long.'

I watch as he rushes out the door, wondering what on earth I have let myself in for. As I try to read his carefully typed notes, a thousand questions whirl around my head. Have I just been privy to the first draft of the novel by a recluse author that the world has been waiting years to read or have I simply transcribed the contents of a delusional mind?

I spend the next couple of hours trying to focus on Charles de Gaulle's rather dry exploits on the battlefields of France and am just circling a copyright query in red pen, about one of the letters Jasper wishes to cite, when my phone buzzes in my back pocket.

I take it out and look at the screen. It's a follow-up notification from the genealogy website I joined a couple of weeks ago, asking if I was *still searching for someone?* It includes the list of Kimberly Harpers from the 2021 census that I've already scrutinized, including the one whom I foolishly hoped I might find here at Lustrum Manor. I'm about to move it to trash when there is a knock on the door.

'Who is it?' I call, stuffing my phone into my pocket and returning to Jasper's notes.

There is no reply.

'Jasper? Is that you?' I call out nervously.

Then the door creaks open and I turn to see a tiny, dishevelled figure standing there.

'Maeve?' I cry, jumping up from my chair. 'What is it? What's happened?'

Her face is plastered in white make-up, her cheeks matted with rouge, her lips smeared with red lipstick. She looks like a child who has been let loose in her mother's toiletry bag.

'I need you to help me,' she says, her eyes blazing as she rocks from side to side. 'I don't want to lose him again.'

'Lose who?' I say, putting my hand around her back to steady her.

'William,' she says, looking up at me pleadingly. 'It was all there last night, the whole story, and I'm worried it will slip away. I thought if I got dressed in my proper clothes, the clothes I used to wear then . . . maybe I could hang on to it a little longer. But my eyesight's not what it was, and I bet I look a dreadful fright.'

She turns to me and smiles, and my heart suddenly hurts for her.

'Come on,' I say, leading her out of the room. 'How about I help you get ready.'

'But won't Jasper be needing you?' she says, looking up at me like a scared child.

'I've got an hour for lunch,' I say, closing the door behind us. 'That's more than enough time to get you sparkling again.'

8

BLYTHE

Paris

25 April 1960

'Smile for the birdie!'

Blythe blinked into the flash of her mother's shiny new Polaroid camera, while silver stars danced in front of her eyes.

'That was perfect, honey,' cried her mother, Hadley, as the developing photo popped out onto her lap. 'Though, Chad, would it kill you just to smile for once?'

She shook her head playfully at her husband.

'You know Daddy hates having his picture taken,' laughed Blythe, as Hadley placed the camera back into its case and laid it on the seat beside her.

'I know,' sighed her mother. 'But surely he could make an exception seeing as we're on vacation. What will my girlfriends at the country club say when I show them this?'

Blythe spluttered as her mother handed her the freshly developed Polaroid. In it her father sat stony-faced while Blythe, eyes closed, beamed into the camera.

'Don't go showing that to anyone, Mom,' she said, handing back the photo. 'I look like I'm asleep.'

'Yes, but still beautiful,' cooed Hadley, stroking her daughter's cheek.

At the end of the table, Chadwick Aston-Laine grimaced as he took a sip of his cocktail.

'Honestly, Blythe,' he sighed, pushing the drink aside. 'I don't know why you insisted on us coming here instead of the Ritz. Jeez, they can't even make a decent Martini.'

'Come now, sweetie,' said Hadley softly. 'There's nothing wrong with a bit of variety. And I have to say, in this case, Blythe has chosen just right. They say any American worth their salt comes to Harry's Bar when they visit Paris.'

She gave her daughter a reassuring smile.

'And by the way, honey,' she whispered to Blythe. 'You made the right choice with that dress. It looks incredible.'

'Thanks, Mom,' Blythe replied, her cheeks flushing. 'Though I'm still not sure about this cashmere wrap.'

'It's perfect,' Hadley smiled, giving Blythe a reassuring squeeze on the arm. 'Honestly, B, you should be a model like I always told you. You have a natural flair for fashion and a set of pins that would give Cyd Charisse a run for her money.'

'Mom, honestly,' groaned Blythe, rolling her eyes. 'People don't say "pins" in Paris. It's . . . well, it's very much reinforcing the primacy of the male gaze.'

'Oh, honey, I have no idea what you're talking about,' laughed Hadley. 'It's a compliment, that's all. Hey, I'm just glad you inherited my legs and not your father's. Talk about chicken drumsticks.'

'Mom!' cried Blythe. 'That's so mean.'

'What are you two whispering about?' said Chad, from the other end of the table.

'Oh, nothing,' said Hadley, taking a sip of her Martini. 'I was just telling Blythe to avoid the chicken fricassee. I hear it's foul.'

She winked at her daughter and the two dissolved into fits of giggles.

'Crazy, the pair of you,' said Chadwick, shaking his head. 'I tell you, I'll never understand women as long as I live.'

'Hey, Chad,' said Hadley, composing herself. 'Isn't that the Graingers over there? Why don't you call them over, ask them to join us?'

While her husband beckoned to the wealthy Chicago couple they had met at the hotel breakfast that morning, Hadley turned to Blythe.

'See,' she whispered, her cheeks flushed from white wine. 'I told you this trip would do you good. I know you love your books and your writing and all that but you can see that too much studying is not healthy. You're starting to think like me now. Making sure you're in the right place at the right time. Knowing instinctively where the important people hang out. You're going to be such an asset to Amory, my darling, you really are.'

Blythe smiled politely at her mother, but inside, her heart sank. For a moment back there, she had thought she and her mother were getting along the way they used to, before Amory and the engagement and finding a wedding dress to rival the one worn by Mom's East Coast socialite heroine, Jackie Kennedy, back in the fifties, became the prime focus of life. Still, best not to rock the boat, not now she had got her parents to Harry's.

'Thanks, Mom,' she said, taking a sip of her slimline tonic with a twist of lime. 'That's sweet of you to say.'

While her father returned to the table with the Graingers, Blythe kept her eyes on the bar. Her mother had got it partly right. Blythe had chosen Harry's for a specific reason. But the 'important people' her mother had in mind were not who Blythe was here for.

She had formulated the plan the previous evening as she walked back from Les Deux Magots, reliving the conversation with William over and over in her head. When he left the table, she had opened up her notebook and scribbled down what he had said so that she wouldn't forget it. Virginia Woolf, Tom Eliot, Gertrude Stein, William's disdain for students and, most importantly, the tiny scrap of information he had shared as he spoke to his friends: 'When I've finished my shift at Harry's.' That was it, the key to making sure she saw him again. Because she had to see him again. She had to experience, even for just a few moments, the happiness she had felt when they were talking together. No one had ever made her feel so understood, so seen.

Back at the hotel, Blythe had quizzed Jean-Paul, the young concierge, about Harry's.

'The famous American bar, mademoiselle? Oh, you must go. You will like it a lot.'

But now she was here and there was no sign of William. She felt deflated and foolish. She looked around the table. Her mother was merrily regaling Mrs Grainger with the details of the forthcoming nuptials. 'Do you remember Jackie Kennedy's wedding dress? Well, that's the look we're going for. You know Blythe has been mistaken for Jackie several times at the Hamptons. They have the same colouring and bone structure, don't you think?'

While Mrs Grainger made polite noises in the face of Hadley's incessant chatter, her husband was embroiled in a heated discussion with Chadwick about the World Series. It seemed, thought Blythe, that the only person not getting what she wanted from this trip to Harry's Bar was her. It was a mistake coming here. Why, she had probably misheard William the other night. After all, this slick Right Bank establishment didn't seem like the kind of place he would work at.

'Mom, I've got a headache,' she said, leaning across the table where Hadley was drawing a sketch of Blythe's wedding gown on a scrap of paper for the benefit of Mrs Grainger. 'I think I'm going to head back to the hotel.'

'Oh, don't be silly, sweetie,' said Hadley, looking up. 'You're probably just dehydrated. I'll order you a soda water. Here's the boy now.'

As her mother clicked her fingers, Blythe turned, and her heart somersaulted in her chest.

William.

'Well, what are the odds?' he said, with a smile as he took Hadley's order.

Blythe felt her cheeks flush as William leaned across the table to collect the empty glasses. He looked so different. Gone were the shabby overcoat and baggy trousers and in their place an immaculate white shirt, bow tie and waistcoat. His face was clean-shaven while his messy hair had been slicked back with oil. He looked as well turned out as one of Amory's fraternity buddies and Blythe couldn't help but feel disappointed.

'Any other drinks, folks?' he said, as he placed the empties on his tray. 'Or just the soda water?'

On hearing this suggestion, Chadwick leaned across the table and barked his order without meeting William's eye before turning back to Mr Grainger and resuming his baseball talk.

Despite the low lighting, Blythe couldn't help but notice William's eyes flash with indignation though he retained his composure.

'My pleasure, sir,' he said wryly. 'Two whisky sours and a soda water coming right up.'

Blythe felt sick as she watched William walk away. She had tried so hard to cultivate an image of bohemian bookishness at the café yesterday, even managing to endear herself to that achingly hip young couple. William had referred to her as his friend, saw her as worthy enough to talk to, but now, in one fell swoop, he had seen her as she really was. The hopelessly square daughter of boorish American tourists. And worse, she had watched her parents treat him like that in silence. Not even having the courage to return his greeting, she had just sat there in her pearls and cashmere like a dumb mannequin.

'If you'll excuse me, I have to use the bathroom,' she said, sliding out of the green leather banquette.

'Do you want me to come with you, sweetie?' said her mother, grabbing for her beaded handbag and making to follow. 'There are some rather rakish-looking young men in here. I don't want you to be hassled by any of them.'

'Don't be silly, Mom,' she said, feeling the invisible noose tighten. 'I'm fine. You enjoy the wedding talk.'

Her mother hesitated for a moment, then, smiling, turned back to Mrs Grainger, oblivious to the fact that Blythe was heading in the opposite direction to the bathrooms.

He was standing at the far edge of the bar, placing each drink carefully on the tray. As Blythe approached, she noticed a stray curl had detached itself from the slicked-back styling and she felt an overwhelming urge to reach out and touch it.

'Hey there,' she said, tapping him on the shoulder.

He turned on his heels, with a look on his face that suggested he was ready for a fight. However, his expression softened when he saw her standing there.

'Hey, indeed,' he said, placing a pencil behind his ear. 'Come to help me carry the drinks, have you?'

'No,' she said, moving to one side to let a portly, drunken man stagger past. 'I just wanted to apologize for the way my dad spoke to you just now.'

'Oh, that was your da?' he said, his eyes flashing. 'I thought he was a hapless beggar you'd found on the street and taken pity on.'

It was Blythe's turn to look startled then. No one had ever spoken about her father like that.

'I'm just kidding ye,' he said, nudging her arm. 'What can I say, kiddo, I'm used to being treated like that, and you know what, it's like the proverbial water off a duck's back. I'm surprised to see you in here though. I didn't think this would be your scene at all. Harry's doesn't tend to attract the literary sort, at least not these days.'

He looked at Blythe and she felt a flutter in her chest. He had remembered their conversation, had actually listened to her. Not many in Blythe's world did that.

'Oh, it isn't my scene,' she stuttered. 'Not at all. In fact, it was my parents' idea to come here. I swear to you. I didn't even know you worked here.'

He looked at her and smiled. If he remembered mentioning Harry's yesterday or had any suspicion that Blythe had come here on purpose, he didn't mention it, much to her relief.

'Listen, you don't have to explain yourself,' he said, placing his hand on her shoulder. 'I get it. Now, tell me, are you free later on?'

'Free?' she said, glancing over her shoulder, aware that her parents, or at least her mother, would be wondering where she had got to. 'What do you mean?'

'I mean, dear Blythe, are you at liberty later on this eventide to avail yourself of a little hospitality at one of Paris's most salubrious of hangouts?' he said, adopting a mock-English accent and sweeping his arms to the side for dramatic effect. 'There's a party tonight at a place I think you'd like. Meet me outside Les Deux Magots at midnight and we'll go from there.'

And with that he grabbed the tray and ducked back into the crowd.

'What do you mean, you don't feel well,' exclaimed her mother as they made their way back to the hotel a couple of hours later. 'I thought your headache had cleared up. You were fine at dinner, giddy even. I'll bet it was that disgusting steak tartare you insisted on eating. I told you it would upset your stomach. I'll have the concierge send a doctor over as soon as we get back to the hotel.'

'No, you don't have to do that,' said Blythe, trying her best to sound convincingly ill. 'It's just a little headache, that's all. You and Daddy enjoy your poker game with the Graingers in the bar and I'll have an early night. I'll be fine in the morning.'

'Are you sure?' said her mother, as they stepped inside the hotel lobby. 'Daddy could get a doctor out just like that, make sure everything's hunky-dory.'

She clicked her fingers and Blythe winced, recalling how her mother had summoned William to the table.

'I'm sure,' she said, kissing her mother's cheek. 'Now stop worrying and enjoy the game.'

Once she was back in her room, a palatial wing of the penthouse suite her parents had booked, with sweeping views of the city, she peeled off what she was wearing and opened the wardrobe where the maid had kindly arranged her clothes after unpacking her suitcase for her.

She had to find the right outfit. Yesterday's choice had been a disaster and tonight's a compromise to suit her mother. When she presented herself to Hadley wearing a simple black Dior shift her mother had grimaced. 'Hmm, I think Grandma's pearls and the cashmere wrap would work well with the dress, sweetie. We want people to see that you're a young lady of breeding, Mrs Soon-to-be-Amory-Vaughan,' she had trilled. And Blythe had agreed because she had to keep her mother sweet if she was to convince her to go to Harry's instead of the Ritz bar, where her parents preferred to spend every evening. Still, she felt her cheeks burn at the memory of William standing there at the table, his eyes silently judging her, her parents, her cashmere wrap.

Recalling how that girl, Estelle, was dressed at Les Deux Magots yesterday, Blythe selected a pair of white pedal pushers and laid them on the bed. Then, crossing the vast hallway, she went to her parents' bedroom and opened the drawers. 'Daddy is always cold,' she thought, as she rifled through piles of neatly folded vests and sweaters. 'He's bound to have packed it.' In fact, she remembered her mother fussing round Rita, the maid, as the flustered young woman tried to pack the cases the night before they left for Paris. 'Make sure Chad has at least two lambswool sweaters,' she had demanded. 'I hear France gets bitterly cold in the evenings.' Anyone would have thought they were heading for the Arctic rather than Continental Europe, though for once, as she found what she was looking for, Blythe was grateful for her mother's overzealous packing.

Pulling the black sweater from the bottom of the drawer, she skipped back to her own bedroom. Standing before the ornate full-length mirror a couple of minutes later, she let out a little shriek of delight. It shouldn't work but it did. With a little adjustment, she had pulled the neck of her father's oversized sweater so that it fell casually over one shoulder, then added a belt round her middle, and she had created a look of effortless bohemian chic. Slipping her feet into her black ballet pumps, she grabbed an armful of pillows from the top of the wardrobe and shoved them in the bed, pulling the covers over. If her mother looked in on her when she came up later, she would think she was fast asleep. Besides, knowing how many bourbons her mother consumed during poker games, Blythe doubted she would even notice.

Once the bed was made, she took her bag from the table and slung it over her shoulder. With one last look in the mirror and a sweep of red lipstick – oh, how her mother would disapprove – she made her way out of the penthouse and into the Parisian night to find William.

'Look at you, kiddo,' he exclaimed, when she arrived at their meeting place. 'Or should I say Audrey Hepburn. That sweater really suits you. Now, shall we?'

Blythe felt a rush of excitement fizzle up her spine as William offered her his arm and whisked her off through the winding, lamplit streets. As they walked, the boulevard became progressively run-down. The pretty architecture around Saint-Germain gave way to blocks of slum tenements with laundry hanging over balconies and beggars slumped in doorways. A woman with over-rouged cheeks and smudged black mascara stumbled out of the shadows and hollered something in French at William who simply shook his head and waved her on.

'So where are you taking me?' said Blythe a little nervously, as William, spotting a pair of gendarmes walking towards them, darted down a back alley. 'Is it far?'

'Just a couple of hundred yards away,' he said breathlessly, slowing his pace as they approached a pretty tree-lined boulevard. 'Sorry about that back there. I always get a little antsy when I see the cops. I suppose it's in my blood to be distrustful of authority.'

Blythe wanted to probe this comment further but before she got the chance William had stopped outside a small building tucked into the corner of the street. Strange place to have a party, she thought. It had a dimly lit glass shopfront where Blythe could see the silhouette of what looked like a display of books, while black shutters were pulled halfway down over the doors. The street was dark, but Blythe could just make out the name, printed in swirling letters above the door.

Le Mistral.

'Here we are,' he said, rapping three times on the glass door. 'Welcome to paradise.'

The door opened and, ducking under the shutters, they stepped inside a narrow, low-ceilinged room. The walls were lined with bookshelves and the air smelt of smoke, dust and fried potatoes. Turning to look out of the foggy front window Blythe gasped as the magnificent outline of Notre-Dame cathedral loomed out of the shadows on the other side of the Seine, which was just yards from the shop. There were a couple of small tables crammed up against the shelves, with stubby red candles wedged into wine carafes in the centre, and a little stove with a copper pan on top. 'What an incredible place,' she whispered to herself, as she ran her fingers along the book spines. William was right, this was nothing short of paradise.

'Come on,' said William, taking her hand and leading her up a step that was almost concealed by the book stacks. 'The party's this way.'

9

BLYTHE

They entered another room, just as narrow as the first with more books stacked floor to ceiling. The walls were painted gold, and the floor was dotted with large cushions upon which were sitting a dozen or so people drinking wine and smoking cigarettes. There was a gramophone wedged on top of one of the book stacks from which was emanating a rich saxophone melody.

'John Coltrane,' whispered William, the scent of tobacco on his breath. 'Medicine for the soul. Come on, let me introduce you to the tumbleweeds.'

'The what?'

But as William took her hand and led her across the room, Blythe's voice was lost amid the music.

'William,' cried a young woman with cropped hair the colour of straw. 'Thank God you've arrived. This party is in dire need of some Irish craic.'

She had a velvety English accent and a languid way of speaking that made it seem as though she was about to yawn. Blythe watched as the woman kissed William on both cheeks, holding her glass aloft.

'I shall do my best to honour the spirit of Behan and keep you suitably entertained,' said William exuberantly. 'Oh, where are my manners? Blythe, this is Paula. A fellow tumbleweed.'

He pressed his hand on the small of Blythe's back and ushered her forward.

'A pleasure to meet you,' said Paula, shaking her hand. 'Any friend of William is most welcome here. Now, go and get a drink. There's some on the side over there. Sam's going to read his new poem in a moment.'

While Paula returned to her cushion William took two glasses of red wine from the counter and led Blythe towards another room. There was an archway leading into it, above which was a handwritten mural. Blythe paused to read it, but the light was faint, and she couldn't quite make out what it said. Something about strangers and angels in disguise.

'Now this is what we call the Old Smoky Reading Room,' said William, handing her a glass of wine as they entered.

In the corner of the windowless room, hunched in a threadbare armchair, sat a handsome older man in his forties with curly fair hair, a neat moustache and a tuft of beard at his chin. He was youthfully dressed, in loose-fitting trousers like William, and a blue shirt with the sleeves rolled up to the elbow. In his left hand he held a cigarette aloft, the smoke swirling about him like mist. *Old Smoky Reading Room*. She could see now where it got its name. Perched on the man's lap was a bowl laden with fried potatoes from which he ate intermittently, while nodding his head at the man sitting next to him who Blythe recognized as Sam from Les Deux Magots last night.

'That's George,' said William, as Blythe sipped her wine. She had never tasted red wine before. It was rich and peppery and burned her throat in a not unpleasant way. 'He owns the shop. The whole tumbleweed thing is down to him, God bless him.'

'What is the tumbleweed thing?' asked Blythe. 'What does it mean?'

'Well, it's George's philosophy of sorts,' said William, his cheeks flushed from the wine. 'He told me once how, during the Depression, he'd trekked across America like a hobo, with barely a cent to his name. Yet, despite the poverty that people were enduring all around him, they still managed to offer hospitality, food and shelter to him. He was a tumbleweed back then, he said, drifting along with no foundations. I guess when he first opened this place and saw how a lot of its clientele – especially young people – were suffering, he wanted to help.'

'How does he help?' asked Blythe, watching as Sam got to his feet.

'He lets people like me – like us, I should say – writers, artists, thinkers, have a bed for the night if we need it,' said William, as inside Blythe melted at those words 'like us'. 'In return he asks us for three things – to read a book a day, to help out in the shop for a couple of hours and to write a single-page autobiography for his archives. How does that sound, eh?'

It sounded like Blythe's dream, yet even as she stood there, as she was welcomed into Mistral's folds, she knew that it would always remain just that, a dream.

'Come on, you two,' cried Paula, appearing behind them. 'Sam's about to begin.'

William guided them back into the main room where they settled on a cushion next to Paula and a bespectacled, thirty-something tumbleweed who introduced himself as Allen while Sam stood in the middle of the floor, his notebook open in his hands. But as he opened his mouth to speak there was a commotion from the front of the shop and suddenly Estelle hurtled into the room.

'Je suis désolée d'être en retard,' she cried, as she hurried over and sat down between Paula and Allen. 'Bonjour, Paula, Monsieur Ginsberg. Continuez, Sam.'

She blew a kiss at him, just as she had at Blythe the previous night. Sam shook his head and smiled before blowing one back and beginning to read.

His voice was soft, velvety rich as he recited a poem entitled 'One Night in Paris'. Blythe closed her eyes, listening as he led the audience through the winding streets, describing a young couple, in their first flush of youth, kissing passionately as they stumbled into a mysterious building deep in the Latin Quarter. Opening her eyes, she glanced at William. He looked back at her, his head to one side, and smiled. Blythe felt a fluttering in her stomach. No man had ever looked at her like that. It was as though he could see inside her, right down to her bones, as though he could read her thoughts, see into her darkest recesses, as though he truly wanted to know her, the real her.

She sipped her wine and turned her attention back to Sam just as his poem was taking an unexpected turn. Leading the audience through his fictional building in the Latin Quarter he described a room where men and women 'partook of each other, without discrimination'. Blythe felt her cheeks flush as he described the young male protagonist being taken from behind by another man, while his female sweetheart pleasured him from the front.

'You all right there, kiddo?' whispered William, leaning across to her. She turned to him and smiled.

'I'm fine,' she said, taking a long glug of wine. 'This is just swell.'

He nodded his head, unconvinced.

It was true, she was fine, if a little stunned. It was like no party she had ever been to before. While Sam broke into his next stanza, she thought of the inane soirées she'd had to attend at the country club with her parents and, latterly, Amory. The soul-crushing small talk, the women huddled together sharing recipes and society gossip, the men sinking whiskies and puffing on Cuban cigars while discussing the movements of the stock market and comparing golf handicaps.

When Sam finished there was a roar of applause. Estelle jumped to her feet and kissed him passionately.

'Hey,' she cried, turning to the tumbleweeds huddled on the floor. 'What say we put the music back on? Liven the place up a bit.'

She raced over to the gramophone and suddenly the room was alive with a sound that Blythe had never heard before. A pulsing, raucous cacophony, that felt like it was penetrating her ribcage.

'Come on, my sweet American girl,' said William, pulling her up from the floor. 'Let's rock.'

Before she knew it, Blythe was dancing round the room with him, her face pressed next to his. As the music intensified, William discarded his jacket and threw it across the room before pulling her back towards him. His sweat drenched her skin, his heart pulsated against hers. Blythe's parents would have been appalled to witness such a spectacle, but Blythe didn't care because for the first time in her eighteen years she felt truly alive.

'What is this music?' she exclaimed, as William twisted her around the room.

'They call it Motown,' he cried, sweat pouring from his brow. 'But we call it the future.'

'I've never heard anything like it,' gasped Blythe, as William pulled her back towards him.

'Music like this ain't for listening to,' he cried, his breath warm against her face. 'It's for moving to.'

And when the song ended they collapsed into a heap on the floor, with Blythe on top of William. Her lips were tantalizingly close to his. She leaned forward but as she did, he rolled out from beneath her.

'Cigarette break,' he cried, gesturing to Sam, who slumped down beside him with a box of Gitanes. 'Come here now, my good man, and tell me about that poem. I think I know where the inspiration came from.'

Blythe pulled her knees to her chest as the two men huddled together. She suddenly felt awkward, like the girl who gets overlooked at the prom. She was hot and sticky, and the threadbare carpet was thick with dust. Getting to her feet, she brushed the grime from her pedal pushers and glanced at William, who was so engrossed in his chat with Sam that he didn't notice her leave the room.

There was a whole wall crammed with shelves to the left of the archway that led to the Old Smoky Reading Room. Running her finger along the cracked spines, she paused at a familiar name, smiling to herself as she recalled the summer of 1959, lying on a sunlounger on the terrace of her parents' holiday home in the Hamptons, a pile of books recommended by her beloved teacher, Mademoiselle DuPont, stacked on the ground beside her. As she pulled out the battered copy of *Tender is the Night*, running her fingers over Scott Fitzgerald's embossed name, she was back in the broiling August heat, imagining herself as Rosemary Hoyt, basking in the attention of Dick and Nicole Diver on the French Riviera as they headed to their doom.

'Scott signed that copy, if I'm not mistaken.'

She turned to see George standing in the archway, a ring of smoke circling from a freshly lit cigarette.

'He did?' exclaimed Blythe, flicking to the title page. Sure enough, there was Fitzgerald's scrawl, the *g* of his surname resembling a mandolin. Above the signature were the words: *For Sylvia, the kindest heart.*

'Who was Sylvia?' asked Blythe, looking up at George. He raised an eyebrow.

'Why don't you come and sit down,' he said, gesturing through the archway to the threadbare sofa, 'and I'll tell you all about her.'

Time seemed to freeze as she sat listening to George telling her, between puffs of endless cigarettes, the story of Sylvia Beach, the woman behind a shop named Shakespeare and Company that resided on the rue de l'Odéon which, in its 1920s heyday, had been a gathering place for the leading lights of the Lost Generation.

'Hemingway adored Sylvia,' said George, flicking the ash from his cigarette into an empty wine glass. 'Said she was the kindest woman he knew. And he wasn't wrong. Though she was also the bravest. The way she stood up to the Nazis when they tried to close her down. Boy, that took some guts. It was a sad day in Paris when that bookstore closed and she was arrested. They say she never fully recovered. It felt like a light had gone out. That's why I opened this place, as a kind of homage to Sylvia and what she was trying to achieve with her shop. I felt there was still something of the spirit of the Lost Generation to be found in Paris, still writers needing space and time to think. At Le Mistral, they can do just that. So how about you, what are you writing?'

He looked at Blythe earnestly, just as William had the previous day when he asked if she was studying at the Sorbonne. Blythe had grown so used to men treating her like an air-headed little woman, first her father, then Amory, that it felt odd to have men like George or William talk to her as though she were on their level. But it felt wretched that, despite all her dreams, she had nothing to show for it, just notebooks full of half-finished stories and scribbled observations.

'I'm just here on vacation from Connecticut. I'm getting married in the Hamptons this fall and . . .' She left the sentence hanging, waiting to see a look of disappointment in George's eyes. Why was he wasting his time talking to a girl whose only prospect was becoming an East Coast trophy wife and mother? 'I do like to write but I haven't finished anything yet.'

To her surprise, George did not flinch. Instead, he reached across and grabbed a notebook from the table by the sofa. Ripping out a page, he handed it to her.

'Here,' he said, his blue eyes twinkling. 'Take this and write down your autobiography – hell, imagine you're writing your obituary. And if it includes spending the rest of your days sipping cocktails in the Hamptons and never writing a goddamn word then so be it. But I suspect, miss, your life may just take you by surprise.'

Before she could answer, she noticed William standing in the archway. His hair was messed up and he was swaying on his feet.

'Oh, there you are, kiddo,' he said, taking his hat from under his arm and placing it on his head. 'I wondered where you'd got to. Listen, it's getting late. Time to get you back to your folks.'

She glanced at her watch. It was almost three a.m. Her heart lurched as she sprang from the sofa.

'Gosh, I didn't realize the time,' she said, folding the paper George had given her and placing it in her bag. 'We'd better go. It was nice to meet you, George.'

She extended her hand, but George just looked at her impassively and nodded, as though their conversation had never happened.

William was strangely quiet as they crossed the Pont Neuf and headed to the hotel. He looked as though he was lost in thought. Blythe recalled the way he had gazed at Sam as the young man read his poem, how engrossed he was in their conversation.

'You and Sam seem like good friends,' she found herself blurting out, unable to hold in her curiosity.

William turned to her, his eyes glistening in the moonlight.

'Sam is a beautiful artist,' he said wistfully. 'A brain the size of Africa and the body of a Greek god.'

'Are you . . .' she began, hardly knowing how to phrase the question. 'Are you two . . .'

'Are we lovers, Blythe?' said William bluntly. 'Is that what you're asking?'

'I . . . er . . . I don't know, I just . . . I'm sorry. I didn't mean to pry, it's just that I didn't think you were . . . you were like that.'

'I'm one of those anomalies, Blythe,' he said softly, pausing on the bridge to look into the water. 'I love men and women equally. Can't see no distinction. A beautiful soul is a beautiful soul regardless. That's how I see it. I know it must sound strange to someone from your background and I understand. I can't imagine my Irish Catholic family being welcoming of it either, but like I said about that Motown music earlier, there's a new world forming, a future where things don't have to be so rigid. I suppose that's what Sam's poem was all about. Do you see?'

Blythe nodded her head, though inside she felt like a stupid child. As the lights of the hotel appeared up ahead, she felt her heart sink – and not just because the night was ending but because, once again, she had got it all so hopelessly wrong. When William had asked her to the party, she had let herself get carried away, imagined herself having a passionate love affair with this beautiful, bookish young man. It was another reminder of her gaucheness, how she didn't fit in, she chided herself as they stopped outside the revolving doors.

'Well, it's been quite the evening,' said William, his soft Irish voice breaking into her thoughts. 'We must do it again some time.'

Her heart leapt. He didn't think she was an idiot. He wanted to see her again.

'Well, we're here for the next month,' she said, her words tumbling out like dropped pennies. 'And I'd love to come to the bookstore again, see George and Sam and Estelle and Paula. Or the café. Or I could come meet you at Harry's.'

She paused, hearing her mother's voice in her head. *'Blythe, you are making quite the fool of yourself. What have I told you about blathering on like that. You're a young lady, and ladies are there to listen, not talk.'*

'I know where to find you,' said William, placing his hand on her arm. Then with a sweep of his head he kissed her softly, on the cheek. She inhaled his scent: red wine, cigarette smoke and citrus soap.

'Oh, and in answer to your question,' he whispered in her ear. 'No, Sam and I are not lovers.'

As he gently pulled away from her, Blythe opened her mouth to speak but he placed his finger lightly on her lips.

'Now, get yourself inside before you're missed.'

And with that he was gone, swallowed up into the Parisian night like the smoke from one of George's cigarettes.

10

ALEXIS

When Maeve finishes speaking, she swivels her chair round to face me. The sharp bob frames her features perfectly and gives the white shade an almost silvery hue. Her face glows in the pale light streaming in through the window and as she lifts her hand to close her notebook, she pauses for a moment to admire her freshly manicured nails.

'You were right, Alexis,' she says, looking up at me with a smile. 'That shade is most becoming. And as for the hair, well, I feel like me again. Thank you for taking the time to help me. It was just what the doctor ordered.'

Taking an early lunch hour, I had brought Maeve upstairs with the intention of freshening her up, giving her hair a quick wash and finding her some clean clothes, but it had turned into an hour-long pamper session that, I have to admit, both of us sorely needed.

After washing Maeve's straggly hair over the sink in the en-suite bathroom, using copious amounts of shampoo to get rid of the grime that had accumulated from weeks of neglect, I had taken the hairdressing scissors I keep with me in my toiletry bag and restored her trademark bob. As I had blow-dried it and set it with a spritz of hairspray which I located at the back of the bathroom cabinet, I recalled the YouTube hairdressing tutorial I had memorized one night in the van. With finances dwindling and without my beloved London salon, I needed to find an inexpensive way to keep my hair tidy. So with the help of a hairdressing kit and a good deal of patience I mastered the art of the trim. But nothing beat the sense of satisfaction of seeing my new-found skills being put to use on someone other than myself. When I saw Maeve's finished haircut, how it brought her back to life, my heart almost burst with happiness.

'Oh, my dear,' Maeve had exclaimed when she saw herself in the mirror. 'You've performed a miracle. I look almost human again.'

'It's amazing what a good haircut will do,' I said. 'Up there with freshly laundered sheets on the feel-good factor scale, eh?'

'You're a good girl, Alexis,' she said, tears suddenly welling in her eyes. 'I'll bet your mother is ever so proud of you.'

Mention of my mother had made my chest tighten. If I answered Maeve honestly then she would ask further questions, questions that I just wasn't ready to answer. I'd spotted a box of rather dated cosmetics on Maeve's dressing table earlier and decided to swiftly move the subject along by suggesting I give her a makeover.

'Why stop with the hair?' I said, grabbing the box. 'I think we should go all out, bring back the Maeve O'Malley of old.'

'If only,' she sighed sadly, glancing at a framed photograph on the wall. It showed Maeve in a gold beaded dress beaming into the camera, a glass of champagne in her hand. 'I know I said you were a miracle worker, but

I don't think even your magic could bring that Maeve back.'

'Well, I'm up for the challenge,' I said, rummaging through the box with its overwhelming scent of Max Factor face powder. 'And I say we bring back the signature red lips.'

Maeve smiled as I held up a black tube of MAC lipstick.

'Paramount,' she cried. 'My favourite shade. I was never without it in the nineties. Then they bloody well discontinued it, so I had to use mine sparingly.'

'You're telling me you've kept hold of this since the nineties?' I exclaimed. 'Maeve!'

'Oh, well,' she shrugged. 'They say quality lasts a lifetime.'

We had met each other's eye then and I found myself, for the first time in years, laughing, really laughing, deep and hearty and unabashed, what my mother would have called a right good belly laugh.

When I'd finished doing her make-up and she had given my efforts her seal of approval, Maeve had said there was something else she would like to show me. Aware of my allotted lunch hour already slipping by, I'd said that if she wanted to get another chapter in as she had seemed so desperate to do when she came to find me in Jasper's study then we would have to get a move on.

'Oh, this won't take long,' she said, taking a key from her bedside drawer and walking across to a pair of double doors on the far side of the room. 'In fact, it will help me set the scene. Come on, you'll see.'

I followed her, waiting while she fumbled with the key, then watched as she flung open the doors and turned to me with a wink.

'Go on,' she said, ushering me forward. 'Pick me out something nice, and for you as well. It will be fun if we look the part.'

She flicked on a light, and I gasped as I found myself in what looked like a vintage atelier. Gowns covered in clear plastic wrapping lined the rails that ran either side of the room. Above them, neatly stacked on broad shelves, were shoeboxes emblazoned with designer names that had once adorned my own wardrobe: Chanel, Prada, Jimmy Choo, Gucci, Yves Saint Laurent. Running my hand along the row of gowns, I gasped as I saw labels that belonged to another age, vintage gems like Halston, Biba, Dior and Givenchy. As a vintage fashion junkie, I felt as though I had died and gone to haute-couture heaven.

'Maeve, I can't possibly wear any of these,' I said, turning to her. She stood at the door looking at me fondly, like a mother watching a child let loose in a sweet shop. 'They're . . . far too precious. Take this one, for example.'

I pulled out a floor-length champagne-coloured beaded number and held it up. The light from the window made it shimmer like gossamer.

'This is a mid-twentieth-century Halston masterpiece,' I said, shaking my head in disbelief. 'The same one that was worn by Audrey Hepburn when she won Best Actress at the 1962 Oscars.'

'You certainly know your fashion history.' Maeve smiled.

'It's my passion,' I said. 'Though being on the road, it's been a while since I last wore an evening gown.'

'That makes two of us,' laughed Maeve. 'So, even more reason why we should dress ourselves up to the nines and get on with the next chapter. Like I said, it helps to look the part.'

'But these gowns are far too precious to just sit around in,' I said, replacing the Halston and pulling out a dazzling midnight-blue, sequinned Dior cocktail dress. 'Besides, I'm not sure I'd be able to squeeze myself into any of them. They're tiny.'

'Nonsense,' said Maeve, edging past me and taking out a dress from the end of the rail. 'Try this one. The colour will bring out your eyes. Go on, I bet it fits you like a dream.'

She peeled off the plastic covering and handed me an emerald-green halter-neck silk gown, cut on the bias and falling in diaphanous folds to the floor. It was the most exquisite piece I had ever seen, a dream of a dress.

'Oh, Maeve, are you sure?' I said, taking the dress and holding it up against me. 'Pieces like this need to be protected.'

'Rubbish,' scoffed Maeve, shaking her head. 'What use is it having nice things if you can't enjoy them? As far as I'm concerned dresses are made to be worn, not kept hidden away like some old museum relic. Now, go and put it on while I find something suitable.'

Ten minutes later we were in her study, perched on our chairs like two ageing movie stars. Maeve was right, the green dress fitted like a dream. It felt amazing to be wearing something special again. Opposite me Maeve sat dictating the chapter, resplendent in a pale pink Chanel shift dress.

Now, as I press 'save' on the document and Maeve continues to admire her manicured nails, I turn over the chapter in my head.

'You know, I'm not sure if we need so much detail on

George at the end there,' I say, my editorial muscle kicking in. 'After all, this is Blythe and William's story, not his.'

'Perhaps,' says Maeve, narrowing her eyes. 'But then without George Whitman there would be no Mistral, no William and Blythe. It was the bookshop that brought them together, you see.'

'One could argue it was rush hour at Les Deux Magots that did that,' I say, leaning back in my chair, the diaphanous folds of the dress skimming the floor like a mermaid's tail. 'If it hadn't been so busy, William wouldn't have had to share Blythe's table, their lives would never have crossed. And yet we don't get to hear the life story of the waiter who seated them so why do we get George's?'

'Are you really comparing the legendary George Whitman to a waiter?' cries Maeve. 'Honestly, without him we have no story.'

'I'm just saying we might have to cut a little bit in the next draft,' I say, using the kind of polite persuasion it has taken me decades to hone.

'Hmm,' says Maeve, with a twinkle in her eye. 'We'll see.'

I'm just getting into my stride and am about to offer another suggestion when there is a knock at the door.

'Oh, there you are. I was wondering where—'

Jasper stands in the doorway aghast.

'What on earth . . .?'

Snapping the laptop shut I jump to my feet, almost tripping over the hem of the dress.

'I'm sorry, Jasper,' I say. 'I know I'm horribly late, but Maeve and I were just—'

'We were having a little pamper session,' interrupts Maeve, giving me a glance that suggests I should stay quiet about the novel. 'Alexis very kindly washed my hair and did my make-up, and I couldn't resist digging out some of my old outfits. She's even given me my old bob back. Do you like it?'

Jasper looks at her with an expression I can't quite place. It's like he's seen a ghost.

'Maeve, you know fine well that Cordelia has offered to wash your hair countless times these last few weeks and you've flatly turned her down,' says Jasper indignantly. 'And as for the bob, I would say that it's rather unsuitable for a woman of your age. You are also aware that I have recruited Alexis to aid me with my edits. She is a staff member and now you have put her in a very awkward position where she very likely felt she couldn't say no.'

'Honestly, Jasper,' I say, shuffling to the chair by the window where I left my cardigan and jeans earlier, 'Maeve really didn't coerce me. It was my suggestion that I do her hair. And, please be assured, I'll work extra time on your edits today to make up for it.'

'Good,' says Jasper, visibly rattled. 'I'll see you in the office once you've got changed.'

Suitably admonished, I make my way to the dressing room to return the dress.

'Thank you, Alexis,' Maeve calls out after me. 'I've had a marvellous time.'

I must admit I enjoyed it too. Dressing up in vintage Halston and working on a new Maeve O'Malley novel is pretty much bucket-list territory for me and, though it terrifies me slightly, I can feel my old passions igniting again, new ideas and editorial suggestions burning up inside me as I make my way along the oak-panelled corridor. Best to leave them to one side for now though, I think to myself, as I step into the dressing room. I have an entire afternoon and evening making sense of Jasper's dry rendering of Charles de Gaulle's diary ahead of me.

Slipping out of the dress I hang it back carefully on the hanger and place the plastic covering over it.

'Thank you, Maeve,' I whisper, as I straighten it out. 'For making me feel like myself again, even if it was just for a little while.'

Once I'm in my own clothes, I pull my hair back in a loose bun and take a look at myself in the mirror. I really should remove the elaborate make-up but the sight of myself with smoky eyes, curled lashes and softly contoured cheeks makes me feel happy, as though a part of me I thought I'd lost for ever has been returned.

Switching off the light, I step out into the corridor and am just heading for the stairs and Jasper's office when my phone vibrates in my hand. I look at the screen. A new email notification. Clicking on it I see that it's an update from Ken the mechanic. He's finished the first part of the work on the van and has included an invoice for £200. All the more reason not to slacken when it comes to my work here, I think to myself, as I close the email. After all, Jasper's writing may be dull but it's my only way of getting out of here and back on the road to find my mother. It is then that I remember the email I'd received earlier. The genealogy company. I'd been about to bin it when Maeve interrupted me. Closing Ken's message, I click once more on the subject line *Still searching for someone?*

As the page loads, something comes back to me, something that has been niggling ever since I arrived here. It was the long pause when Jasper heard my mother's name over the intercom, a delay which, at the time, I'd put down to him having difficulty hearing me over the noise of the traffic. But now, after being here and watching him up close, I can't shake the feeling that he knows more about my mother than he is letting on. There is something Jasper Hardy is keeping from me, and I intend to find out what it is.

11

ALEXIS

I didn't plan on confronting Jasper immediately, but he can tell by my demeanour when I stagger into the office that something is the matter. Though at first, he assumes that it is Maeve and the impromptu dressing-up session that has unsettled me.

'I've told her time and time again that she must put the past behind her,' he says, pulling out a chair for me to sit on. 'It doesn't do her or those around her any good to be constantly revisiting a life that has long gone. I'm sorry you had to get embroiled in it, Alexis, and I do apologize if my tone was rather curt earlier. It's just . . . well, to new-comers, Maeve can seem like a ray of sunshine, an exciting, spontaneous free spirit, and being around her when she's like that is addictive. But when you've lived with her as I have and been privy to moods that can change on a six-pence, well, I'm afraid it's made me rather self-protective.'

'No, I understand, Jasper,' I say, trying to focus my thoughts. 'I should have been firmer with Maeve, told her that I had to work. I can see how stressful this is for you which is why I offered to help. And I'm so grateful for this job, I really am. But it's not Maeve who's unsettled me.'

And then, before I know it, I've told him everything, about my mother leaving when I was a child, my father's recent death, the discovery of my mother's diary and my quest to find her using the same mode of transport she left in, though I'm careful not to mention what happened with my job and marriage along the way. 'And then there's this,' I say, showing him the census notification. 'Which is the reason I came here in the first place. Everything matched. Her name, her birth date. I was sure this was it. Jasper, look, I'm sorry to go on like this but are you certain that you don't know my mother, that she didn't stay here?'

He takes the phone and looks at the screen, shaking his head. 'I am absolutely sure,' he says, handing it back to me. 'I have never heard of or met this woman. As you may know, Mrs Hardy and I bought Lustrum Manor in 2018, and since then there's only been us and Cordelia living here. I'm sure we'd notice if someone else had sneaked in.'

He lets out a rather awkward laugh as he collects the next chapter from the printer tray and places the papers into a neat pile on the desk, ready for me to edit.

'But this is a census record,' I say, staring at the notification as though I can somehow find the answer on the screen. 'An official document. And it quite clearly states that this was my mother's place of residence in March 2021.'

'Like I said, I think we would have noticed if we'd had a house guest,' he says, glancing at me over his glasses. 'I don't know, maybe this Kimberly Harper – er, sorry, your mother I should say – got mixed up. Perhaps she was staying at the pub, the Lustrum Arms. That's also on Spring Lane and offers rooms to rent. She may have filled out that census online and it automated the address from "Arms" to "Manor".'

'That's a thought,' I say hopefully. 'I'll get in touch with the pub and ask them.'

But then I think of my mother, how she loved that camper van of hers and hated being confined indoors, and an idea comes to me.

'What about the land?' I say. 'I mean, the grounds are extensive here. Is it possible she could have camped out there, in her van?'

He looks at me with a tense expression and I realize I have probably said too much. After all, this man gave me a job and a place to stay when I was in dire need and he's dealing with a heavy workload and a sick wife. The last thing he needs is me pestering him about my mother who, it's becoming increasingly clear, he has never met.

'Look, I'm sorry, Jasper,' I say. 'I shouldn't be unloading on you like this. As you say, there must be some mistake.'

'Oh, you're not unloading, dear,' he says, his expression softening. 'I was just thinking that the only possible explanation for her to put this address on the census is the outhouses?'

'The outhouses?'

'Yes. We have a number of them, most in a state of dereliction,' he says, gesturing out of the window to the vast swathe of land extending from the terrace. 'The previous owner rented them out to local farmers but when we arrived we let it slip, and since Maeve has been unwell it's rather fallen down the list of priorities. Anyway, what I'm getting at is that it's not beyond the realms of possibility that someone could seek refuge in one of those outbuildings without us knowing.'

'You mean my mother could have squatted here?'

'Squatting is rather a harsh term,' he says, his cheeks flushing. 'Sometimes people find themselves in desperate need and have no choice but to make use of whatever amenities or shelter they stumble across. Though I'm not saying your mother did that. From what you tell me she was a very respectable woman. It doesn't sound like hiding out in some old barn would be something she would do.'

It's exactly the kind of thing she would do, I think to myself though I don't say this to Jasper. Of course, it all makes sense. There's no other way my mother could have been living in a place like this. She could have easily found somewhere hidden to park her camper van, if she still had it. And squatting would have appealed to her free-spirited nature, her disdain for authority. I'll never forget her calling my primary school teacher a boring old fart after he asked her not to smoke in the parent-teacher meeting.

'My mother was a restless soul,' I say, taking the printed sheets from Jasper. 'Always itching to be on the road, heading for the next destination. It looks like Lustrum Manor was just another pin on the map in 2021. But that was four years ago – she could be anywhere now.'

'You know, I must say, speaking with my historian hat on, that these genealogy sites are to be taken with a pinch of salt,' says Jasper, shaking his head. 'Most of them don't have any affiliation to official records. That census information could be a load of nonsense for all we know. In fact, it would have to be. I mean, who has heard of someone filling in a census while squatting in an outbuilding? It doesn't make sense.'

'Unfortunately, when it comes to my mother, nothing makes sense,' I say, a familiar lump settling in my throat.

'I'm sorry, Alexis,' Jasper says gently. 'It must be hard not to have . . . what do they call it these days, closure?'

'Well, I suppose some mysteries are just not meant to be solved,' I say, taking out my red pen. 'Do forgive me, Jasper. You're not paying me to cry over my mother, and I'm aware I've already wasted enough of your time today. Now, rest assured Charles de Gaulle will get my undivided attention for the rest of the afternoon.'

'Thank you, Alexis,' says Jasper, getting up from his chair. 'I suppose after all this morning's drama, Charles's reflective notes may be just the balm you need. I'll leave you to it.'

I work steadily through the afternoon and have the edits finished by six. However, as soon as I put my pen down, my head fills with thoughts of my mother, the idea of her hiding out here, possibly scared and alone, the prospect that she will just keep running and I will never find her, and that familiar knot of anxiety starts to gnaw at my chest. I need some air. And I need some answers. Taking my jacket from the hook by the front door, I head out into the grounds in search of the outhouses.

It is a beautiful evening, warm with just a hint of a breeze, and despite the drama of the day I feel a deep sense of peace wash over me as I walk across the courtyard and follow the moat around the manor. All around me, the mullioned windows glint and sparkle in the light of the setting sun. Passing the west wing, I recognize the curved bay glass of Maeve's study and wonder what she is doing in there. Preparing the next chapter, ready for tomorrow's session? Or perhaps she is lying on the chaise longue catching up with the Richard Osman audiobook I spotted on her desk earlier. As I ponder, a figure appears at the window. Maeve? I raise my hand to wave at her but as I do something odd happens. It might be the sun shining in my eyes, a trick of the light or my own harried brain, but for a brief moment I see my mother's face at the window. I blink and look again. But there is nothing there. A shiver flutters through me despite the warmth of the evening and, quickening my step, I make my way towards the grounds.

Beyond the vast lawn, there is a walled area with a rusting iron gate. The outhouses Jasper mentioned seem to be located at the far end of the grounds. Despite the dwindling light in the sky, curiosity gets the better of me and I head towards the gate. The latch is rusted and stiff but when I manage to get it open and step inside, I am greeted with the most beautiful surprise. A walled garden.

Though a little wild and overgrown it must have been exquisite in its prime. There is a rose-covered arbour on the far side of the garden, underneath which stands an old-fashioned love seat made from twisted willow. It reminds me of *The Secret Garden*, another book I adored as a child. Why doesn't Maeve come here to write? I think to myself as I step across the knotted, overgrown beds. It would do her the world of good to come and breathe in the fresh air. I make a note to mention it to her tomorrow. Perhaps we could tidy it up together, bring it back to life.

When I reach the end of the path, the sun is just about to dip behind the trees and I lift my face up towards its golden light. Intuitively, I stretch my arms into the Salute to the Sun, my favourite yoga pose for easing my twisted muscles – being behind the wheel of the van pretty much constantly this past year or so has taken its toll on my back – and close my eyes, feeling every muscle and sinew relaxing. As I repeat the movement, I can't help but think about my mother. Perhaps she came to this secret garden when she stayed here. I can see her, up to her elbows in soil, pulling up the weeds just as she did in our garden back home when I was a child. Just as Tara and I had done with our little patch in Richmond. Tears prick my eyes as I remember that first evening, sitting out on the patio side by side, exhausted from a day of lugging boxes and furniture up several flights of stairs but happy to be finally in the house of our dreams, the sum of our collective hard work. 'Here's to us,' Tara had whispered, clinking her glass of gin and tonic against mine. 'May our eternal summer never fade.' She was paraphrasing a line from the reading my father had given at our wedding, Shakespeare's Sonnet 18, an ode to love everlasting, to unions that grow stronger with time.

Just then the sun disappears behind the trees and a chill breeze ripples through the air. I feel desperately alone suddenly, as though I am the last person left on earth. What had seemed blissful just a few moments earlier now feels wretched and rotten. Digging my phone out of my pocket, I retrieve the last number and wait.

'Hello.'

Her voice is tentative, wary.

'Darling, it's me,' I say, trying to keep my tears at bay. 'I . . . I just wanted to see how you were.'

'I'm OK,' she says, with an audible sigh. 'Where are you? I can hear birdsong.'

I look up. A dove has settled on the arbour above my head and is cooing to its mate.

'It's a long story,' I say, relieved to be speaking to her at last. 'But I think I may be a step closer to finding Mum.'

'That's . . . that's great,' she says, a note of tension in her voice. 'I guess that was what you always wanted.'

I want to tell her that what I always wanted was her, that it is complicated, that my mother's leaving made me feel I wasn't worthy of love and happiness and a secure home. But I don't say any of this. Instead, I tell her about the van breaking down and Lustrum Manor and the fact that the woman who lives here is Maeve O'Malley, none of which impresses Tara, and rightly so.

'Listen, I have to go, Alexis,' she says wearily. 'I've got an opening statement to prepare for tomorrow. I'm in court all week so it's pretty full on. Look, I'm glad you're having a nice time. And I hope you find your mum, I really do, but it's hard talking to you like this. You said it was only going to be a few months and you've been gone for more than a year.'

'I know, darling,' I say, panic rising at the sense of finality in her tone. 'But please don't shut me out. Can I call you again, perhaps when the case is over? Sunday, maybe?'

'Maybe,' she says resignedly. 'Bye, Alexis.'

She rings off and I sit for several moments staring at the screen. Loneliness permeates my bones. Above me, the dove takes flight and as I watch it soar across the sky, I feel a sense of purpose returning. I'm going to make this right, I tell myself as I get up from the bench and walk out of the gate.

The outbuildings loom at the back of the property. I stride further away from the manor and make my way through an intersecting field, using my phone torch to see the path in the fading light. As I walk, I mull over the conversation with Tara in my mind, analysing her tone, her words, the fact that she rang off before I had the chance to say goodbye. But put myself in her shoes. She has every reason not to trust me and to erect boundaries to protect herself. It is what I had done when my mother left but those boundaries were book-shaped, my protectors were authors like Maeve whose brave characters had guided me through the fog of abandonment. I have spent years living with the consequences of my mother's leaving and now, as I reach the edge of the outbuildings, I feel like I still have a sliver of a chance of resolving it. Maybe if I do that then I can build my bridges back to Tara. Maybe then all of this will not have been in vain.

My head is bursting with what-ifs as I reach the outbuildings and push open the corrugated-iron door of a medium-sized barn, disturbing a nest of swallows as I do. My heart flips in my chest as the birds swoop over my head and make their bid for freedom out of the open door. Looking around me, I feel a deep sense of despair. It is just an abandoned old barn with animal feeding troughs wedged into the walls and straw scattered across the stone floor. The air smells faintly of cow dung and I press my hand to my mouth as I step gingerly over the decaying hay bales. My mother may have been a free spirit but there is no way she would have spent more than ten minutes in this dump let alone lived in it. Besides, whoever heard of someone filling in a census from the confines of a cow barn. None of it makes sense.

But then, as I am about to turn and go, the torchlight from my phone catches something. A brightly coloured bit of paper wedged against one of the troughs. As I draw closer, I see that it's a page from one of Maeve's *Time Traveller* books, the *Journey to Post-War Paris*. I recognize the colourful drawing of the terrace outside Les Deux Magots, the very place Maeve has been writing about these last few days. How odd that it has ended up here, I think to myself, running my finger along the edge of the paper, serrated where it was ripped from the book. When I look closer, I see someone has written something in the top corner of the picture. The paper is faded and weather-worn, the ink smudged and the writing almost illegible, but I can make out a few words: *Mummy and Daddy. Where . . . began.*

How strange, I think to myself, placing the paper in my pocket, and making my way to the door. Whatever can it mean? Yet as I step out into the cool evening air, I hear something that makes my skin prickle.

'Alexis?'

It's my mother's voice. Calling me.

'Alexis, where are you?'

I scan the field. There is no one there. Just my mind playing tricks again. The temperature has dipped and I zip up my jacket. As I make my way back across the field, I feel a deep sense of despair. After a year of dead ends, I'm no closer to finding my mother – why on earth could I have thought she would have stayed in that barn? – and I've pushed Tara far away. Why didn't I just allow myself to be loved? Tara loved me unconditionally and I threw it all away, just like my mother did to me and my dad. Is this my reality now, I ask myself, this loneliness? Did my mother take away my chance of ever being wanted when she walked away that day? Does she even give me a second thought?

'Alexis!'

The voice again. I look up and see a figure striding across the grass towards me. But it is not my mother, it is Cordelia. She looks frazzled. Her blonde hair has come loose from its usually neat bun and her mascara is smudged. She looks like she has been in some sort of scuffle.

'Oh, thank God,' she cries. 'I've been looking for you everywhere. I saw a light from the window. What are you doing out here?'

'I was just exploring the land,' I say, rather taken aback at Cordelia's brusque manner. 'The walled garden is so beautiful. I was thinking perhaps I could help spruce it up a bit, get Maeve, er, I mean Mrs Hardy, out here for some fresh air.'

'I'm afraid Mrs Hardy has just had the mother of all meltdowns,' sighs Cordelia. 'That's why I was looking for you. Poor Jasper's in there trying to calm her down but she insists on seeing you, says she needs to get the next instalment down, whatever that means.'

'Oh, it's the novel,' I say, following Cordelia back to the house. 'She's writing a new one. But I told her I would only be able to do it in the evenings so it wouldn't get in the way of my work for Jasper.'

'She's writing a novel? Jesus, that's all we need,' says Cordelia, shaking her head. 'More delusions.'

'I wouldn't call it a delusion,' I say. 'Writing is her profession. She was a hugely successful author in her day. And honestly, Cordelia, when she is dictating the story to me, she couldn't be more lucid.'

'So she's managed to hoodwink you too,' says Cordelia, pausing as we reach the courtyard. 'I knew it.'

'Hoodwink?' I say, flinching as I hear raised voices coming from inside. 'What do you mean?'

'It's just a very difficult situation,' she says, shaking her head. 'Mrs Hardy – Maeve as you call her – is growing worse each day and Jasper is doing everything he can but she's not the easiest person to deal with. Jasper is worried she's been skipping her medication which is why she had that episode the other day when you found her. I'm afraid without the pills another breakdown is inevitable.'

'Poor Jasper,' I say with a sigh. 'He's got a lot on his plate, that's clear to see. And I'm happy to help. The job has been a lifesaver. You see, without my van, I'm pretty much homeless.'

Cordelia frowns.

'I can't imagine living in a van,' she says. 'But then I do love my creature comforts. I'm really boring. Honestly, most nights I'm in my dressing gown in front of Netflix by seven and I'm out like a light by nine. The idea of being on the road without a proper bed and bath makes me shiver.'

'I was like that too once, believe it or not,' I say, as we make our way across the lawn. 'Anyway, as for Maeve, well, she was one of my heroes when I was growing up. I had every one of her books. It was those wonderful stories that inspired me to pursue a career in publishing. It just seemed like fate that she stepped out in front of my van that day. If I can help her in any way, then I will.'

'You do realize how sick she is?' says Cordelia, lowering her voice. 'Jasper has laid it all out, hasn't he? I know how he likes to bury his head in the sand and make out things aren't as bad as they are.'

'He told me about the confusion, yes,' I say, squinting my eyes as we cross the little stone bridge in the dusk. 'The fact that she hasn't been herself for some time.'

'I'm afraid that's not the half of it,' says Cordelia, with a heavy sigh. 'Do you know about William?'

My head feels fuzzy suddenly. There's the William who Jasper warned me about, the phantom trigger for all Maeve's ills, and then there's the charismatic young Irishman of the novel who in my mind is a perfect mix of Brendan Behan and Paul Mescal.

'He mentioned something,' I say. 'But he didn't elaborate. I got the impression that William was some manifestation of Maeve's condition though the novel she's writing has a William in it too and I'm not sure if that's just coincidence.'

'Listen, Alexis,' says Cordelia, turning to me, a look of utter resignation on her face. 'You have to understand. She's not writing a novel. She's just performing for attention. I've seen her do this countless times before and it never ends well.'

'Cordelia, what did you mean when you said the confusion's not the half of it?' I ask, growing increasingly uneasy. 'And who is William? The real one, I mean?'

'Listen, you didn't hear it from me,' says Cordelia, leaning closer. 'And you have to promise me that you will not breathe a word of it to anyone.'

'I promise,' I say, an icy chill rippling through me.

'Mrs Hardy is a complicated woman, some might even go so far as to call her disturbed,' says Cordelia, reducing her voice to a whisper. 'And that was the case long before the confusion set in. This goes back years. As for William, he's not a manifestation of her illness, he's her . . . well, he's what you would call her guilty conscience.'

I am about to probe further when the orangery door bursts open and Maeve comes marching down the steps, closely followed by Jasper who looks like he has just been dragged through a bush. His cardigan is askew and there is an angry red mark on his cheek.

'Alexis, thank goodness you're here,' Maeve cries, rushing to my side. Her mascara runs in black rivulets down her face and the sleeve of her dress is torn.

'Maeve, Jasper,' I cry, shocked at the state of them. 'What on earth has happened?'

'She was just a little unsettled that she couldn't find you,' says Jasper, his steady voice belying his ruffled appearance. 'But look, dear, here's Alexis now. All's well, eh?'

Maeve grips my arm, her eyes burning into me. She looks like a terrified child. I can't understand it. She was so settled and happy when I left her earlier.

'Come now,' says Jasper, extricating Maeve's hand from my arm. 'Let's get you back in the house.'

As we make our way up the steps, he leans in and whispers to me. 'I don't think she took her medication this morning. And she's refusing to have it now. Alexis, I hate to ask this, but do you think you might be able to convince her to take it? She quite clearly trusts you.'

My stomach sinks as I recall seeing Maeve throwing her pills away again earlier. She seemed so sprightly, particularly after the dressing-up session, that it hadn't concerned me. Now, seeing how worried Jasper is, I feel terrible.

'Of course,' I whisper back to him. 'Whatever I can do to help.'

'Are you still there, Alexis?' says Maeve, turning to me as we step inside the orangery.

'I'm here,' I say, giving her a reassuring pat on the arm. 'Shall we go and sit by the fire in the drawing room?'

'No,' she says, gripping my hand. 'We're going to my study. That's why I was looking for you. I have to get it down before I forget. We don't want to lose him again, do we?'

'Lose who, dear?' says Jasper softly, still holding on to her.

'Why, William, of course,' she cries exasperatedly. 'Who else?'

12

BLYTHE

Paris

April 1960

'Blythe, that is far too much butter. Think of your waist-line. You'll never fit into any wedding gown at this rate.'

Hadley Aston-Laine shook her head in dismay as her daughter, ignoring her protests, proceeded to smear not only creamy French butter but also a thick dollop of raspberry jam onto her croissant.

'You should have ordered the grapefruit and black coffee like me,' she said, watching in horror as Blythe took a great bite out of the pastry. 'After all, it's only five months until the wedding and you've still a good ten pounds to shed before then. Don't you, agree, Chad?'

Her father looked up from his day-old copy of the *Wall Street Journal*, a barely touched plate of smoked salmon and scrambled eggs congealing in front of him.

'Sorry, what was that?' he said, his mind three thousand miles away on the trading floor.

'Mom thinks I'm fat,' said Blythe, taking another defiant bite from her croissant. 'And that I should live on air and water for the next five months.'

'Don't be ridiculous,' said her father, rolling his eyes. 'You're as ripe as a peach, sweetie. No man wants a brittle stick insect, I can tell you that for nothing.'

Her mother glared icily at him as he took a forkful of cold scrambled egg before returning to his paper.

'I did not say you were fat, sweetie,' Hadley sighed. 'I just think that—'

But before she could finish, a young man appeared at the table beside Blythe.

'Mademoiselle?'

Blythe recognized Jean-Paul, the concierge she had probed for information on Harry's Bar.

'There is a delivery for you,' he said, his English impeccable. 'At the front desk.'

'For me?' said Blythe, dabbing her mouth with a napkin. 'Are you sure?'

'You are Blythe Aston-Laine, no?' he said, his mouth curling slightly.

'Yes, but I wasn't expecting a delivery.'

'Oh, my goodness,' her mother suddenly whooped, her eyes lighting up. 'I'll bet it's a gift from Amory. You know how romantic that young man is. Oh, sweetie, hurry down and see what it is.'

It was the happiest her mother had looked all week. With a sigh, Blythe got up from the table and followed Jean-Paul down to the front desk.

But when she got there, instead of an elaborate bouquet of flowers or a basket of fruit, there, to her delight, was William.

'Your delivery, ma'am,' said Jean-Paul, with a wink, giving William a friendly pat on the arm.

'Well, this is a pleasant surprise,' said Blythe, as the concierge left them. 'Though you could have just asked for me in the usual way without all this subterfuge.'

'Ah, I didn't want to rouse any suspicions, you know,' he said, blushing slightly. 'With your folks and all.'

'I suppose you're right,' said Blythe, her stomach fluttering at the sight of William who, back in his white linen Henley shirt and pinstriped dark trousers, looked as though he had just climbed straight out of the pages of an E. M. Forster novel. 'Though Daddy wouldn't notice anything outside Wall Street this morning. So why are you here?'

'I was just passing,' he said coyly. 'And . . . I . . . well, I just wanted to, you know, say hello.'

Blythe was rather taken aback by his bashfulness. The William she had seen so far had been something of an extrovert. This new version, though surprising, was rather endearing too.

'Hey, I have an idea,' she said, pulling him to one side as a group of American tourists bundled up with cameras and street maps marched through the lobby. 'Are you free today?'

'Er, for most of it,' said William, shaking his head as one of the tourists, a bullish-looking man wearing a Red Sox baseball cap, started ringing the concierge's bell loudly. 'I have a shift at the bar at five. Why?'

'I thought we could do something,' said Blythe, feeling emboldened. 'I don't know, have an adventure. I need some mental stimulation, William. Some conversation that doesn't involve stock prices or the calorie content of a grapefruit. I've written next to nothing since I've been here, and the whole reason for coming to Paris was precisely that, to be inspired, to write.'

'I know just the place,' said William, his face lighting up as he whispered a name into Blythe's ear.

'Perfect,' she said, a shiver of excitement running through her as she pressed her face next to William's.

'But what will you tell your folks?'

'Leave that to me,' she said, beaming. 'Give me two minutes.'

As he watched her scurry through the lobby, William felt a rush of something he hadn't felt before in his twenty-one years on this earth. It was a heady mix of excitement, lust, curiosity and danger underscored with something else, something that he had felt in his bones when he first set eyes on Blythe Aston-Laine at that table outside Les Deux Magots, a feeling that she was his past, present and future, that she was his salvation and his downfall.

'A guided tour of the Louvre,' exclaimed her mother, when Blythe ran back to the dining room. 'Now that is just adorable. Trust Amory to think of something so perfectly romantic.'

'Are you sure you don't mind?' Blythe said, crossing her fingers behind her back as she stood by the table. 'You know, I could always just come to lunch with you and Mrs Grainger as planned if you prefer.'

'And turn down Amory's generous gift? Don't be ridiculous,' said her mother, coiling her manicured fingernails around her pearl necklace. 'Hey, do you want to take my camera to get some photos for Amory? I can fetch it from upstairs if you like?'

'No thanks, Mom,' Blythe replied, her heart fizzing with excitement. 'You know me, I prefer to live in the moment.'

'Sensible girl,' muttered her father from behind the

newspaper. 'Your mother's permanently attached to that damned camera.'

'Oh shush, Chad,' sighed Hadley, rolling her eyes. 'You're such a bore. Well, Blythe, if you're not going to document the day with photos, at least make sure you buy Amory a little something to say thank you in return. Men just love those personal touches. Now off you go and have fun. Go on, go, go, go.'

And with her mother's whoops of delight ringing in her ears, Blythe did just that.

'I feel like I died and woke up in heaven,' she gasped, as they walked through the sunlit corridors of the Louvre a half-hour later. 'To be this close to such incredible masterpieces is just . . .'

Her voice caught in her throat. She felt tears welling in her eyes. Then, as if he knew, William took her hand and squeezed it tenderly.

'I know,' he said gently. 'I remember the first time I came here. In fact, I'll be honest with you, it wasn't an entirely positive experience.'

'Why is that?' asked Blythe, her eyes drawn to the fresco of *Prometheus Giving Fire to Man* on the ceiling above, the robed celestial figures frozen in time.

'It's hard to explain,' continued William, his hand still clasping hers. 'I guess, like you, I'd come to Paris with these expectations, these dreams. I had wished it, imagined it in my head for so long, that when I actually came here it felt almost too much, like I couldn't breathe, like I was drowning under the weight of all this beauty, this magnificence, this creativity. It felt like there were no boundaries, no rules, and I didn't know where I belonged in it all. It took me a while to learn the language of Paris, and I'm not talking about French. I'm probably not making any sense here.'

He turned to her and smiled, his blue eyes glinting in the sunlight pouring in through the arched windows.

'It makes perfect sense,' said Blythe. 'In fact, that's how I felt when you took me to Le Mistral the other night.'

'I could see that,' William replied, turning to her. 'That's why I kept you close. It can be . . . a lot, that place.'

'How long did it take you?' asked Blythe, as they stepped into the sculpture gallery. 'To shake off that feeling?'

'I don't think I have,' he replied. 'Not fully. Here, let's sit awhile.'

He gestured to a bench by the window.

'You see, kiddo,' he said, as they took a seat, 'when you come from a background like mine, you get used to feeling like an outsider. Sure, my folks were literate, they raised me on tales of Queen Maeve of Connaught and Grace O'Malley, my da could recite Yeats's poems by heart, while Ma got me onto Joyce and Wilde. But they were poor – my da was a labourer and my mother cleaned rich people's houses. That was the reality, earning a living, making sure we had a roof over our heads and food in our bellies, yet not forgetting all this stuff – art, poetry, literature. As my ma used to say, that was what fed the soul. But then I look at the other folk at Mistral, the tumbleweeds, the so-called starving artists, and most of them come from monied backgrounds, they're all running away from Mummy and Daddy and play-acting at being poor, but they've been raised to believe they deserve a seat at this table.'

He gestured to the room at large.

'They never feel like they don't belong,' he said, his voice trembling with emotion. 'It doesn't enter their mind. Yet, for me, it's like I must prove myself every day just to get a foot in the door.'

'I understand,' said Blythe, rather taken aback by William's passionate outburst. 'But being monied doesn't necessarily mean you get an easy pass. I mean, look at me. I've never felt as hopelessly gauche as I have these past few days in Paris. Sure, my parents have money, but that doesn't matter a jot when you come up against people like Paula and Sam and George, and you, for that matter. You're all just effortlessly cool, confident in your own skin, while I'm this awkward American tourist trying to keep up.'

'That couldn't be further from the truth,' said William, stroking her hand. 'First of all, I'm about as effortlessly cool as a lump of lard and as for being confident in one's own skin, why, I've never met anyone as assured as you. That's why I . . . that's why I like you so much, Blythe. You don't care what other people think, you're not part of any clique, you're happy just to be you. And I think that's grand.'

He paused and looked at her and Blythe felt as though his eyes were searing her soul.

'I think you're grand too,' she said, smiling as she mimicked his accent. And then, underneath the gaze of some of the greatest masterpieces in the world, she leaned forward and kissed him.

The kiss seemed to last an eternity yet could only have been seconds. And in those precious moments it had felt to Blythe that the world had ceased to exist, that they were the only two people alive, their coming together the only thing that mattered.

'Would you mind awfully,' she said, when they finally came up for air, 'if I did some writing?'

'Here?' said William, raising his eyebrows.

She nodded.

'Sure,' he said, taking his slim notebook from his pocket. 'But if it's all right by you, I'd like to relocate to do it.'

He pointed to an archway at the other side of the room.

'There's something in there I think you'll like. Come on, let's go and see.'

An hour later, her fingers smudged with black ink, Blythe read back over the words she had written in her notebook.

Sunlight streams through the window, illuminating the angel and casting his wings in a perfect golden glow. Their bodies entwined, his lips tantalizingly close to hers, there they stay, locked in an eternal embrace while the world passes by, oblivious. 'Do it,' she implores of him, her arms wrapped around his neck, stone turned to skin, dust turned to breath. 'Set me free from this marble prison, this rigid tomb. Kiss me, kiss me like we will never see tomorrow, and bring me, even for just this moment, back to life.'

With a sigh, she placed her fountain pen back into her pocket. In front of her was *Psyche Revived by Cupid's Kiss.* Antonio Canova's sculpture remained unmoved, as it had done for centuries. Yet something inside Blythe had stirred, a block had been released, she was writing, really writing for the first time in months.

'Ah, you're back in the room.'

Closing her notebook, she turned to see William, who

had been sitting on the bench alongside her all this time, lost in his own story. She smiled at the crumpled pieces of paper lying in his lap.

'I'm sorry,' she said, composing herself. 'I just felt so moved. It's the most powerful image I have ever seen.'

'No need to apologize for expressing yourself,' said William, nudging her playfully. 'Unfortunately, I just can't seem to find the words today.'

He gestured to the crumpled pages on his lap.

'Seems my mind is elsewhere,' he said, kissing her lightly on the lips. 'But I'm glad to hear you've been inspired. I told you, there's something about this piece.'

She looked around at the vast room they were sitting in, the ornate carved ceiling, the glass windows reflecting the light of the sun on the priceless art within, and she sighed contentedly.

'Thanks for bringing me here,' she said, breathing in the dusty air. 'It's just what I needed.'

'We brought each other here,' said William, his eyes following a group of American tourists who had gathered round the sculpture. 'It's funny but when we were sitting side by side just now, I felt so at ease, like I was under no compunction to speak.'

'Same,' she said, following his gaze. 'Safe in each other's silence. I could never write like that with anyone else.'

They both grimaced as a large man with a camera round his neck loudly enquired of the tour guide if there was a need for Cupid to be cupping Psyche's breasts. 'Gee, pal, we have kids here. They don't want to see all that.'

'It's hard to find like-minded people,' said William, turning his attention back to Blythe. 'My ma used to say, once you do you must hold them close, 'cause they're as rare as hens' teeth.'

Blythe laughed; a real unabashed chuckle that made her stomach hurt. And she realized she hadn't laughed like that since she was a child.

'Happy?' said William, nudging her shoulder playfully.

'I am,' replied Blythe, composing herself.

'Writers always feel happy once the story comes,' he said, blinking as a shaft of sunlight hit his face. 'It's a blessed relief. Many's the time I've thought I'd lost the ability, that I'd never write another word, and then, like some sort of alchemy, it happens. So are you going to tell me what it's about? Your story?'

Blythe felt her cheeks flush. She gripped her notebook, fearful that her words might somehow spill out of it into the room.

'Well, it's a different story to the one I'd originally planned,' she said. 'It's just taking shape, really. But I suppose the key theme is one of coming back to life, of crossing paths with someone who ignites your passion, makes you think that anything *is* possible.'

He looked at her, his blue eyes deep and dreamy, and she felt, like Psyche, a yearning that consumed her whole body.

'And anything is possible, my sweet American friend,' he said, kissing her inky fingers with his soft lips. 'But right now, I have a pressing engagement with a heap of books at Le Mistral. Come on, you can give me a hand.'

13

BLYTHE

'Whichever poor soul died sure had good taste,' said William, as Blythe crouched beside him. 'Just look at it all.'

They were emptying a box of books that George had just taken delivery of from a friend who dealt in house clearances.

'Good taste and a love of the Bloomsbury set,' said Blythe, as they separated the Woolfs from the Forsters, the Sackville-Wests from the Stracheys, and piled them neatly along the floor. 'In fact, that's what we should create, a Bloomsbury section.'

'Good idea,' said William, standing up and regarding the shelves. 'I say we clear out the old city guides from the second shelf and we'll put the new section there. No one ever picks up those dusty old guides. I'll stick them under the counter. Now, you can either alphabetize those Bloomsburys or put them in order of publication date, it's up to you.'

He pulled the old guidebooks down from the shelf, a plume of dust motes fluttering in their wake, and took them back to the counter where an old man in a Fedora was waiting to be served.

As Blythe stacked the Bloomsburys she ruminated over that moment in the Louvre in her head. The way William had looked at her just before the second kiss. The velvet softness of his lips on her fingers, the feeling deep inside her that something of great importance had just passed between them, an intensity that seemed to match the essence of the sculpture, its half-naked figures entwined for eternity. She could sense the story rising in her, almost begging to be let out. Taking her notebook and pen from her pocket she was about to carry on where she had left off when she felt a presence looming over her.

'Hey, Blythe.'

She looked up and saw William. He was with Paula, who was dressed in a man's shirt and baggy trousers and smoking a cigarette from a tortoiseshell holder. Brushing the dust from her skirt, Blythe got up from the floor to greet Paula.

'Darling, you look as beautiful as ever,' said the older girl, kissing Blythe on both cheeks. 'While I look a royal mess.'

'Remind me, both of you, to never take a call from my mother when I'm trying to clear my head,' she sighed, drawing on her cigarette and blowing smoke circles towards Blythe. 'Honestly, the woman drives me mad.'

'What's up with Lady Lawson today?' laughed William, placing his hand on the small of Blythe's back. She felt a surge of electric warmth rising up her spine, yet he kept his gaze firmly on Paula and her tale of family woe.

'Well, she was on her second gin and Dubonnet and it's still mid-morning in London so make of that what you will,' said Paula, with a shrug. 'And she was calling to tell me that I've been invited to a reunion of my classmates from Cheltenham Ladies' College, and wouldn't it be an awful shame if I missed it because of some stuffy old magazine. Oh, and for good measure, she told me that if I carried on messing around with writing I'd never find a husband. Men can't stand their wives working, apparently. Were you aware of that, Blythe?'

Blythe felt her cheeks flush as she thought of Amory and her own mother's insistence that once she was married, Blythe's role would be that of wife, homemaker and hostess.

'I . . . er . . . I . . .' she stuttered, all the bravado and confidence of the morning now evaporated.

'Blythe's not into all that marriage nonsense,' said William, squeezing her hand gently. 'She's far too busy with her stories.'

'I quite agree,' said Paula, taking another drag of her cigarette. 'Though in my case I'll have to wait until women can marry each other for it to make sense to me, if you know what I mean. Poor Mummy always thought it was a phase I went through at school and she's still holding out for me to be swept off my feet by some Mr Darcy character.'

'He'd have to be a brave man to try that with you,' laughed William. 'You'd likely throw him in the Seine.'

'You know me too well, darling Will,' said Paula, with a wry smile. 'Anyway, enough of all that. I'd love to hear what you're working on, Blythe. William told me the two of you were writing at the Louvre today.'

'Blythe's penning a love story,' said William, his eyes brightening. 'Inspired by Cupid and Psyche no less.'

'Sounds fascinating,' said Paula. 'I was just telling William about the new literary magazine Sam, Estelle and I are setting up. We're looking for stories for the first issue. You should submit yours when it's finished.'

'Oh gosh, no,' exclaimed Blythe, stuffing her notebook

back into her pocket. 'I couldn't possibly. It's not even a proper story, just a bunch of thoughts.'

She stumbled slightly as she grabbed her handbag from the floor and slung it over her shoulder. The room suddenly felt close. Paula's smoke mixed with the fusty smell of the books and the scent of stale cooking oil from George's fried potatoes made her feel nauseous.

'All stories are just a bunch of thoughts, really,' said William, turning as the door opened and Sam walked in.

'Hey, my friend,' cried William, rushing to embrace him. 'Good to see you.'

'You too,' said Sam, glancing at but not acknowledging Blythe. 'Estelle's running late but she'll be here by six.'

'Right, we can start without her,' said Paula, grabbing Sam's arm. 'Come on, George is waiting in the back room. He thinks he may know of a place we can get it all printed. Anyway, must dash. Spread the word, won't you, William. And, Blythe, if you change your mind about that story, you know where we are.'

She disappeared down the narrow corridor in a cloud of cigarette smoke.

'You should take her up on that offer,' said William, joining Blythe by the bookshelves.

He paused, his eyes fixed on her.

'What?' she said, feeling self-conscious suddenly. 'What is it?'

'I was just wondering if you're going to tell me what your love story's about,' he said, casting his eyes across her newly created Bloomsbury section. He slid out *Mrs Dalloway* and placed it after *The Voyage Out*. 'Sorry, I'm a stickler for chronology.'

He stepped closer to her, dangerously close. Her heart began to pound. She heard her mother's voice in her head. *'Blythe Aston-Laine, what in God's name do you think you're doing? Have you forgotten that you're engaged to be married?'*

'It's just a bunch of scribbles, that's all,' said Blythe, stepping back. 'I'm not a writer.'

'What makes you say that?' asked William, leaning his head against the shelf, his dark curls falling across his forehead. 'You certainly sound like one.'

'It's all just part of the dream,' said Blythe, with a sigh. 'Paris, books, writing. I've lived all this in my head for years. Now I'm here and, well, it still doesn't feel real. Honestly, William, I'm no writer – I can't even stack Virginia Woolf's novels in the right order – I'm just a fraud.'

'Hey,' said William, taking her by the shoulders. 'Let me tell you something. I have met a lot of people in my life, most of them crooks and charlatans and rogues on the make, and you, my friend, are no fraud.'

'I don't mean in the literal sense,' she said, that familiar heaviness settling in her chest. 'I mean when it comes to actually becoming the person I have dreamed of being. There is no point in me submitting stories or getting inspired because my whole future has been planned for me. This last year I . . .'

She rubbed her finger round the hefty diamond on her finger, the ring that seemed to get tighter every day.

'You don't talk about him,' said William. 'The man who gave you that.'

He nodded towards the ring.

'There's nothing to say, really,' she said, taking a book from the shelf and flicking though it to distract herself.

'He's a good person, a sweet soul. I've known him all my life, but I don't love him.'

'So why are you with him?' said William, taking the copy of *A Room with a View* from her trembling hands and placing it back on the shelf.

Blythe felt her cheeks burn. No one had asked her this before. Why, she hadn't even asked it of herself.

'He's my father's second in command at the family firm,' she began, not meeting William's gaze. 'Daddy has no son, so he needs someone to leave the business to, a safe pair of hands. And if Amory marries me then the business stays in the family.'

She looked up. William raised his black bushy eyebrows, aghast.

'No wonder you were so taken by *Cupid and Psyche*,' he said, shaking his head and letting out a derisive snort. 'It's the closest thing you'll get to love if you let your folks plan your life like this.'

He laughed and it felt like a knife through Blythe's heart. She sank to the floor, wedging her knees to her chest, tears pricking at her eyes. William knelt down beside her and placed his hand on her arm.

'I'm sorry, kiddo, I didn't mean it the way it came out,' he said soothingly. 'I guess I'm just rattled that some other guy gets to be with you, gets to spend the rest of his life with you.'

He reached out and stroked her cheek.

'Being with you at the Louvre today, Blythe, it was like . . . it was like coming home. Those kisses, I—'

But before he could finish Paula appeared in the doorway.

'William, why are you still here? It's almost five. You said you needed to scoot to Harry's for your shift.'

'Damn it,' he exclaimed, staggering to his feet as Paula returned to the back room. 'I'm sorry, kiddo. Gotta go. Wait here for me, will you? I'll be back at eleven.'

He kissed her cheek, grabbed his overcoat from the chair behind the counter, then hurried to the door.

'Wait for me,' he said. 'You promise?'

Blythe knew she had to get back to the hotel but, lost under his spell, she nodded her head.

'I promise.'

And as William stepped out into the early-evening bustle, she heard herself cry out after him.

'I'll wait for you for ever, William Kenneally.'

14

ALEXIS

As I approach the beginning of my second week here, life at Lustrum Manor has fallen into something of a routine. From nine a.m. until four p.m., I work steadily on Jasper's Charles de Gaulle biography, familiarizing myself in the process not only with the former French President's thoughts on his time in the trenches but also with the dry, laboured, sterile tone of Jasper's writing. Perhaps I am being harsh, perhaps I am simply unaccustomed to the academic 'voice', though I have certainly read plenty of biographies in my time, but there is just something lacking in Jasper's writing, a passion, a spark, a heart, something that sadly seems to be reflected in his outward demeanour, a chilliness that no quantity of toothy smiles, cups of tea and shepherd's pies can help to dispel. It is tricky because, on several occasions, I have found myself torn between simply editing – which is what Jasper is, to my eternal gratitude, paying me handsomely for – and rewriting the whole thing.

My mother, and my quest to find her, is never far from my mind though the mystery of her whereabouts remains frustratingly unsolved. The idea that she may have stayed at the Lustrum Arms was ruled out when I paid a visit to the pub one evening and was told by the landlord that the accommodation wing had been closed in 2021 due to lockdown restrictions. Still, though disappointed to have another lead prove to be a dead end, I am determined not to give up. Jasper's opus may be dull but the money I'm earning from it will get me back on the road within a couple of weeks. Besides, it has been good to reignite my editing skills though I've had to temper my usual brutally honest approach with a liberal sprinkling of tact and diplomacy.

Now, with a dozen chapters to go, I have reached the delicate stage where I must suggest ways in which we can bring more life into his subject without causing Jasper great offence, thus having to navigate the dilemma faced by editors the world over: how to create the best possible piece of work without damaging the author's fragile ego.

Still, if passion and intensity are lacking in Jasper's opus, they are positively overflowing in Maeve's. In fact, as we have revised and edited the opening chapters this last week, I have found myself having to rein her in, reminding her not to overwhelm the reader but to drip-feed William and Blythe's burgeoning relationship and keep the reader guessing. To be honest, it has surprised me that, as a seasoned author, Maeve doesn't exercise this restraint naturally. Perhaps it is her delicate state of mind or the fact that her bestselling books had been love letters to a time and place rather than a person, but I can't help but feel that there is more to this novel than she is letting on. The emotional reaction she has to William while telling the story is visceral, to the point where sometimes after writing a scene between him and Blythe she seems physically and mentally spent and has to lie down to recover. This evening is no different and as Maeve finishes dictating the chapter she lets out a wail of anguish.

'Maeve?' I say, pressing 'save' on the document and closing the laptop. 'What is it?'

A tear falls down her cheek as she closes her notebook. I watch as she shifts in her seat and turns to me. The visible change in her this last week is incredible. Gone is the grubby dressing gown and unkempt hair. Instead, she now makes sure to blow-dry her newly bobbed hair and apply her make-up each morning as well as showcasing an array of new outfits daily, from tailored trouser suits to brightly coloured shift dresses. Today she looks immaculate in an elegantly understated Prada midi-dress paired with soft pink suede ballet pumps, and is a million miles away from the distressed old lady who ran out into the road. And yet, there is still that look in her eye, the haunted terror that won't seem to subside.

'It's just . . . I,' she says haltingly, 'I feel as though time is running out. There's so much more to say and so little time. And I'm tired, Alexis. I really am.'

'Writing a novel is a huge undertaking,' I say, recalling the pep talks I had given over the years. 'It must take it out of you, mentally and emotionally. That's why I've always been in awe of authors like you who wrote so prolifically. Wasn't it a book a year at one point?'

'In my heyday, yes,' says Maeve, pulling out a tissue from the box on the desk and dabbing her eye. 'And I loved it. I thrived on those deadlines. All those young people who fell under the spell of the *Time Traveller* series. They used to queue up outside bookshops overnight whenever a new one came out. Their loyalty gave me the energy to keep producing. Still, you're right, it does take it out of me. And I know Jasper worries about my well-being but I've always simply taken it for granted that the emotional and mental strain is just part of being an author, the price we pay for our craft. However, this one is different. It is more than just a story.'

I nod my head, though I can't help but think about what Cordelia said about William, the fact that he was a manifestation of some dark aspect of Maeve, and a shiver flutters through me. I want to ask her about this but I daren't. She has come so far this week, not clashing with Jasper as much and making sure she takes her medication, that I don't want to set her back.

'I know what you're thinking.'

Maeve's voice snaps me out of my troubled thoughts.

'You think I'm letting my emotions get in the way of the story,' she says, rising from her chair and walking to the window. 'That's what all my editors used to worry about. They knew that I would cling on to my darlings for dear life.'

She turns to me with a rueful smile.

'But I always capitulated in the end,' she whispers. 'I always killed them.'

The air in the room turns chilly suddenly. I take my trusty Bella Freud sweater from the back of the chair and pull it on.

'Maeve, we should head to bed now,' I say. 'It's getting late.'

'But this one is different,' she says, seeming not to hear me. 'This one I'm in control of. No contract, no publisher, no editor, just me.'

She turns from the window and smiles.

'And this time I'm keeping every one of my darlings alive.'

I am just helping Cordelia to wash up the supper dishes when Jasper appears at my side. The oven dish is caked in burnt mince and I'm almost breaking out into a sweat trying to scrub it off.

'Here, I'll sort that,' he says, taking the dish from me and plunging it into the hot water. 'I pay you for editing, not housework.'

'Are you sure?' I say, drying my hands on the tea towel while Cordelia stacks the dishes onto the rack.

'Absolutely,' he says, briskly. 'I have a few things I need to discuss with Cordelia this evening and what better way than over a sink of dirty dishes.'

'If you didn't cremate the shepherd's pie each time, it wouldn't take so long,' says Cordelia, shaking her head. 'Or you could always get a dishwasher, you know, enter the twenty-first century like everyone else.'

'As I've told you time and again, a dishwasher would look horribly out of place in this glorious old kitchen,' he says, playfully patting her with the tea towel.

I stand by the sink, feeling rather awkward, like I'm playing gooseberry somehow.

'I'll leave you to it,' I say, grabbing my phone from the table.

'Oh, Alexis, I've left your first week's wages in an envelope on my desk,' says Jasper, not looking up from his scrubbing. 'I should have given you them on Friday, but it completely slipped my mind. You can grab it on your way up.'

'Thank you,' I say, feeling even more awkward. Wages in an envelope, I think to myself as I walk out of the kitchen and head down the corridor. Like a schoolkid in her first Saturday job. Is it just me or did I hear Jasper and Cordelia laughing as I left the room?

'So that's a grand for the work on the engine,' says Ken, jabbing his calculator with an oil-matted finger. 'Received with thanks.'

He hands me the receipt along with an invoice for the rest of the work and I wince as I look at the figure still to pay.

'Happy for us to get to work on the rest of the repairs?' he says, shoving the calculator back in the drawer and coming round to my side of the counter.

'Yes, definitely,' I say, tucking the receipt and invoice into my pocket. 'Like I said, I need to be back on the road as soon as humanly possible and I've got two more weeks of work for Jasper Hardy at Lustrum Manor which will cover the outstanding bill.'

'No worries,' he says, folding his arms across his chest and regarding me curiously. 'So, how's it going up at the manor?'

'All good,' I say cautiously. 'I'm editing Jasper's new book and also doing some work for Maeve – er, Mrs Hardy.'

'Strange business that was,' says Ken, shaking his head.

'Oh, she's a lot better now,' I say, assuming he is talking about Maeve's roadside antics. 'In fact, she seems to be thriving which is great to see.'

'I wasn't talking about Mrs Hardy,' he says, glancing outside to where Jasper is sitting in the car looking rather impatient. He had agreed to drive me here but has a marking deadline this afternoon so I can't linger long. 'Though I'm glad to hear she's feeling better. No, I was thinking about all that business with the old Lord Lustrum, terrible it was. The village haven't forgiven them.'

'Forgiven who?' I say, my heart quickening. 'I don't quite know what you mean?'

'All I'll say is,' he whispers as, outside, Jasper starts up the engine, a sign for me to hurry up, 'that when it comes to Lustrum Manor, nothing is as it seems. If I were you, once your van is ready, I'd get out of there as fast as you can.'

15

ALEXIS

Sitting in Jasper's study that afternoon I try my best to focus on cutting down a particularly lengthy and dense passage on de Gaulle's early education, but Jasper's convoluted sentences blur in front of my eyes. All I can think of is what Ken said earlier about getting away from here as fast as I can. Out of the window I see Cordelia walking across the courtyard with a basket of kindling in her arms. She looks pensive, her eyes darting from side to side as she makes her way towards the orangery. Then Jasper appears. He puts his hand on her arm, but she pushes it away. She glares at him angrily, shaking her head as he tries to talk to her. Then he does something strange. He leans across and strokes her hair. She looks at him for a moment, her expression softening. Then, handing him the box of kindling, she walks off towards the orangery, Jasper shuffling in her wake.

Unsettled, I return to the document on my screen, but my brain just won't focus. I'm starting to feel like there is something strange going on at Lustrum Manor, though I'm not quite sure what. I can't stop thinking about Ken's reaction when I told him I was working here. He's a solid, pragmatic man but, for just a moment, he looked fearful. If only Jasper hadn't been waiting for me in the car, then I could have pressed Ken for more details. I am so preoccupied with thoughts of this I don't notice Jasper coming into the study until he appears beside me and, much to my shame, I let out a terrified scream.

'Oh gosh, dear,' he exclaims, placing his hand to his chest. 'I didn't mean to startle you. I just wanted to let you know that it's four o'clock and I shall be needing the study now.'

'Of course . . . er . . . yes,' I say, saving the document with trembling fingers. 'And sorry I screamed. I was just . . . just so engrossed in this chapter I didn't hear you come in.'

'Well, that's good to hear,' he says, taking his glasses from his top pocket. 'How about we have a debrief tomorrow morning. You can let me know where you are with it.'

My heart sinks. I have made next to no progress on the chapter today, so distracted have I been by Ken's comment. Still, if I start extra early tomorrow, I can make up for lost time.

'Sure,' I say, coming out from behind the desk. 'That sounds great.'

He nods, then sits down in the spot I have vacated and takes out his own laptop.

'I'll leave you to it,' I say, heading for the door.

'Thank you, Alexis,' he says, his back to me. 'Oh, and just one other thing. Cordelia tells me you were looking in the old barn the other day. I want to make it clear that, though you're free to explore the grounds, the outbuildings are strictly out of bounds. They're in a dreadful state of disrepair, a health-and-safety hazard as they say, and, well, I would hate for anything to happen to you.'

He turns and looks at me over the rim of his spectacles, his eyes cold and expressionless.

'Of course, Jasper,' I say, opening the door. 'Understood.'

But as I step into the corridor my body turns to ice. I need some answers and there is only one person in this house whose word I trust.

'You're early,' says Maeve, when I burst into her study a few moments later. 'I thought we were due to start after dinner as usual.'

She is sitting on the window seat, dressed in a teal cashmere polo neck and black cigarette pants. Her feet are bare, and I notice she has painted her toenails cherry red. She is stroking Daphne who is sitting on her lap while an audiobook reverberates round the room.

'Darling puss,' she says, as the cat jumps down and goes to lie in a shaft of sunlight. 'All she does is sleep these days, which is just as well because it means she pretty much stays in here most of the time. Jasper's allergic to cats, you see, comes out in a dreadful rash if Daphne so much as looks at him.'

She glances up at me and smiles.

'Alexis, you look terribly pale. Is everything all right?'

'Do you mind if I switch this off a moment?' I say, gesturing to the PC on her desk from which the audiobook is blaring.

'Go ahead,' she says, with a nod. 'I'm afraid my attention wandered during that last chapter. As always, I was thinking about my own. Now, what's the matter, darling? Come and tell me.'

Pausing the audiobook, I take a deep breath before going to join Maeve at the window seat.

'I received this a couple of weeks ago,' I say, bringing up the census page on my phone and handing it to her. 'It's the reason I came to Lustrum Manor in the first place.'

'No use showing me that tiny print with my shoddy eyesight,' she says, handing the phone back to me. 'I won't be able to make head nor tail of it. What does it say?'

Taking a deep breath, I tell her everything. From 25 December 1988 right through to 21 March 2021. When I have finished, I realize I am crying.

'Oh, my dear,' says Maeve, placing her cup on the floor and sweeping me into her arms. 'I had no idea what you had been through. In my mind, I saw you as having a wonderfully stable childhood with a solid, heart-of-gold mum. It's a testament to your own strength that you are so assured and grounded. It must have been heartbreaking for you to have her leave like that.'

She strokes my hair gently.

'But then she must have had her reasons,' she says softly. 'Motherhood . . . well, it is the most beautiful and yet terrifying thing. Not many of us are brave enough for it.'

I sit up and wipe my eyes with the back of my sleeve.

'I got used to not having her there,' I say. 'I built up this wall of steel around myself, made sure no one could hurt me like she did. Then I poured every ounce of energy and passion into my career. I trained myself not to think about my childhood, about her. But then my dad died in October 2023. I found my mother's diary when I was clearing out his house a few weeks later and something inside me just snapped. I can't describe it. After that nothing else mattered but finding her. I rather lost my head, dropped everything, my entire life, and went off in search of her in that old camper van.'

'It all sounds exhausting,' says Maeve, handing me a tissue.

'It was. It is,' I say, dabbing my eyes. 'Not least because every time I feel I'm getting close it turns out to be another false lead and I'm back where I started. Like that notification. Some would call it kismet, the fact that you ran out into the road that day, then my van broke down and I had to stay here in the very place that, according to these census records, my mother lived in 2021. But I'd already stopped at Lustrum Manor and spoken to Jasper. He is adamant that no one else has lived here but you, him and Cordelia since you bought it.'

'Ah, now, that's not strictly true,' says Maeve, getting up from the window seat and going over to her desk.

'What do you mean?' I ask, watching as she pulls open the top drawer of her desk.

'Well, if I'm not mistaken,' she says, taking out a small leather diary, 'Jasper took on a gardener, an older woman in her sixties, to help around the grounds a few years ago. It was during Covid. We couldn't find a gardener for love nor money – everyone was shielding, you see. It was starting to get out of control and Jasper, God bless him, tried to stay on top of it but he had his writing and teaching to deal with. Oh, he used to get ever so cross at trying to log on to those Zoom calls for his lectures. I'm afraid he's something of a technophobe. Cordelia was working full-time at the chemist and what with the pandemic things there were busier than ever. But the garden was starting to look unsightly so I was delighted when Jasper said he'd found a woman to help with it.'

'And this woman?' I say, my heart racing. 'She stayed here?'

'As far as I know, yes,' says Maeve, flicking through the pages of the diary. 'What was the date on the census again? I have my 2021 diary here and I'm sure I would have made a record of it.'

'The twenty-first of March,' I say, the date already imprinted on my mind.

'Ah, yes, here it is,' she says, bringing the diary over. 'She started on the first of March. You'll have to read it as my eyes won't even work for my own handwriting.'

She laughs wryly and hands me the book, her finger holding open the page.

New gardener starting today, I read Maeve's entry for the first of March. *Jasper dealing with the induction etc. One month trial period. I wish I could go and meet her, get some fresh air in the beautiful grounds, but Jasper is insistent that I shield, that I am high risk and that I cannot be exposed to anyone who might be carrying this terrible virus. Let's hope that . . .*

I pause, my voice catching in my throat. Beside me, Maeve flinches in her seat.

'What is it, dear?' she says, putting her hand on my arm. 'What does it say?'

I clear my throat, try to steady my mind and my voice, but as I read on my whole body begins to tremble.

'It says, *Let's hope that Kimberly Harper lives up to her glowing references and restores our walled garden back to its former glory.*'

'Kimberly Harper,' gasps Maeve, as I flick through the remainder of March which, surprisingly, shows mainly blank pages. Maeve's daily life at that point appears to have drawn to a complete halt. 'Is that your mother's name?'

I nod my head, my chest tightening with trepidation as I

skim the entries. There is no mention of my mother until the very last day.

'*The thirty-first of March*,' I read aloud. '*Sadly, Jasper had to let KH go. Very disappointing. What will happen to the walled garden now? I feel so bad that I am cooped up indoors. If only I could get out there and tend to it myself but Jasper is insistent that it is too risky for me to leave the house. Anyway, I don't even think I would have the energy for it. I am feeling so tired these days.*'

'She didn't pass the trial period,' I say, closing the notebook and turning to Maeve. 'What happened?'

Maeve sighs and looks out of the window.

'This is very awkward,' she says, shaking her head. 'And I feel rotten telling you.'

'Please, Maeve,' I say, panic and dread rising through me. 'I need to know what happened.'

'Well, as I said, it was Jasper who dealt with her day to day,' says Maeve, turning to me with a reticent expression. 'In fact, I barely saw her. I think I only met her a couple of times at most. Jasper was adamant that she keep her distance. I wasn't to be disturbed. I remember feeling embarrassed that he'd instructed her like that, as though I was some grand celebrity, which isn't me at all. But Jasper was ever so fearful about me catching Covid. He basically had me locked away up here during this time, saying that I was in the high-risk bracket. Anyway, initially he was thrilled with her, said she was a marvellous worker. The grounds had been a mess when we bought the place and she was starting to get everything in order. Then, all of a sudden, he let her go with immediate effect. I woke up one morning and she was gone.'

'But why? What had she done?'

Maeve sighs deeply before answering.

'Well, at first Jasper was rather cagey,' she says. 'Just said that she wasn't up to scratch. But that was nonsense because he'd spent the previous few weeks telling me how wonderful she was. Anyway, finally I got it out of him.'

She looks at me and grimaces.

'I'm afraid, dear,' she says, putting her hand on my shoulder, 'he found she'd been entering the manor and stealing.'

'Stealing?' I cry, jumping up from the seat. 'No, that's just crazy. My mother was many things, but she wasn't a thief. There must have been some mistake.'

'Sadly, it's true,' says Maeve, looking up at me, her hand on her chest. 'Several of my first editions were found in her bag. It looked like she was planning on selling them. Cordelia was there too and corroborated the story. Jasper hadn't wanted to tell me because it had been his decision to hire her and, well, he can't stand being made to look foolish.'

I slump back down on the seat, my vision clouded by tears.

'I can't . . . I can't believe my mum would do that,' I say, as Maeve gently rubs my back. 'It makes no sense.'

Grabbing the diary I flick through the sparse pages, desperately trying to find some explanation, some vindication for my mother, but there is nothing.

'I suppose Jasper will have kept more of a record of her time here than I did,' says Maeve, taking the diary from my shaking hands and placing it on the floor. 'He's meticulous in those matters.'

'But what I don't understand is why Jasper would lie to me,' I say, twisting the sodden tissue in my hands. 'Both times I told him about the census he said, quite clearly, that my mother never lived here.'

'He probably thought he was doing the right thing, the kind thing,' says Maeve gently. 'Shielding you from the truth. After all, nobody wants to know that their mother is a . . .'

She leaves the sentence hanging and we sit in pained silence for what seems like a lifetime.

'Anyhow, you can ask your mother all of this when you find her,' says Maeve, breaking the impasse. 'You still want to find her, don't you?'

'Of course I do,' I say, wiping my eyes. 'But she could be anywhere. God, she could be dead for all I know.'

'Don't say that, dear,' says Maeve softly. 'You should always have hope. Listen, what about that census thing. Surely it has more detail.'

'Not until the next census, which isn't until 2031,' I sigh.

'All right,' she says, handing me my phone. 'Well, what about the genealogy site itself? Now you know that the Kimberly Harper mentioned is in fact your mother, surely you can find more information on her specifically, besides the census? I don't know, electoral rolls, perhaps?'

'I hadn't thought of that,' I say, taking my phone and opening the genealogy company's latest email. 'Let me have a look.'

I click on my mother's name and a new page opens. A profile page.

'It looks like she signed up to this genealogy site,' I say, scrolling down. 'But she hasn't been very active on it.'

'I wish these sites had been around when I was writing my *Time Traveller* books,' says Maeve, peering over my shoulder. 'They would have been enormously helpful.'

'Hmm,' I say, clicking on 'profile details'. 'Hey, it says here that she has been a member since January 2021. So that's before she arrived at Lustrum Manor. And, oh my goodness, there's a section marked "current location" with a map. According to this, she updated her location in April 2021, after she left here.'

'Oh, that's wonderful, Alexis,' says Maeve. 'See, I told you not to lose heart. There's always a way. Is she still in the UK?'

'No,' I say, enlarging the page and showing it to Maeve. 'She's here.'

Maeve squints at the page.

'Paris. The Latin Quarter.'

She looks up at me in disbelief.

'How strange,' she says. 'That was the area around Le Mistral.'

'Yep,' I say. 'Or rather, Shakespeare and Company as it is today.'

'Paris,' says Maeve. 'Is there any reason why your mother would be there?'

'Not that I can think of,' I say, minimizing the page, then typing 'Shakespeare and Company' into Google Images. 'But I just want to check something. My goodness . . . of course . . .'

'What is it?' says Maeve, peering over my shoulder. 'You've gone all pale again.'

'Look,' I say, handing Maeve my phone and pointing to the collage of pictures on the screen. 'Look at that one, on the book bag, halfway down. The emblem. A circle with the image of Shakespeare inside.'

'Yes?' nods Maeve, her brow furrowing. 'What about it?'

'Hold on a moment,' I say.

I grab my bag from under the desk and pull out the tattered copy of *The Time Traveller's Journey to Belle Époque Paris*. Turning to the title page, I gasp.

'What is it, dear?' says Maeve, as I return to the window seat.

'Look,' I say, holding open the page on which is stamped, underneath my mother's Christmas inscription, the distinctive Shakespeare and Company emblem.

'Ah, one of my favourites,' says Maeve, her eyes misting over as she reads the inscription. 'It was such a pleasure to write. Gosh, published in November 1988, just in time for the Christmas market. But what does it mean regarding your mother?'

'It means,' I say, taking the book from her and clutching it to my chest, 'that she bought that book in Paris just before she left. It means that, unbeknownst to me or my father and for reasons only known to her, my mother had visited Shakespeare and Company just before Christmas 1988. And if that website is to be believed, she was staying close by, in the Latin Quarter, after she left Lustrum Manor in 2021.'

'But why?' asks Maeve, as Daphne jumps back onto her lap. 'What connection did she have to Paris?'

'None, as far as I'm aware,' I say, placing the book back into my bag. 'But there must be some reason why she kept returning to Shakespeare and Company and I intend to find out.'

16

BLYTHE

Paris

1960

'When you said you were taking me to dinner, this isn't quite what I had in mind.'

Blythe laughed nervously as William shimmied up the drainpipe and reached his hand along the window ledge. They were in a little back street just along from Les Deux Magots where they had met a few moments earlier.

'And I told you, kiddo,' William called down from the ledge, 'that this is the best table in town. Now, are you coming up or what?'

Blythe glanced around her. The street was deserted save for a stray dog lying languidly in the late-afternoon sun. When, three days after their visit to the Louvre, William had suggested meeting for dinner, she had dressed accordingly in a close-fitting black crêpe dress and peep-toe kitten heels, perfect for the Ritz but useless for climbing up drainpipes.

'Here, I'll pull you up,' said William, extending his arm for Blythe to hold on to. 'On a count of three. Are you ready?'

Blythe took a deep breath and nodded her head.

'One, two, three . . .'

She grabbed hold of William's hand and with a whoosh he hoisted her onto the ledge.

'There,' he said, kissing her on the forehead. 'Nothing to it.'

'Are you kidding me?' gasped Blythe, catching her breath. 'If I'd have known I was going to be shimmying up drainpipes I'd have come prepared. These heels were not meant for climbing. Now, remind me why you've brought me here.'

'I think that should be pretty obvious,' said William, pulling her closer. 'One, my years of living as an impoverished Irishman in this city have given me something of an insider knowledge into . . . how can I put it . . . "street survival". And I happen to know that in the heat of summer, fresh food often spoils, so the Parisians, particularly in this part of town, like to keep their cheese and their saucisson, their fruit and cream, out on the window ledge. See.'

He gestured to the little spot beside him on the ledge where, sure enough, clustered on a red-and-white gingham cloth, was a selection of cheeses – a ripe, round Camembert and a wedge of Brie – a plump saucisson and a dish of ruby-red strawberries, beside which stood an elegant porcelain jug.

'A veritable feast and it won't cost us a penny,' said William, picking up the jug and taking a sniff. 'Cream, as I suspected. Lovely.'

'But isn't this stealing?' said Blythe, glancing at the windows behind them. 'This food belongs to someone. It doesn't feel right that we should just take it.'

'Which leads me to the second point, my darling moral girl,' smiled William. 'The chap who lives in this apartment is away for the weekend. I know that because I saw him leave this morning with a hefty suitcase and heard him tell the neighbour he was off to the coast and wouldn't be back until Monday. I tell you, in another life I could have been a detective. Now, this food is not going to stay fresh until then. It would be a mortal shame to let it go to waste, don't you think?'

He raised his eyebrows and Blythe began to laugh, both at his expression and at the ludicrousness of the situation.

'Oh, William Kenneally,' she sighed, kissing his hand. 'If I live to be one hundred, I don't think I will ever meet anyone as unique as you.'

'I should hope not,' he said, taking a napkin from his top pocket and laying it out on the ledge between them. 'I'm what they call a one in a million.'

'My mom would be appalled if she could see me now,' said Blythe, as William broke off a piece of cheese and fed it to her.

'Which bit do you think would offend her the most?' asked William, taking a strawberry from the dish and slipping it into his mouth. 'The breaking and entering, the eating without cutlery or the unsavoury company?'

'Oh, definitely all three,' laughed Blythe, reaching out to wipe strawberry juice from William's chin. 'As well as the sloppy eating.'

'I suppose this would be frowned upon in the country club,' said William, taking a sip of cream from the jug and handing it to Blythe.

'Everything is frowned upon in the country club,' said Blythe, taking the jug. 'Though I don't want to think about that right now. I want to enjoy this moment, this perfect evening in Paris.'

'Hey, speaking of perfect,' said William, 'there was another reason why I wanted to bring you up here at this hour. Look at that.'

He pointed ahead. Blythe gazed out across the rooftops and felt her heart soar.

'William,' she whispered, as the evening sun illuminated the spires of Notre-Dame in a triumphant blaze of glory. 'I've never seen anything so beautiful. It looks like a painting.'

'Heaven's glory, eh?' whispered William, taking her hand in his. 'Or, as I like to call it, magic hour. That fleeting moment when the world seems to stand still, when the city holds its breath, when there's no need to rush, no need to be anywhere but here.'

As the sun dipped, he turned to her and Blythe saw, to her surprise, that he had tears in his eyes.

'William, what is it?' she said gently.

'It's just . . . well, it's a lonely business, life,' he said, smiling sadly. 'I suppose I've got used to being on my own, being resilient, telling whoever will listen that I'm a libertarian and I can do it all alone but that's nonsense. Truth is I've only ever wanted to feel how I feel right now.'

'And how *do* you feel right now?' asked Blythe, putting her head on his shoulder.

'Safe,' he whispered, kissing her head. 'Blythe?'

'Yes, William?'

'Would you hold me?'

They stretched out on the ledge then, William's head on her chest, his arms around her waist, and they lay in perfect silence, safe in each other's arms.

'I can feel your heart,' whispered William.

'It belongs to you,' said Blythe, stroking the hair on the nape of his neck. 'You know that, don't you?'

'Yes,' he whispered. 'And mine is yours.'

'William,' she said. 'I don't want this to end. I don't want to go home at the end of the month.'

'Don't think of that now,' he said gently. 'Just be here, in this moment. The future doesn't exist. It hasn't happened yet.'

Suddenly, the silence was punctured by the sound of bells, chiming the hour.

'Eight o'clock already,' said Blythe with a sigh.

'Ah, damn,' said William, sitting up.

'What is it?'

'It's just, there's this party Paula and Estelle were organizing,' he said, running his hand through his hair. 'The magazine crowd will all be there. They wanted me to go and . . . well, I should show my face.'

'Of course,' said Blythe, adjusting her dress. 'I'll head back to the hotel, let you go and see your friends.'

'Hey,' he said, kissing her nose. 'Don't be such an eejit. I'm not going anywhere without you.'

He smiled at her, and she felt as though her heart would burst.

'What you said before,' she said. 'About being lonely. You're not the only one who feels like that, I . . .'

'You don't have to explain,' he said, squeezing her hand gently. 'I know. We're two sides of the same coin, you and me, kiddo. Now, let's see if those heels of yours will survive the descent.'

The party was taking place in the docks, an area of the city into which Blythe had not yet ventured. The wind blowing in from the river was bitterly cold as they made their way along the quay. 'Here, take this,' said William, removing his overcoat and draping it over Blythe's shoulders.

'Are you sure?' she said. 'Won't you be cold?'

'Don't be daft,' he said, with a laugh. 'I'm Irish. This weather is practically tropical compared to Sligo. Right, then, here we are.'

They had stopped outside an old stone warehouse. Stubbing out his cigarette, William took her hand and pushed open the stiff metal door. The warehouse, which reminded Blythe of the indoor arenas from her horseback-riding days, was packed with people. Some stood huddled at the side, sipping drinks and smoking cigarettes, while an adventurous few were dancing on the long trestle tables that ran the length of the room. The air was thick with cigarette smoke and the only light came from the candles dotted around the tables. As William took her hand and led her across the room, she saw Paula and Estelle, arms entwined as they danced wildly to the beat of the music.

'Hey, William! You made it.'

Paula, noticing them, had jumped down from the table and was making her way through the throng, her glass of red wine held aloft. She was wearing what looked to Blythe like a brassiere along with a full-bodied taffeta skirt and, bizarrely, a pair of hobnail boots with the laces undone.

As Paula reached across to embrace her, Blythe felt the woman's breasts press against her and she quickly pulled away, her face flushing with embarrassment.

'Dressed for the occasion as always, Paula,' said William, glancing sideways at Blythe who was standing with her arms folded across her chest. She didn't want to meet his eye, didn't want him to see the shock on her face.

'Ah, you know me, William,' laughed Paula, taking a drag of her cigarette. 'I get too hot when I dance and have to shed my clothes. Years of convent school repression will do that to a girl. Now, come on, you two, no more standing around like dummies, come and jive with us.'

Blythe put her hand up to protest but before she knew it, she was being pulled onto the table by Paula who proceeded to dance with William in a way that could only be described as indecent, hips grinding against his, hands cupping his backside. Blythe, swaying in time to the music, an African drumbeat that was getting progressively faster, knocked into a young man who was in the process of climbing onto the table.

'I'm sorry,' she cried, as the young man regained his balance. He looked up at her and her heart sank.

'Sam.'

'What are you doing here?' he asked, his eyes darting behind her, then settling on William and Paula who were now dancing in such a frenzy that Blythe felt sure they were going to send the table flying. 'I didn't think this was the kind of place girls like you frequent.'

'William brought me,' she stuttered, feeling awkward suddenly.

'Of course he did,' said Sam. And, with a shake of his

head, he pushed past her and slithered himself in between Paula and William.

'Blythe,' said William, pushing Sam aside and taking her hand. 'Come on, let's go and get a drink.'

As they jumped down from the table and William paused to kiss her, she could feel Sam's eyes boring into her.

'I don't think Sam likes me,' she said, as William led her across the room.

'Ah, don't be daft,' said William. 'He's just very cautious around newcomers. Once you get to know him, you'll see he's a grand fella.'

Blythe smiled though inside she knew that it wasn't caution that was influencing Sam's behaviour towards her, it was pure old-fashioned jealousy.

'Right, why don't you grab those seats while I get us some drinks,' said William, gesturing to a pair of oversized cushions wedged against a stone pillar. 'I won't be a sec.'

While William joined the lengthy queue for drinks, Blythe sat down and for the first time was able to fully take in her surroundings.

As she watched the hot, shadowy figures twisting and turning in time to the music, she felt words rippling through her head. From this angle she could see the whole room, the bodies pressed together: Paula, now devoid of her skirt, dancing in a frenzy down the middle of the table, Estelle stamping her feet in time to the music like a flamenco dancer, Sam swaying awkwardly from side to side and, in front of her, waiting patiently in the queue, oblivious to it all, William. Her William. As she sat drinking in the outline of his back, his broad, straight shoulders, the solid self-assurance that no one else in this room, not least the extroverted dancers, possessed, she felt something unfurling inside her like a coiled snake. A story. She would have to be quick if she wanted to capture it, just as it was sounding right here, right now, in her head. Grabbing a chunky candle from the floor beside her, she took out her trusty blue notebook with its gold embossed star and began to write, the words pouring, like liquid, onto the page. As she scribbled, a bottle of red wine appeared by her feet. Looking up, she saw William heading towards the swell of the crowd.

'I'll be right back,' he shouted above the din. 'Paula's roped me into something.'

He beamed at her and then, as he disappeared into the throng, Blythe took a long swig from the bottle and continued to write and drink until the room began to blur and all she could see were words, dancing like sprites across the landscape of the page. Then, suddenly the music paused, and the crowd hushed.

'Mr William Kenneally, ladies and gentlemen.'

Paula's haughty voice snapped her out of whatever spell she was under, and she looked up to see William, his hair slick with sweat, standing on a makeshift plinth with an open book in his hand.

'This poem,' he announced to the hushed audience, 'is called "A Song to the Siren":

'In the dark of night you come for me
And sing your silent song.
You are the one I am waiting for.
Your kiss will right my wrongs.'

As William's soft Irish voice caressed each word, Blythe staggered towards the table where he stood, her head spinning. Drunk on wine and lust and something deeper, something she would only later recognize as love, she beamed to the room in general, opened her arms and cheered every verse. '*This is about me,*' she wanted to cry to the gathered crowd, who stood enraptured by William. '*He loves me, don't you see?*' she screamed silently. '*He loves me as I love him.*'

Her legs buckled beneath her. She tried to grab hold of the table but ended up stumbling, like a fool. As William finished his poem to rapturous applause, he noticed her, and pulled her up onto the table.

'Hey, kiddo,' he whispered, as she fell into his arms. 'I think you've had a bit too much vin rouge. You need to line your stomach if you're going to drink like that and you barely touched our rooftop picnic. Let's sit and have some food.'

She nodded her head, like a child, as he lifted her gently down from the table and onto a pile of cushions that were spread out at various points around the floor. Once he had settled her, he disappeared into the crowd before returning a couple of minutes later with a tray of French bread, butter and cheese.

'Here,' he said, breaking off a piece of bread and dipping it into the butter. 'Have some of this.'

She leaned towards him as he fed her the soft bread and deliciously rich butter which she ate ravenously, as though she had been starved for days. '*Butter, Blythe!*' she heard her mother exclaim from somewhere in the mists of her past. '*You know that will just go straight to your hips. How will you fit into that beautiful wedding dress if you get all fat?*'

'*Go away, Mom,*' she muttered under her breath, as

William fed her another piece, his fingers brushing her lips. *'Go away, wedding and Amory and dieting and all of it. Just go away.'*

'Someone was hungry,' said William, brushing a stray crumb from her cheek. 'And not just for food.'

He looked at her and his eyes seemed to penetrate through her skin, through her bones, all the way down into her soul.

Emboldened, she grabbed him and pulled him to her. As their lips met, she could taste the creaminess of the butter, the tang of red wine, on his tongue. It was the headiest, most sensual taste she had ever encountered and from that moment on she would always associate those two things – butter and red wine – with William, and love.

The kiss seemed to last a lifetime and, so engrossed was she in William and his soft caresses, she didn't notice Sam standing above them, his face contorted with rage. She didn't see him take the little blue notebook that she had left on the floor beside her and clamber up onto the table. Only when she heard his voice and felt William pull away as if he had been shot, did she realize what was about to unfold.

'Ladies and gentlemen,' boomed Sam, holding Blythe's notebook aloft. 'Tonight, we have a very special treat. A preview of the work of a dazzling – no, a beguiling – young woman who has come here all the way from the US of A, a real Yankee Doodle sweetheart. And she's so wholesome, folks, she's even got a pretty little heart on her notebook. Would you look at that. Ain't it just the cutest thing?'

'Sam, what the devil are you doing?' snapped William, leaping to his feet and rushing to the table.

'Her name is Blythe Aston-Laine,' continued Sam, ignoring William's pleas. 'And boy, does she know how to spin a good old yarn. Here we are, ladies and gents:

'Her body rose to meet his and in that moment all pain and sadness fell away. He was her and she was him, one heart, one mind, one soul. Years of searching had brought her to this place, this moment of surrender, a sanctuary made of flesh and bone. They could hide here, perhaps for ever, close out the world and stay inside this cocoon until the day they drew their last breath. For without him there was no tomorrow, without him there was no light, without him . . .'

As she heard the contents of her notebook, her unedited writing, her private thoughts, spilling out from Sam's mouth and into the crowded room, Blythe felt as though she had been punched in the stomach.

'Sam, get down from there now, you damned fool,' cried William, his voice shaking with rage as he reached up and grabbed the notebook from his friend's hand.

'Ah, William, calm yourself. It was just a bit of fun, what's wrong with you.'

Sam's voice was the last thing Blythe heard as she ran out of the warehouse. She had no idea where she was going but she knew she couldn't go back there, couldn't see the looks on the faces of those people, hear their laughter as they mimicked her ridiculous attempt at literature, the silly, gauche little American girl with her cutesy notebook who thought she could compete with the big boys.

With these thoughts whirling through her head, Blythe ran into the darkness of the docks. She had no idea where she was or how to get out of there. All she knew was that she had to keep on running, away from Sam, from the laughter, from the humiliation.

But as she took the left turn that she hoped would lead her back to the main road, she found herself faced with a brick wall, a dead end. Somewhere in the distance a dog barked, and a male voice screamed expletives in French. She had to find her way out, had to get back to the safety of the city and the hotel. Turning on her heels she started to run the other way but as she reached the end of another alley, she felt a set of hands on her shoulders. She screamed, tried to fight the person off, but they were stronger than her. Overpowered, she felt herself falling as her legs went from under her and the world turned black.

17

ALEXIS

'You've made an early start this morning, dear. Listen, Cordelia and I are just popping to Waitrose. Can we get you anything?'

I look up from my edits to see Jasper's head poking round his study door.

'I woke up at five and couldn't get back to sleep. Thought I'd crack on with this chapter,' I say, glancing at the time on the corner of the screen. It is just coming up to eight o'clock. 'Er, nothing for me from the shop, thanks. Though Maeve's running low on hot chocolate so you might want to stock up on that.'

'Ah, yes,' he says, with a grimace. 'Heaven forbid we run out of her precious, and hideously expensive, French chocolate. Why she insists on it is a mystery to me when the ordinary stuff is just as good. Anyway, I won't keep you. I can see you're making good progress there. We'll be about an hour or so. We have a couple of errands to run after we've been to Waitrose.'

With that he disappears, and I sit and wait until I hear his car pull out of the drive. Then I set the laptop aside and look around the study. Maeve had said that Jasper keeps a record of everything, and I have spent two days waiting for the right opportunity to search for any reference to my mother. But where to start?

The desk drawers yield nothing but packets of Post-its, spare biros and numerous boxes of paper clips. Moving across to the filing cabinets on the wall opposite, I open the top drawer of the first one and see several storage boxes, neatly stacked. My heart sinks. If there are any documents pertaining to my mother in here it will be like searching for a needle in a haystack. However, if I want to find the evidence I am looking for I have no choice but to plunge in.

I spend the first ten minutes working my way through the boxes, pulling them out and inspecting them one at a time. The first couple contain signed publicity photos of Maeve down the years. I smile at her progression from young, twenty-something, rather conservative author in the black-and-white shots from the late sixties – with her neatly curled hair and sensible twin sets, she looks like a newsreader or a *Blue Peter* presenter – all the way through to the flamboyant 1980s celebrity with her red lipstick, dyed black Anna Wintour-style bob and trademark designer dresses.

The next box is crammed with an array of colourful envelopes. I pick one up. It is bright red with a border featuring Snoopy, the cartoon dog. I smile at the childish writing on the front, the vague address:

Maeve O'Malley, Writer of Time Traveller's Journey, Matador Publishing House, London, England.

And yet it must have reached Maeve as the envelope is open, the letter seemingly read.

Dear Maeve,

You are my favourite writer in the world and I would like to ask you a question. If you could actually travel back in time where would you go and who would you meet? Also, may I have your autograph.

Yours sincerely,
Polly Harris

Just three short lines and yet the adoration this little girl felt is palpable. Maeve was someone who understood, she was more than a writer, she was a friend and confidante. I glance at the yellowing note – and imagine little Polly sitting down to write it. I can feel her excitement as she sealed the envelope and carefully wrote out the address, wishing and hoping it would reach its recipient, because I was that little girl once. And, seeing the piles of envelopes, I know that Polly and I were just two out of millions who had fallen under Maeve's spell. I remember the letter I wrote to Maeve a few months after my mother left. My life had been turned upside down and the only constant I had were the *Time Traveller's Journey* books. When things got too much I could just open one up and transport myself to another time and place. I wrote all this in my letter, telling Maeve that I wanted to publish books like hers when I grew up. Like Polly, I had addressed the letter to Maeve's publishers and fixed it with a first-class stamp. But I had made the mistake of giving it to my father to post. A week passed and I hadn't heard anything though I figured that an author as famous as Maeve would be inundated with post and it would take her a while to reply. But as the weeks turned to months, it became clear that I was not going to hear from her. Her rejection, because that is what it felt like, had stung and it took me weeks to be able to think about Maeve or read her books without feeling a sense of shame. Maybe she thought my letter was too personal, perhaps there'd been spelling mistakes, or she just didn't like the sound of me. That bloody letter haunted me for years. And then, a week after my father died, I was sorting through his stuff and found it in one of his old briefcases. He'd forgotten to send it. I saw my childish handwriting and started to cry, for the sad little girl I was back then, for the mother I had lost and for the fact that Maeve, my idol, had not ignored me after all.

And here I am still searching for my mother and finding nothing.

I place Polly's envelope back into the box and notice I have tears in my eyes. Remembering that letter of mine made me think of Tara, the only person in the world I have ever told the story of it to. She knew what I had gone through as a child, and she made sure our home life was as calm and safe as mine had been chaotic and unpredictable. And in return, I had, like my mother before me, taken a metaphorical grenade and blown it all up.

I neatly stack the brightly coloured letters into piles. Then, as I reach the bottom of the box, I pull out an A4 Jiffy bag addressed to Maeve at Matador. It has a courier sticker attached to the top right-hand corner but half of it has been peeled off. I can just make out the fragment of a date: '—ly 2020'. July 2020? Something about it tells me that it doesn't belong here amongst the fan mail. Turning it over, I see that the envelope has been opened. I know I shouldn't but curiosity gets the better of me and I place my hand inside and pull out the contents.

It is a Polaroid photograph, black-and-white and very grainy, but I can make out the figures of two men locked in an intimate embrace. The shot seems to have been taken from a distance. Though rather blurry I can see that the men are standing by a wall down what appears to be an alleyway. I stare at the photo, wishing I could zoom in and see who the men are. One of them has his back to the camera. His hair is light, and he is wearing a polo-neck jumper. The other man's face is partially obscured by curly dark hair that falls across his forehead. The fair-haired one has his arms around the other man's shoulders, and they are kissing. My heart thuds inside my chest as I stand here looking at the image. It is not at all what I had expected would be in the envelope.

Then I turn the picture over. There's an inscription on the white border, written in permanent marker. I read it and my legs buckle.

'What the hell,' I gasp out loud, stumbling back into the desk. Then, composing myself, I read it again. There, in spidery handwriting that looks just like Maeve's, are written six loaded words:

William. The night I killed him.

18

BLYTHE

Paris

1960

The next thing Blythe knew she was flying through time and space, carried aloft like a bird soaring through cloudless skies. She felt warmth spread through her body, though a cold breeze ruffled her hair. Was this it? Was this death? In that darkened space, she saw her life, all that had been and all that could have been, spread out in front of her on a giant cinema screen like the ones at the drive-in movie theatre back home. She saw her horse, Major, his black coat glistening in the sun, his breath curling in tendrils from his velvety nostrils, and she felt a deep, overpowering sense of joy. He had been her best friend and confidant, the first living being to steady her and, at the same time, make her feel free. The next face she saw was her teacher, Mademoiselle DuPont, horn-rimmed spectacles resting on an aquiline nose, lips painted pastel pink, the scent of lavender soap fluttering in her wake as she walked up and down the aisles of the classroom, a well-worn copy of *The Sun Also Rises* in her hands, her soft French accent caressing Hemingway's words and transporting Blythe out of the room, out of the stultifying world of upper-class East Coast America, and away across the ocean, to Europe, to France, to Paris. The scene folded in on itself then, like origami, and the screen darkened before a new image flickered slowly to life. This image made Blythe's body turn to ice. A lone figure sitting in a chair by a window, a Miss Havisham locked in purgatory, a sense of hopelessness and despair all around. Thick cobwebs hung from the ceiling, shrouding the figure in a terrifying cocoon of dust and decay that Blythe could feel inside her own body. She blinked her eyes, but the vision had disappeared and she realized, to her horror, that she was inside it, inside the figure, inside the cobwebs. She thrashed her arms about, clawing desperately at the thick webs, but they seemed to grow stronger and stronger until they clung to her body like a second skin. She tried to scream but no sound would come out. And then, when she thought there was no escape, she felt a hand grip hers and pull her from that room. She felt the fresh air on her skin as she opened her eyes and saw his face.

'William.'

'Oh, Blythe, thank God. Thank God.'

'Where am I?' she stammered, blinking her eyes as she came to. 'What happened?'

'You passed out,' said William, placing his hand on her forehead. 'Ah, good, you're cooling down now. Though I'm not surprised you heated up. It was awful stuffy inside that party. Too many people.'

Blythe looked around. They were sitting on a bench outside the hotel. It was dark, though she could make out the twinkling lights of the Pont Neuf in the distance.

'How did we get here?' she asked, recalling those hands on her shoulders, the terror as she had tried to run. 'Last thing I remember I was in an alleyway at the docks.'

'Yes, that's where I found you,' he said, brushing her hair from her face. 'After you ran out of the party I quickly followed suit.'

'It was you?' she said, as the events of the last few hours come back to her in fragments. 'I thought it was some attacker.'

'Yeah, well, I don't know if it was the shock or the drink or a combination of the two, but you passed out right there in front of me,' he says, his expression uncharacteristically serious. 'I didn't know what to do. In the end, I figured you needed to be with your folks, so I scooped you up and carried you back here.'

'You carried me all this way?' she said incredulously.

He nodded his head, then looked down at the ground.

'Listen, he shouldn't have done that to you,' he said, looking up. 'Sam. He was out of order. But, you know, he gets awful jealous sometimes. It's a bit much, if you know what I mean.'

'Why would he be jealous of me?' asked Blythe, the throbbing in her head beginning to subside.

'Oh, I don't know, maybe 'cause I've talked about you incessantly these last few days,' said William bashfully. 'Or that, since I met you, I can't stop writing poetry, and that I live for the next time I can see your face and hear your voice.'

He stops, then takes a cigarette from his top pocket and places it between his lips.

'What can I say?' he continues, patting his trouser

pockets for a box of matches. 'I'm a fool for love, always have been.'

'But what about you and Sam?' asked Blythe, her heart almost exploding in her chest. 'It's clear that he likes you, that he sees the two of you as . . . as an item.'

'An item!' he laughed, as he lit his cigarette and tossed the spent match on the pavement. 'Now there's a term I've never heard used outside Hollywood.'

'You know what I mean,' said Blythe, her cheeks burning.

'It's not like that here, Blythe,' said William, turning to her. 'What may seem outlandish in Connecticut or Sligo or wherever holds no weight here. Men kiss men and sleep with men, then they do the same with women and no one cares. It's just lust and bodies and feelings with no heavy labels, no expectations. I'm a live-and-let-live kind of fella and what works for Sam and Estelle and Paula and the rest of them is their business. They're my friends and I love them. But as for being an item with Sam, you're way off the mark. I only have eyes for one person and I'm looking at her now. But, sadly, she's engaged to another man so . . .'

'William, you know how I feel about you,' said Blythe, holding his hand. 'Lord, the whole warehouse knows, thanks to Sam reading out my story.'

'But they were just words, Blythe,' he said, taking his hand away. 'And for all I know they could be fiction.'

'What are you saying?'

'I'm saying that words aren't enough,' he said, looking up into the night sky. 'It's all well and good having some fun on holiday, one last fling before you get married, but . . . but I have feelings for you, kiddo, and I've got a horrible feeling my heart's going to get broken here.'

'William, you know my situation,' pleaded Blythe tearfully. 'I meant everything I said earlier. Without you there is nothing.'

'But you see, Blythe, that's not true,' he said, turning to her. 'Without me there is your fiancé and your family and the country club, there's your life.'

'I don't want that life,' she whispered, her voice choked with tears. 'I just want you.'

'And I want you,' he said, holding her hand to his heart. 'Like I have never wanted another person in my goddamned life. But, listen, kiddo, I've bared my soul to you. And I need to know that you're serious, that you're not just playing with me, having a bit of fun with a penniless writer before heading back to your real life. I've laid it all out there for you, how I feel. There's nothing more I can say. What happens next is down to you.'

'What do you mean?'

'I mean you can either be with me or you can stick to your old life,' he said, getting up from the bench. 'The choice is yours. Let me know what you decide.'

Blythe's head was spinning as she walked into the hotel lobby. He wanted her to choose between him and her life in the US. How would that even be possible? How would they do it? So preoccupied was she with these questions she didn't notice her mother sitting on the Chesterfield sofa by the reception desk until the last minute.

'Blythe?' her mother gasped, looking up. 'What are you doing here? I thought you were in bed.'

'I . . . er . . . I couldn't sleep,' she stuttered as she rushed over to Hadley. 'So I went for an early-morning stroll to clear my head.'

It was then that she noticed the suitcases by her mother's feet, Blythe's included.

'What's with the suitcases, Mom?' she said. 'I thought we were here until the end of the month.'

'So did I,' sighed her mother, taking a long drag of her cigarette. 'But Daddy's been called back on urgent business. He's just sorting out the bill with the concierge and we'll be on our way after breakfast.'

'But Mom, we can't leave,' cried Blythe, panicking. 'I have plans. I've made friends here and—'

'Plans change,' said her mother, stubbing out her cigarette in the glass ashtray. 'And you have friends aplenty back home. I'm sorry, Blythe, but the vacation's over. Time to say farewell to Paris.'

19

ALEXIS

My back is aching as I stand outside Maeve's bedroom door twenty minutes later. I had exerted myself piling the boxes back into the cupboard while the early-morning sun blazed through the window and all I want is a cold shower, but I know I need to show Maeve this photo. I knock on the door, then gently push it open. As I step inside, I see Maeve sitting up in bed. She's listening to her audiobook at full volume.

'Hello, dear,' she says, looking up. 'What's that you've got there?'

Now that I'm here I'm not quite sure what to do. The envelope I'm holding in my hands was addressed to her and I opened it. What if she gets angry? What if she tells Jasper I was rifling through his things?

'Alexis?' she says, pausing the audiobook. 'Is everything all right?'

I realize there is little point keeping it from her and that actually it would be a relief if Maeve could reassure me as to what the inscription means, so with a deep breath I go over to the bed and sit down on the edge.

'I found this,' I say, handing her the envelope. 'And I swear to you it was already opened. I didn't unseal it.'

A frown passes over Maeve's face as she takes the envelope.

'Where was it?' she asks, her voice and hands trembling.

'In Jasper's study. In a box amongst some fan mail,' I say, my heart pounding. 'It was stuffed right at the bottom. I was trying to find some record of my mother being here but there was nothing and then . . . then I found that.'

'Why do you look so serious, Alexis?' she says, with a nervous laugh. 'What's in here? Some sort of bomb?'

Her voice trails off as she turns the envelope upside down and the Polaroid lands face up on her lap. She looks down at it and her whole body begins to shake uncontrollably.

'Maeve, it's OK,' I say, alarmed. 'Maybe you can look at this later, when you're ready.'

I reach for the photo, but she bats my hand away.

'No,' she cries, sweeping it up. 'Leave it. I need to see.'

I stand up and go over to the chair by the window. Best to give her some space. But as I sit down, I hear Maeve let out an anguished howl.

'I . . . I can't believe it,' she cries, rocking to and fro, the photo clasped to her heart. 'How is this possible? Who took this?'

'Maeve,' I say gently. 'Who is he? The man in the photo?'

'He was my William,' she whispers.

'And he's the inspiration for the character in the novel?'

'He is so much more than that,' she says, as she lifts the picture up to the light and reads the inscription.

'What the—?'

She lets out a howl and almost drops the picture.

'What does it mean?' she gasps, looking up at me.

'Well, I thought you'd be able to tell me that,' I say, coming over to sit with her. 'As you wrote it.'

'I wrote it? What are you talking about?'

She looks at me, her face riven with tears.

'That's not my handwriting,' she whispers. 'It's my mother's.'

'Come now, Maeve,' I say, trying to keep her calm. 'There must be some explanation.'

'Is there a postmark?' she says, wiping her eyes. 'If I know where it was sent from then I'll have my answer. Have a look will you, Alexis.'

I lean over and grab the envelope from the floor.

'It's partly torn but it looks like it was sent in July 2020,' I say. 'That's all, I'm afraid.'

'Are you absolutely sure the handwriting is your mother's?' I say, wondering, to my shame, if this might be another of Maeve's delusions. 'It looks very like yours?'

'I would recognize it anywhere,' says Maeve, with a sigh. 'And of course it looks like mine. My mother was the one who taught me to write. But how did she come to have a Polaroid of William in her possession and why would she say she killed him?'

'Maeve,' I say, trying to keep my voice steady. 'Now might be a good time to tell me about William. I know he's a character in your book, but Jasper and Cordelia seem to think that—'

'I don't care what they think,' she snaps, still clutching the picture. 'And as for William, I will tell you everything in good time. But first, I need to know the meaning of this Polaroid and my mother's words. Also, if this package was sent in 2020, why am I only just seeing it now?'

'Well, it was right in the middle of lockdown,' I say, looking, once more, at the postmark. 'Perhaps Jasper was distracted with all the worries of that period, his Zoom lectures and what have you, and simply mislaid it.'

'Perhaps,' she says, her eyes narrowing. 'Or perhaps someone just didn't want me to see it. I feel like so much has been kept from me these last few years, no wonder I've not been myself. Jasper seems to think he's protecting me, looking after my best interests by keeping me in here and fussing, but it just leaves me feeling like I can't breathe.'

She throws the covers back, gets out of bed and goes to the window, her hands trembling as she presses them to the glass. I glance at the antique clock on her bedside table as its metal fingers creep towards nine a.m.

'I need to clear my head, work out what that picture means and how it got here,' she says. 'And I can't do that if I'm cooped up here. I need to get out, need to get back to my old self, even if it's just for a day.'

'What are you suggesting?'

'I'm suggesting we book a taxi to the train station,' she says, turning to me with a stoic expression despite the tears. 'You and me, Alexis, are going to take a trip to London.'

20

BLYTHE

Paris

1960

'I'm not doing it,' Blythe cried, as her father returned from the front desk, tucking the hotel bill into his thick wallet. 'I'm not going back yet.'

'Come now, sweetie, don't make a scene,' said her mother, her eyes darting from side to side. 'You knew the vacation would have to end at some point. It just happens that we're going home a bit earlier than planned. Anyway, I thought you'd be happy to be getting back to Amory. You must be missing him like crazy.'

'I am,' said Blythe, the scent of William's Gitanes still clinging to her clothes. 'It's just . . . well, like I said I've made plans.'

'Oh, yeah,' said her father, his heavyset figure looming over her. 'What plans?'

Many years later, Blythe would recognize that moment not just as the one that would change her life for ever but also as the one when she truly became a writer. Because, standing there in the lobby of the Ritz hotel, she concocted a story so elaborate and yet so believable, she convinced her parents, at least partly, that she should stay on in Paris until the end of the summer.

'A course in French etiquette,' her father had scoffed. 'What in God's name is that? And why would a well-bred American girl like you be in need of it?'

'Well, it takes place in one of the most sought-after salons in Paris,' said Blythe, fully invested in her story now. 'Run by Madame Roux, granddaughter of one of the oldest aristocratic families in France and a close friend of Jackie Kennedy, no less, another alumna of the course. As Madame Roux said to me just the other day, from fashion to art to high culture, all the best things begin in Paris. What a coup it would be for me to absorb high-end Parisian etiquette and take that back with me to Connecticut. Imagine the parties, the events, the menus. I would be the perfect hostess. And think how proud Amory would be to have a wife with such Parisian chic.'

Her father went to protest but Hadley put her hand out to stop him.

'I think she might have a point, dear,' said her mother, her eyes glinting with thoughts of her daughter becoming a society trailblazer. 'Think of what she could learn from someone like Madame Roux. And, oh my, you could get an introduction to Jackie Kennedy and invite her to the wedding. It would make the society pages, no question.'

'What are you saying, Hadley?' demanded Chadwick, a look of utter bewilderment etched across his face.

'I'm saying that if this course is good enough for Jackie Kennedy, then it's good enough for our little girl,' she beamed. 'Oh, Blythe, this is too exciting for words.'

'Hang on a minute,' cried Chadwick, holding up his

hands, an act of both surrender and exasperation. 'Where are you going to stay? And how much does this thing cost?'

'I'd stay with Madame Roux, of course,' said Blythe, thinking on her feet. 'And as for the cost, well, it's . . . it's one thousand dollars.'

'A thousand bucks? Are you kidding me?'

Chadwick Aston-Laine's face turned purple.

'Oh, Chad, come on,' said Hadley, running her fingers along her husband's arm. 'I'd say that was a sound investment. With a priceless return.'

'It'd better be,' said Chadwick, his expression softening. 'But before I agree to anything I want to meet this Madame Roux. See if she's kosher.'

'Of course,' said Blythe, her heart pounding. 'Just give me a minute. I'll go call her from the phone at reception.'

And as she made her way to the concierge's desk, she thought back to the previous evening, to Paula dancing on the table, and the next part of her plan came into play.

Hadley Aston-Laine had been mesmerized as the formidable 'Madame Roux', clad in fox fur and pearls and clutching a white fluffy poodle, regaled her with anecdotes from summers spent with the Kennedys on the French Riviera. Five minutes was all it took to convince the Aston-Laines to hand over traveller's cheques to the value of a thousand dollars, plus some spending money for Blythe, and send their daughter on her way.

'You'll keep in touch, sweetie,' said her mother, tearfully pulling Blythe into her arms as Chadwick loaded their cases into the taxi. 'Call me every evening, no matter how late. You promise?'

'I promise, Mom,' Blythe had said, inhaling her mother's distinctive L'Air du Temps perfume and feeling a twinge of guilt. 'But you mustn't worry. I'm going to have the most incredible time.'

'I know that, honey,' said her mother, stroking Blythe's hair. 'But you're my baby. I'm always going to worry about you. And listen, if there's any problem, anything at all, you get on that telephone, and your daddy will have you on the first plane out of here.'

'I'll be fine, Mom,' said Blythe, extricating herself from Hadley's arms. 'Now you two have a safe trip home. And please, try not to worry.'

'Easier said than done,' said Hadley, climbing into the back of the taxi. 'When you're a parent you never stop worrying. You'll find that out for yourself one day.'

'You be good now,' said Chadwick, kissing his daughter on the cheek before joining Hadley in the taxi. 'And as your mom says, call us every day, you hear me?'

'Loud and clear, Dad,' said Blythe, fear and excitement rippling through her.

'We love you, baby girl,' Hadley called out through the open window as the taxi pulled away. 'Have a swell time.'

And that, though she didn't know it yet, would be the last time she ever saw her parents. An invisible curtain had come down on her old life and, from this moment onwards, nothing would be the same again.

21

BLYTHE

Later that evening, free of her parents and with a new-found sense of purpose, Blythe presented herself, suitcase in hand, on the doorstep of Le Mistral.

'So you've made your decision?' said William, opening the door, his expression a mixture of shock and relief. 'You've chosen us?'

'There was never any doubt,' she replied. 'Now are you going to let me in? It's freezing out here.'

The shop was deserted, eerily quiet, and as she walked across the threshold, Blythe felt a surge of contentment. Pressing his finger to his lips, William led her through the Old Smoky Reading Room and up the narrow staircase. When they reached the top, he paused as though trying to decide something. Blythe stood, her face inches from his, taking in his features as though seeing them for the first time. The deep-set eyes framed by thick dark lashes, the heavy brows, the lump on the bridge of his nose, the dark hairs on his top lip, the contours of his cheekbones, the shadow of a scar just under his left eye, the way his dark curls fell over one side of his forehead, and the warmth of his breath as he whispered in her ear.

'There's only one bed, Blythe,' he said, his voice rippling through her. 'Looks like Paula's taken residence in the other room tonight.'

He drew back then and looked at her, his eyes twinkling with merriment.

'Listen, we should hit the sack. It's late and I need to sleep but I swear to you I shall be a perfect gentleman,' he said, guiding her towards the door on the right. 'I'm a good Catholic boy after all.'

There had been a moment, as she stood in the doorway looking at the sagging mattress pressed up against the bookshelves, when Blythe hesitated. She thought of her parents who were probably halfway across the Atlantic now, happy to think that their daughter was safely ensconced with Madame Roux and immersing herself in the finer details of French etiquette. What would they say if they could see her now?

'You can go on the inside,' said William, removing his jacket. 'That way you won't catch the draught from the window.'

He smiled as he pulled back the blanket and something in Blythe stirred. This was everything she had ever wanted. To be away from her parents and her stifling life, heady on wine and books and Paris. She felt light and unencumbered.

'You know I'm not Catholic,' she said, peeling her dress over her head. 'And I have no desire for you to be a perfect gentleman. At least, not tonight.'

She had never been undressed in front of anyone before, but this felt like the most natural thing in the world.

'Are you sure?' he whispered, kissing her lightly on the mouth, his warm breath sending shivers through her body.

'I've never been more sure of anything,' she said, unbuttoning his shirt and running her fingers through the wiry hairs on his chest. 'I want you, William. I want to be with you.'

With that he pulled her towards him and kissed her deeply. Then, slipping off his shirt, he lifted her onto the bed.

Afterwards, as they lay entwined in each other's arms, their bodies sticky with sweat and lust, Blythe closed her eyes and replayed every moment. His soft mouth exploring every inch of her body, his fingers caressing her, the heady sensation as he moved inside her, the sharp fleeting pain that soon gave way to a pleasure she had never known. The sense that for as long as she might live, there could never be another person who would make her feel as cherished, as whole, and as safe as William Kenneally had that night.

'Well, kiddo,' he whispered, his breath hot against her face. 'I sure am glad your parents booked you into that etiquette school.'

She turned to face him, and they both burst out laughing.

'You know, I still can't believe they bought the story,' said Blythe, resting her head on his chest.

'Neither can I,' said William, stroking her hair. 'But then Paula is quite the convincing actress. I think she missed her vocation.'

'You should have seen my mother's face when Paula came sweeping into the hotel,' said Blythe, wrapping her legs around William's. 'She was mesmerized.'

'I wish I could have been there to witness it,' laughed William. 'Though it doesn't surprise me. Paula's folks are landed gentry back in England. She knows all the tricks.'

Blythe lifted her head from his chest and kissed him deeply on the mouth. His lips were soft and warm.

'I suppose your mother would see this as living in sin,' he said, between kisses.

'Oh, she would,' laughed Blythe. 'And she would wonder why Madame Roux had transformed into a skinny, penniless Irishman.'

'Hey, less of the skinny,' he cried, turning on his back. 'And I'll have you know I come from a long line of aristocrats.'

'Oh, yeah?'

'Yeah. My great-grandfather was Lord McGinty of the Sligo Road. Heir to a one-bed bothy and a poteen factory.'

'So then, William Kenneally, you know my story,' she whispered, running her fingers along his taut stomach. 'Now what about yours? And don't give me any more of Lord McGinty and the poteen factory 'cause I'm not buying it.'

'I don't have one,' he said, his eyes fixed on the ceiling.

'Oh, come on,' said Blythe playfully. 'Everyone has a story.'

'Well, I suppose mine is still in development,' he said, his voice tinged with sadness. 'Paris is my new chapter, shall we say. The last one didn't have the happiest of endings.'

He turned on his side and took her hand in his.

'You see, Blythe,' he continued, 'I have the opposite problem to you. Where your family is overbearing and controlling, mine is . . . well, mine doesn't exist any more. My blood family, that is. The great thing about Paris and this shop is that I've been able to create a new family out of complete strangers.'

'Your angels in disguise,' said Blythe, remembering the inscription above the door.

'I suppose so,' he said gently. 'Though I had an angel, my mother. She was the finest human being I have ever known. Soft and kind and funny, she made me feel like I could do anything, she made me feel safe. It was Ma that filled my head with stories. Her father called her the seanchaí, that's the Gaelic term for the storyteller and every family has one. She used to say that I was the next seanchaí, but that I had to go and tell my stories far and wide, get away from that little town on the west coast of Ireland, and go see the world.'

'Your mother sounds wonderful,' said Blythe.

'She was,' he replied, with a deep sigh. 'She had the gentlest heart and the finest mind and yet she didn't realize it, thought that she was just another wife and mother made for cooking and cleaning and looking after babies. I used to think that if only she had known how brilliant she was, then she could have lived a different life, a better life. Reminds me of someone else I know.'

He stopped and kissed the tip of Blythe's nose.

'What happened to her?' she whispered, feeling his breath on her face. 'To your mother.'

'She died when I was sixteen,' he said. 'Swiftly followed by my da. Broken heart, they said. He couldn't live without her. After that, nothing was the same again. Six months later I packed my bags and like James Joyce many years before me I made it all the way to France.'

'She'd be proud of you,' said Blythe. 'You're doing what she said you would, taking your stories out into the world.'

'Well, I don't know about the stories but I'm taking

myself out into the world,' he laughed. 'And for that, yes, I think Maeve O'Malley would be proud.'

'Maeve O'Malley?'

'That was my mother's name,' he said softly. 'After the warrior Queen of Connaught. O'Malley was her maiden name.'

'Maeve O'Malley,' said Blythe, rolling the name over and over in her mind. 'That's beautiful.'

'So was she,' said William drowsily. 'So are you.'

With that he fell asleep. Blythe lay there wide awake as the sun crept through the window slats. A new day, she thought to herself. And she didn't want to waste a second of it.

Leaning across the bed, she took her dress from the floor and pulled it over her head. Then climbing over William's sleeping form, she tiptoed out of the room.

When she reached the bottom of the stairs, she heard voices coming from the Old Smoky Reading Room.

'Five hundred copies! That's an incredible amount. I say we crack open a bottle of George's claret and raise a toast.'

It was Estelle speaking. The excitement in her voice was palpable.

'Let's stick to coffee for now,' replied Paula, laughing. 'I still have over a dozen submissions to read through for the next issue.'

Blythe's heart felt as though it would explode with happiness as she stood listening. Those young people were truly living – they were free to express themselves as they wanted, free to pursue their talents and look to the future with excitement. And, for the next few months at least, she was part of them.

'Blythe! I didn't know you were here. Are you coming to join us?'

She looked up and saw George heading towards her, a box of books in his hands and a cigarette hanging out of the corner of his mouth.

'Yes,' she cried, skipping after him towards the Old Smoky Reading Room. 'Yes, I am.'

22

ALEXIS

London

'Good afternoon, darling Hector. My usual booth, if you will.'

The elderly maître d' looks as though he has seen a ghost as Maeve strides through the door, which in a way he has. Despite her sadness, she insisted on making an effort for today's trip. Her white hair is swept into an elegant chignon, her face is glowing and perfectly made up with an added swish of MAC Paramount on her lips, and her slim frame carries off the plum velvet trouser suit and black polo neck to perfection. Inspired by her, I have paired my black ribbed Stella McCartney crew-neck sweater with a black pencil skirt, thick tights and a pair of bright red Prada spike-heeled ankle boots that Maeve has kindly loaned me. It has been a while since I have donned business-lunch wear and I have to say it feels pretty good.

'Er, of course, Ms O'Malley,' he says, tucking two leather-bound menus under his arm and leading us across the restaurant. 'And may I say how nice it is to see you. It must be what . . .?'

'At least eight years,' says Maeve, nodding regally to the other diners as we pass. 'Though it seems like only yesterday.'

'Here we are,' says Hector, pausing by the booth. 'Do take a seat and the waiter will be with you shortly to take your order.'

'Oh, just send over my usual,' says Maeve as we slide into the green leather banquette. 'A glass of champagne and a shepherd's pie with some Tabasco on the side. Alexis, will you have the same?'

'Sounds great. I'm starving,' I say.

'Then make that two, Hector,' says Maeve, handing back the menus.

'See, the world hasn't changed all that much, has it?' says Maeve, as he departs. 'I can still get the best seat in my favourite restaurant. You know, I used to sign all my book deals here.'

'In the age of Docusign that sounds wonderfully decadent,' I say, as a young waiter arrives with our drinks.

'The age of what?' says Maeve, frowning. 'No, actually, don't tell me. I'd rather stay blissfully ignorant.'

'It must have been an amazing time to be an author back then,' I say, as Maeve leans forward to clink my glass. 'Back when deals were struck over long boozy lunches.'

'Yes, it was,' says Maeve, pausing to take a sip of her champagne. 'Ah, that's lovely. But then, as I've been out in the wilderness since Covid, I have nothing to compare it to. I suppose if I was still getting published today, I'd have all sorts of obstacles to face, not least the world that lurks inside those things.'

She gestures to my smartphone that I've placed on the table beside me.

'Novelists like me were once accused of not living in the real world,' she says. 'But when I look around me now,

I think we're the only ones still inhabiting the world fully, feeling every emotion, every pain while everyone else numbs themselves inside that virtual space. Still, I don't blame them. It's tempting just to retreat, I suppose, to block out the world. We've all been there.'

She looks at me and it feels as though she is peering into my soul.

'It's funny, Alexis,' she says, taking another sip of champagne. 'How I've spent the last week or so spilling out my story and yet, apart from the mystery of your mother, I still know very little about you.'

'There's nothing to tell, really,' I say, shifting uncomfortably in my seat. 'I'm just a middle-aged woman enjoying the freedom of the road.'

She goes to speak but is, mercifully, interrupted by the arrival of our food. Her delight at the shepherd's pie overrides any desire for further questioning of me, thankfully.

'Now Jasper has tried to recreate this since we've been in Kent but has never succeeded, poor chap,' she says, sprinkling a liberal measure of Tabasco sauce onto the pie. 'But what he doesn't get is that this isn't just any old shepherd's pie, it's a moment in time, a memory of the person I used to be. Like Proust's madeleines, I taste this and I'm back in my old life, writing books, toasting new deals, marching round this city as though it were my own.'

She pauses, overcome with emotion. Her hands tremble as she lifts her fork and eats a morsel of fluffy potato. As I watch her, I see my mother that last day. Sitting at the kitchen table, a paper hat from the Christmas cracker on her head, trying her best to look enthusiastic about the turkey, sprouts and pigs in blankets piled on her plate, a misty look in her eyes that I thought was due to the wine she had drunk but which I later identified as the moment she made her mind up to leave. And yet it wasn't a triumphant or euphoric expression, rather one of resignation. There was no other option. She wanted to be somewhere else. Nothing, not my father, not the house, and, sadly, not even her daughter, could compare to what she craved. The freedom of sitting at the wheel of her VW and heading out into the unknown. I see the same look in Maeve's eyes when we sit together at Lustrum Manor, a sense that she is a caged bird desperately trying to set herself free, using the only means she has ever known: her stories.

'All that's missing is my darling Bella,' says Maeve, dabbing her eye with her napkin.

'Who's Bella?'

'She's the one who lived through all this with me,' she says, gesturing theatrically to the room at large. 'God, I miss her.'

'What happened to her?' I say, taking a sip of champagne, its buttery fizz warming my throat.

'She died,' says Maeve sadly, her eyes filling with tears. 'Heart attack. It was so quick, mercifully she didn't suffer but . . . but for me, when I heard the news . . . it was such a shock. She'd been my friend and editor for over thirty years. I used to say she knew me better than I knew myself, as a writer and as a person.'

'She sounds like an amazing woman.'

'Oh, she was,' says Maeve, smiling sadly. 'You remind me of her in a lot of ways. The same quiet tenacity, the same even temper and calm disposition. I wish you could have met her, wish Jasper could have too.'

'Jasper never met her?' I say, the champagne making my cheeks flush.

'Sadly, no,' says Maeve, draining her glass. 'We got together a few months after her death. Gosh, I was in a sorry state back then. I was just so lost without her and then . . . there was Jasper. He was such a rock during that time. Truly, I don't know how I would have got through it without him. But, God, what I wouldn't give for one more lunch with Bella or one more afternoon in her office. When I say office it was more like a library, floor-to-ceiling books, first editions. If anywhere used to settle my mind it was Bella's office. I hope her successor maintained it. Really, it was such a special place. In fact, that's just given me a splendid idea.'

She catches the waiter's eye and does the old-fashioned scribbling sign for the bill that I haven't seen used by anyone in years.

'Now, come on, Alexis,' she says, as the young man arrives with the bill. 'And we'll head off.'

'Where are we going?' I say, grabbing my bag from under the chair.

'You'll see,' she says, placing a wad of crisp twenty-pound notes on the table. 'But I promise you, you're going to love it.'

As the cab pulls up outside the imposing building on the Strand, I feel as though the oxygen has been sucked out of my lungs.

'Maeve, what are you doing?' I say, as she pays the driver and strides towards the painfully familiar revolving doors. 'I . . . I can't go in there.'

'Don't be silly, dear,' she says, beaming at the impassive doorman. 'It may seem intimidating to the uninitiated but you've just as much right to be here as anyone else. Now, come on, let's see who is trying to fill Bella's shoes. They'd better be up to the task.'

I feel sick as she grabs my arm and marches me into the building.

'But whoever it is can't be here,' I say, as the neon-yellow reception desk comes into view. 'Matador Books are based in Bloomsbury.'

'They were,' says Maeve, pushing the glass door open. 'But they moved here last year when they merged with Scion.'

The name, writ large in black typography above the reception desk, makes my blood freeze. I remember the avalanche of paperwork bearing that logo arriving at the house in the days following my exit, the words 'urgent' and 'legal department' screaming out at me in thick red lettering. How can I possibly have found myself back here? I was slowly getting better, I was focused on finding my mother, finding my feet again, until that fateful day when I met Maeve. Now she has brought it all hurtling back to me and I have no way of escaping.

'May I help you?'

Thankfully, the young receptionist who poses the question is new. I think of Dawn, the kindly East End stalwart who ran the reception desk when I was here, the look of sadness and pity on her face as I was guided from the premises that terrible morning. Thank goodness she is not here today to witness this most unceremonious of returns.

'Ah, yes,' says Maeve, adopting the voice I have come

to recognize as the 'chat show' voice, the one reserved for the likes of Hector and this young woman. It's a million miles away from the croaky whisper she adopts back at Lustrum Manor. 'We're here to see whoever is in charge at Matador Books.'

'Sorry, do you have an appointment?' says the girl, frowning as she adjusts her headset.

'Bella Holstein was my editor,' repeats Maeve, her mouth twitching. 'Tell the new one that Maeve O'Malley is here to see them.'

'I'm not familiar with that name, I'm afraid. Is anyone expecting you?' says the girl, looking a little flustered. 'Oh, here's Heidi, she might be able to help. Heidi, these ladies are looking for the person who replaced . . . sorry, what was the name of the editor again?'

'Bella Holstein!' exclaims Maeve, raising her hands in the air. 'Dear God, girl, how can you be working in a publishing house and not be familiar with the name of Bella Holstein, the finest editor of her generation?'

'Bella Holstein was the editorial director of Matador, darling,' says a voice from behind.

As we turn from the desk my stomach lurches when I see the whippet-thin Heidi Berenger walking towards us. Please God, anyone but her.

'She died a few years ago,' she drawls languidly, addressing the receptionist. 'Sadly. Her role was spread out across various departments so there is no specific replacement. Ladies, a word of advice, we don't accept unsolicited submissions.'

'Unsolicited submissions?' gasps Maeve, swaying on her feet. 'Do you know who I—'

'Come, Maeve,' I say, guiding her to the seating area before she can finish uttering the immortal words. Two plush velvet sofas are perched on either side of a glass cabinet bearing first editions of Scion's bestsellers. As I settle Maeve onto the seat, I spot five of mine, their titles staring back at me, almost teasingly.

'Alexis,' cries Maeve, her eyes clouded with tears. 'You were right. We shouldn't have come here. I don't know what I was thinking. It was just, the lunch, the champagne, it brought it all back and I thought if I came here I could somehow find her again, the spirit of her.'

'Alexis Harper?'

I look up to see Heidi Berenger standing by the sofa.

'Ah, I thought it was you,' she says, raising a perfectly arched eyebrow. 'Though you look . . . well, you look so different. More relaxed.'

'Hello, Heidi,' I say, willing there to be a fire alarm test or a bloody mass evacuation so I can take Maeve and flee back through those damned revolving doors. 'Good to see you.'

'None of us could believe what happened,' she says, twirling her identity lanyard between perfectly polished red fingernails. 'You were at the absolute top of your game and then whoosh, it all came crashing down.'

She clicks her fingers, and the noise seems to rouse something in Maeve.

'I want to go home, Alexis,' she says, getting up gingerly from the sofa. 'I can't be here any more.'

'Of course, Maeve,' I say, taking her arm. 'You've had a big shock. We'll head straight to the station.'

I nod to Heidi as I pass but when we reach the glass entrance, I hear her let out a shriek.

'Oh, my God,' she cries. 'Is that . . . is that Maeve O'Malley?'

My hands trembling, I bundle Maeve through the revolving door and out onto the street where, mercifully, a black cab with a yellow light is trundling towards us.

'"We don't accept unsolicited submissions,"' cries Maeve, as I flag down the cab and help guide her inside. 'Well, at least that would have given Bella a laugh if she'd heard it. I'm their biggest-selling author. Who actually was that woman? And why was she saying all those things about you?'

As I instruct the driver to take us to Victoria station, I feel all the tension I have held inside my body these last few years begin to dissipate. There's no more running now. It's time to come clean.

'Let's get on the train first,' I say, placing my hand protectively on her arm. 'And then I'll explain everything.'

'You promise?' she says, her eyes narrowing.

'I promise.'

23

ALEXIS

As the train hurtles out of London towards the suburbs and the Kent countryside beyond, I take a deep breath. Maeve, sitting across the table from me, waits for me to speak. It's my turn to tell my story.

'Gosh, where do I begin?' I say, desperately trying to find the words.

'I suppose,' says Maeve, 'like all good stories, you should throw the audience in at a pivotal point. The moment everything changes for the heroine.'

'Funnily enough,' I tell her, 'it was the night I finally met you, my favourite childhood author, that it all started to unravel. Though I didn't realize it at the time.'

'Really?' says Maeve. 'How so?'

'It's a long story,' I say, with a sigh.

'Well, you know how much I like those,' smiles Maeve.

And so, as she settles back in her seat, I climb into my time machine and rewind eight years.

'Now for the penultimate award of the evening: Editor of the Year 2017.'

Time seems to stand still as the host, Irish chat-show legend Gregory Lane, holding a shiny gold envelope in one hand, gestures to the big screen behind him.

'And the nominees are . . .'

The room falls silent as a montage of faces appears on the screen alongside a brief summary, narrated by Gregory, of our achievements. My fellow nominees, my peers. Some are friends, some, as the smug face of Felix Carrigan-Blake looms from out the screen, not so much. And then there I am, or at least, the thirty-one-year-old me. The black-and-white photo, taken in 2012 on the roof terrace at the vast Scion headquarters on the Strand the day I took over from legendary editor Valentina Morris, shows a rather wide-eyed and green version of the woman I am now, sitting here waiting on the words of this affable Irishman. Over the last five years I have launched the careers of fifteen bestselling authors, one of whom won the Booker, and two the coveted Baileys Women's Prize for Fiction, all of them making either the top or upper echelons of the *Sunday Times* bestseller list. I hear Gregory Lane recount my achievements – 'An editor referred to in the industry as having "the Midas Touch"' – and yet still, sitting here in my impossibly glamorous Stella McCartney gown, holding the hand of the love of my life, my wife, Tara, who I live with in a beautiful house by the river in Richmond, still I cannot quite believe this is real, that I am here amongst such an illustrious crowd. I have entered the inner sanctum, a golden world only very few are granted access to. Yet though I hear what Gregory Lane is saying about me, see my glossy photo on the screen, inside I am still that scared little girl hiding behind her books, shielding herself from her parents' chaos with a bunch of words printed on paper. What is it Tara always says, tongue in cheek? That reading is a form of madness, staring at a bunch of symbols on a page until you spin off, hypnotized, into another world. What can I say, she is a lawyer and logic is her thing.

'And the winner is . . . Alexis Harper, Scion Books.'

Tara's words ring in my ears as I make my way onto the stage and before I know it, after thanking my mentors, my authors, my peers, I find myself recounting her words to the audience.

'But it is more than that,' I tell them, clutching the gold trophy, a beautifully engraved feather quill, to my chest. 'The millions of readers my authors have enchanted with their stories, and the messages we receive every day telling how a particular book has changed a person's life, saved them in their hour of need, made them laugh, made them cry, made them see the world and their place in it differently, are a testament to that. For I learned long ago that a story is a form of magic, a life force all its own, a strange form of communication that has been around since the dawn of time and will continue to exist long after every person in this room is gone.'

I hear a whoop of applause and as I descend a woman in the front row whose face I cannot see clearly, for the lights are in my eyes, clasps my hand and whispers, 'Well said, my dear.'

Her voice is familiar, rich and low with the faint hint of East Coast America.

When I return to my seat, Tara reaches across and kisses my cheek. 'Congratulations, my love, though you could have done without mentioning my theory on reading.'

She's part joking but I can sense a sharpness to her voice that takes the sheen off my happiness, and as the CEO of Brotherton Books takes to the stage, I find myself going over my speech in my head. Have I embarrassed myself? Said too much? Did I forget to thank Tara in my speech? My cheeks flush and I can feel the stirrings of a headache. I am just about to excuse myself to go to the loo when the screen bursts into life and, suddenly, I am seven years old again.

A montage, set to the melancholy strains of the Beatles' song 'In My Life', begins to play. The first clip shows a dazzling woman with Elizabeth Taylor eyes, black bobbed hair, bright red lipstick and her trademark Gitanes cigarette, holding court on the Michael Parkinson show where the host is asking her if she'll ever stop writing. 'All I will say is, Michael,' she drawls, exhaling a ring of smoke into the air between them, 'they're gonna have to prise the pen from my hand if they want me to quit and I tell you, dear, I have the tightest of grips.' The audience explodes into laughter, then the montage switches to the exterior of Hatchards bookshop on Piccadilly some time in the late eighties where a queue of excited young fans waiting to meet their idol talk to the camera about what she means to them. As I sit here listening, I find myself nodding my head in agreement. These fans were me, their devotion was real, as was mine. The impact this woman had on my life is indescribable. The pain in my head subsides and is replaced with a flurry of childish excitement for, suddenly, to rapturous applause, she is there on the stage. Maeve O'Malley. My childhood hero, the woman who opened the door, literally, to my career. She is older, her black hair threaded with silver, a little shrunken, her gold evening dress rather dated, her incredible cornflower blue eyes dimmed somewhat, but as she begins to speak, I am overjoyed to find her as charismatic and eloquent as ever as she holds the audience under her spell. And as she steps down from the stage and takes her place in the front row, I realize that she was the person who congratulated me earlier, who clasped my hand.

When the ceremony ends, I leap from my seat and push my way through the crowd.

'I have to find her,' I say, when Tara asks why I am in such a rush to leave the auditorium.

'Who?' she cries after me, but I am already making my way down the stairs towards the foyer.

As I push past puzzled colleagues who hoped to stop and chat, to congratulate me on my win, I recall how, in all my years of publishing, I have never met Maeve O'Malley, though there have been several 'almost' meetings: a literary lunch that was cancelled last minute, the cocktail party I had arrived at five minutes after she left. I was starting to think that it was fate keeping us apart, that the old adage 'never meet your heroes' was true, and that the universe was conspiring to protect me from disappointment. But she clasped my hand and said wonderful things to me just now. Tonight, of all nights, I need to get the universe on side and tell her how much she means to me.

And there she is, being led towards the exit by a bearded man in a tweed jacket.

'Ms O'Malley,' I cry, but my voice is drowned out by an announcement over the tannoy that the bar will be closing in ten minutes and the hem of my expensive dress catches on my shoe, almost sending me tumbling down the last couple of steps.

To the bewilderment of those around me, I take off my

silver shoes, tuck them under my arm, then run across the foyer. I push my way through the revolving doors just in time to see a sleek SUV, with Maeve O'Malley's distinctive black bobbed head in the back of it, drive swiftly away.

'Never mind,' says the doorman, when I limp back into the foyer, muttering about having just missed her. 'There'll be another chance. Famous author like her is always popping up somewhere.'

'Little did I know,' I say, blinking back into the present day, where Maeve sits before me, hands clasped, tears in her eyes. 'Little did any of us know what would happen next.'

'Jasper said it was becoming too much,' says Maeve, her voice barely a whisper. 'London, the literary whirl, my crushing grief over the loss of Bella. He said it would do us both good to get some country air, said he'd seen an amazing historic house for a fraction of what it would cost in London. So, in early 2018, I rented out my beloved Hampstead flat and made an offer on Lustrum Manor. That night, the night of the awards, though I didn't realize it either, was my swansong. But you, dear. I knew I recognized you from somewhere. Now it all makes sense. Still, what I can't get my head around is how you went from the dazzling heights of that evening to – and forgive my bluntness – slumming it in a beaten-up old van.'

'It happened gradually,' I say, shuddering as I think back to the interminable Tube journeys, the crying that would not stop, the fatigue, the twenty-four-hour emails and calls, the working through weekends and holidays, the slow descent into despair and exhaustion. An incremental chipping away at my mental health. 'And yet it had all started so well. For the first decade of my career, I was deliriously happy.' I recount it to Maeve, as though recalling someone else's life. The excitement of discovering a new author, the 'pinch me' moment of seeing the book race up the charts, the indulgent glitz of award ceremonies, the business trips to Paris and New York, the trophy house by the river in Richmond, my marriage, and the weird thrill of hearing us described as 'the ultimate power couple'. 'It was a dream life,' I tell her, with a sigh. 'But dreams have a funny way of becoming nightmares.'

'Oh, I know all about that,' says Maeve, nodding her head ruefully.

'That night at the awards ceremony had been the catalyst,' I say, my chest tightening as the past comes surging back. 'It was almost as though, with that award, I had reached the top and there was nothing more to strive for. It all felt pointless somehow. All that success, all that ambition, and yet I was still that little abandoned girl inside. And the one person I wanted to be proud of me was still missing. My success hadn't brought my mother back – it had only made me more disconnected from everything. And still, people envied me, younger colleagues wanted to be me. Yet the more successful I became the more the stress piled up. I tried to tackle it by delegating duties, bringing in more assistants. But I find it very hard to let go and often ended up doing it all myself anyway. The problem was that I felt if I delegated, it would distance me from the authors and the stories, the very reason I had been drawn to book publishing in the first place. Ironically, it was this pig-headedness that led to my own demise and the loss of the authors I had fought so hard to keep. That's why these last few weeks have been so special. Working on your draft, I've felt myself coming back to life.'

'My draft,' whispers Maeve dreamily. 'If only it were that simple. But, yes, I could see it in your eyes while we were working. I saw a light coming back into them that hadn't been there when you first arrived. Like I said before, you remind me so much of Bella. Oh, my darling Bella. If anyone knew the dark recesses of my mind it was her.'

'I'm sorry, Maeve,' I say. 'Here I am talking about myself as though I'm the only person to have experienced loss. It must have been so hard to lose such a great friend as Bella and then to have it all brought back up again today.'

'Don't be silly, dear,' she says, smiling sadly. 'Bella, more than anyone, could identify with what you're describing. Funny how I thought her role would have been filled by someone just like her, that Matador, in fact the whole world, would be going on as usual, after almost a decade away. But life, and publishing, has moved on. It was foolish of me to think I could just reappear and take up from where I'd left off as though nothing had happened.'

'It's not foolish,' I say, remembering the spark in Maeve's eyes as she marched into the Matador offices, a spark that has been sadly lacking at Lustrum Manor. 'That was your life, your world. The only one that made sense. I can relate to that because that's how I felt.'

'So what changed?'

'Everything,' I say, sighing. 'It seemed like, overnight, I became a manager, a corporate suit obsessed with sales figures and forecasts. And the worst thing, the thing that depressed me the most, was that I stopped reading for pleasure. I learned to skim-read, my editorial brain leaping, almost unconsciously, onto areas that required attention. It was great for my authors but something inside me died. I found I was losing the greatest part of reading, the sense of wonder and magic. Books suddenly became work, hard work. I came to associate them with sales figures and spreadsheets rather than art, than stories. Me, the girl who, growing up, had never been without a book in my hand. It felt like, bit by bit, my whole identity was being taken away from me.'

'So what happened next?'

'My dad died,' I say, a familiar lump of grief settling in my chest. 'It happened while I was away at Frankfurt Book Fair in October, 2023. I was exhausted and on edge. I had back-to-back meetings with agents and editors from all over the world, eighteen-hour days, with drinks and dinner meetings, and conference calls that often went on long into the night. I was just stumbling back to my hotel room when my phone rang.'

I pause, remembering the enormity of that moment. The perfunctory words relayed to me by an overworked NHS doctor.

'A heart attack was the official cause of death,' I say, as the light fades outside the train window. 'But the truth was that my father had given up on life long before he took his last breath. His life stopped the day my mother left him.'

'My dear,' says Maeve, placing her hand on mine. 'I'm so sorry. Truly I am.'

'I should have told someone,' I say, my heart pounding as I recall what happened next. 'Should have taken the rest of the week off. If I had then the mistake wouldn't have been made and I wouldn't have reacted as I did.'

'What mistake?'

I look up at Maeve, the writer I have spent almost my whole life idolizing, the woman I have come to know this last couple of weeks, the friend and confidante I never thought I would find, and I hesitate. Will she hate me when she finds out what I did? But I know, after everything she has done for me, I owe her some honesty.

'There was a new author,' I say, closing my eyes so I don't have to see her response. 'Unknown at the time but a multi-million seller now. She had written the novel every publisher had been hankering for, a piece of speculative fiction that had captured the mood of post-pandemic Britain perfectly. There'd been a seven-way auction but, after a long lunch with me and my assistant, Jenny, the author had agreed to sign a three-book deal with us. It was stunning news and the team at Scion were deliriously happy. I'd left Jenny to draw up the contract while I went to my room to freshen up. That's when I'd got the call about my dad. I was in such shock, I missed seven calls from Jenny and countless emails. By the time I was back at my desk, the damage had been done.'

'What happened?'

'We missed the signing deadline,' I say, slowly opening my eyes. 'And I missed all those calls and emails from Jenny which had been relaying the author's queries on certain aspects of the contract she wasn't happy about. Instead of answering those calls and explaining to Jenny what had happened to my dad I'd just sat there in a trance on the floor of the hotel, unable to move, unable to speak. Some time that evening, the author met with and signed with another publisher who agreed to offer more money and more favourable terms.'

'It happens,' says Maeve, with a shrug. 'It's business. And you, my darling, had had a terrible shock. It's not your fault.'

'Oh, it was pretty cataclysmic,' I say, my voice trembling with emotion. 'But I could have explained about my father when I got back to the London office the next day and, though it was a huge loss for Scion, they would have understood. But my head was all over the place and I'm afraid that instead of asking for leniency I went on the defensive and took it out on Jenny. This anger I didn't know I had inside me came spilling out, all aimed at her. I told her she was an idiot, that she should have come and hammered down my door. Basically I laid the entire blame for the loss of the author at her feet.'

'Oh,' says Maeve, raising her eyebrows, though her expression is sympathetic.

'My behaviour was deemed unacceptable, and it was suggested that I take some time off,' I say, recalling my unceremonious removal from the building by two security guards. 'Though the legal document that arrived the next day made it clear that my position had been terminated.'

'You were fired.'

'Well, to avoid repercussions – they knew my wife was a lawyer – they took the redundancy route, stating that my role was to be redistributed,' I say, the tears I have spent the past half-hour trying to hold back now coming forth. 'Still, unlike a sacking, I at least left with a few months' pay.'

'Alexis, it must have been such a shock,' says Maeve, reaching into her handbag and handing me a tissue. 'And, yes, it was wrong that you lost your temper like that but you're only human and your father had just died.'

'It was a shock,' I say, wiping my eyes. 'But what with the funeral and the sale of my father's house there was still a lot to deal with. I had to keep my focus somehow and then . . . well, then I had my epiphany. A month later I was clearing out my father's house and I found my mother's diary. When I read it, something clicked inside. I knew I had to find her. And I knew I couldn't go on living as I had been. Wallowing around the house in Richmond, being snappy at Tara all the time. Something had to give. Then, just after Christmas, I was shopping in town when I saw a camper van parked outside Richmond station. It was bright yellow, just like Mum's, and had a *For Sale* sign in the window. It seemed like a message from the universe. A week later the van was mine. I never told Tara and I'm ashamed to say this now, but once the sale had gone through and I had collected the van, I went home, packed some things and left her a note saying I'd be gone for a little while. It was cowardly of me, but I knew that if I saw her face she would convince me to stay. I had to get away, I had to find my mother.'

'So that's how you came to have your camper van?' says Maeve, with a smile, as the train slows down on its approach to Haughton.

'Yes,' I say, recalling that day. 'And it was so strange because when I got behind the wheel, I felt something inside me burst into life. It was like my mother's spirit and all her unfulfilled dreams had taken root in me. The hours after that are still a blur. All I really know is that I'd just lit a match under my seemingly perfect life. That was over a year ago and here I am in another world. Gone are the six-figure salary and the designer clothes. I live day to day, taking on work when I need it. I'd managed to avoid editorial commissions until you and Jasper. I just couldn't face being back in that world so I mainly took on ad hoc bar work or waitressing. I even did a couple of night-carer shifts at a nursing home, practical work, the kind that can be left behind at the end of the day. How freeing it's felt after years of living, breathing and sleeping my career with no room for anything else. And now, with the information I found on the genealogy website about my mother being in Paris in April 2021 and the fact that she must have visited the shop in 1988 to buy me that book for Christmas, I'm one step closer to finding her. If I manage that then none of this will have been in vain.'

Opposite me, Maeve is silent, her lips pursed.

'I suppose you think I'm an awful person,' I say, as the lights of Haughton station come into view. 'That I'm horribly selfish for just driving away like that. That I'm no better than my mother.'

'I don't think that at all,' says Maeve, a tear falling down her cheek. 'Nor do I think ill of your mother. She did what she had to do. As for you, well, I do hope you find her and if you want my opinion, I think what you did was very brave. If only I had half your courage, then maybe I'd be able to tell you my truth.'

'What truth?' I say, as the train pulls into the station. 'What do you mean?'

'Ah, we're here,' says Maeve, grabbing her bag and getting up from the seat. 'I suppose the truth, like every good plot twist, will have to wait.'

24

ALEXIS

It is just getting dark when the taxi drops us off at the gates of Lustrum Manor, but the house is ablaze with lights and music.

'Good grief,' exclaims Maeve, as we walk up the drive-way. 'What's going on? It looks like they're having some sort of party.'

The drawbridge is flanked by tiki torches and the sound of orchestral music fills the air. As I guide Maeve over the bridge, I feel a strange sense of unease.

'Look at all these candles,' says Maeve, as we make our way across the courtyard to the orangery. 'Who in heaven's name put them here? It can't have been Jasper. He hates candles.'

Her words hang in the air as we open the door of the orangery. It has been decked with glittering fairy lights and sitting at a table in the middle of the room are Jasper and Cordelia, a bottle of wine and two glasses between them. They are both smartly dressed – Jasper in a dark suit and tie, his unruly hair slicked back, while Cordelia is wearing a bright floral cocktail dress. Her blonde hair has been blow-dried into bouncy waves and her face is glowing with soft, flattering make-up. She looks a million miles from the frazzled woman I have been accustomed to seeing this last couple of weeks. For a moment, they don't notice us standing there and carry on chatting. Finally, Jasper looks up and lets out a gasp that is half surprise half yelp.

'My goodness, thank God you're back,' he cries, jumping up from the table and striding towards us. 'I couldn't believe it when you texted to say you'd gone to London for the day. Alexis, really, you had no right to take her off like that without consulting me. She is not a well woman.'

'It was my idea, not Alexis's,' says Maeve sternly. 'And I am perfectly well, thank you. Now, what's all this then?'

She gestures to the table bedecked with flowers and candles.

'And why are you both dolled up?'

Jasper's face flushes.

'Er, well,' he says, taking Maeve's arm and guiding her into the room. 'It was . . . it was . . .'

'It was a drinks evening organized by the history department,' says Cordelia, with a sigh. 'Jasper didn't want to go there alone. You know how socially awkward he can be. So I went along with him.'

'A drinks evening?' says Maeve incredulously. 'You never mentioned it to me. I thought your only plan for today was the trip to Waitrose this morning. And anyway, it's only nine o'clock. Shouldn't you still be at this do?'

'I'd forgotten all about it until I saw it in my diary this afternoon,' says Jasper, taking Maeve's coat. 'I thought I should show my face. After all, the university has been so good to me these last few years, keeping me on for part-time lecturing. But like Cordelia said, you know how I am with crowds. And it was full of loud drunken students. We stayed for the first hour, then slipped away. Besides,

I couldn't settle as I was worried sick about you. Thank God you're home safely. Now, why don't I make you a nice hot chocolate and get you settled in bed? I bet you're exhausted, my darling.'

With that he takes Maeve's arm and whisks her out of the orangery.

'What a nightmare,' says Cordelia, gesturing for me to join her at the table. 'Here, have a glass of wine. It looks like you need it.'

I sit down wearily, my mind still churning over the events of the day, the look on Heidi Berenger's face when she saw me.

'Thank you,' I say, as she pours me a glass of red. 'And, yes, it has been a long day.'

'Honestly,' says Cordelia. 'These two just don't pay enough for the amount of stress they throw at me. Take tonight. I was all set for a night in front of the TV and I end up in the middle of some hideous university gathering. These shoes are killing my feet too.'

She stretches out her legs and kicks off her high heels, swaying tipsily in her seat. It is clear she's had rather a lot to drink this evening.

'Anyway, what was all that about?' she says, taking a sip of wine. 'The trip to London?'

'Oh, it was nothing,' I say, keeping Maeve's confidence. 'I just thought it would be nice to have a change of scene. It can get a bit claustrophobic in here.'

'You're telling me,' says Cordelia. 'I don't know how they do it, really I don't. Both of them cooped up in their rooms, barely getting out. It's not healthy. That's why I said I'd take Jasper to the event tonight. I told him not to worry about Maeve going to London, that you were with her and would make sure she was all right, but he wouldn't listen. You should have seen how nervous he was. No wonder people give them a wide berth.'

She shakes her head and sighs.

'Speaking of which,' I say, as my head begins to clear. 'I don't suppose you remember a woman called Kimberly Harper? She came here in 2021 to work as a groundskeeper or gardener but didn't pass the trial.'

'Oh, her,' says Cordelia, refilling her glass. 'God, yes. That was during lockdown, wasn't it? Kimberly Harper. That's right, Jasper let her go 'cause she asked too many questions.'

'Really?' I say, leaning forward. 'What sort of questions?'

'Mad stuff, according to Jasper,' she says, her voice thick with alcohol. 'But then Maeve has always been a target for cranks. It seems she was just a deranged fan trying to get close to her idol but Jasper soon sussed her out.'

'She was asking questions about Maeve?'

But Cordelia doesn't answer. She is staring at the door, a look of horror on her face. I turn round and see Jasper standing there, his face etched with fury.

'Alexis, you must be exhausted after your train journey,' he says, walking over to the table. 'Why don't you head up to bed.'

It is more of a command than a question.

'Yes,' I say, getting up from the table. 'I could do with an early night.'

'Oh, and before I forget,' says Jasper, reaching into his pocket and pulling out a brown envelope. 'This is for you. It's your wages.'

'But the next lot isn't due until the end of the week,' I say, as he hands it to me.

'I know, but see it as an advance,' he says, smiling. 'A little thank-you for all your hard work both with me and Maeve. I know that what you're doing with her is above and beyond the line of duty and I'm grateful for that, I really am.'

'Gosh, thanks, Jasper,' I say, surprised that he isn't issuing me another ticking off for taking Maeve to London. 'I can pay the final instalment of repairs with this.'

'That's what I thought,' he says, glancing at Cordelia whose head is slumped on the table. 'You'll soon be out of here and back on the road, eh? Now, do excuse me, I'm going to have to brew some strong coffee for this one.'

'Of course,' I say, tucking the envelope into my pocket. 'Night, Jasper. Night, Cordelia.'

She lets out a low groan as I leave the room but when I step out into the corridor I hear Jasper's voice. Tiptoeing back to the door, I press my head against it and listen.

'What the hell do you think you're playing at?' he hisses. 'Talking to her like that.'

'I don't know what you mean, Jasper,' she slurs. 'My head is throbbing, and I just want to go to bed.'

'I'm talking about Kimberly Harper,' he says, his voice uncharacteristically menacing. 'For God's sake, Cordelia, do you know how dangerous it could be if Alexis got wind of all that?'

'I didn't say anything wrong,' Cordelia wails. 'I didn't give anything away.'

'Only because I walked in and stopped you,' he says. 'Now, I have no idea what this trip to London was all about but you and I are going to have to take things up a notch now.'

'What do you mean?'

'I mean, we were almost caught out tonight. And I have a horrible feeling that Alexis is treading perilously close to the truth.'

'So what do we do?'

'I don't think we have much choice any more,' he says. 'I think it might be time to do what we discussed.'

'What? This soon?'

'I'm afraid so, Cordelia. Otherwise, both of us are finished. Now, you'd better get to bed and sober up, because you're going to need a clear head. It's time we take our plan to the next level and end this once and for all.'

25

BLYTHE

Cimetière du Montparnasse

July 1960

'Are you going to tell me who died?'

Blythe held on to William's arm as they followed Paula, Sam and Estelle through the labyrinthine gravestones, her forehead glistening with sweat. The French summer was now well under way and Blythe was still acclimatizing to the intense heat.

'Everybody, I guess,' laughed William, his blue eyes glinting in the morning sun.

'Very funny,' hissed Blythe, punching his arm playfully. 'I mean, why are we here in this cemetery? Isn't the magazine going to press today?'

'That's right. *La Voix* hits the stands at noon,' he says, taking her hand in his. 'With my short story on page six. Say, Blythe, I wish you'd have submitted something like Paula asked. First edition of a literary mag is pretty special.'

'I told you,' said Blythe, as the group ahead came to a halt beside a chimney-shaped gravestone. 'I'm not ready yet.'

'Still?' said William, raising his eyebrows. 'It's been two

months and no one besides you has been privy to the contents of that strange little notebook of yours.'

Blythe dropped his arm and was about to retort that there was nothing strange or little about her notebook and nor would she be rushed when Sam raised his hand.

'Thanks for coming, all of you,' he said, a single red rose tucked beneath his arm. 'Paula asked if we could mark this day, the day a mighty fine new literary magazine goes to press, by doing something special. And considering the spirit of the enterprise, I could think of no better way than by paying our respects to this man here.'

He gestured to the stone, a family memorial with several names featured. A shaft of bright sunlight illuminated the second name down on the marble frontispiece. Blythe crouched in front of the stone and, shading her eyes from the harsh light, whispered it to herself.

Charles Baudelaire.

'A writer whose spirit we all agree encapsulates not only Paris,' continued Sam, as the other tumbleweeds gathered round the grave, 'but the essence of what all of us here are bound together to create: a life dedicated to the power of words. A series of sounds exhaled into the ether, a cluster of symbols scribbled on a page, and yet what magic, what sorcery they unleash once you know what to do with them.'

Blythe looked up as Sam, with tears in his eyes, laid the rose on the grave. Paula, Estelle and William clasped each other in a tight embrace. She could have joined them, could have bowed her head respectfully at the resting place of the great poet, yet she stayed kneeling on the ground, her back to the group. Because, despite William's assurances and her own eagerness to throw herself wholeheartedly into the world of the tumbleweeds, there was a part of her that would always feel like an outsider. Her words, contained in her trusty notebook, were not meant to grace the pages of *La Voix*, she knew that. Her stories were still gestating. One day they would reach an audience, and it would be the right one.

'That was beautiful,' said Paula, as she and Estelle strolled towards the grand wrought-iron gates. 'A perfect way to mark the birth of *La Voix*.'

Following them, William, Blythe and Sam played an awkward game of pathway politics, with Blythe holding William's hand while Sam held his gaze. Would it always be like this? thought Blythe. Would a life with William mean a life in which Sam was forever hovering on the periphery? And though William insists that Sam is a good man, Blythe will never forget how he had humiliated her so horribly when he read out the contents of her notebook at the party that night. What was not in doubt was the fact that Blythe and William were in love and that neither of them could imagine a future without the other. And though William would be happy to stay here in Paris alongside the tumbleweeds and the ever-present Sam, Blythe had other ideas.

The realization had come to her one evening in Le Mistral. It was quiet, just George reading in his chair and a couple of tumbleweeds stacking books out front. William and Sam had gone to see a play put on by an experimental theatre group down by the docks, Paula and Estelle were upstairs working on the first edition of *La Voix*, and for the first time in weeks, Blythe found she could hear her own voice. It had been a throwaway remark by George that lit the flame. He'd looked up from the book he was reading and regarded Blythe thoughtfully. 'You ever feel you were born in the wrong time?' he asked her. 'Or the wrong place?'

'I don't know,' she'd replied. 'I've never really given it much thought.'

'Well, take us, for example,' he continued. 'Two misplaced Yanks sitting here in this run-down corner of Paris. Why aren't we in Missouri or Connecticut? What is it that we're searching for? And why Paris of all places?'

Blythe ruminated on the question. Had she been searching for something in Paris or had she just been trying to escape? From Connecticut, from her parents, from Amory and all that stifling social nonsense? And it could have been anywhere really, Paris was just the place her father was doing business in. It was the city Mademoiselle DuPont, her beloved teacher, had lived in and Blythe had been so spellbound by the woman who had introduced her to the works of Hemingway and Stein that she would have travelled to the moon if Mademoiselle DuPont had recommended it. But, and she asked herself this sincerely, if she could have chosen the destination, the place she really wanted to make a life in, would Paris have been that choice?

'I suppose I'm still working it out,' she said.

George had smiled then and returned to his book.

'London,' he said, as Blythe headed out of the room. 'I think that's the place for you. Don't ask me why, I just feel it. In my bones.'

So, over the next few days, London had become the beacon shining on Blythe's horizon, the north star she knew she had to head towards. She hadn't told William her plan yet as it was still formulating in her head and growing more pressing as each day passed. To go to London with William and be a writer. That was all the plan consisted of at this point, but it made more sense to her than anything else in her life thus far. The logistics would look after themselves. All she had to do was get to London and then her life, her true life, could begin.

'See you back at the shop,' called Paula, as she and Estelle exited the gates. 'Publication day party starts at noon and you are all going to be there.'

'What a day to be alive,' said William, as Sam fell back to light a cigarette. 'My first time in print. You know, Blythe, I think this is the beginning of great things for us, for all of us. Wait here a second.'

He patted her arm, then ran back to Sam to catch a smoke. Blythe shook her head. 'No, I won't wait here,' she muttered crossly. 'I'm not your lapdog.' The sun blazed on her face as she made her way out of the gates. Shading her eyes, she saw a man standing on the pavement, a dark shadow against the bright blue sky. As she drew closer, Blythe felt the skin on the back of her neck prickle, her heart stutter in her chest.

'Amory?'

The word, as it left her lips, sounded like a lament.

'Blythe, darling.'

He rushed towards her and swooped her into his arms. Never, in all the years she had known him, had she seen him so demonstrative.

'What . . . what are you doing here?' she cried into the folds of his jacket.

'I've come to take you home,' he whispered, stroking her hair. 'And make you my wife.'

26

BLYTHE

Paris

July 1960

'It was a shock seeing you standing at the cemetery gates like that,' said Blythe, as Amory marched them through the lobby of the Ritz. 'How did you know I was there?'

'Well, I went to the address your parents gave me, thirty-seven rue de la Bûcherie,' he said, as they stopped outside the lift. 'To find that it was a dusty old book-shop. Funny place to have an etiquette school, don't you think?'

He pressed the button for 'up', then looked at her quizzically.

'Not really,' said Blythe, thinking on her feet. 'Madame Roux is . . . well, she's rather eccentric and she believes that being well read is an important part of the etiquette train-ing, hence why she's based at Le Mistral.'

'Hmm,' said Amory, clearly unconvinced. 'Well, there was no sign of your Madame Roux when I turned up, just some four-eyed square behind the front desk who smelt like he needed a good shower. It was him who told me where you'd be. A pilgrimage, that's how he described it. I mean, come on, Blythe, these people would have had their heads flushed down the toilet at my college, and rightly so.'

'They're my friends,' said Blythe, trying to supress the anger that was growing inside her. 'They're good people.'

'I'm sure they are,' said Amory, as the lift doors opened, and they stepped inside. 'And I'm glad these classes of yours have been worthwhile, I really am. But this will all be a memory soon. We're heading home to our families, our real friends. Now let's go see our rooms.'

Blythe felt her chest tighten as he pressed the button for the seventh floor, and all the old fears and anxieties she had buried these last few months came tumbling back.

'Rooms?' she said, as they ascended.

'Yes, darling. Rest assured, I booked two separate ones,' said Amory. 'I am a gentleman even in this lawless city. Hey, did you know they have original Monets hanging in the master suite up here? Imagine falling asleep beneath a masterpiece. Remember when we were kids and our parents signed us up for summer school art class? I loved that. I remember the tutor saying I had an excellent eye for design. You were hopeless as I recall, though you did excel in the creative writing segment. Probably all those books you constantly had your nose in. I'd say you've been lucky these last few months to have been exposed to the highest of Parisian culture. It's going to stand you in good stead once the season begins back home. The conversations you can bring to our gatherings. Say, I hope you've polished up your French too. That's going to be mighty helpful when it comes to European clients.'

As the elevator reached the seventh floor, the art deco doors opening with a creak, Blythe felt as though her head was about to burst. She had forgotten Amory's propensity for incessant, inane chatter.

'I hope you don't mind us not flying back immediately,' said Amory, taking her hand as they stepped out into a lushly carpeted corridor. 'Thought it might be nice for us to have a few days together in the most romantic city in the world.'

'No, I don't mind,' said Blythe, letting go of Amory's clammy hand. 'But I'll need to collect my stuff from Madame Roux's place. I should go over there in case I miss her.'

'Now?' said Amory, pausing outside Room 709, his face drawn. 'But I only just got here. Surely it can wait? We have a lot of catching-up to do.'

Wrapping his hands around her waist, he tried to kiss her mouth, but she turned away.

'Amory,' she cried, taking the key from his hand. 'Contain yourself. We're not married, remember.'

'Hey, I'm not trying any funny business,' he said, as she opened the door. 'I just missed you, that's all. Can't a man kiss his own fiancée?'

'Of course,' said Blythe, aware that she would have to tread carefully to avoid arousing Amory's suspicions. 'I just need to freshen up, that's all. Say, how about I meet you down at the bar in about an hour.'

'Sounds good,' he said, his large brown eyes softening so that for a moment he looked like the little boy she had once known. 'What'll I order you?'

'The usual,' she said, without thinking.

'And what would that be?'

Her heart twisted in her chest. William would know. If

she were with him he would be uncorking a bottle of red, purchased from the liquor store on the corner, which they would drink on the rooftop curled up in each other's arms. The idea of drinking red wine with Amory made her feel queasy so instead she smiled her best smile and told him to make hers a lime soda.

'Sure thing,' he winked, kissing her forehead. 'Don't be long now.'

She watched him disappear down the corridor and, once she was sure he was gone, she closed the hotel room door and skipped away in the opposite direction.

An hour, she told herself, as she ran down seven flights of stairs. Just one hour to find William and let him in on her plan.

When she got to Le Mistral, the party was in full swing. Jazz music rang out, the air was thick with cigarette smoke and excited voices. Copies of *La Voix* covered every available surface, and men and women Blythe had never seen before stood nose to nose in the cramped space, clutching chubby glasses of wine in their hands.

'Excusez-moi,' Blythe called out above the din, as she squeezed through the tightly packed crowd. 'Pardon.'

'Blythe, over here.'

She looked up to see Paula standing on a raised platform at the entrance to the Old Smoky Reading Room. Extending her hand, she pulled Blythe up to join her.

'Where have you been?' she hissed into Blythe's ear, her breath sour from wine and cigarettes. 'You've missed the speeches.'

'I'm sorry,' said Blythe, raising her voice over the din.

'It's a long story but my fiancé turned up unexpectedly and has booked us into the Ritz.'

'Did you say fiancé?' cried Paula, with a gasp. 'Jesus, Blythe. You're a dark horse. I had no idea. Listen, wait here. You look like you need a drink.'

Paula jumped down from the platform and disappeared into the crowd, returning a few moments later with a half-drunk bottle of white wine.

'Sorry, we seem to have run out of glasses,' she said, offering Blythe the bottle.

'I can't stay, unfortunately,' said Blythe, scanning the room.

'You have to get back to Mr Ritz, I get it,' Paula sneered.

'No, I just need to find William,' said Blythe, her heart pounding. 'It's rather urgent.'

'Oh, William and Sam went to grab some food,' said Paula, taking a swig from the bottle. 'Said they were going to work on some poems over lunch, but you know what Sam's like. He'll be trying to woo William with his sonnets.'

Blythe felt that familiar ache in her chest, the reminder that this was William's home, his friends, and no matter how much he said he loved her, he would always put them first.

'It's all right,' she said, jumping down from the platform. 'I don't need him. I can do this myself.'

'Do what yourself?' Paula called out after her. But Blythe didn't answer. She had had it with Le Mistral, with William and Sam and the bloody tumbleweeds, with Paris, with the whole lot of it.

*

'Goodnight, my sweet. Tap on the wall if you need me. I'm just next door.'

Amory kissed her hand, then clutched it to his chest.

'Where's your ring, darling?' he said, pulling away.

'Oh, it's at the jeweller's,' she replied, her heart pulsating as she thought back to earlier that day, rushing from Mistral to the pawnbroker's, the elation she felt when she had secured the deal. 'I've lost a bit of weight these last few weeks and it was feeling rather loose, so I arranged to get it resized. I hope you don't mind but I was terrified it would fall off and get lost.'

'Very sensible of you,' he said, kissing her forehead. 'That ring's a family heirloom.'

Guilt stirred in Blythe's chest. Had she done the right thing? But then she remembered her plan – London, writing, freedom – and her resolve returned.

'I'd better get to bed, Amory,' she said, extricating herself from him. 'I'm awfully tired.'

'Parting is such sweet sorrow,' he sighed. 'Who wrote that again?'

'Groucho Marx,' said Blythe sarcastically, as she pulled her hand away. 'I'll see you in the morning, Amory. I really have to get some sleep.'

Bemused, Amory smiled, then slunk away.

Closing the door, Blythe grimaced as she thought back to earlier that day. How interminable the afternoon with Amory had been. Returning from the bookshop, she'd found him in the bar of the Ritz, wondering where she had got to. She'd explained that she'd fallen asleep in her room after he left her, which he appeared to believe. After that they had done a little sightseeing before stopping for dinner at an overblown, soulless place by the Tuileries, recommended by a client of Amory's. When Amory had suggested a nightcap at Harry's Bar, she had affected a headache and let him fuss over her as he bundled them both into an overpriced taxi and headed back to the Ritz.

'Your parents can't wait to see you,' he said, as they walked through the lobby, where a lone pianist was playing a Gershwin number. 'Your mother, especially. Wait till you see the colour scheme she's come up with for the wedding reception. Peaches and cream. She said it's *Vogue*'s top combination for the season.'

As he prattled on beside her, Blythe felt like they had swapped identities. Amory was the excitable bride, while she was the reticent groom dragging her feet. No wonder her mother loved him so much – he was the daughter she had never had.

Now, sitting in her room on the edge of the opulent queen-sized bed, she realized that if she didn't come up with a plan soon there would be no London, no writing career, no freedom, only Amory and charity luncheons and peaches and cream. Her eyes filled with tears as she lay back and looked at the ceiling, its intricate cornicing blurring in front of her like the melted icing of a wedding cake.

She closed her eyes, willed herself to sleep but it was hopeless, her brain simply would not stop whirring. Just then there was a knock at the door. Her heart sank. What does he want now? I'll pretend to be asleep, she told herself. Then he'll go away. She listened. There was another knock, more insistent. Getting to her feet, she crept to the door and pressed her ear to it.

'Blythe,' whispered a familiar voice. 'It's me.'

With trembling hands, she unlocked the door. William stood there. His hair was all messed up, his shirt rumpled. The momentary elation Blythe had felt when she heard his voice gave way to revulsion. Had Paula been right? Had Sam planned to coax William into bed? Because by the look of him he'd succeeded.

'How did you get up here?' she said, pulling him inside. 'And keep your voice down. Amory's just next door.'

'My pal Jean-Paul let me up,' he said, his jaw tensing. 'Amory's next door, is he? So that was the slick fella I saw you walk off with at the cemetery today? When Paula said you were staying at the Ritz with your fiancé tonight I thought that might be the case. Happy ever after, eh?'

'How can you say that?' Blythe hissed, tears springing to her eyes. 'You know how I feel about marrying him. It's the last thing I want. In fact, I don't even want to be in Paris any more. It's not the right place for me. I'm going to go to London and be a writer.'

'And yet here you are in the Ritz hunkering down in your separate bedrooms like a good little girl. See, Blythe, you say you don't want Amory and your high-society, vacuous American life, but I don't see you putting up a fight. Your parents, Amory, they call, and you come running.'

The ice in his voice chilled the air.

'I could say the same thing about Sam,' she snapped back. 'The big-headed poet whistles and good little William runs after him like a dog chasing scraps.'

'You know nothing about Sam,' he cried, raising his hands to his head. 'And you know nothing about how tough it is to exist like this. Do you know that Sam literally grew up in orphanages back in Philadelphia, that he has to make his writing work or it's back to Philly and the factory line, that he doesn't have a trust fund to fall back on like Paula, or you. See, it's all right for you to come and try it out for a few months like some actress performing in a play. But then you get to go back to your life of luxury while the rest of us are left behind trying to scrape a living. But you know what, Miss Connecticut, I wouldn't swap places with you for all the money in the world. 'Cause it takes guts to do what we do, to dedicate our heart and soul to art and poetry and writing at the expense of all the trappings of a so-called ordinary life. And you, despite your notebook and your grand proclamations, don't have the courage to cut the cords of your privileged life. Jeez, you can't even write a one-page autobiography or show me any of your stories. And I think I know why. Because you're terrified of how your life will really pan out. Fifty-plus years of playing hostess in small-town America. That's what I see.'

'Stop it,' cried Blythe, sinking to her knees. 'Just stop it. That's not true.'

She pressed her hands to her ears and squeezed her eyes shut. In the darkness she saw the life ahead of her spiralling out of her control, like an uncoiled thread. She saw a picket fence and three children in neat white pinafores, she saw Amory walking up the path with a briefcase in his hand. She saw a bookshelf full of unread books, notebooks with empty pages, a record player with the lid tightly shut. And she saw herself standing at the window, a glass of gin in her hand, her stomach starved from dieting, her soul starved of creativity, and she let out a silent scream that vibrated through her entire body.

'Hey, I'm sorry, kiddo. I didn't mean to be so mad. I got you, baby. I got you.'

William's arms were wrapped around her. She opened her eyes and saw, through a blur of tears, his face next to hers.

'I'm not the person you think I am,' she whispered. 'I'm not going back there. I swear to you. I can't. I'm going to get out of here and I came to Le Mistral today to find you because I want you to come with me.'

'Really?' he said, lifting his head up. 'You're serious?'

'I've never been more serious about anything in my life,' she said. 'Besides you.'

He smiled but his expression was pensive.

'Where would we go?'

'London,' she said, her heart fluttering with excitement. 'We could find work there, take our writing seriously, look to get it published. Oh, William, imagine it, just the two of us.'

'London,' he said, his eyes narrowing. 'You know, Blythe, I'm not too fond of the English. See, they have this nasty habit of killing my countrymen. It kind of puts a fella off, you know. That's why I like Paris. I feel safe here.'

'That was a long time ago, William,' she said, shaking her head. 'Things have changed over there. London is a hub for people like us now. It's alive with writers and musicians and artists.'

'But how do you know this?' he said. 'You've never been. Are you sure you're not just running away from m'laddo next door?'

'I know it in here,' she said, placing her hand on her heart. 'Paris has been wonderful, but I don't feel I truly belong. There is something in London that's calling me.'

'You're dead set on this?'

'I am.'

'Then I'm in,' he said, holding her face with both hands. 'I'm in, because, damn it, Blythe, I love you. And I'd follow you to the ends of the earth if I had to, God help me. But I want to ask you something.'

She nodded her head.

'You do realize this is not going to be easy. We'll have to find work, a place to stay. London doesn't come cheap. And if we do it, there's no going back.'

'I know that, William. But I don't want to go back. I want to go forward. With you.'

'OK. So we'll do it. But you promise you'll see this through? You won't change your mind and run back to him and your folks?'

'I promise.'

He looked at her then and Blythe felt as though the world had shifted on its axis. Nothing, after this, would ever be the same again. They had committed to each other; they were going to escape here and build a life together. And it had all been her idea. Pulling him towards her, she kissed him deeply. She was in control. Not Amory, not her parents. She wanted William. She loved him and he loved her. As she peeled off her clothes, felt the warmth of his skin next to hers, it seemed as though her soul was soaring. Though she had made love to William countless times these last few months, this time felt different. It was as though she was finally stepping out of the girl she had been, sweet obedient Blythe Aston-Laine, and taking on another form. As she took William inside her, felt his light kisses on her neck, her breasts, her belly, she felt, for the first time in her life, truly free.

And later, as they lay on the floor, spent, entwined in each other's arms, she realized that something had changed irrevocably. She was someone else now, someone new.

'I feel different,' she whispered.

'That's because you are,' he replied, pulling her close. 'What we've unleashed can't be put back in the box.'

'I don't want to go back,' she said, tears pricking her eyes. 'I just want to be with you. And this plan of mine is perfect. I have enough money to get us to London, rent a place – George has given me the name of a friend of his with a spare room in Highgate – and to live on for the rest of the year.'

'And where did that sort of money come from?' he said, scowling.

She held up her ring finger and smiled.

'That ugly old rock?' he gasped. 'You . . . you . . .?'

'I pawned it, yes,' she said triumphantly. 'Earlier today. I told Amory I'd left it at a jeweller's to be resized and he believed me. Little does he know that the ring he gave me to signify my bondage has ended up securing my freedom. Now, Amory and I are due to fly home the day after tomorrow, in the afternoon. All we have to do is give him the slip that morning and head to the ferry terminal. I have the sailing times in my bag. From there, we'll be free.'

'Yes, but you don't think your folks and Amory wouldn't come after you?' he said, with a sigh. 'Your da's a powerful man, Blythe. He knows people in high places, I'll bet. Once Amory found out you'd run off, he'd tell your folks and they'd put out a search party, alert the ports. Even if we got to England, we'd be constantly looking over our shoulder. No, what we need is to make a proper escape, a clean one.'

'What do you mean?'

'Look, if you go missing, they'll be looking for Blythe Aston-Laine turning up at the ferry terminal or the London docks or what have you,' he says, lying back on his elbows. 'What we need to make sure of is that the person who leaves Paris is not you. It'll be a massive decision, kiddo, but the truth is if you mean what you say and you want to start a whole new life then you're going to have to remove all trace of Blythe Aston-Laine.'

'But how would I be able to do that?' she said, her stomach knotting with anxiety at the realization that her slapdash plan might fail at the first hurdle.

'I have an idea,' whispered William, his breath warm against her ear. 'But I'll need to check a couple of things first.'

He gently extricated himself from her and picked up his clothes, which were scattered around the floor.

'I'll have to tread carefully,' he said, with a reassuring smile. 'But I should be able to sort it.'

'It is legal, isn't it?' she said, watching as he pulled on his trousers. 'I don't want you doing anything that could get you into trouble.'

'Don't you worry about that,' he said, his eyes twinkling. 'I'll be fine. But the thing is, it might take a little time. You said you and Amory are due to fly back to the US the day after tomorrow. Now, are you all right to spend tomorrow with old laughing boy next door, do a little sightseeing or whatever?'

Blythe nodded her head.

'Just, whatever you do,' said William, 'don't make him suspicious. Keep him sweet, you know?'

'I think I can do that,' she said, though the thought of being amorous with Amory made her feel sick.

'Good,' whispered William, kissing her cheek. 'Leave this with me. I'll send word to you when it's sorted. Happy?'

'More than I've ever been,' she smiled, as they tiptoed to the door. 'I love you, William Kenneally.'

'I love you too, kiddo,' he whispered, as he stepped into the corridor. 'More than you know.'

27

ALEXIS

The following morning, exhausted from a sleepless night tossing and turning as I tried to make sense of what Jasper and Cordelia had been talking about, I trudge down to the kitchen where I am surprised to find Maeve sitting at the table, notebook in hand. She looks up as I enter and gestures to the laptop opposite her.

'I've had an early start,' she says brightly. 'I came down to see if Daphne had sneaked in here. She wasn't in her usual spot by the study window this morning so I thought she must have come looking for food but her bowl's untouched. You haven't seen her, have you?'

'No,' I reply, stifling a yawn. 'But I'm sure she'll turn up once hunger gets the better of her. Cats always do.'

'I suppose so,' says Maeve. 'Though it's most unlike her. Anyway, it feels good to be up and about early. The editorial notes you left me were spot on. I wonder, do you have time to make a crack on the next chapter?'

'Maeve, you know I can't help you during the day,' I say, taking the coffee pot from the range and pouring myself a large mug. 'Jasper's paying me to work on his book from nine until four each day. Speaking of which, I should get going.'

'Oh, that won't be necessary,' says Maeve, flicking

through her notebook. 'He's gone out with Cordelia. Some meeting or other. He'll be out most of the day. He left a note for you.'

As I bring my coffee over and sit down next to her, she hands me a scrap of paper with Jasper's neat handwriting on it.

Alexis, I'm afraid I won't be requiring your services today. And please, can you make sure Maeve takes her medication this morning. Thanks, Jasper

As I read the perfunctory message, I think back to the previous evening, the conversation I overheard. Did Jasper know I was listening? Because this note sounds like an admonishment of sorts. I drain my coffee and take the cup over to the sink to rinse. Maeve's pill box is sitting on the counter. I go to pick it up, then something makes me stop. She has been so happy and clear-headed these last few weeks and I know that she has thrown every pill Jasper has given her into the bin when she thinks he's not looking. She is a world away from the trembling, confused old woman dressed in rags that I first met that day out on the road. When Jasper had first explained the importance of his wife's medication, I had trusted him implicitly – there was no reason not to. Now I am not so sure.

I stand by the window for a moment. The sun is blazing onto the grounds, and I feel compelled to get out of this cloying house and into the fresh air.

'I have an idea,' I say, turning to Maeve. 'As it's such beautiful weather and I have an unexpected day off, how about we take the laptop outside? We could work in the walled garden. It's such a beautiful space. How does that sound?'

237

Maeve looks at me as though I've just suggested we run naked through the streets but then her face softens, and she smiles brightly.

'You know what, that sounds like a splendid idea,' she says, clasping her notebook to her chest. 'I've struggled with this chapter because what happens is so . . . painful. Perhaps if I'm out in the sunshine like I was when I first met him it will be easier to find the words.'

'You mean when the reader first met him?'

'No, dear, I meant when *I* first met him.'

'Are you saying that . . . that William is real?'

She looks down at the notebook and gently strokes the cover. Then, glancing up at me, her blue eyes blazing, she smiles.

'Come on,' she says, getting up from the table. 'Let's go and sit in the sunshine. Once we've written the next chapter, I think it will all become clear.'

28

BLYTHE

Paris

July 1960

'Sculptures, my dear? Do we really have to? You know I find them awful tiresome. All that flesh on display. Better to go see the *Mona Lisa*, surely? One to tell the folks back home about.'

While Amory consulted the guidebook for the location of the famous painting, Blythe stood in front of *Psyche Revived by Cupid's Kiss*, drinking in every little detail. When she had last seen this sculpture, she had been a virgin. And though the magnificence of it had inspired a story, it had been one she could not place herself in. Back then, it had seemed almost too much, the passion of it, the nakedness, the sensuality – those things were out of reach for Blythe, lovemaking was something that other people did, not her. Yet now she was looking at the artwork through new eyes. She had experienced the heat and passion conveyed by the sculpture, she had lain naked in a man's arms, been revived by his kiss. Now she felt it, not just in her body, but in her soul. She knew exactly what it was that the sculptor was trying to say through this piece: that love has the power to bring a person back to life, to set them free. Tomorrow morning, all being well, she would be boarding a train with William, bound for London and a new life. If she had to endure a couple of hours of Amory gawping at the *Mona Lisa* and eating overpriced tea and cakes at the Ritz, then it would be worth it.

'Found it,' said Amory, rolling the guidebook up and tucking it under his arm. 'It's back this way. Now, let's leave these dusty relics and go see if the world's most expensive painting lives up to the hype.'

As Amory guided them out of the sculpture gallery, Blythe turned to take one last look at Psyche and Cupid. 'Not long now, my love,' she whispered to herself. 'Then we will never be parted again.'

'I have no idea what you're talking about, honey. What man?'

'The man in the hat and overcoat who has been following us for the last five blocks. Surely you saw him.'

It was late afternoon, and they were making their way back to the Ritz after a day of sightseeing that had so far taken in, as well as the Louvre, the Eiffel Tower, the Champs-Élysées and the Jardin du Luxembourg, an area they didn't linger long in as Amory dismissed it as a den of iniquity. Somewhere around the Sixth Arrondissement Blythe had become aware of the heavyset man walking a few steps behind them. When they had stopped to look at the jewellery in Tiffany's window, the man had stopped too and bent to tie his shoelace. Blythe had caught his eye as they paused to cross the street. Something about his facial expression, the heavy brows, the steely eyes, the way his hands were balled into fists, sent shivers through her. Now, as they approached the hotel, she saw that he had taken a seat on the bench outside, his face hidden behind the open pages of *Le Monde*.

'There,' she hissed to Amory as they drew near. 'On the bench. You see him?'

'Darling,' said Amory, turning to her and placing his hands on her shoulders, 'what I see is a man reading a newspaper and minding his own business. Look, I get it, you're on edge. This has been a nice little break for you these last few months but once we're back home all your focus will be on preparing for the wedding. Sure, it's still a couple of months away but it will be here before you know it and there's so much still to organize. You're feeling that, I guess, hence the nerves. Come on, let's go inside and have a little afternoon tea. Cake always cheers a lady up, so I'm told.'

Cake was the last thing Blythe wanted but she knew she had to keep Amory sweet for just a little longer. Following him into the lobby, she glanced back and saw that the bench was empty. The man was gone. Perhaps it had just been in her head, after all. The nerves at what she was about to do giving way to paranoia.

While Amory marched ahead to the tea salon, Blythe became aware of the concierge, Jean-Paul, gesturing to her.

'I have something for you, mademoiselle,' he said, his voice lowered.

At the door of the salon, Amory turned and raised his hands as if to ask what was going on.

'A phone call from my parents,' she called to him. 'You go on ahead. I'll be right there.'

Once Amory was out of sight, Jean-Paul slipped his hand into his pocket and pulled out a white envelope.

'From Mr Kenneally,' he said, his eyes darting to the side. 'He said he'll be with you at the agreed place at seven-thirty tomorrow morning. And you're not to let anyone see this, it's to be opened when you're both on the train. Does that make sense?'

'It sure does,' said Blythe, her stomach fluttering with excitement as she tucked the envelope into her pocket and headed to the tea salon. Just one more night, then it would all be over.

When she entered the tea salon, Amory greeted her with a broad grin.

'Darling, I just have to make a quick phone call too,' he said, pouring her a cup of Earl Grey tea. 'I won't be long. And have some of those cakes while you wait. They're delicious.'

As he slipped out of the salon, Blythe took a piece of paper out of her handbag. The timetable for tomorrow's ferry crossings. She scrutinized it, sketching out the journey in her head. The weather would be fine. It would be a calm sea, blue skies and bright sunshine, the perfect conditions. She and William would get a drink, then step out onto the deck and watch as the coast of France slowly disappeared. While the breeze blew through their hair she would tell William their story, how they would settle in Highgate, go for long walks on the heath and drink in pubs with names like the Spaniards and the Flask. They would make money from their writing, slowly but surely, taking extra work here and there to pay the rent. As the money from the pawning of her engagement ring dwindled, they would have to tighten their belts, but it would be worth it because they would begin and end every day in each other's arms. Blythe closed her eyes and pictured the two of them in some rickety bed high in the eaves of an old Highgate town house. She felt the warmth of William's naked body curled around hers, the soft touch of his fingers as they worked their way inside her. It was so vivid, so real, she found herself letting out a little gasp.

'Penny for them.'

She opened her eyes and saw that Amory had returned.

'I was just . . .' she stuttered, trying to compose herself.

'Daydreaming as usual,' he said, with a wry laugh. 'So tell me, how were your folks earlier? On the phone?'

'Oh . . . yes,' she said, remembering the lie. 'They were . . . they were just checking our flight times for tomorrow.'

'Two o'clock sharp,' said Amory, a strangely gleeful look in his eye. 'Then we'll be home where we belong. Now, my darling. I have a little bit of business to attend to this evening – nothing exciting, just a drinks meeting with a contact of my father's. He may be able to provide parts for the new factory at a fraction of the cost of our current supplier. Terribly dry and dull so I don't expect you to come with me.'

'I will if you want,' said Blythe half-heartedly, remembering her promise to William that she keep Amory sweet so he didn't suspect anything. 'After all, I am your fiancée.'

'Ah, that's kind of you, honey,' said Amory, squeezing her cheek the way a fussy aunt would pet a child. 'But it's more business than pleasure, this meeting. I have to keep stone-cold focused and if you're there that pretty little face of yours will just distract me. No, better you get an early night tonight. I'll organize room service for your supper, then you can turn in and get your beauty sleep. You've a big adventure ahead of you tomorrow.'

Yes, I have, thought Blythe, excitement fluttering through her body as she drained her tea and said goodbye to Amory. And you, Mr Vaughan, don't know the half of it.

'Souvenirs?' Amory had exclaimed, as he stood before the bathroom mirror, shaving foam matted to his face. 'At this hour of the morning? Shouldn't you be packing? You do realize we have a flight to catch in a few hours?'

Blythe had assured him that she was aware of the time and the flight but that she just felt it would be sweet to run along to the little vendor by the bridge and pick up a couple of silly trinkets for her mom and dad. 'They love that kind of thing. Remember when we were kids and your folks and mine took us on that day trip to Coney Island? And Dad bought a bunch of those little Ferris wheel ornaments for his worker guys on the factory floor? See, my parents have money but they're not as cultured as you, Amory. They don't appreciate art the way you do.' Throwing in this added bit of flattery had softened his demeanour some-what and he'd put down his razor and kissed her on the nose. 'Besides,' she said, her heart fluttering with excite-ment for what was to come, 'there's no rush. I'm all packed and ready to go.'

'Well, don't be long,' he said, wiping away a puff of shav-ing foam that had landed on her cheek. 'Or I'll send out a search party.'

His words rang in her ears as she ran into her room, grabbed her packed suitcase, and made her way to Les

Deux Magots. Lugging the heavy case along the street, the early-morning sun bathing the pavement in pale golden light, Blythe thought she saw that man again, loitering by the entrance to the Métro. But as she crossed the street and headed for the terrace, she glanced back, and he was gone. It could have been a trick of the light or just her own paranoia making her see things that weren't there. Everything will be fine once William gets here, she told herself as she took her seat in Siberia and waited.

Ten minutes passed, then fifteen, twenty. Panic began to rise in her chest. The train to Calais they had planned to be on would leave in one hour.

'Where are you, William?' she muttered to herself, tucking a stray piece of black hair back under her yellow headscarf. She had to be careful not to make herself conspicuous. If she was discovered now, then it was all over. 'You said you'd be here.'

'Blythe!'

She looked up, her heart lurching with hope. A man stood on the other side of the street, his hand raised in greeting. The glare of the morning sun temporarily obscured the man's face and for a moment Blythe allowed herself to believe that it was him. He had come just as he promised, her William. The Cupid to her Psyche.

But then the sun shifted position in the sky, and she saw with a clarity that made her heart quicken, the sharp hawkish cheekbones, the immaculately coiffed hair, the finely tailored suit.

Amory.

He put his foot forward to cross the street but then fate – the gods, serendipity, call it what you will – intervened and a hulking great delivery truck tore round the cobbles before screeching to a halt right by Amory, barring his way across the road and, more pertinently, obscuring his view of Blythe.

She had all of a few seconds to make her move. While the driver, a barrel-chested old Parisian with a mop of unruly white hair, clambered out of the truck to offload his crates of bottled beer, Blythe leapt into action. With Amory safe behind the truck, and leaving her suitcase behind, she darted into the café, through the kitchens, and out into the back yard. Thanks to William, she knew the labyrinthine streets of the Latin Quarter like the back of her hand – they had been her playground that whole glorious late spring and summer of 1960. A halcyon period she prayed would never end.

What we've unleashed can never be put back into the box. That is what William had told her, and it was true. *You are stronger than you think, you just need to believe in yourself.* He had told her that too. But was she strong? she asked herself as she reached the Pont Neuf, the sky an intense cornflower blue. Could she actually do this on her own?

The question burned inside Blythe's head as she ran across the bridge, dodging and weaving through the tourists and early-morning strollers. William's envelope rustled in her pocket as she ran. She had less than twenty minutes to get to the Gard du Nord to make the train. Once she got to London, she would call Le Mistral and ask to speak to William. There had to be an explanation for why he hadn't shown up. They would talk on the telephone and arrange for him to get the next train. She would be with him soon and all would be well.

But before she could reach the other side, she felt some-one grab her arm. She turned and her heart flipped in her chest. It was the man who had been following her yesterday. Wriggling out of his grasp, she tried to make her escape, but he caught her again, pressing her against his chest.

'Get off me,' she cried, pulling at his fingers. 'Whoever you are. Just let me go.'

Summoning every ounce of strength she had, she shoved her elbow into his chest. Winded, he stumbled backwards. There was a crash as he hit the ground. He was obviously injured but she had no time to look back and see. She had a train to catch.

Fifteen minutes later, breathless and sweating, she took her seat on the eight a.m. Calais-bound train. As the guard approached to inspect tickets and documentation, Blythe slipped her hand in her pocket and took out the neat white envelope. Inside was a passport and a note written in William's distinctive spidery hand.

My love,

With the help of some of my more 'unsavoury' contacts at the docks I managed to purloin a passport for you. I am longing to begin our new life together and will not rest until I am back in your arms.

Yours eternally,
William

PS I was put on the spot with regard to choosing a name for you. In the end, I decided to pay tribute to my other great love. Ma would have given anything to have the life you're about to live but I know that you will do the name justice and be its greatest legacy.

Blythe opened the passport and smiled. She was no longer Blythe Aston-Laine, the good little girl who did as she was told, she was a courageous young woman whose stories were going to captivate the world. All she needed, she thought to herself, as she handed the passport to the guard, was for William to be with her soon, and her dream would be complete.

'Maeve O'Malley,' said the guard, opening the passport and looking from it to her. 'This is you?'

'Yes,' replied Maeve, warmth spreading through her body. 'This is me.'

PART TWO

29

ALEXIS

The walled garden, despite its unkempt appearance, is show-ing signs of spring. Red and yellow tulips cluster jewel-like amid the weeds while on the arbour around the cracked gate tiny pastel-coloured buds are sleepily waiting for June when they will burst forth into a riot of pink roses. This time of year always makes me think of my mother. I can see her now, in our small suburban garden, hair scraped back from her face, hands covered in soil as she pulled out weeds and tended to her beloved roses. Even as a child I could feel the sense of peace that emanated from my mother when she was gardening. It was palpable. A similar feeling overcomes me as I sit here now watching Maeve. She is standing by the sundial, her back to me. The folds of her pale pink chiffon dress ruffle in the breeze, her white hair shimmers in the sharp morning sun and she looks, for a moment, like an angel, a being transported here from another place in time which, in a way, she is.

'This book?' I say, closing the laptop that I have bal-anced on my knee. 'It's not a novel at all. It's your story. You're Blythe.'

She turns to me and smiles sadly and in that moment I see all the women she has ever been: the little girl who loved horses, the intense teenager bursting with words, the gauche young woman who arrived in Paris that warm spring day, the bold young writer who boarded a train and shook off her past, the famous and celebrated author whose stories mesmerized a generation and, in the deep melancholy of her elderly eyes, the scared, confused octogenarian desperately hoping that her words, like spells, would ward off whatever health horrors had beset her and solve the mystery of what had become of her great love. Her William.

'I had an extraordinary life,' she says, weaving her way through the overgrown flower beds. 'I enjoyed success beyond all measure, even had a second chance at love with Jasper, who, as I told you, was such a rock to me when Bella died, but at the heart of it, there was always something missing, a great big void where he should have been.'

'I can certainly relate to that,' I say, thinking once again of my mother, as Maeve joins me on the bench, the scent of Chanel No5 wafting through the air.

'I've spent decades trying to make sense of it,' she says, shaking her head. 'Wondering why he never came that morning. Had he meant what he said, that he loved me and wanted to start a new life together? Or was he just humouring me? Telling me what I needed to hear so I'd have the courage to get on the train and escape Amory and the future my parents had planned?'

'It sounded as though he truly loved you,' I say. I have a memory of my father, who rarely spoke of my mother in the years after her disappearance but instead blocked out his pain with work and duty, driving me to school one day. 'Landslide' by Fleetwood Mac had randomly come on the radio and I turned to see tears streaming down his cheeks. It was the first and only time I saw my dad cry. I think of

Maeve and William, my heartbroken dad and my restless mother, me and Tara, all casualties of love.

'If he didn't, then he deserved an Oscar for his performance,' says Maeve, her soft voice bringing me back into the moment. 'How can you love someone and leave them like that? But then, is that just the story I've told myself all these years?'

'Maeve, now that I know this is not just a novel, that William was a real person, we really need to talk about that photo.'

Beside me she lets out an anguished gasp.

'The writing on it,' I say, treading carefully. 'It's very like yours.'

'I told you, my mother and I had identical handwriting,' says Maeve, her voice trembling. 'She must have written that, but it just doesn't make sense. How could my mother, who was back in Connecticut at that point, have killed William? And more to the point, why would she?'

'Is the other man in the picture Sam?'

'Yes,' she whispers. 'Though it can't have been taken before I left. William swore to me that he loved me and that he would meet me. He wouldn't have kissed Sam, not after everything we had experienced together. I'm sure of it.'

She takes a deep breath, then continues.

'For years I've had these terrible nightmares,' she says, her frail hands trembling. 'William is calling out for me, but he's trapped somewhere, and I can't get to him. The day I met you, I'd woken from yet another one. I'd always known, deep inside, there was more to William standing me up all those years ago, but I had no way of finding the answer. Of finding him. For so long I have felt that the best way to remember, like any story, was to start from the beginning. If I wrote it all down, every little detail, from the first moment I met William, then maybe I would find some clues. But every time I tried to type, my hands just seized up, or I felt foggy again and had to rest. Then I'd get frustrated and snap at Jasper or Cordelia. I think they just assumed that William was a character I was working on, though a fairly troublesome one going by my mood whenever I spoke of him. That morning, I ended up throwing the laptop down and running into the road in frustration. Then you appeared. And when I heard you had some editing experience, I knew it was my chance. It was as though you had been sent, like an angel.'

She looks at me and smiles and I feel, for a moment, what it must be like to have a mother.

'And yet, here we are all these chapters in and I'm still none the wiser,' she says, with a sigh. 'It's all so frustrating.'

'Hey, how about we take a break now,' I say, getting up from the bench. 'We'll walk into the village, have a bite to eat at the Lustrum Arms and I'll pay my next instalment at the garage.'

'Oh, I don't know if I can,' says Maeve wearily. 'Would it be an awful chore for us to drive there instead? I'm afraid that last chapter has taken everything out of me.'

'How can we drive?' I say, confused. 'Jasper has taken the car.'

'Correction,' says Maeve, her face brightening. 'Jasper has taken *his* car. Now, let me go and fetch my coat and I'll meet you by the old stable block over there. I think you're going to like this.'

*

Ten minutes later we're hurtling down to Haughton, and I am at the wheel of one of the most beautiful cars I have ever seen. An oyster-pink classic Rolls-Royce, which could have come straight out of the pages of *The Great Gatsby*. And beside me, resplendent in a vintage fur coat and silk headscarf, Maeve is pure Daisy Buchanan.

'The car was a little gift I gave to myself when I hit sales of ten million back in 1988,' says Maeve, as we glide down the road. 'Complete with cassette player, which probably makes me sound like a dinosaur to you. It was my dream car though I haven't driven it much these last few years. Jasper says it's rather vulgar.'

As Maeve takes a cassette out of the glove compartment, my thoughts return to the previous evening, that unsettling conversation I overheard between Jasper and Cordelia.

'But then Jasper has always liked things just so,' says Maeve, putting the cassette into the car radio. 'He can be a fusty old trout sometimes but he's harmless. I was rather lost when we met and, even now, despite our quarrels, I don't know what I'd do without him.'

'Where did you meet, if you don't mind me asking?' I say, my voice almost drowned out by Helen Shapiro's 'Walking Back to Happiness'.

'Ah, this reminds me of my early days in London,' says Maeve, tapping her foot in time to the music. 'Such a bitter-sweet time. Every song I heard would make me think of William and our poor sweet little . . . Sorry, dear, what did you ask me?'

'You and Jasper,' I reply. 'Where did you meet?'

'At a memorial party for Bella, a few months after her death,' says Maeve. 'Her funeral had been family only but this was a large affair, full of publishing folk. Jasper could see I was upset and made a beeline for me with a large G and T. You know, I had ruled out marriage all my life. How could I even think of it when I had given my heart to William? But that day, mourning my lovely friend and talking to this kind man who shared my love of books and history, something changed. I think Bella was overseeing it from above. She knew about William. In fact, she was the only person I told and she kept my confidence and took the story with her to the grave. But she worried about me, thought that I was blocking love out, that I was lonely, and she gently encouraged me to move on from William, though I never took her advice. Funny, but I think my meeting Jasper at her memorial party was Bella's last little gift to me, a nudge from the heavens to tell me that it was safe to love again.'

'Yes,' I say, unease rippling through me. 'It's vital to feel safe in a relationship. Strange how you stood back from the spotlight when you got together with Jasper.'

'Well, Jasper's never been impressed by fame and all the nonsense it brings,' says Maeve, oblivious to my concerns. 'He thought I could do with a break, and I suppose he was right because at that point I was a bit like you were a couple of years ago, just burnt out. I rather lost my appetite for writing when Bella died, the spark had gone. So I just . . . disappeared.'

'And Jasper encouraged this?'

'Not as such, no,' says Maeve, turning the music down a little. 'But he did think I needed to get out of London. It was not long after my Author of the Year Award. They used to call it the Lifetime Achievement Award which, I don't know, just made me feel very old all of a sudden. He told me about this amazing house that had just come on the market in the Kent countryside and persuaded me to view it. I could tell he'd fallen in love with it. And he was right, London was a bit too much for me at that point, I needed a rest. So, I remortgaged my flat in Hampstead, rented it out and bought Lustrum Manor. Jasper and I got married there and for a while all seemed well.'

'What changed?' I ask, as the village comes into view.

'I'm not sure really,' says Maeve, shading her eyes from the sun pouring through the windscreen. 'It was a subtle change. It began with my eyesight failing and I started having the nightmares about William. Then Covid came and everything ground to a halt. The moat was practically sealed off. The university closed and even when it re-opened, there was still just skeleton staff and Jasper's hours were drastically cut.'

'It was a brutal time,' I say, recalling the stress of those days. 'So many people lost everything.'

'Indeed,' says Maeve, with a sigh. 'Though Jasper is pretty resilient and he swiftly rerouted. That's when he started writing his historical tomes. The advances for those were rather modest but, combined with some ad hoc Zoom lecturing, which he hated – and of course my royalties – we were fine. And we could afford to keep Cordelia on, who'd been with us from the beginning.'

'It was Jasper who hired her, was it?'

'Well, it wasn't as official as that,' says Maeve, as we drive into the village. 'Cordelia was an old family friend, born and bred in Haughton. They'd known each other for years. Now Jasper doesn't trust many people, but he'd trust Cordelia with his life. And I have to agree. She drives me mad sometimes with her fussing, but she's got a good heart. Ah, here's the garage coming up on the left. Mind how you park the old girl. She's a delicate soul.'

'I must say it's nice to see you out and about, Mrs Hardy,' says Ken, wiping his hands on his overalls as we enter the repair shop. 'You're looking ever so well.'

'Thank you, dear,' says Maeve, looking hopelessly out of place amongst the grease and grime of the workshop. 'It's been a while since I've ventured into the village. But now I'm here, I really should book my little car in for its MOT. Jasper said he'd do it but I'm not sure he's got round to it.'

Ken's face falls at the mention of Jasper.

'No,' he says, as I hand him the cash. 'I haven't seen him in here for a long time. Nor in the village. We were wondering if all was well up there.'

'Oh, yes, everything is fine,' says Maeve, the chat-show persona creeping back in. 'We've just been busy, that's all. Jasper's up to his eyes with work and I've begun writing a new novel.'

'I shall keep my eyes peeled for it,' says Ken, handing me the receipt. 'Or at least I'll let my wife know. She's the big reader. I'm more of a TV man myself. Can't resist a good murder mystery.'

He laughs and it echoes round the workshop.

'Anyway,' he says, turning to me. 'That van of yours is coming on great. It did need a lot of work but I haven't had to wait on parts being delivered because, as luck would have it, I had some spare VW ones out back. All being well, it should be ready in a couple of days.'

'That's wonderful, Ken,' I say, watching as Maeve

wanders back out onto the forecourt. 'I'll pay the last instalment when I come to pick it up. It will be great to be on the road again.'

'So how are things up there?' he says, nodding towards Maeve, who is standing by the Rolls, her face to the sun. 'And you can speak the truth, now Mrs H is no longer in earshot.'

'I'm not sure, to be honest,' I say, tucking the receipt in my pocket. 'It seems fine on the surface if you know what I mean but there's just something about Jasper and Cordelia that I can't quite put my finger on.'

'It's like I was telling you last time you were here,' says Ken, lowering his voice as he leans across the counter. 'It was a very strange business what happened up there.'

'Yes, I was meaning to ask you about that,' I say, glancing to check that Maeve is still safely outside. 'We got interrupted last time. You said something about a Lord Lustrum.'

'That's right,' says Ken, folding his arms across his broad chest. 'Salt of the earth, he was. An aristo but one with a heart if you know what I mean. He was the mainstay of this village, the thread that held it together. He donated thousands to the school, the village hall, the little league football team. And it wasn't just money, he took part in village life. Opened the summer fete every year, turned on the Christmas lights, made sure the old folks got a big box of firewood straight from his land every winter. Oh, and he liked a pint too. Every Friday night you'd find him holding court in the Lustrum Arms regaling us locals with his stories of travel and his time in the army. He was a great raconteur with a sound mind and then . . .'

He pauses and shakes his head.

'Then what?' I say.

'Then, Cordelia Baker returns and starts working for him,' he says incredulously. 'It all leads back to her. I mean, I'm not one to judge but that girl had been a tearaway since she was a nipper. Shoplifting, underage drinking, joyriding, you name it she was into it. It was so bad her parents washed their hands of her and moved out of the area. She dropped out of school and spent her teens sofa-surfing and getting up to no good. She had been about to be sent to prison when Lord Lustrum stepped in. Being the big-hearted man he was he thought she deserved a chance so he asked the magistrate if her sentence could be converted to community service which she could serve working up at Lustrum Manor. She did that for a few years before running off when she turned twenty-one.'

I scratch my head as I try to equate the polished, super-organized Cordelia with the young tearaway Ken is describing. But then I think back to last night, her drunken demeanour, and I think I may have had a glimpse of her previous self.

'What happened?' I say, unease creeping through my bones. 'To Lord Lustrum?'

'Well, that's just it,' says Ken, with a shrug. 'No one really knows. One minute he was fine and dandy, up and about the village, the next he just . . . well, he just disappeared.'

'Disappeared?'

'No one saw hide nor hair of him,' says Ken, folding his arms across his chest. 'Though Alice at the village stores said he was still getting his deliveries made but everything was going through a housekeeper. After all that time, must have been over twenty years, Cordelia had returned and was working for him full-time. Now the Lord had no children and no living relatives but as I said he was well liked in this village so after a few months of this a bunch of us went up there to see what was going on. And that's when things took a very strange turn.'

'What do you mean?'

'Well, when we arrived everything was boarded up,' he says. 'And it looked a right state. The moat was full of algae, the grounds had gone to ruin, that lovely walled garden that had been Lord Lustrum's pride and joy was overgrown and full of weeds. I remember going apple scrumping in the orchard as a kid, sitting up in the trees looking out over those grounds and thinking how magnificent it would be to live in such a magical place. I tell you, it broke my heart seeing it in such a state of disrepair.'

'And did you find him?' I say, aware of the time ticking and Maeve waiting for me outside. 'Lord Lustrum?'

'Well, that's just it, there was no sign of him,' says Ken, with a sigh. 'She was there, Cordelia, all snooty and grown up, telling us we were trespassing. As if she owned the place, her of all people, the local tearaway. Honestly, if I hadn't seen it with my own eyes I wouldn't have believed it. Anyway, she soon realized we weren't budging so she told us that Lord Lustrum was ill, that he'd been diagnosed with dementia and was unable to receive visitors.'

'Dementia,' I whisper, my skin prickling. 'And did you see him? Lord Lustrum?'

'No,' says Ken, shaking his head sadly. 'As I said, she wouldn't let us. Though I did take a peek inside and saw that fella sitting in the drawing room, feet up in front of the fire as though he owned the place.'

'Which fella?'

'Your boss,' says Ken, raising an eyebrow disdainfully.

'Jasper Hardy. Next thing we knew the house was up for sale and there was an obituary to Lord Lustrum in *The Times* saying he'd passed away after a long battle with dementia. It even mentioned Cordelia, said she'd nursed him to the end.'

'And when was this?' I say, my chest tightening with panic.

'2018,' says Ken. 'Spring of the year. The two of them stayed at the house while it was up for sale. And they never left.'

Ken glances at the door before continuing.

'When Cordelia Baker came back, that, as they say, is when it all went wrong,' he says. 'For the house, for the village and for poor old Lord Lustrum. But anyway, I'd better not say any more.'

He nods his head and I turn to see Maeve standing in the doorway.

'Come on, Alexis,' she says, beckoning to me. 'Let's go and get that lunch. I'm absolutely starving.'

The Lustrum Arms is quiet when we arrive, and we take a seat by the window that looks out onto the village square.

'It's ages since I've been here,' says Maeve, handing me the paper menu. 'Jasper never liked it but then he's never been one for pubs. Here, dear, can you read that for me and see if they have a ploughman's on there. I have a craving for some cheese and pickles.'

'And what about Cordelia?' I say, Ken's words ringing in my ears as I peruse the menu. 'She must have liked it here, having been born and bred in the village.'

'I don't think this is quite her scene,' says Maeve, taking off her fur and placing it across the banquette. 'She's more champagne than cider, is Cordelia.'

'I'm sure she is,' I say, smiling as the barmaid comes over to take our order.

'Two ploughman's, please,' I say, handing her the menu. 'A lemonade for me and what would you like, Maeve?'

'Oh, lemonade is fine,' she says distractedly. 'Thank you.'

As the barmaid walks away, I take a deep breath and turn to Maeve. I have to tell her what I heard and here, away from Jasper and Cordelia, is the only place to do it.

'Maeve, there's something I want to talk to you about,' I begin. 'I don't quite know how to say it but—'

'Maeve O'Malley, is that you?'

'Jonathan Farrow,' cries Maeve, jumping to her feet.

I turn round to see a man standing behind me. He is about Jasper's age, mid- to late sixties, well built with a bald head and a white goatee beard. He is dressed smartly in a navy pinstriped suit and is holding a briefcase in one hand and half a pint of beer in the other.

'Please, won't you join us,' says Maeve, patting the seat beside her. 'This is Alexis. She's my editor. Alexis, this is Jonathan Farrow, our family solicitor.'

We shake hands and Jonathan sits down.

'You look so well,' says Maeve, sizing him up. 'Have you lost weight?'

'Well, it's been a long time since we last saw each other, Maeve,' says Jonathan. 'So very likely I have. And you look remarkably well. I'm surprised.'

'Surprised?' says Maeve, her smile fading.

'Yes,' says Jonathan, taking a sip of his beer. 'Under the circumstances. Jasper said you've been ill, so ill you couldn't work or deal with any legal affairs. I was very sad to hear it when I called him.'

'Jonathan, I have no idea what you're talking about,' says Maeve, putting her hand to her chest. 'When did you call Jasper?'

'Gosh, it must be four, five years ago now,' says Jonathan, pausing as our food arrives.

When the barmaid leaves, he continues.

'You see, I'd received something from your publisher, Matador.'

'Nothing serious, I hope,' says Maeve, looking startled. 'I'm not being sued, am I?'

'Oh, no, nothing like that,' smiles Jonathan. 'No, they had received correspondence from lawyers dealing with your mother's estate in the US. I understand you were estranged from your parents and had been for some time. The publisher was the only address they could find to contact you.'

Maeve goes so pale that I fear she is about to pass out.

I lean across and take her hand.

'Maeve, are you all right? Do you need some air?'

'I'm . . . I'm fine,' she says, pulling her hand back. 'Go on, Jonathan. You say my mother's estate? When did she . . . when did she die?'

'In 2016,' he says gently. 'Though we didn't get the correspondence until 2020. Probate had taken many years and most of their money had been swallowed up by debt and your mother's care-home fees.'

'I don't care about the money,' cries Maeve. 'I never did. I walked away from my parents and their materialistic world when I was a girl. No, I want to know what was sent to me. You said correspondence.'

'Yes,' says Jonathan. 'It was a package addressed to you at Matador. As I said, I called Jasper when it arrived and asked if I could talk to you as I needed you to sign to collect it, but he said you were seriously ill and weren't to be troubled by anything like this. He came to the office, saying because of your fragile mental state, he would sign on your behalf. As he is your husband, I was happy with that and gave him the package. He opened it and pulled out a Polaroid. I could tell he was shocked by whatever was on it because he hurriedly put it back in the Jiffy bag. He pulled out the remainder of the contents, a rather weighty letter, read it then handed it to me. He said that he would take the Polaroid but would leave the letter with me. I asked him what I should do with it and he said . . . well, he said that I should just bin it.'

'He said what?' gasps Maeve, her voice trembling. 'Please tell me you didn't, Jonathan?'

'Of course I didn't,' he says. 'It's not mine to destroy and I would get in serious trouble if I did.'

'So where is it now?' says Maeve. 'This letter.'

'Safely filed away in my office,' says Jonathan. 'Across the square.'

He gestures out of the window.

'And now that I have you here,' he continues, 'how about you come and collect it? The estate went to such lengths to get it to you. I feel it must be of some importance. What do you say?'

'I say it's divine providence that we came in here,' says Maeve, her eyes clouding with tears. 'I've been rather foolish, Jonathan. Not seeing things that have been happening right under my nose.'

She glances at me, and I know that when it comes to Jasper the penny is starting to drop.

'And now,' she says, taking her coat from the chair. 'I think it's time I knew the truth.'

Once we're back in the car, after collecting the letter from Jonathan's secretary, Maeve sits in silence, clutching the faded envelope to her chest.

'Are you all right?' I say, placing my hand on her shoulder. 'Do you want to take a few moments?'

'No, it's fine,' she says, with a nod. 'You just drive.'

Switching on the engine, Maeve's cassette bursts into life and 'Walking Back to Happiness' resumes. I go to switch it off, but Maeve puts her hand out to stop me.

'Leave it,' she says gently. 'It'll help.'

As I drive, and Helen Shapiro sings of reclaiming what she had lost, beside me Maeve puts on her spectacles and opens the envelope.

Tears course down her face as she turns the pages of the letter and lets out an anguished cry.

'Maeve?' I say, as she folds the note and places it in her lap. 'What does it say? Tell me.'

'Not yet,' she says, turning to me, her eyes swollen with tears. 'Let's get home and settled first. Then I'm going to need your help.'

'Of course,' I say gently. 'Whatever you need me to do I will.'

'I know that, darling Alexis,' she says, her voice wracked with emotion. 'I've known it since the first moment I met you. You're a good girl. A diamond. And I need you to help me finish this story. It's time. Now, thanks to my mother's letter, I know how it really ends.'

30

AMORY

Paris

July 1960

Thankfully, Blythe fell for the story that I had a business meeting to attend tonight. The last thing I needed was for her to get suspicious and follow me. And if she had she would have seen that I had spent the last three hours drinking bourbons in some dive bar along from the Ritz. Now I'm not a heavy drinker but tonight's assignation is going to require a bit of Dutch courage. But I will see this through. There is no way I'm letting Hadley down now. Like her, all I want is to protect the girl I love.

Speaking of which, it seems Blythe has finally twigged that we're being followed. And though it's mean of me, the fact that she's getting so spooked has made my day. 'Cause now the mask has fallen and what I see in front of me is not the sophisticated Parisian ingénue she's trying to be, but the scared little girl who's strayed too far from home, the spoilt kid who still needs her daddy though she's too proud to admit it. She forgets that we've known each other since we were babies. I know who she is. She can't fool me, and she hates that. Case in point, our trip to the Louvre just now. Who was she trying to kid standing in front of that naked statue, trying to make out I was some kind of philistine 'cause I didn't show it enough appreciation? Jeez, little does she know that I have more appreciation for the female form than that bog-trotting oaf she's messing around with. See, that's why Hadley sent me here, why she hired Monsieur Reynard, the best PI in the city, to trail Blythe these last few months. It's because she knows, like any good mother, that her cossetted little daughter is easy prey. The fact that Blythe thinks she's been going it alone in the big city all this time makes me laugh. She's just a spoilt little rich girl playing dress-up. Still, best not to let anything slip. Hadley would kill me if our secret got out. So I pleaded ignorance and played with her head a little.

'I have no idea what you're talking about, honey,' I said, putting a protective arm around her shoulder. 'What man?'

'The man in the hat and overcoat who has been following us for the last five blocks,' she cried, her eyes blazing. 'Surely you saw him.'

I watched her as we crossed the street, her neat little head darting this way and that, fear rippling through her like the surface of a placid lake disturbed by a pebble. Let her panic, I thought to myself, let her think Monsieur Reynard is some deadly attacker who's going to spring out at her from behind a bush. It's all she deserves, letting herself be paraded across town by another man. As we approached the hotel, she froze suddenly.

'There,' she hissed, pointing her finger. 'On the bench. You see him?'

Of course I saw him. Reynard was sitting there in plain sight, keeping his side of the bargain. But I played dumb.

'Darling,' I said, giving her the old puppy-dog stare, 'what I see is a man reading a newspaper and minding his own business. Look, I get it, you're on edge. This has been a nice little break for you these last few months but once we're back home all your focus will be on preparing for the wedding. Sure, it's still a couple of months away but it will be here before you know it and there's so much still to organize. You're feeling that, I guess, hence the nerves. Come on, let's go inside and have a little afternoon tea. Cake always cheers a lady up, so I'm told.'

As I ushered her into the lobby, I gave a wink to Reynard who waited a beat before following us inside. I strode ahead to the tea salon, itching to get Blythe out of the way so I could speak to Reynard but when I turned round, I saw she was chatting to the pretty-boy concierge.

Catching her eye I gestured to her to see what was going on.

'A phone call from my parents,' she responded. 'You go on ahead. I'll be right there.'

It's all good, I told myself. Hadley's just checking to see if Blythe's with me. Once I've spoken to Reynard I can telephone Hadley, put her mind at rest. After all, it's not just my future marriage that's at stake here, it's my 50 per cent share in the family business. It's imperative I play this right and get Blythe safely back to Connecticut. I was all smiles when she returned to the tea salon a few minutes later.

Once she was happily ensconced at the table with a slice of cake and a pot of tea, I slipped away on the pretence of making an important phone call. Reynard was waiting for me in the lobby.

'You found him?' I said, making sure no one was in earshot.

'I did indeed,' said Reynard, a thin smile creeping across his leathery face. 'And it seems our Mr Kenneally has a very – how can I put it – complicated and colourful private life. Though I think we should discuss this somewhere quieter. It's rather . . . delicate information.'

'Is it that bad?' I said, guiding him to the billiard room which, at this hour, was deserted save for an elderly couple sipping port in a booth by the window.

'It's pretty damning,' replied Reynard.

Settling ourselves in a pair of Chesterfields at the far end of the room, making sure we weren't in earshot of the other patrons, I listened carefully as Reynard filled me in.

'It seems,' he said, his eyes scanning the room, 'that Mr Kenneally has a male friend in whose company he is often to be found. A very – how can I put this – handsy male friend. If you know what I mean.'

'Holy shit,' I spluttered. 'You're telling me Kenneally is a nancy boy? That he's playing around with some dude? This is dynamite. What a filthy pair of degenerates. What was Blythe thinking being anywhere near that guy? Still, she's led a very sheltered life. I doubt she even knows this kind of thing exists.'

'It is, as you say, damning,' said Reynard. 'Though, in France, not illegal. However, I overheard Kenneally at Harry's Bar telling his boss he was planning on moving to London, where it is. And the friend, Sam, is a US citizen so if he wanted to return home his "activities" here could make life difficult for him. Also, there are still some tough laws governing this sort of thing here, including a lesser-known clause that doubles the penalty for indecent exposure for homosexuals.'

'What does that mean?' I asked, glancing to check the elderly couple were not privy to this.

'Well, according to my lawyer contact,' said Reynard, lowering his voice, 'it means that those carrying out their perversions "publicly" could still be punished. Sometimes up to three years in prison.'

'I see,' I said, an idea forming in my mind. 'A public display of affection might get him.'

'Possibly,' said Reynard, leaning back. 'Without such a display we have nothing but we could make life difficult for Kenneally and his friend in London and the US were we to talk. For now, it is simply a case of warning Kenneally off. I've spoken to Madame Aston-Laine and she's happy for me to confront him this evening.'

'Ah, see, now,' I said, trying to contain my glee at the idea that had just come to me. 'I know Hadley's paying you for this, but I think I should be the one to deliver the killer blow, so to speak.'

'You mean, the warning?' said Reynard.

'Yes, sorry, of course,' I said, patting his arm reassuringly. 'The warning. Show up and confront him with this intel that he's been seen getting handsy with another man, tell him he has to cut all contact with Blythe or else we talk to the authorities in London. I think, as Blythe's fiancé, that should come from me, and I know Hadley would agree.'

'If that is what you think is best,' said Reynard, handing me a photo. 'This is Kenneally, so you know who you're looking for. I took it earlier today when I tailed him to the docks. He was talking to a rather unsavoury character and looked like he was up to no good. Afterwards he stopped at Les Deux Magots café to drink coffee with a group of young scruffs. I overheard him telling them he would be back at the bookshop, Le Mistral – where he is currently staying, courtesy of the eccentric proprietor – by ten-thirty, after collecting his wages from Harry's Bar, where he works.'

'That's not all he'll be collecting tonight,' I said, my mind racing. 'Many thanks, Monsieur Reynard, for your sterling work these last few months. You are a gentleman.'

'You're most welcome,' he said. 'Though I may add that my services are still ongoing. For my and Madame Aston-Laine's peace of mind, I shall remain here while you attend to Kenneally, to keep an eye on Mademoiselle Blythe and make sure she doesn't leave the hotel.'

'Understood,' I said, getting up. 'Now, if you'll excuse me, I'd better return to my fiancée before she starts worrying.'

It takes me fifteen minutes to reach the Latin Quarter, enough time to gather my thoughts and prepare my little speech. I have no idea how many people may be in the crummy little bookstore, so my plan is to catch him as he approaches and conduct our little tête-à-tête someplace private.

What I hadn't bargained on was the fact that this Kenneally guy appears to have a hundred doppelgängers. Every last man I see is dressed in that same scruffy garb I saw in the photo – grubby half-mast pants, hobnail boots, oversized coats and unkempt hair. Jeez, this place is something else, and to think that just across the river there's a whole district dedicated to the finest men's tailoring in Europe. Chadwick would be appalled if he could see just how low his darling daughter has sunk, but I guess all good girls have to rebel at some point. Best to get this out of her system now rather than further down the line. Still, I shall be requesting she takes a good long shower before she comes anywhere near me on our wedding day.

Just then I hear laughter. I look up and see what appears to be a couple of hobos walking down an alleyway towards me. They're talking loudly. One of them keeps trying to hold the hand of the other, like some dame who won't take no for an answer. And then I hear something that makes my ears prick up.

'Shall I stay over at the bookshop tonight, William?'

I step closer and see him. Thin and lanky, with a stupid grin plastered across his face and a pair of blue eyes that sets him apart from his fellow scruffs. Here he is, William Kenneally. Our filthy Paddy scum.

I hang back behind a row of Vespa scooters as the other guy leans across and lights Kenneally's cigarette. Then, just in case, I reach into my bag and take out the Polaroid camera Hadley lent me for the trip. 'Make sure you take some good shots,' she'd said, clearly meaning of her darling daughter with her beloved fiancé. But as I stand here watching this pair of deviants, holding my breath as the blonde-haired one leans closer, I know that I am not just going to get a good shot, I'm going to get the shot of a lifetime.

It happens in seconds. Blondie leans in and grabs William, presses his mouth against his, pulls his body indecently close.

Boom.

I get it. The shot.

They pull apart, blinking into the white light. Blondie, terrified, runs off into the night.

'Hey, stop that,' cries Kenneally, charging towards me. 'You've no right to be taking my picture. Quit it, you hear me?'

I lower my camera and look directly into his eyes.

'What . . . what are you doing here?' he stammers. 'Why did you take those pictures and . . .'

He lets the sentence fade away, then does as any coward would and runs.

'It's too late, William,' I call after him, seeing that he's heading for a wall. 'You can't undo this. You're dead, now, you hear me? Dead.'

I catch up with him moments later. He's standing with his back pressed to the wall, a condemned man waiting for his executioner.

'Mr Kenneally,' I say, striding towards him.

But before he can respond, I pin his arms behind his back so he can't move.

'What the hell is this?' he cries as I smash him into the wall, keeping his arm twisted behind him.

'This is your five-minute warning,' I hiss, rage burning inside me. 'Now turn around, you piece of shit. I got something for you.'

He turns, those blue eyes full of fire now. Blood trickles from his cheekbone which has been grazed by the wall.

'This,' I say, taking out the newly developed Polaroid photo and pressing it in front of his face. 'Your late-night homosexual fumbling.'

The colour drains from his face and his arms go limp.

'You've got this wrong,' he says, his voice shaking. 'That wasn't what it was. We're just friends.'

'That's none of my concern,' I say, whipping the photo back under my jacket. 'What matters is that this is a piece of evidence showing you engaging in a homosexual act. That's illegal in London, isn't it, William? And isn't that where you're headed next? It would be an awful shame if the shiny new life you're planning on creating in England is over before it's even begun. But, hey, even if you stay here in Paris, life might get a little difficult were I to show this photo to the authorities. I hear something like that is rather frowned upon, even in decadent Paris.'

'What do you want from me?' he says, his voice low, menacing.

'I want you to stay away from my fiancée, Blythe Aston-Laine,' I say, pressing my elbow into his chest. 'See, neither me nor her family want her being anywhere near a man who engages in such sordid and immoral acts.'

'That is not what happened, I told you. That picture is not what it seems,' he says, gasping for breath as I exert more pressure. 'And how do you know about me and Blythe?'

'Her mother's had a PI follow her these last few months,' I say, watching his face redden. 'Wise move as it seems she wasn't studying anything but the laws of the great unwashed. And remember who you're talking to. There is no you and Blythe. There is only me and my fiancée. You're just some deviant who crossed her path.'

'Oh, yeah,' he cries, yanking my hand away and coming at me with a roar of rage. 'So how come I was in her bed last night?'

The alleyway suddenly seems to close in around me. There's a ringing in my ears that gets louder and louder, like a train whistle. I see this punk's face in front of me and then I see him lowering himself onto Blythe, violating her – the woman I am due to marry, the woman whose family wealth I have set my future upon – and something in me explodes.

Grabbing his head, I smash him back into the wall, once, twice, three times, before he falls to his knees. With a kick to the back, he falls flat like an animal waiting to be put out of its misery. And this I duly deliver as I rain down kick after kick after kick into the back of his head, until there is no more sound, no more movement, no more William Kenneally.

31

HADLEY

Connecticut

October 17th 1960

. . . and that is what Amory told me when he returned to the US without you. It was meant to be a warning, sweetie, that is all, but it got out of hand. And I don't know whether William was just goading him or whether you did indeed partake in extramarital relations with him, but you can surely see that to Amory it was a red rag to a bull. Your father is horrified as you can imagine and says that he has washed his hands of you. As for me, well, I am just very disappointed. You had everything to look forward to, a wonderful life to create with Amory, and now it is all ruined.

I don't even know why I am writing this letter because I have nowhere to send it to, not knowing where you are, whether you are dead or alive. But, oh, Blythe, if only you knew the trouble you've caused back here.

Your loving mother

September 23rd 1998

Dearest Blythe,

What a surprise I got this morning when the nurse switched on the television set, and I saw your beautiful face beaming out. I'm not one for TV, but the other residents tell me that the David Letterman show is a big deal. I see you've changed your name, which made me sad as the one I gave you was so pretty, but you still have your beauty queen looks and your mighty fine way with words. An author. Who would have thought it. And a bestselling one at that. I understand that you're already a huge star in England and Europe. How wonderful. If only I wasn't stuck in this nursing home, I would have quite the boast for my bridge chums. The nurses thought I was kidding when I said that you're my daughter. They told me that the woman on the TV is British and has never mentioned any American family. They think I'm getting confused in my old age, but I tell them I know my own child. Oh, Blythe, my sweet girl, I never doubted you would do something great with your life. I just wish I could have been there with you to enjoy the ride but then, as you know, I've always been a coward.

Still, for once in my life, I'm going to be brave and tell you something you should have been told a long time ago. Your father is dead now and Amory got married, eight months after returning from Paris, to an oil baron's daughter from Texas. He moved south and set himself up for life. I suppose he never gave you or William Kenneally another thought though the story has haunted me for years. I look back at the letter I wrote you in 1960 and it sounds like I was excusing Amory, but you see I felt so guilty. If I hadn't hired that PI to follow you in Paris, if I hadn't been so obsessed with what our social circle might think and just let you be with the man you loved and not the man your father and I thought you should have loved, then none of it would have happened. And I would still have my beloved daughter in my life. But then there was the other side of me, the coward, that just said leave it alone, what's done is done. But now, all I can see is that the man you loved was killed in cold blood and, as far as I know, you have gone out into the world completely

278

unaware of that, perhaps even hoping you'll one day see him again. And how could you have known? Thankfully, the death was never reported — I scoured the international newspapers for months afterwards — and Monsieur Reynard told us that he saw you running towards the railway station that morning. I tried to look for you, Blythe, but your father urged me to stop, told me that you had disgraced the family name and were on your own now. It broke my heart but I had to obey my husband. I'm not brave like you, Blythe. Like I said, I'm a coward.

I am so sorry, my darling. Take this letter as my one act of goodness in a lifetime of mistakes. One day, I'll be gone, buried next to Daddy in the family plot, and when that day comes, I will arrange for this letter to be sent to you. I don't want you to hear this now, while you're doing so well. I want you to keep smiling that beautiful smile and living that amazing life that you always deserved. I just hope that when you do get this letter and find out what really happened to William, you're surrounded by people who love you. That's all I ask.

Goodnight, my sweet girl.

I remain always,
Your loving mother

32

ALEXIS

'Oh, Maeve. I'm so sorry,' I say, closing the laptop for what feels like will be the final time. We are sitting in her study as outside the sun sets on what has been the most emotionally draining of days. When we returned there was no sign of Jasper or Cordelia and, to Maeve's further distress, no sign of Daphne the cat either. The house was deathly quiet as we made our way upstairs, Maeve refusing any offer of food or drink until she had got the story out. Her pain, as she sat dictating it to me, was palpable, grief pouring out of her along with the words.

'All this time I've been living my life blissfully unaware that he died the night I was set free,' she says, clasping her hands on the desk in front of her. 'And it was the thought of him being out in the world, writing his stories, doing whatever the hell he pleased, as he always did, that gave me the strength to do what I did, to keep showing up and being the person he knew I could be. At least now I can feel assured that I did the right thing in getting away from my family. Boy, I knew they were toxic but to keep this a secret all those years, to collude in Amory's evasion of justice, well, it's just barbaric. Amory got married, she says in the letter, he likely had a brood of children, grandchildren, lived a full and happy life, all the things that William should have had but was denied by the actions of my family and that beast of a man. I don't know whether Amory is still alive, but I hope his conscience has eaten him up all these years. I'm not a vengeful person but I wouldn't wish him a moment's peace. What he did was unforgivable, and he was never punished for it.'

'Yet it seems your mother had something of a conscience,' I say, as Maeve gets up and walks across to the window. 'In her own twisted way she did the right thing in the end.'

'She didn't care about me,' says Maeve, her voice loaded with contempt. 'All she cared about was saving face. If you see, in the first letter, written just after it happened, she's making excuses for Amory and then, years later when she finds out I've become a success, she's suddenly sorry and saying she loves me. You think she'd have felt that way if I'd become a Parisian waitress just scraping by? Of course not. I was right to get the hell away from them all. I just wish I could have done it with William at my side.'

She lets out a gasp and sinks to her knees. Rushing to her aid, I scoop her up and guide her to the sofa.

'I thought he'd just had a change of heart,' she says, looking at me with tear-glazed eyes. 'I thought he'd had some fun with me, then gone on his merry way. Now, in light of what actually happened, I know that he really did love me. He was heading to Le Mistral that evening to bed down before meeting me at the café the next morning. If Amory hadn't found him, I could be sitting with William now, having had a long and happy life together. Instead, I had to escape into fantasy worlds, write about love instead of actually having it. Oh, William Kenneally, what fun we might have had.'

She leans her head against my shoulder, the scent of

Chanel No5 and fresh linen drifting about her, and I'm overwhelmed with a deep sense of sadness, as though all her pain and grief is seeping into me.

'I still need to find him,' says Maeve, lifting her head. 'Even if it's just a grave. I mean, surely someone . . . someone must have found him that night.'

'Maeve, try not to think about that,' I say, aware of her agitated state. 'It will only upset you.'

'The people in the Latin Quarter were good folk,' she says, taking a handkerchief from inside her cardigan sleeve and dabbing her eye. 'They would have taken care of him, made sure he got a proper burial. Alexis, you have to help me find him. Do you think you can do that?'

'I'll try,' I say tentatively. 'Though what is it you want me to do?'

'You said you wanted to find out why your mother listed the Latin Quarter as her location on that genealogy site. I know that's where you'll be heading next, once your van is fixed, and I want you to take me with you,' she says, looking at me pleadingly. 'To Paris.'

'Paris?' I exclaim. Though Maeve is right and I should be heading there to see what I can find out, it is only now that I have really entertained the idea. 'Are you sure? It's been a long time, Maeve. We can't be certain we'll find any trace of William there.'

'I know,' she says, with a steely expression in her eyes. 'But we can at least try. And if we don't find anything then I can just go and sit in a quiet spot and pay my respects. Will you do it, Alexis? Will you help me?'

'Of course,' I say, though my gut is telling me this may be a big mistake.

'Oh, thank you, darling girl,' she says, getting to her feet. 'Now, I'm exhausted and should probably go to bed. We'll book the tickets first thing tomorrow. But I'll need my passport. You'll find it in the larger of the two filing cabinets in Jasper's study. That one is always locked but he stores the key under the plant pot on his desk.'

'Maeve, I don't feel comfortable going through Jasper's files,' I say, as we leave her study and head out into the half-lit corridor.

'But you must,' she cries, pausing by the door, her eyes blazing. 'You have an alibi. If he sees me in the study, he'll get suspicious, and I can't risk him finding out about this trip. He wouldn't understand and he'd try to stop me. This has to be our little secret, do you understand?'

I nod my head but as I watch her disappear down the hallway towards her bedroom I feel a deep sense of unease. No, I don't understand, Maeve. I don't understand any of it.

The house is quiet as I make my way down the stairs and head to Jasper's study. I check my watch. It's almost ten o'clock and there is still no sign of Jasper and Cordelia. Though I'm curious as to where they've been all day, I'm thankful they are still out as it gives me the chance to do what I need to do.

Stepping inside the study, I see that Jasper's desk is uncharacteristically tidy. Where usually there are half-drunk cups of coffee, scattered papers and books plastered with Post-it notes, now there is just the computer, the lamp and the plant pot. It seems rather strange. Closing the door quietly behind me I walk towards the desk. A shaft

283

of moonlight pours in through the window, illuminating the rather grubby glass, the thick layer of dust along the windowsill. I lift up the plant pot. The key is nestled beneath it. Taking it, my eye is drawn to movement outside. I hear a car door slam. In the darkness I can just make out Jasper and Cordelia exiting the car. They have been out all day and most of the evening. Where could they have been? Stepping back so they don't see me, I watch as they walk, hand in hand, up the path towards the house. Then, to my astonishment, they pause and share a passionate kiss.

'What the hell?' I cry, staggering backwards and cracking my knee on the edge of the desk.

But there is no time for the shock of what I've just witnessed to sink in. I need to find Maeve's documents and get the hell out of here.

With trembling hands, I insert the key into the lock on the filing cabinet. The first drawer opens with a loud creak. I see yellow folders marked *Jasper* and *Maeve*. Taking out Maeve's I flick it open and see the passport, as well as some other papers. Deciding there could be more documentation she might need, and not wanting to have to make another covert visit to the study, I grab the whole folder, close the cabinet and return the key back under the pot.

But as I reach the door, I hear voices coming up the corridor. Jasper and Cordelia. My heart leaps inside my chest. What do I say if they come in? That I couldn't sleep and came to finish off some editing? The file burns in my hands as their footsteps draw closer. I have nowhere to hide it and Maeve is counting on me to get it to her and get the two of us to Paris, an idea that, after what I have just witnessed, is not so silly after all.

'Thank you for coming with me today. And for the dinner. I still can't quite believe we've done it. When they said they were oversubscribed, I thought that was it, until you talked them round and secured a home visit. It's almost too good to be true. And that's all down to your tenacity. God, I don't know where I would be without you.'

It's Jasper speaking. They are right outside the study now.

'I'm with you every step, darling Jazzy,' replies Cordelia. 'As I always have been. Now, remember, hold your nerve. We're almost there.'

He says something inaudible, and they walk away. I am tempted to go straight to Maeve and tell her what I have just heard but she was so drained after reading her mother's letter and desperately needed to rest. No, I think to myself, as their footsteps recede, I'll leave it until the morning when both of us are clearer headed. And when I'm sure Jasper and Cordelia have gone, I peel open the door and make a run for the stairs, not stopping until I reach the relative sanctuary of my bedroom where I get into bed and place the folder safely under my pillow.

When I arrive at Maeve's study the following morning I find her sitting by the window, her mother's letter open on her lap.

Stepping inside, and closing the door behind me, I stand for a moment, frozen to the spot. I want to tell her what I heard last night but I have no idea where to begin.

'The more I read this the worse it gets,' she says, putting the letter down beside her on the window seat. 'Funny how my mother's handwriting is crystal clear to me though I can't read anything else. But that feels less a blessing than a curse. And there's still no sign of my darling Daphne. I've been up since dawn searching for her. Sorry, I should have said good morning, Alexis. It seems my manners have gone as well as my nerves. What's that you've got, dear?'

She gestures to the folder I have clasped in my hand.

'I brought the whole thing,' I say, walking over to Maeve and handing her it. 'Thought you might need it.'

'Oh, he's created a file now, has he?' says Maeve, with a giggle. 'He's so well organized. Ah, good, here's my passport. And it hasn't expired, thankfully.'

Placing the passport to one side, she sifts through the rest of the folder.

'Now, Alexis, do bring the laptop over here,' she says. 'We can look at the ferry times.'

'You want to get the ferry?' I say, my nerves steadying.

'I thought it would be more fitting,' says Maeve, looking up with a smile. 'That's how William arrived in France.'

'In that case, we'll have to wait a few days. My van's not ready yet.'

'No need to wait,' says Maeve brightly. 'We have my car. You took to it rather well on our little trip yesterday.'

'Maeve, I'm not insured,' I say. 'It was only by the grace of God that we weren't stopped. I can't risk being held by border police. That's the last thing we need.'

'Hmm, that's a bore,' says Maeve, placing her hand to her mouth. 'Ah, there's my old chequebook. Not much use for that these days.'

As she pulls it out a wedge of papers, held together with a clip, falls to the floor.

'Oh dear,' says Maeve. 'What a mess I'm making.'

'Don't worry, I've got it,' I say.

As I bend to pick them up, I see a note with *Matador*, the name of Maeve's publisher, stamped at the top.

'*Dear Maeve,*' I read aloud. '*Please find attached this package sent to us by Mrs Hadley Aston-Laine who requested we forward it to you.*'

Flicking to the next page, I read on:

'*My dearest Blythe, here it is, the photograph. Though I didn't physically do it, I will always blame myself for William's death. I hope one day you will forgive me. Your loving mother.*'

'Now we know why she wrote "the night I killed him" on that photo,' I say, handing it to Maeve. 'She blamed herself for William's death.'

'As well she should,' says Maeve angrily, gripping the note.

'Hang on a sec,' I say. 'The accompanying note, from Matador, is dated 2020, same as the letter we collected from Jonathan yesterday. Didn't he say Jasper took the envelope with the Polaroid in it but left Jonathan with the letter to bin? This note must have been in the envelope along with the picture.'

'But why . . .' says Maeve, shaking her head in disbelief. 'Why didn't I see it? Why did Jasper hide it from me?'

'Maybe he didn't know the note was in there,' I say. 'It's not very big.'

'The Polaroid, the letter, now this,' says Maeve, her voice cracking. 'They were all addressed to me. Did he think he was protecting me somehow by hiding them? I know that he worries about my well-being. That must be it.'

'I'm not sure, Maeve,' I say, feeling increasingly uneasy.

As she puts the note aside and continues to leaf through the rest of the papers that fell out of the file, I think back to what I overheard last night. Jasper and Cordelia are up to something, and it seems like it's a lot more serious than just hiding letters. Yet Maeve still thinks Jasper's simply protecting her well-being. It's no good, I have to speak out.

'Maeve,' I say, my heart pounding. 'There's something I need to tell you. About Jasper.'

But she isn't listening. She has pulled out a sheet of paper from the pile and is staring at it.

'Oh, my goodness,' she cries, putting her hand to her mouth. 'I can't read the small print but look at that subject header.'

She hands me what turns out to be a letter, dated a week ago. It is stamped with the name of the solicitor, Jonathan Farrow, and marked in red type: *REQUEST FOR POWER OF ATTORNEY*.

'My eyesight may be poor, but I can see what that is,' she says, her voice trembling. 'And it's been processed by Jonathan. Why the hell didn't he tell me about this when we were with him yesterday?'

'Jesus, this is lies, all of it,' I say, reading the document. 'They're saying you've lost control of your faculties, that you have dementia that is so advanced there is no other option but to . . .'

'To what?' says Maeve, trembling. 'Tell me, Alexis.'

'"To hand over all control to the named persons",' I continue. '"Who are as follows . . ."'

I pause, not quite believing what I am seeing. Gathering myself I carry on, my hands shaking.

'"Who are as follows: Mr Jasper Hardy and his wife . . . Mrs Cordelia Hardy."'

33

ALEXIS

'I don't understand, Alexis,' cries Maeve, clearly horrified. 'How can she be his wife? It doesn't make sense. He and I were married in a small but beautiful ceremony here in the grounds, with Jasper's friend, a Humanist minister, officiating. Jasper organized everything, from the paperwork to the flowers to the food. I didn't have to do a thing, just say "I do".'

She pauses then and lets out a resigned sigh as though the penny is finally dropping.

'How could I have been so stupid?' she says, shaking her head. 'Describing it all to you now, it's clear it was all just a scam, but I didn't suspect a thing. I trusted him. He was my rock, my kind and gentle Jasper. How could he . . .? None of it makes sense. Oh, God, I need some air. Come with me, won't you?'

'Of course,' I say, helping her up. 'But I think we should take these with us, for safekeeping.'

'Yes,' she says, stumbling to the door. 'Whatever you think best.'

Grabbing my bag from the back of the door, I shove the papers inside, my hands trembling with rage, but I know I will need to keep a cool head. Whatever it is we have just stumbled upon, it seems to me that Maeve is in grave danger.

*

'I suppose I've always known, deep inside, that something untoward was going on,' says Maeve, when I tell her I saw Jasper and Cordelia kissing. 'Though I was too scared to admit it.'

We are in the walled garden, sitting side by side on the bench underneath what was once the rose arbour. The air is cool and still, somewhere above us a dove is cooing gently and the sun glistens on the paving stones, bathing them in soft silver light. It is an idyllic scene, a moment of perfect tranquillity, and yet here we are contemplating the very worst of human nature.

'He must have thought I was a soft target,' says Maeve, twisting her linen handkerchief around her fingers. 'An aged public figure, past her prime and desperate for affection after my darling Bella died. No wonder he was so insistent I give up my home in Hampstead and live all the way out here. It was all part of the plan, their plan. But, oh, Alexis, do you think I'll be in trouble with the law? I mean, in marrying him. It's bigamy, isn't it?'

'You weren't to know,' I say, my mind whirring with questions. 'He's the one who'll be in trouble. That's if your wedding was actually legal which, from what you've told me, sounds highly unlikely. It's just astounding that someone could be so cruel and calculating.'

'You know, the more I think about it,' says Maeve, 'the more I see what he was doing, right from the start. I know for a fact that I don't have dementia. The only thing that has gone downhill for me, health wise, has been my eyesight and a bit of arthritis in my hands. But he made me think I was losing my mind, played with my head. Not all at once, but bit by bit. He chipped away and chipped away until I didn't know what to believe any more.'

'He was very good at it,' I say, anger burning inside me. 'He had me convinced for a while. Telling me how vital it was that you take those pills. And as for your state of mind, he and Cordelia almost gaslit me into believing that William was some dark secret in your past, so much so that, for a moment, I thought you might have killed him yourself. And for that I feel terrible.'

'You mustn't, dear,' says Maeve, patting my arm gently. 'It was those two playing with your head, making you believe their twisted lies. As for the pills, well, for the last week or so I've made sure I haven't taken any that he gave me. In fact, you'll find a nice little collection in my top drawer. You know, once you arrived and we began work on the story, that's when it all started to become clear. I knew I didn't need those pills, that they made me feel drowsy and sick, but before you came I . . . well, I think he'd just broken me down.'

She sighs deeply, as though expelling every stress and strain of the last decade.

'I wonder,' she says, blinking into the sun, 'if this place wasn't all part of the ruse. Not just the money side of it but the layout too. It was all designed to add to my sense of disorientation. Having each room reflect a different historical period, which he would change on a whim. He used to tell people in the village that the manor's new interior decor was all down to me but none of it was my choice. My life, my career, my home, he took it all away, like it had never existed. And then you arrived, Alexis. My God, where would I be if you hadn't turned up that day?'

She looks at me and smiles sadly.

'We need to get out of here,' she says, shading her eyes from the sun. 'We need to go to Paris, just as we planned. See if we can find William's resting place. And hopefully also find some answers about your mother.'

'But, Maeve, I told you, I can't risk driving that car. I'm not insured.'

'Which is why we're going to take yours,' says Maeve determinedly. 'Now, pass me my handbag. You said yesterday there was one last instalment to make. I'll give you my debit card and you can go and pay Ken. I'm sure he'll have had those repairs done by now. He's a good chap.'

'That's incredibly generous of you,' I say, my heart lifting at the prospect of being reunited with my van and getting out of this house of horrors. 'And I'll pay you back, I swear.'

'Don't be silly,' says Maeve, as she scrambles in her bag for her card. 'It's the least I can do. And besides, you've earned every penny of it. I imagine you can just scan it on Ken's card reader, but I'll give you the PIN just in case.'

The sun beats down on the ivy-clad wall creating strange and beautiful shadows and, just as before, I get an overwhelming sense of my mother having been here. I can see her floating across the lawn and through the rose arbour into the garden, her chestnut hair floating in the breeze.

'Maeve,' I say, turning to her. 'Do you think Jasper might have been lying about other things too? My mum, for example. You see, I don't think for one minute that she would have stolen those books. There must have been some other reason why he fired her.'

'Her van,' says Maeve, her eyes widening. 'I remember

now. As she was leaving, I heard her say something about being stuck on the property. She said her van had broken down and Jasper—'

Before she can finish her sentence, her expression hardens. She stands up from the bench and strides out of the gate.

'Maeve,' I call after her. 'What is it?'

Then I see them. They are standing in the courtyard deep in conversation. They don't seem to notice Maeve until she is almost upon them.

'Ah, there you are,' says Jasper, his face twitching. 'We've been looking for you. Why don't you come inside, it's getting rather chilly.'

'Don't you tell me what to do,' thunders Maeve. 'Don't you ever tell me what to do.'

'My dear, whatever is the matter?' he says, glancing nervously at Cordelia who has taken a step backwards.

'I know what you've been doing,' says Maeve, turning to me for reassurance. 'I know what you've stolen from me, what you've hidden from me, and what you planned to do with me. I know everything, Mr and Mrs Hardy.'

Cordelia gasps.

'Maeve, I . . . I don't know what you're talking about,' says Jasper, his mouth tightening. 'You're not making any sense. Why don't you come inside and—'

'I said, don't tell me what to do,' says Maeve, lurching towards him, her fists pummelling at his chest.

'Stop,' cries Cordelia, rushing to Jasper's aid. 'See, Jasper, she needs help, serious help.'

'Yes, I do,' cries Maeve, as I pull her away. 'I need help to get away from you. How could you be so cruel, so conniving? To trick me like that, to try to make me think I was losing my mind, to take my career, my home, my life. But the worst thing, Jasper, is that you hid that photograph from me. You told Jonathan Farrow that I wasn't in a fit state to see my mother's letter, so that it's only now, all these years later, that I get to find out what happened to William. You couldn't let me mourn the man I loved, the only man I've ever loved. You even took that away from me.'

'Like I said, my dear,' he says, his face impassive, 'you're not making any sense. William isn't real, is he? We all know that. He's just a figment of your broken mind.'

The next moment seems to happen in slow motion. Jasper reaches out to take Maeve's arm and she swings her fist into his cheek. He stumbles to his knees. Cordelia lets out a scream.

'You bastard,' cries Maeve, as Jasper, recovering his composure, grabs her with both hands. 'You're going to pay for what you've done to me. I swear, you're going to pay.'

'Enough of this,' he says, his left cheek flaming red. 'You need to rest. Come on.'

'Maeve,' I say, rushing to her side. 'Jasper, let me take her indoors.'

'No,' whispers Maeve, so that only I can hear. 'You go and see if you can get the van and come straight back, even if you have to call a taxi. Be quick, now. I'll be waiting.'

With that she strides into the dark folds of Lustrum Manor, Jasper and Cordelia following reluctantly in her wake.

34

ALEXIS

Adrenaline courses through me as I run out of the gates and onto the narrow B road that leads to the village. Cars thunder past as I stumble along the pothole-riven grass verge, my phone pressed to my ear.

'*You've reached the offices of Jonathan Farrow. I'm afraid there's no one here to take your call right now but if you leave a message, we'll get back to you as soon as we can. Thank you.*'

'Jonathan,' I say breathlessly, as the beeps subside. 'This is Alexis Harper. I met you yesterday at the Lustrum Arms. I was with Maeve O'Malley. Jonathan, I have to speak to you urgently. Please call me back as soon as you get this message.'

I leave my number, then click off, noticing the time on the screen. It's just coming up to eight-thirty. Still early. Maybe Jonathan Farrow hasn't arrived for work yet. Maybe – and I pray this isn't the case – neither has Ken.

Sticking my phone back in my pocket, I run down the hill, not stopping until I see the reassuring sign for *Dawson's Motor Repair Workshop* coming up on the left.

'Bloody hell, love,' cries Ken, as I burst in and almost prostrate myself onto the counter. 'What's happened? Here, let me get you a drink.'

While Ken fiddles with the water dispenser, I try to catch

my breath and gather my thoughts but when he hands me the plastic cup, my hands shake so much I almost drop it.

'Come on, take a seat over here,' says Ken, guiding me towards the fold-out seats in the waiting area. 'And tell me what's happened.'

'There's . . . there's no time,' I say, as I slump down in the chair. 'I have to pick up the van and get her out of there. You said it was practically ready.'

'Get who out of where?' says Ken, as I gulp down the water. 'You're not making any sense, love.'

'Ken,' I say, turning to him. 'I know you said it might take a couple more days, but I need the van urgently. I can pay you the outstanding amount right away. Is there . . . is there any way you can hand it over . . .'

My head starts to spin, and I pause, try to steady myself.

'Hey, slow down, love. Take a deep breath,' says Ken, looking worried. 'As for the van, well, the bulk of it's done. The engine's been repaired, the gearbox fixed, and fan belt tightened so it's roadworthy. There's some rust patches on the left-hand chassis that need attention but I wouldn't say that was essential.'

'You mean I can have it back?' I say, leaping to my feet. 'I can . . . I can get out of here?'

'Technically, yes,' says Ken, folding his arms across his chest. 'Though I wouldn't recommend you driving, the state you're in. Anyway, it'll take at least twenty minutes to sort out the paperwork.'

'I haven't got twenty minutes,' I cry, thinking of Maeve's anguished face as she headed back into the house. 'She needs me.'

'Listen, you won't have twenty minutes if you jump

behind that wheel and crash into someone,' says Ken firmly. 'You'll be dead.'

He looks up then as a young man appears in the doorway, clad in the same blue overalls.

'Ryan, son,' he says. 'Can you bring the VW round to the forecourt? I might need you to drive this lady home too.'

'I can't. I've got that MOT to finish,' says Ryan, with a shrug. 'Told the customer it'd be ready by ten.'

'I'm fine, Ken, honestly,' I say, as Ryan disappears to get the van. 'Look, I've stopped shaking.'

I hold out my steady hand. Ken looks at me, unconvinced.

'So are you going to tell me what's happened?' he says, taking my empty cup and throwing it in the waste bin. 'I assume this has something to do with our "friends" at the manor?'

I take a deep breath. I really don't have time to go into this now but I feel so shaken by what has happened that I find myself recounting the whole sorry tale to a flabbergasted Ken. When I finish, he sits for a moment, stunned.

'I knew that Cordelia Baker was a wrong'un,' he says, with a sigh. 'And there was always something a bit iffy about that Jasper fella but playing with the old woman's head like that, well, it's just heinous. Still, she did the same to Lord Lustrum if rumours are to be believed.'

'I just have to get her out of there,' I say, my eyes darting to the doors, praying that Ryan will hurry up with the van. 'She's not safe.'

'I should have known something like this would happen,' says Ken with a sigh. 'The last woman who went to work there ended up in a sorry state.'

'Which woman?' I say, my chest tightening. 'When?'

'A few years back,' says Ken. 'Pandemic time, so four, maybe five years ago. As I said, us villagers barely saw the Hardys and Cordelia, and during lockdown even less, so we had no idea who was living and working there. But this one day, I was in here by myself. It was late afternoon and getting dark. I was doing the books when this woman burst in, older lady in her mid- to late sixties, I'd say and dressed rather peculiarly in a shaggy coat and long skirt, like something out of that programme our Ryan likes to watch, *Daisy Jones and the something-or-other*. Anyway, she was terribly distressed. Said she'd had to leave her van on their estate, as it wouldn't start. Poor woman didn't have the money to repair it.'

When he finishes, my skin prickles as I remember what Maeve said about my mum when Jasper threw her out. She said her van had broken down.

'Kimberly Harper,' I say, turning to Ken. 'That was her name, wasn't it?'

'I can't really remember but it rings a bell,' says Ken. 'All I know is that she was in a bad way, all agitated. Said she'd been working the grounds at Lustrum Manor and had been suddenly told to leave.'

'For stealing books,' I say, knowing what is coming. 'Jasper fired her.'

'No,' says Ken, his brow furrowing. 'No, that wasn't it. He threw her out because she'd got the job under false pretences.'

'What do you mean?'

'Well, she'd recently found out who her biological mother was,' says Ken. 'I remember that because it resonated. I'm an adopted kid too and I recognized something in her, a sadness. That's what led her to Lustrum Manor, but old Jasper Hardy was having none of it and sent her packing. He probably feared he'd lose out on a big inheritance. People like him only ever think of money. Anyway, I felt so sorry for her that, when she said she couldn't afford the repairs, I ended up buying the van off her. Promised to hold on to it for a year or so in case she came back with the cash, but I never heard from her again and had to scrap it. It's how I had those rare parts for you.'

'So you're saying that . . . Kimberly's mother was . . .?'

'Mrs Hardy,' says Ken, getting to his feet as Ryan pulls up outside. 'Or at least that's what she believed. I suppose we'll never know, eh? Right, here's our lad with the van. I'll get the paperwork ready, then you can be on your way.'

35

ALEXIS

Despite the elation I thought I'd feel being back behind the wheel of my beloved camper van, my head feels as though it will explode as I drive the short distance back to Lustrum Manor, gripping the steering wheel to stop my hands from shaking. Exhaling deeply, I try to process what Ken told me. My mother – for his description of Kimberly and the fact that she had a VW camper van left me in no doubt that it was her – had not been fired for stealing, she had been thrown out by Jasper because she was trying to find her birth mother.

Maeve.

Which means the woman who I grew up idolizing, the woman I have spent the last few weeks helping write her story, is my grandmother. And she is, if everything I have learned so far is true, in grave danger.

For Maeve is not the first victim of Jasper and Cordelia. Poor old Lord Lustrum had suffered a terrible fate at their hands. Yet both Maeve and the late Lord appeared to be part of something bigger, some elaborate plan hatched by Jasper and Cordelia that is still ongoing, the aims of which I am still having difficulty fathoming. But one thing is for certain, whatever it is they are up to, I have to get her out of there.

I am a few metres from the entrance when my phone rings. Pulling onto the grass verge, I take it out and see an unknown number on the screen.

'Maeve,' I cry. 'Is that you?'

'Alexis, it's Jonathan Farrow returning your call.'

My jangled nerves turn to anger as I rage down the phone at the solicitor, telling him what a snake he is, asking how he could have sat there so nonchalantly with Maeve yesterday when he had effectively signed her death warrant.

'Alexis, I have no idea what you're talking about,' says Farrow when I finish my rant. 'I have neither signed nor ratified any Power of Attorney document for the Hardys and if my name is on there then it has been forged. Tell me, are they at the manor now?'

'Yes,' I say, trying to calm myself. 'Jasper and Cordelia have Maeve in there. I'm just on my way to get her out.'

'Right,' says Jonathan, his calm voice a balm. 'Well, I think we should get the police involved. I'm just about to board a plane with my wife. We're off to Majorca on holiday but you have my number. If you could send me a photo of that document right away, then I can call the relevant authorities from my end and report it. This is fraud, Alexis, plain and simple.'

He rings off and I quickly take the Power of Attorney document out of my bag. Laying it flat on the passenger seat, I take a photo of each page, then forward them to Jonathan. Once the message is sent, I put the document back into my bag before sitting for a moment, my hands on the wheel, looking at the gates of Lustrum Manor. They are still open, thankfully, and yet something tells me it would be wiser to park the van up here on the grass verge outside rather than on the driveway. I know that the lock system for the gates is operated from within. All it would take is the press of a button by Jasper or Cordelia and the van would be trapped. I will have to be careful if I am to get her safely out of there.

But as I lock up the van and proceed through the gates on foot, I am alarmed to see an estate car parked outside the front door. As I draw closer, I see the words *East Dover Care Services* printed on the side in red lettering and my stomach flips over.

'What?' I cry, rushing up the steep stone steps. 'Oh, no. Please, no.'

I try the door. It is locked. Rifling in my coat pocket, I take the spare set of keys Jasper gave me when I started work and, with trembling hands, try to unlock the door but it seems to be bolted from the inside. I go to pull the heavy iron knocker, then pause. Think, Alexis, I exclaim. If they've bolted the door they're hardly going to come and let you in.

Casting a careful glance around me, I creep round the side of the house, then dart across the drawbridge and into the courtyard. It is eerily quiet, not a soul about. Looking at the mullioned windows looming above me with their imposing metal bars, I think about poor Lord Lustrum, trapped against his will in his own home, and a chill ripples through me. What kind of monsters prey on elderly people like this? Monsters that act in plain sight, I tell myself, as I tiptoe across the courtyard towards the orangery.

Standing well back I observe the scene taking place behind the floor-length glass as though watching a movie on a screen. There is Jasper playing the role of genial host to perfection, that studied look of weariness etched across his face as he sits pouring tea for the oblivious care worker, a chubby, bespectacled young man who can be no more than twenty-five years old. Creeping closer, I see the leading lady, Cordelia, dressed in a baggy cardigan and jeans, her face devoid of make-up, her hair scraped back in a bun, every inch the exhausted relative burdened with the care of a dementia-stricken loved one. So far so predictable. But then as I reach the steps, I see a sight so horrifying it makes my legs buckle. There, huddled in a wicker chair in the corner of the room, is Maeve. Her head is lolling to the side at a disturbing angle, her arms hang loose over the edges of the chair. There is no movement coming from her, no sound. I have to do something.

'Maeve, it's all right,' I cry, pushing my way through the glass doors. 'I'm here now and I'm going to get you out.'

Jasper, Cordelia and the young man look on aghast as I rush to Maeve's side.

'Sorry,' says the young man, leaning forward in his chair. 'Are you another family member?'

'Maeve,' I say, taking her arms gently and pulling her towards me. 'Maeve, can you hear me? It's Alexis.'

Her body is limp but on hearing my voice she opens her eyes. They are milky and glazed. She opens her mouth as if to speak, then slumps back in the chair.

'What have you done to her?' I cry, leaping to my feet. 'She was perfectly fine when I left. What the hell have you done?'

'Alexis, calm down,' says Jasper, placing his teacup on the table. 'This is not your concern.'

'Not my concern,' I cry, my body trembling with rage. 'You are abusing a vulnerable woman in plain sight, a woman you have duped into being here. Listen, I know everything. About Lord Lustrum, about this place, about—'

'In answer to your question, David,' says Cordelia, smiling wearily at the young care worker. 'This woman is not a relative, she's a disgruntled ex-employee that Jasper and I had to dismiss. She'd been meddling with Mrs Hardy's medication and she was caught trying to steal her Rolls-Royce. We believe she was inflicting cruelty on a vulnerable old lady. She even sank so low as to hide Mrs Hardy's cat in the basement which, as you can imagine, caused Mrs Hardy no end of distress.'

I gasp as Daphne slinks from behind the armchair Maeve is sitting on, then lies down at her feet.

'What are you talking about?' I cry, incredulous. 'Maeve and I have been looking for Daphne for days. Why the hell would I hide the cat? And I've never been near the basement. I didn't even know there was one. As for the car, Maeve suggested I use it to drive to the village. If I was going to steal it I'd hardly come back with it, would I?'

'We said we wouldn't call the police,' continues Cordelia, her voice chillingly steady. 'But, Alexis, you're really not leaving us much option. And with photographic and recorded evidence of your misdemeanours, I wouldn't really rate your chances.'

She looks at me and for the first time I notice it, the cold-hearted evil.

'You're lying,' I cry, crouching by Maeve to try to coax her up. 'This is all nonsense, and you know it. You're trying to hoodwink this poor guy just as you did me and Maeve and Lord Lustrum.'

'I'm sorry but none of this is helping Mrs Hardy,' says David, as I try in vain to rouse Maeve. 'In fact, I'd say you're causing her more distress.'

'You see, this is what we've had to put up with the last few weeks,' says Cordelia, dabbing fake tears from her eyes. 'We employed this woman in good faith to care for Mrs Hardy and it turns out she's nothing but a crook.'

'You did no such thing,' I cry. 'Jasper employed me to help with his editing. It's a pack of lies. I'm not Maeve's carer, I'm . . . I'm her granddaughter.'

'As you can see,' says Cordelia, her eyes blazing with a mix of shock and rage as she steps between me and Maeve and bundles me towards the glass door, 'this woman is deluded. We get a lot of them coming here. Crazed fans of Maeve's, claiming to be related to her. She's just another one of them. Now, come on, Ms Harper, you've caused enough trouble.'

She gives me a sharp jab in the base of my back, which almost sends me tumbling down the steps, then slams the door shut behind me. I hear the key in the lock and turn to see her standing on the other side of the glass, her face fixed with a triumphant smile.

Staggering back across the courtyard, my heart lurching in my chest, I try to gather my thoughts. I could call Jonathan Farrow, but he's on a plane bound for Majorca. I could go back to the garage, tell Ken what has happened. He could summon the villagers, confront Jasper and Cordelia once and for all. Oh, come on, Alexis, I sigh, this is real life not *Game of Thrones*. And all that would happen is that Cordelia would repeat her accusations against me, which, if I'm honest, to an observer with no clue as to what has gone on these last few weeks, could seem highly plausible.

Back in my van, I sit for a moment, my phone clasped in my hands. There is only one person who can get Maeve out of here.

Pressing 'call' I close my eyes and wait. It's picked up after three rings. Between choked sobs I just about get the words out.

'It's me,' I cry. 'I need your help.'

36

ALEXIS

Of all the locations I may have imagined us one day reuniting in, the coffee shop at Canterbury train station was certainly not one of them. And yet now that she is here, sitting opposite me, her beautifully manicured fingers cradling a Styrofoam cup of coffee, I realize none of that matters. Just being in her company makes me feel safe, as though the leaden events of the last twenty-four hours, indeed the last fifteen months, have been lifted from my shoulders and I can breathe freely.

'You know I could have just dumped your call,' she says, looking up at me, her green eyes turning golden in the light of the sun pouring in through the window. 'I mean, Christ, Alexis, it's been well over a year of no contact save a few confusing phone calls. And now you just expect me to drop everything and help you.'

'I know, and I'm sorry,' I say, wanting desperately to touch her hand but knowing it would not be the right thing to do. Not yet. 'And believe me when I say I will explain everything, I swear I will. I just need to get Maeve out of that house first.'

'You promise me?' she says sternly. 'Once this is sorted, we'll talk? You won't just run away again?'

'I promise you, Tara,' I say, blinking away the tears that I've spent the last twenty minutes trying to keep at bay. 'From the bottom of my heart.'

'All right,' she says, taking a deep breath. 'Now tell me everything.'

As I give her a potted round-up of the past few weeks, she leans forward in her seat, clasping her hands tightly, and a sense of relief floods through me. My Tara. Champion of lost causes, lawyer extraordinaire. If anyone can help solve this, it's her.

'I still can't believe you found Maeve O'Malley,' she says, when I finish. 'Your childhood hero. And to think that she could be your grandmother. It's like you had a second sense about it.'

'To be honest, I haven't had time to let it sink in properly,' I say, aware of the clock ticking. 'For now, all that matters is that we get her out of there before she's carted off to some care home. Do you think that's possible?'

'If what you've told me about this Hardy couple stacks up and Farrow gets back to us ASAP to confirm the fraud on the Power of Attorney document, then I think we have a chance,' says Tara, draining her coffee. 'As for her being taken away, I'm pretty sure that guy was just there to assess her. And I'm also pretty sure he would need to have Maeve's GP confirm her condition before any decision is made. The whole thing sounds dodgy and Jasper and Cordelia are quite clearly not acting lawfully. But, Alexis, we're going to have to tread carefully and you're going to have to do exactly as I tell you, no rushing in all guns blazing. Is that understood?'

'Yes,' I say. 'Of course.'

But as I follow Tara out into the car park I know, deep inside me, I will do whatever it takes to rescue Maeve.

'Right,' says Tara, pausing by the front steps of the manor. 'Leave the talking to me and don't, whatever you do, lose your temper with them. And they haven't to know that I have any personal connection to you, OK?'

I nod my head, my stomach churning with nerves.

'Right, here goes.'

While Tara rings the bell, I take a cursory look around the drive. The care worker's car has gone though Jasper's Jag is parked in its usual place at the side. 'Please,' I whisper, as a light goes on in the hallway, 'please let her be all right.'

'Can I help you?'

The door has opened, and Jasper stands there, looking his usual dishevelled self. I draw back in the shadows while Tara introduces herself.

'Well, I have no idea what this is all about,' he says, grinning nervously. 'But you'd better come in.'

As Tara makes her way inside, briefcase in hand, I emerge and follow suit, to Jasper's horror.

'Oh, for goodness' sake, what now?' he says, blocking my way. 'Cordelia told you earlier, your services are no longer required.'

'I'm not here in a professional capacity,' I say, pushing past him. 'I've come to find Maeve.'

'This is preposterous,' he cries, the temper I have always suspected he was harbouring finally bursting forth. 'I'll have you arrested for trespass.'

'Darling, what is it?'

I turn to see Cordelia at the foot of the stairs. No longer

playing up the 'exhausted' image for the care worker's benefit, she has replaced the dowdy outfit she was wearing earlier with a floral midi-dress. Her face is fully made up and she has a glass of champagne in her hand.

'Celebrating something?' I say, anger burning inside me.

'Alexis,' whispers Tara, coming to my side. 'You have to keep calm.'

'Call the police, Cordelia,' says Jasper, clearly agitated now. 'This is harassment and trespass. Quick, darling.'

Placing her glass on the grand sideboard, Cordelia pulls her phone out of her pocket.

'I really wouldn't do that if I were you,' says Tara, her voice as cool as ice.

'Oh yes, and why not?' says Jasper, visibly rattled.

'Well, actually, what I should say is please do call them,' says Tara, her tall imposing figure dwarfing Jasper. 'You see, we came here to offer you the opportunity to confess of your own accord before we call them. And for you to vacate Ms O'Malley's property.'

'Confess to what?' cries Cordelia scornfully. 'Have you any idea who you're talking to? We own this house.'

'But that's not true, is it?' says Tara, turning to me with a nod. 'The deeds clearly show that Maeve O'Malley is the sole proprietor of Lustrum Manor.'

'Yes, but Jasper's her husband,' says Cordelia. 'And therefore has rights to it. Also, his wife has dementia, she's lost control of her faculties. David, the care worker, has been visiting at various intervals for the past year and has seen her decline. We are all in agreement that she needs specialist care, Maeve included, which is what she told David earlier this afternoon.'

'Where is she?' I say, my voice trembling with rage and fear. 'What have you done with her?'

'She's in a safe place,' says Cordelia, with icy calm. 'Where she can spend her final days in peace, being cared for by professionals.'

'But there's nothing wrong with her,' I cry. 'This is criminal, what you've done. Tell me where you've sent her.'

'Alexis,' hisses Tara. I catch her eye and she puts her finger to her lips.

'Enough of this,' says Jasper, striding over to Cordelia and taking her phone. 'I'm going to call the police myself. This woman is a menace. Moreover, I shall tell the police who you really are. A mad fan of Maeve O'Malley's who inveigled her way into this house with some cock-and-bull story about a car breaking down and, now, that you're related. You're nothing but a stalker and a dangerous one at that.'

He presses the emergency button on the phone and presses it to his ear. As he waits for it to pick up, Tara edges alongside him.

'And you, Mr Hardy,' she says coolly, 'are nothing but a fraud. Please, do get the police over here. I think they'd be interested to see the documentation we have in our possession. Retrieved from your filing cabinet is the following: the letter addressed to Ms O'Malley that you fraudulently signed for, the pile of forged prescriptions from the local pharmacy, and, oh, the counterfeit Power of Attorney document on which you faked the signature of a solicitor, Jonathan Farrow. All of which you had filed, perversely considering the nature of the documents, in a folder marked "Maeve".'

'What?' says Jasper, stopping the call, the colour draining from his cheeks.

'That's right,' says Tara, not missing a beat as the phone clatters to the floor. 'And I also have reason to believe that your marriage to Maeve O'Malley was not legally binding. Another fraud. And if you are not her legal husband then you have no claim whatsoever on this house or any of her assets. In addition, I understand that, despite your unfounded claims, Ms O'Malley is very much in control of her faculties. Now, you have two choices, Mr Hardy: you either tell us where Maeve is, or I call the police.'

'Jasper, don't listen to her,' cries Cordelia, black mascara running in rivulets down her face. 'She's bluffing. She doesn't have any such paperwork. How could she? You burned the other copy of the Power of Attorney on the fire, like I told you.'

He turns to her with a look of defeat and shrugs.

'I'm sorry, darling,' he says, slumping to the floor. 'I kept it. I thought we might need it.'

'I don't believe them anyway,' says Cordelia, her face pink with rage. 'They can't possibly have that document. The cabinet was locked.'

'And the key was under the plant pot,' says Tara calmly. 'It was a yellow folder, wasn't it, Alexis? Do show them.'

Cordelia lets out an anguished wail as I pull the file out of my bag and hold it up for them to see.

'Now,' says Tara, turning to me with a nod. 'The name of the place you've sent Maeve to? You have thirty seconds.'

While Jasper splutters out the name and directions to the care home and Cordelia paces the hall in a rage, I make my exit. Running down the steps, I take out my phone.

Jonathan Farrow's calm voice is a blessed relief after the vicious sniping of the Hardys.

'The police have the screenshots,' he says, the sound of tinny Spanish music in the background. 'I've confirmed it's not my signature and that the Hardys are a flight risk. They should be at the manor shortly.'

'All done?' says Tara, rushing out of the door as I end the call a couple of moments later.

'All done,' I reply.

Then, holding hands, we make our way back to the camper van.

'Right, let's go and find her,' says Tara, pulling on her seat belt as I start up the engine.

And in that moment, I'm not sure who she's talking about: Maeve, me, or my mother, but it doesn't matter. As we pull away, we see a set of blue lights in the rear-view mirror, hear the whirr of a police siren as it hurtles towards Lustrum Manor.

Justice will be served. Maeve is free at last.

37

MAEVE

George Whitman knew the importance of being hospitable to strangers. Why, he even proclaimed it on the walls of his beloved bookshop, knowing full well that any one of the tumbleweeds that floated through his door could be an angel in disguise. And never had that sentiment been more pertinent than at the moment when Alexis, the stranger who has proven to be my guardian angel, swooped through the door of the care home.

My head is foggy from the medication Jasper and Cordelia forced down my throat, so what has happened in the immediate aftermath of my release is still quite sketchy. All I know is that the people who sought to cause me pain and heartache, to defraud and undermine me, are being dealt with, and that my life is my own again. Alexis tells me that the deeds to Lustrum Manor and my beloved Hampstead flat, which Jasper and Cordelia had been letting out at an exorbitant rent, are safe and that I am free to go home. But as I sit here, wrapped up warm in the back of her cosy camper van parked up at a motorway services just outside Dover, I know that there is only one place I want to be right now, only one place to conclude this story. But first, it is clear that there are things Alexis needs to get off her chest.

'Now that we've had time to catch our breath,' she says to me, as I cradle a mug of hot chocolate in my hands, 'can we talk about Kimberly? She believed you were her mother. Was she right?'

Placing the mug on the pull-out table, I close my eyes and return to that autumn day in 1960.

'I'd been in London six weeks when I realized something was amiss,' I say, remembering the acute terror as though it were yesterday. 'William and I had been so passionate, so in love, we hadn't always taken precautions. I was naive, still just a child myself really, and it hadn't even entered my mind that I could end up . . .'

I pause as my mind skips forward to the doctor's surgery on Highgate Hill, the look of disgust on the GP's face as he confirmed both the pregnancy and my lack of marital status. 'You know there is only one option for you, Miss O'Malley, don't you?'

His words burned into me as I left the surgery and hurried across Hampstead Heath. It had all been going so well. I had found work as an assistant in a small publishing house in Bloomsbury and, through George's contact, digs in a sweet little cottage in Highgate Village which I shared with two other young women. I'd still had no word from William but by then I had resigned myself to the fact that he no longer wanted to be with me. When I'd called Le Mistral, Paula had said that neither William nor Sam had been seen since I left, that the rumour was they'd gone travelling round Europe together. When I heard that, it had felt like a knife to my heart, but it also served as confirmation that the Paris part of my life was over and if I was to have any chance of achieving my dream of being a writer I would have to throw myself wholeheartedly into my new life in London. But what I hadn't reckoned on was a baby, an illegitimate one at that.

'It was a different time back then,' I continue, looking up at Alexis and Tara who are huddled together in the front seats of the van. 'Though I would have loved to keep the baby, I was very young and, more pertinently, unmarried. It simply wasn't done. So, with the aid of some baggy jumpers and loose-fitting skirts, which didn't look too out of place in bohemian North London, I disguised the pregnancy as best I could and then . . .'

My eyes fill with tears as I recall the bare walls of the austere maternity home the GP had booked me into, the sharp, judgemental stares of the midwives, and how I screamed and hollered and pushed my child, the child William and I had created, out into the world that cold March morning.

'They took the baby away immediately,' I say, my voice catching in my throat. 'All I knew was that it was a girl, and that she had my eyes and William's chestnut hair.'

'And you didn't know where they had taken her?' says Alexis, her face etched with sadness.

'No,' I say, wiping my eyes. 'I was just expected to go home, get on with my life and forget about it, though I never did. It might not have seemed so, as I presented such a confident, happy facade to the world, but there wasn't a day that passed when I didn't think about my little girl and wonder where she was. How cruel that she had come to find me, and that monster kept her away. He couldn't even let me have that.'

'And because of him we have no idea where my mother

might be now,' says Alexis, her eyes filling with tears. 'And without her van, it's even harder to imagine where she might be or if she's safe. It's like I've lost her all over again.'

'But you've gained something too,' says Tara, gesturing to me with a smile. 'Both of you have.'

'And it's been the greatest blessing of my life,' I say, reaching forward to hold my granddaughter's hand. 'After all the losses we've endured, to have found each other feels like nothing short of a miracle.'

Alexis smiles and squeezes my hand.

'So, where to now?' she says, as I settle back into my seat, and she starts up the engine.

'Dover Port,' I say, without hesitation. Alexis and Tara turn round in unison, the pearly lights of the motorway services sign illuminating their stunned faces. 'And the next ferry to France.'

'But I thought you'd want to go home first,' says Alexis, turning her attention back to the road. 'Gather your thoughts. Make sure everything is as it should be.'

'I have no desire to ever set foot in that house again,' I say, the smell of burnt shepherd's pie still lingering in my nose. 'It's not my home. It never was. It was just part of their ruse. No, it's time to do what we set out to do before all this torrid business was uncovered. To find William.'

'You're sure?' says Alexis, her warm smile penetrating my bones.

'I'm sure,' I say, leaning back into my seat and closing my eyes.

38

KIMBERLY

April 2021

Paris in springtime. The perfect place to be. Yet as the cab driver heads across the Pont Neuf, I feel a deep sense of sadness that nothing – not the mid-morning light hitting the surface of the Seine and turning its milky waters momentarily golden, nor the reassuring bulk of Notre-Dame to my left, nor even the general sense of happiness that permeates the air as we enter the Latin Quarter – can alleviate.

I hoped to be returning here with good news, some photographs maybe or perhaps even a message from Maeve to William. Instead, all I have is the dog-eared copy of *The Time Traveller's Journey to Post-War Paris* minus a page, and a sickening feeling of dread.

It had been a chance meeting with a shamanic healer in Antibes that had set me on the road that led to Paris and then Lustrum Manor. In deep meditation, I had confessed to the healer how I walked out on my husband and child on Christmas Day 1988 and how the guilt of that action had eaten into me every day since. As my conscious mind gave way to the subconscious, I told him that I had recently found out that I was adopted but had kept this secret from my husband and daughter. I didn't know why I couldn't share this with them but I knew that, for as long as I could remember, I had felt like an outsider, that I didn't belong. Though I loved my daughter dearly, I had married far too young, searching, in my older husband, for a sense of family, a surrogate father figure. I could still feel that shame burning inside me as I recounted my story, the sense that I was unwanted and had, in turn, continued the generational curse and abandoned my own family. But there was no judgement from the shaman. Instead, he simply listened as I revealed how I had climbed into my camper van that day and driven all the way from my home in the North East to Dover Port, music blaring to drown out my thoughts. I told the shaman how I had driven onto the ferry as though in a dream and disembarked at Calais, then on to Paris, where I stopped, almost instinctively, at the bookshop in which, just a couple of months earlier while on a shopping trip with friends, I'd bought my daughter a copy of the latest Maeve O'Malley as a stocking filler. It was strange because it felt as though some invisible force was compelling me to go to France, to revisit that bookshop, buy a copy of another of Maeve O'Malley's books, and keep driving on and on, down the country across Europe and beyond, as though searching for something. I told him how, once I had started, I could not stop. As the months turned to years and then to decades, it became harder to go back. For what would I say if I did? How could I possibly explain to my husband and child why I had just upped and left them, seemingly without a second thought? So I kept going, living the life of an itinerant, finding work along the way, sleeping in my van. I became part of a community – the stragglers, the hippies, the wanderers – and was welcomed with open arms at gatherings and festivals that celebrated rather than condemned people like me. And it was in that spirit that I wound up at the Healing Flame festival in Antibes, where men and women decades younger than me danced with abandon, their faces and bodies covered in pastel chalk, and for the first time in almost forty years I felt old and out of place. I sat on the beach, a lonely woman on the verge of sixty, and wept as the sun set against a glorious lavender sky. I thought of my little Alexis, her pale face at the bedroom window as she watched me drive away, the ache in my heart that has never healed. That is when he found me, the shaman, and put me in the trance that would transform my life. When I came round, he held my hand and told me that the root of my unsettledness was a deep sense of loneliness, of not belonging. 'You've been running in the wrong direction,' he told me. 'Trying to escape home when you should instead be trying to find it. Find your parents and you will find your peace.'

And so, with a laptop and the help of a genealogy site, I started the year by searching for my birth family, sending off vials of spittle to determine my DNA which was then uploaded. Nothing happened at first but then, in the middle of February, two matches appeared: one in Connecticut and one in Paris. The Paris link had more detail. A man named William Kenneally who was putting together a family tree.

I had been wary at first, didn't want to get my hopes up, but all that went out of the window when I met William a couple of days later at his poky little studio apartment in a rough part of Saint-Germain-des-Prés, for he was my living double. We both shrieked when we saw each other, so close was the resemblance. Same hair colour, same smile, same bone structure. It was uncanny. And it wasn't just the looks. We were two sides of the same coin. Free-spirited, with a love of music and dancing and a hatred of being cooped up inside. I felt so at ease with him I was able to open up about my past and what I had done. I told him how I had looked Alexis up online and found that she had become a hugely successful editor working for the illustrious Scion Books, and lauded by her peers as 'the best in the business', I confided in him my fear that if I tried to get in touch with her, she would, quite rightly, tell me to get lost. I felt, as I have done every day since walking out, like the worst mother in the world but William didn't judge. Instead, he just listened and told me that, though I was scared she would reject me, one day I'd be reunited with Alexis and that she would forgive me. 'Age humbles us,' he told me, his soft Irish accent still evident though he'd spent years away from his homeland. 'It makes us see the foibles of our elders in a different light, makes us realize that they were just human too.' And his words comforted me. It was as though, in William, I had found not just my father but a kindred spirit. Then I realized time was running out.

'I'm dying,' he told me, as we sat on the terrace of his favourite café later that day. 'They say I'll be lucky if I get two more years. Emphysema. All those Gitanes. But listen, kiddo, I've spent years thinking that the greatest love I knew, the girl I still dream about at night, probably hated my guts. I reckoned she'd been told a bunch of lies about me and that she thought I'd cheated on her. I'd been warned not to go near her, and I heeded that warning, even though it broke my heart. You have to believe me, I had no idea she was pregnant when she left, and I can't imagine how hard it must have been for her to give you up. But what I remember of your mother is that she was tough. What she did that day, how she escaped her family to go off to a strange new country all by herself, well, that takes courage and she had that in spades. Of course I heard about her success. You'd have to be a hermit not to be aware of her. And though I always knew she'd make it, and I was incredibly proud of her, that success just put even more distance between us. If I'd tried to get in touch with her, particularly after what she'd been told about me, she'd have thought I was just trying to bask in her spotlight and sent me packing. See, I wasn't brave like your mother. I was scared, terrified in fact, of being rejected by her. But now things are different. I haven't long left and you appearing in my life like this, well, it seems like a sign. So, even though she's probably forgotten all about me, if I could see her, just one last time, I could die happy. I'm too frail to travel now but you could do it for me, couldn't you? Try to find her. Will you do that for me, kiddo? Will you try?'

And I promised him I would.

Now, almost two months later, I am back. And I am going to have to tell him that I couldn't honour the promise I made.

My eyes cloud with tears as I pull up outside his apartment, the horror of what I experienced at Lustrum Manor still fresh in my mind. Yes, I may have found her, his great love, but I didn't even get the chance to tell her who I was. Jasper, her husband, kept her locked away, said she was in poor health and had to be shielded from people in case she caught Covid, which would be deadly. I tried to assure him that I was regularly testing and coming back clear, but he was taking no chances. Sure, I could have just slipped a note under her door telling her who I was, but I was scared that in her frail state such news might give her a heart attack. In the end, in a last-ditch attempt, after I'd been banished from the house, I'd ripped out a page from my *Time Traveller* book and left it in the outbuilding with a little message for Maeve. Jasper had said they'd been talking about converting it into an outdoor writing space for her. It was a long shot, but I thought that maybe one day, perhaps when she was in better health, she would come in there while overseeing the conversion, spot my little message and realize who I was. I even updated my location on the genealogy site to the Latin Quarter in the hope that if she found it and came looking she might just come across William. But I know all of that was just wishful thinking on my part. I know deep down that she will never find the message in the outbuilding because she's virtually a prisoner in that house. Nor will she ever look me up on a genealogy site because, as far as she is concerned, Kimberly Harper was just some fake gardener who rocked up at her house and tried to steal her books. But worse than any of that is the fact that soon she won't remember anything or anyone. Not her husband nor her books, not even William. How do I tell him all this? How do I explain that I never got the chance to introduce myself to Maeve as her daughter, and that I can never go back there because Jasper framed me for theft? How do I put into words that William has lost the love of his life all over again to dementia?

Paying the driver, I climb out of the cab and head to

William's door. Pushing it open, I step inside and my heart flips inside my chest. The place is empty, all his stuff is gone.

'William?' I cry, yanking open the wardrobe, the cupboards, the bathroom door. 'William, where are you?'

As I sink to my knees in despair, I cry out for them, the parents I had spent my life searching for, the daughter I had abandoned. My voice reverberates around the empty room, a stark reminder that I am once again alone, and that no one, not William nor Maeve nor my beautiful Alexis, is coming to find me.

39

MAEVE

'Well, this is where I leave you.'

Tara wraps her belted camel coat around her tall, lean body as we stand by the ticket office.

'You're not coming with us?' says Alexis, and the disappointment in her eyes cuts through my heart.

'It's probably not a good idea,' says Tara, the wind blowing her bobbed blonde hair across her face. 'We still have so much we need to address, so much we haven't even begun to talk about yet, and I don't want to let that get in the way of you searching for your mum in Paris. Besides, I have meetings this week that I can't get out of.'

Alexis nods her head and watches as Tara turns to leave.

'What rot,' I cry, stamping my foot on the asphalt. Tara turns and looks at me, bemused.

'Maeve,' says Alexis, putting her hand on my arm, 'it's fine. Tara and I will catch up when we get back.'

'I say what rot because you two don't realize how lucky you are,' I say, as Tara walks back to us. 'It's clear you love each other very much. Alexis was overworked and grief-stricken by her father's death. She had a breakdown, made a silly mistake at work, and had to get away. And, yes, she could have been more honest with you, Tara, found a way to solve the problem together, but she didn't and here we are. Now, you can go home to London and let it all stew or you can get back in the van and join us on this road trip.'

'Maeve, please,' says Alexis, blushing. 'Tara has commitments in London.'

'No, she's right,' says Tara, her expression lightening. 'Why waste another second, eh?'

She links both our arms and as we head back to the van, Alexis whispers 'Thank you' in my ear.

'No need for thanks,' I whisper back. 'It's simply the correct order of things. And besides, there deserves to be at least one happy ending to this story.'

Alexis's phone rings as we set our bags down in the hotel room, and I stand by the window and look out across the Latin Quarter.

'I bet it's changed a lot since you lived here,' says Tara, coming to stand beside me while Alexis takes the call in the other room.

'In some ways, yes,' I reply, watching a pair of young men holding hands as they cross the street. 'And many things are for the better, though I feel that, deep in its soul, Paris will never change.'

'And it's stayed with you all these years,' says Tara, as Alexis comes back into the room. 'In your heart.'

'Yes, Hemingway's *Moveable Feast*,' I sigh, turning from the window. 'A spirit that once experienced stays with you always. And yet, if I am truly honest, it wasn't Paris that stayed with me, beautiful and evocative though the city is, it was the man I met here. I could have encountered William in Pittsburgh or Paris or Poland and it would have been the same. He . . . he spoke to my soul in a way that no other human being ever has before or since. That's why I need to find his resting place, say goodbye properly.'

'Well, we might be one step closer,' says Alexis, grabbing her jacket from the back of the chair. 'Before everything came to a head with Jasper and Cordelia, I'd put some feelers out through my old connections at Scion's French division and sent a message to the management of Shakespeare and Company, formerly Le Mistral, to see if they had any information on William, or if my mother had visited there recently.'

'Oh, but that's a long shot,' I say, with a sigh. 'I can't see them keeping tabs on customers. There must be hundreds coming in and out each day. As for William, well, it was so long ago and from what I recall no one really kept a record of the tumbleweeds after they left, they just drifted in and out, true to their name. There were the mini autobiographies George requested from each of them, of course.'

I feel a pang of remorse then as I recall how I never did get round to writing the autobiography George had asked me for. All the years of writing that followed and yet, back then, it seemed as though the words just refused to flow. I feel bad for that, a broken promise.

'Though they would only give a sense of their lives before and during their time at the shop,' I continue, picking up my train of thought. 'Not where they went afterwards.'

'That's what I thought,' says Alexis, helping me into my coat. 'But then I've just had a call from a woman named Sabine whose grandmother used to hang out at the shop back in the sixties. Sabine is working on a book about the tumbleweeds. The current manager of the shop had forwarded my query email to her, and she got back to me a couple of days ago to say she was meeting a man who worked there in the summer of 1960. He had agreed to come to the shop to help Sabine with the research. Apparently, he's got loads of documents relating to the tumbleweeds, bits of writing, autobiographies and other stuff. She said she'd call me when he arrived and ... well, Maeve, he's there now and I think you might just want to go and meet him.'

As I step into the cool dark labyrinth of the shop that though now named Shakespeare and Company will always be Le Mistral to me, the decades peel away and I'm eighteen years old again.

Nodding my head at the young person with blue spiked hair and a ruby nose ring who is standing behind the counter, reading a copy of Aldous Huxley's *Brave New World*, I make my way back through the very time portal I spent my professional life trying to recreate. The air fills with the scent of Gitanes and red wine and somewhere in the distance a scratchy jazz record plays on the gramophone. I see the tumbleweeds huddled together on the floor, clad in their loose woollen sweaters, tight capri pants and ballet pumps, their voices echoing off the shelves. I smile as I see Paula and Estelle, their lithe bodies entwined, as they dance to the music. I see George almost obscured in a cloud of smoke, sitting hunched over a bowl of fried potatoes and the one-page autobiography of whichever new tumbleweed has floated through the doors. I see the bookshelves crammed to bursting point, I see the sign with the quote about angels in disguise. I see fragments of the past jostling to emerge from the solidity of the present. I see everything.

Everything but him.

'Blythe?'

A man's voice, addressing me with the name I gave up in 1960. I turn, expecting to see my father or, God forbid, Amory, but instead I see someone who makes my legs buckle, my heart pulsate in my chest.

'So, it is you,' he says, coming towards me, his youthful, chiselled features still visible beneath the mask of old age. He is wearing a light-coloured blazer and navy slacks; his hair, white with flecks of gold, is combed neatly back from his face. The only sign of infirmity is the elegant walnut walking cane he is gripping on to. 'These ladies said it was, but I had to see it to believe it. Hey, what say we go get a hot chocolate, for old times' sake?'

I try to answer the question but all that I can muster is his name which falls from my lips like a detonating bomb.

'Sam.'

40

ALEXIS

The old man sits between us at the table in the far corner of the terrace. When Sam had suggested going for drinks, Maeve had been insistent: it had to be Les Deux Magots and it had to be this particular table.

'They called it Siberia,' says Sam, stirring sugar into his black coffee while Maeve sips her creamy hot chocolate. 'William and Blythe. It was their little in-joke. As always, I felt out on the edge of it all.'

'You were the human Siberia,' says Tara, laughing. Her joke goes down like a lead balloon but the fact that she cracked it makes me love her even more. 'Never change,' I whisper to myself, as I watch her sip her Pernod.

'I need to know what happened,' says Maeve, looking up at Sam with her shoulders hunched as though waiting to be delivered a blow. 'The day I left for England.'

'It was the night before,' says Sam, with a sigh. 'Around ten-thirty. William and I were on our way back to Le Mistral. I'd bumped into him outside Harry's where he'd just collected his last wages. He looked so upbeat, so handsome. And I was like a moth to a flame. I had no idea he was planning on leaving with you but maybe I had some sort of second sense 'cause that night I just wanted to stay by his side. I suggested I walk with him to Le Mistral and when we got close I hinted at coming in with him and staying the night but he was having none of it. All he wanted was you.'

Maeve lets out an anguished sob. I put my hand on hers, give her a reassuring squeeze. This must be hell for her to hear.

'Though I must say,' continues Sam, oblivious to Maeve's distress, 'that guy of yours was careful. He left no trace.'

'Amory Vaughan was no guy of mine,' says Maeve, her body stiffening. 'He was nothing but a thug and, in the end, no more than a cold-hearted killer.'

Sam looks at her, his cup half-raised to his lips.

'A killer?' he says, placing the cup down. 'Jesus, that's dark. Who did he kill?'

'Stop playing mind games, Sam,' snaps Maeve, her eyes blazing. 'I've had enough of that these past few years.'

'I'm not playing any games,' he says, raising his hands up. 'I swear. I have no idea what you're talking about.'

Maeve starts to tremble. Taking a blanket from the back of the chair I place it over her shoulders, then turn to Sam.

'William,' I say sadly. 'Amory Vaughan killed him that night.'

'Are you kidding with me?' says Sam, with a wry chuckle. 'Amory Vaughan didn't kill William. He just roughed him up a bit. You know William, he was made of tough Irish iron. Sure, he got a bit of a beating, but by the time I ran back to find him he was on his feet. He did have severe concussion though – repeated blows to the head will do that to you – so I got him to the nearest hospital just to be on the safe side.'

'What?' cries Maeve, throwing the blanket from her

shoulders. 'I . . . I don't understand. If he didn't die then . . . then why didn't he come looking for me?'

An awkward silence fills the air as we sit pondering the question. Finally, Sam leans across the table and takes Maeve's hand in his.

'I can't answer that question,' he says softly. 'Because when I left William in the hospital that night it was the last I saw of him. He told me, as he passed in and out of consciousness, that Amory had taken a photograph, a damning one, and that both of us were in danger. I told him Amory had only got a shot of us kissing, that this was Paris, two men kissing wasn't a big deal here. But William said Amory had threatened him with some obscure indecency clause, made out he was going to twist the facts to make it look like we were doing something much worse. Now that could have been a load of hokum for all we know, something Amory invented to intimidate William. But real or not, it did the trick because William was scared, real scared. As for him not coming to find you, well, perhaps I do know the answer after all. That fiancé of yours made it clear that he knew people in high places, not just in France but the US and England too. It seems William had no choice but to stay in Paris and lie low.'

'What a piece of work,' says Tara, shaking her head.

'Quite,' says Sam with a sigh. 'Anyway, I told William that somehow we'd get through this but he was heartbroken at losing you. He got real angry, said it was my fault for kissing him, that I'd ruined his life. Then he told me to get the hell out of the hospital and leave him alone.'

'Oh, Sam,' whispers Maeve. 'I . . . I'm so sorry.'

'You haven't got anything to be sorry about, my dear.

None of this was your fault,' he says, his voice heavy with sadness and regret. 'You know, the young me would have told you that William didn't give a damn about you. He'd have told you that he was the great love of William's life and that you were nothing more than a cute summertime fling.'

'And would you still say that?' whispers Maeve, tears running in thin rivulets down her papery cheeks.

'What do you think?' says Sam, smiling gently. 'One thing I've learned in this long – and some would say, eventful – life of mine is that age wises you up, it makes you see things for what they really are rather than what you want them to be.'

He takes a deep breath, lets go of Maeve's hand, then leans back in his chair and addresses his words to the violet evening sky.

'You were the one and only true love of William Kenneally's life and there wasn't a damned thing I could do about it,' he says, his voice cracking with emotion. 'He would have followed you to the ends of the earth and back. But though Amory Vaughan didn't kill him that night, he did take a life, the life William should have led with you.'

He sits up, wipes his eyes and continues.

'It warms my heart to see you two openly together and in love,' he says, turning to me and Tara. 'But the world of the early 1960s was a very different place. It didn't matter that William was in love with Blythe, that he intended to run away to England with her and set up home, have a bunch of kids or whatever. Amory Vaughan and the Aston-Laine family were never going to let that happen. Amory had that photograph and he was going to use it whichever way he could, to blow up whatever life William had planned. He knew what would happen if he came to find you, Blythe, and he knew that you would suffer too. He wouldn't allow himself to do that, he just couldn't.'

'Was he . . . was he happy?' says Maeve, her words muffled by her sobs. 'Did he manage to have . . . a good life?'

'Well, I doubt it was the extraordinary one you guys had planned,' says Sam, with a sigh. 'Though the truth is I don't know. You see, after losing William's friendship, Paris just wasn't the same for me. So, in the fall of 1960 I took off travelling round Europe, earning my way by working in various bookshops.'

'And William?' I ask, as the setting sun throws purple shadows onto our faces. 'Did you ever hear what happened to him?'

'Well, I kept in touch with Paula and Estelle over the years and they told me there'd been various sightings of him though he gave the bookshop a wide berth,' says Sam, leaning back into his chair. 'So it seems he never left Paris, which would make sense as I think he was terrified of what might happen if he did, whether your mother's goons would be on his tail.'

Maeve lets out a heavy sob of despair.

'William,' she whispers. 'My beautiful man.'

'Oh, but it wasn't all tragic,' says Sam, his expression lightening. 'I think he still managed to raise some hell. Apparently, he was spotted leading a charge of students in the Paris riots of '68.'

'That sounds like William,' says Maeve, smiling sadly. 'Always the rebel.'

'I moved back to the States from Europe in 1970,'

continues Sam. 'But Paula sent me regular updates on all things Latin Quarter over the years.'

'And are you still in touch?' says Maeve, pulling the blanket tighter round her shoulders. 'Would she know where William might be?'

'Sadly, she died ten years ago,' says Sam. 'But her granddaughter, Sabine, the young woman who was corresponding with Alexis, managed to get a lot out of Paula in her final months for the history of the tumbleweeds book, particularly with regard to characters like William. According to her, there was talk he was found dead in the alleyway outside the shop, or that he was seen waiting for a bed for the night, forgetting that it wasn't the 1960s any more; there was also the rumour that he was spotted on the Pont Neuf, peering into the water, and that a body had been retrieved the next day. And then there were various sightings of him propping up the bar at Harry's in the late noughties, looking as spritely as he had in his youth. Who knows if any of these were actually him? The crude answer being, no one knows what happened to William and I have a feeling we never will.'

'That was William,' whispers Maeve. 'Always the enigma. It is only right that it remains that way.'

'Though he did leave something,' says Sam, reaching into the leather satchel that he has placed by his feet. 'And though it doesn't tell you what actually happened to him, it gives a sense of what he wished *would* happen.'

'I don't understand,' says Maeve, watching as Sam pulls out a piece of yellowing paper from his satchel.

'Sabine gave me this at our meeting earlier,' he says, handing Maeve the papers. 'A shopworker had found it and passed it on to her, thinking it might be helpful for the book research. Sabine had been trying to work out who the two people in it were. Of course, she would never have realized it was you because the name is different. It had been found a few years earlier, rolled up and placed in a tiny hole above the archway. The one with the mural on. You remember it?'

'Angels in disguise,' whispers Maeve, taking the paper with trembling hands.

'Something like that,' says Sam, with tears in his eyes. 'Now, I'm going to leave you to read that in peace. After all, it's your story, not mine.'

He gets up from the table, shakes hands with me and Tara, then pauses by Maeve's chair. Her head is hunched over the paper, but she looks up as Sam touches her shoulder.

'It's been good to see you, Blythe,' he says, taking a handkerchief from his blazer pocket and dabbing his eyes. 'You take care, now.'

Maeve nods her head, but as he walks away she calls out to him.

'Thank you, Sam. And by the way, it's not Blythe. It's Maeve.'

He smiles, doffs his cap, then disappears into the early-evening rush of Boulevard Saint-Germain.

'What did he give you?' I ask, gesturing to the paper that Maeve is clutching in her hands.

'I have no idea,' she says, with a bittersweet giggle. 'You know how bad my eyesight it. I thought you might be able to do the honours.'

She hands it to me and as I read the faded, elegant handwriting, my eyes fill with tears:

The Life of Blythe Aston-Laine and William Kenneally: A Work in Progress.

William made the train with just seconds to go. Blythe shook her head as she watched him ambling along the aisle towards her.

'You're late,' she said, pulling him down into the seat. 'As always.'

'Got here in the end though, just as I promised.'

'Oh, William Kenneally, what are we doing?' she said, laying her head on his shoulder.

'I have no idea, kiddo,' he replied. 'But I have a feeling it's going to be quite the adventure.'

As the train hurtled out of the station leaving Paris and all its dreams behind, William closed his eyes and saw, spread out in front of him, the life he and Blythe were going to create.

He saw two writing desks. He saw a house bursting with life, with ideas, with laughter and conversation. He saw friends old and new gathered round a long kitchen table, putting the world to rights over copious glasses of red. He saw the two of them making a difference through their work, fighting the system and changing it, one word at a time. He saw them travelling the world side by side, seeing places he never could have imagined as a small boy in rural Sligo. He saw quiet moments too, gentle ones. His child whooping with delight as they rode a sledge across a snowy field. He saw books with his and her names on the spine, he saw the two of them lazing in bed, still hungry for each other despite the passing of time. He saw her black hair flecked with white, her beautiful face becoming more beautiful with age. He saw the children grown up and thriving, grandchildren and in-laws, more life, more noise, more love. Then he saw them, when the time finally came to say goodbye, hands clasped together, souls entwined for eternity.

'Are we there yet?' whispered Blythe, lifting her head from his shoulder and looking out of the window. 'I feel like we've been on this journey for ever.'

337

'Not long now,' he said, kissing her forehead gently. *'Besides, what's the rush? This is just the first chapter, kiddo. And I intend to savour every moment of it.'*

When I finish William's autobiography, I place it on the table, and we sit for a few moments in stunned silence.

'Well, I don't know about you, but I could do with another drink,' says Tara, breaking the impasse, as the waiter approaches.

'Absolutely,' says Maeve, pushing her hot chocolate aside. 'Though I'm ready for something stronger.'

As Tara places the order, Maeve turns to me, her face swollen with tears.

'So we've solved the mystery of William,' she says quietly. 'And I got to hear, through that beautiful autobiography, how he wanted our lives to turn out, how he truly felt about me. But what about Kimberly? She's still out there somewhere. I wonder if we'll ever find her.'

'I've spent my life missing her,' I say, as the waiter returns with three glasses of Pernod and places them on the table. 'But if we've learned anything this evening it's that some people, no matter how much you will it, just don't want to be found. My mother, I realize now, is one of them.'

'And yet part of me thinks that you will find her, when the time is right,' says Tara, placing her hand on mine. 'All that matters is that you have faith in her, as I have always had in you. This last year or so has been one of the most difficult of my life but I never doubted that you'd come back to me, Alexis. And bizarrely, it took you finding Maeve to make that happen.' She turns to Maeve and smiles. 'You know you were her hero when she was a child, don't you? And she had no idea you were her grandmother.

Those books of yours, well, I have no doubt they saved her.'

'And she saved me right back,' says Maeve, lifting her glass. 'My darling granddaughter. Well, here's to absent friends. May they be safe out there on the road.'

We raise our glasses and drink to our ghosts.

'Look at that,' Maeve says, pointing to the sky. 'The sun is setting at last.'

She leans her head on my shoulder and, as she does so, something falls out of her coat pocket. Tara bends down to pick it up.

'You've dropped something,' she says, pushing the little blue notebook, the gold-embossed heart glinting in the evening light, across the table. The little book she was writing in when she first met William that April evening in 1960. It seems she has kept it with her all these years.

We watch as Maeve folds the autobiography and places it inside the notebook.

'There,' whispers Maeve sleepily. 'Now he's with me for ever.'

'The story he wrote was so beautiful,' says Tara, her eyes welling up.

'Yes,' says Maeve, with a smile. 'It is what they call words to live by.'

She closes her eyes, and we sit and watch the velvet sky, three lost souls now found, until the light fades.

41

WILLIAM

Hôtel-Dieu Hospital, Paris

20 October 2023

The old man lying in bed number three in the intensive care ward is what the nursing staff here refer to as an 'âme désolée': one of those patients who arrive alone, receive no visitors and, ultimately, pass on without so much as a goodbye from a loved one. A desolate soul.

Sofie Barbier has just arrived for her twelve-hour shift during which she will work through the night, attending to the needs of the dozen elderly patients spread across the ward. All is still as she makes her rounds, save for a solitary light coming from the bedside lamp of the patient in bed number three. Sofie smiles to herself. It has been two weeks since he arrived here, with final-stage emphysema. His was a sorry tale. He'd been evicted from his apartment in March of 2021 and had spent the next two years living on the streets and in various hostels, a dying man. Eventually, his body wracked with pain, he had dragged himself to accident and emergency and been transferred here. And yet despite his suffering, no amount of breathlessness or super-strength medication seems to be able to stifle his insatiable appetite for reading. Tonight, as she peeks round the door, she sees, stacked up on the floor beside him, the pile of Hemingway, Baudelaire, Fitzgerald and Stein that he requested from the hospital library to reread before the end came, and in his hand a thick wodge of papers.

'Bonsoir, William,' she whispers as she steps inside, careful not to wake the sleeping inhabitants of beds number one, two and four. 'You are up late this evening. Would you like a warm drink to help you sleep?'

'No, thank you,' he says, looking at her over the rim of his half-moon spectacles. 'There'll be plenty of time for sleeping when I'm dead. Though I would like to ask a favour of you.'

'What is it?' says Sofie, sitting down on the edge of the bed.

'I'd like you to take this to the post office for me,' he says, handing her the bundle of papers. 'I'll pay for the package and the postage, of course. I just need to make sure it gets there.'

Sofie looks down to see what he has given her. What she reads makes her heart hurt.

'Where would you like me to send it?'

'Pass me that copy of *A Farewell to Arms*, would you?' he says, his voice croaky from the medication. 'I put the note with the address in there for safekeeping.'

Sofie does as he asks and picks up the book from the floor.

'You are quite the reader,' she says, handing it to him. 'I always wanted to read more though I never seem to have the time.'

'I had the opposite problem,' he says, opening the book. 'Always had plenty of time, too much if the truth be told. Now that time is coming to an end, the books have all been read, but there's one more story that still needs to be told. Here, take this.'

He slides a scrap of paper from inside the book and hands it to Sofie.

'If you could make sure the package is sent to this person at this address, I would be eternally grateful.'

'It would be my pleasure,' says Sofie, with a smile. 'This is quite an impressive address, no? Even I have heard of it.'

'Well, she is quite an impressive person, her mother told me,' says William, leaning back into the thick pillows. 'The best in the business. If anyone can be trusted to get that out into the world, it's her.'

'I will send it by the morning post,' says Sofie, getting up from the bed. 'It may take about a week to get there though.'

'I don't care how long it takes as long as it reaches my granddaughter,' says William.

'Your granddaughter,' says Sofie, with a gasp. 'My, you must be so proud.'

He nods, his eyes glistening.

'Now, if we send it via a courier, they will let us know when it gets there,' says Sofie, tucking the sheets around him. 'How does that sound?'

'Perfect,' says William, closing his eyes. 'I can rest easy now.'

London

27 October 2023

It is Clara Taylor's first day interning at the London offices of Scion Books and she is still finding her feet.

'Check the post room for parcel deliveries each morning,' the office manager had told her as she ran through her list of duties. 'And make sure they get to the right recipient, on time and in one piece. Understood?'

The gravitas of the task weighs heavily on Clara as she pulls the trolley full of packages out of the post room and into the lift. 'Prioritize deliveries to the editors on the second floor, everything else comes after that.' Heidi's words ring in her head as the lift doors open, and she steps out into the vast hub of the second floor.

Looking down at the bulky package on the top of the pile, the recipient's name printed in bold permanent marker, the sender's rather stark Parisian address stamped on the courier label, Clara has a second sense that this should be the first delivery. Parking up the trolley, she takes the package and the half-dozen other envelopes addressed to the same recipient and makes her way to the large corner office overlooking the Strand.

She knocks on the door and waits. There is no reply. Remembering what the manager had said about editors sometimes being out of the office for lunch meetings, she opens the door a fraction, sees that there is nobody there, and steps inside.

The room, unlike the other offices, is bare and barren. There are no photos displayed on the shelves, no piles of manuscripts on the desk, no potted plants, no books, no half-drunk cups of coffee. In fact, it looks as though whoever occupied this office has long gone. Still, thinks Clara, best to leave the post here anyway, just to be on the safe side.

Placing the packages on the desk, with the Parisian one on the top, Clara looks out at the sweeping view from the window, a spectacular vista that takes in the whole of the city.

'One day,' she whispers to herself, as she steps away. 'One day I will have an office like this, and I'll spend my days discovering new authors, new stories. One day I'll be just like Alexis Harper.'

Hôtel-Dieu Hospital, Paris

27 October 2023

Sofie Barbier arrives for her night shift feeling refreshed. After a briefing at the nurses' station, she makes her way to the ward to begin her rounds. The first port of call, bed number three. She wants to tell William that she has received text confirmation that his package arrived safely in London that morning. But as she approaches the room, she has a feeling, a nurse's knowing, deep in the pit of her stomach. One doesn't spend twenty years in this job without acquiring some kind of second sense. So when she opens the door and sees that bed number three is empty and stripped of its covers, that the pile of books has been placed in a cardboard box bound for the Emmaus thrift store down the street, she is not surprised or even saddened. It was time.

'Sleep well, William Kenneally,' she whispers as she passes the bed. 'May all your dreams be sweet ones.'

42

ALEXIS

Richmond

30 April 2025

'Welcome home, darling.'

I feel the warmth of Tara's hand on the small of my back as I walk once more into the house I left sixteen months earlier.

'I know it's going to take some getting used to after being in the van for so long,' says Tara, closing the door behind us. 'But I want you to know there's no rush. One step at a time, eh?'

'One step at a time,' I whisper, inhaling the familiar scents of lilies and strong coffee. 'That sounds like the right idea.'

'Why don't you put those down in your study,' says Tara, gesturing to the boxes of books Maeve pressed into my hands when I helped move her back into her beloved Hampstead flat earlier this week. 'We can sort them later. I'll go and make lunch. Cheese and pickle?'

'Perfect,' I say, kissing her on the cheek.

As she heads to the kitchen, I take a deep breath and open the study door.

All is just as I left it, save for a layer of dust on the bookshelves and a stack of plastic crates on the desk. Placing the box of books on the floor, I wander round the room, reacclimatizing myself. It was always such a peaceful space, a place where I could think clearly unlike my office at Scion where all sense of peace and tranquillity and clearheadedness seemed to evaporate.

Maybe, I think to myself, as I flop down into my ergonomic chair, maybe this could be my new, permanent workspace. Funny that what I was looking for was here all along, right under my nose.

The idea began to form when we were on our way back from Paris. I shared it with Tara and Maeve who, to my surprise, were as excited as I was. Though my old colleagues might find my plan to set up my own independent publishing house ludicrous, with Tara's help and a major new novel from Maeve O'Malley to debut with, I feel confident I can make it work. As Maeve always says, find the opening line and the rest will come. Well, here it is then, I think as I settle into my chair, the opening line of my next new chapter.

Pulling the plastic crate that is wedged precariously on the desk towards me, I open the lid and see a perfunctory note with the Scion branding across it:

FAO Alexis Harper. Contents from office.
Kind Regards, Clara Taylor (Publishing Intern)

'Well, thank you, Clara,' I say, taking a bulky brown Jiffy bag from the top and ripping it open. 'You've probably got my job by now.'

I shake my head ruefully as I pull out the contents of the package but as I place the sheaf of papers on the desk in front of me my heart lurches in my chest.

Forbidden Love
A Memoir
By
William Kenneally

The day passes slowly as I sit locked in place, reading the words of a man I never met but feel I have known for ever. The light fades outside, the sandwich Tara brought for me hours ago turns stale and congealed, the coffee cools to tepid brown water in the mug.

It is midnight when I finish the story of my grand-father's life. And as I place the papers into a neat pile, I lean back in my chair and smile. That was it. The miss-ing pieces Maeve had been scrambling to uncover: the life William had gone on to lead without her. And, in the end, that life was not as extraordinary as Maeve's — odd jobs in bookstores across Paris, bits and pieces of bar work when his health prevailed, some English tutoring in a night school and a handful of love affairs, though none seemed to go the distance. And yet it was in those simple moments, in the ordinary ups and downs, the triumphs and losses, the joys and pains, that William's life was made extraordinary. After all, I think to myself, as I go to head upstairs to find Tara, isn't that what we all want from life: a simple story beautifully told? But then, as I stand up from the desk, something flutters out of the manuscript. A note.

Dear Alexis,

What I didn't include in the manuscript is that your mother found me. Kimberly adored Paris as I did and even lived and worked for

a time in the old bookstore. Funny how history repeats itself, eh?
Anyway, she told me all about you and your prestigious career at
Scion. She'd been following your progress from afar and had heard
that you were the best in the business. Who better, I thought, to over-
see my manuscript than you, which is why I looked up your work
address and sent this package there. Alexis, I want you to know
that despite what happened, your mother loves you very much. My
dying wish is that you find it in your heart to forgive her. She is so
proud of you. As am I.

Yours,
Your loving grandfather,
William

Epilogue

The British Book Awards

Grosvenor House, London

May 2027

The evening is drawing to a close. Beside me Tara squeezes my arm and gestures to the statuette I am clutching in my hands. In all my wildest dreams, never did I imagine that Words to Live By, the independent publishing house I set up from my home study two years earlier, would end up winning Imprint of the Year. Still, though all my debut authors have been an absolute delight to work with and I am so excited at what they will go on to create, there is one major factor that allowed the company to thrive and to give me the capital to invest in new and upcoming authors.

'And now for the final award of the evening,' says the host, the impossibly glamorous TV presenter Sadie Swanson. 'Book of the Year.'

As the names of the nominees are announced, I look across the aisle and see my grandmother. She is dressed in the beautiful gold vintage Halston gown she wore to the 2017 book awards, where we'd had our first fleeting encounter. Her white hair is pinned up in a neat chignon and the trademark red lipstick is happily back in place. She is a million miles away from the cowed old lady who ran out in the road in front of me two years earlier. Now reunited with her beloved Daphne the cat and living between Hampstead and a Latin Quarter pied-à-terre, with a study that overlooks Boulevard Saint-Germain, she truly has come back to life. Her eyes shine as she listens to the stats Sadie Swanson is reading from her cue card.

'Five million sales worldwide. Winner of the Women's Prize for Fiction. The most anticipated comeback of the century,' she says, beaming out into the audience. 'It is my pleasure to announce that the Book of the Year for 2027 is . . .'

The auditorium descends into a collective hush. Clasping Tara's hand I close my eyes as I hear seven words that set my heart on fire.

'. . . *The Extraordinary Lives of Maeve and William.*'

My grandparents' stories entwined at last in the pages of a bestselling memoir.

After the ceremony, I rush to her side, knowing how much she hates crowds, and guide her carefully out of the auditorium. Well-wishers gather in the entrance, many of them women of my age, clutching their childhood copies of *The Time Traveller's Journey* for Maeve to sign. One of them, older than the rest, steps forward. In her layered maxi-dress and shaggy fur coat she looks rather out of place amongst the evening gowns and dinner jackets. At first I think she might be a reporter keen to rehash the Jasper and Cordelia trial that took place last year, in which they admitted, on top of a series of frauds, that they were indeed a married couple and that the wedding ceremony Jasper had conducted at Lustrum Manor for him and

Maeve was not valid. Their subsequent imprisonment and the fact that the case featured someone as high profile as Maeve attracted a lot of media attention. But as the woman draws nearer, I see her face, the familiar blue eyes, the Brigitte Bardot gap in her front teeth, and I realize this is not a reporter looking for the latest scoop. It is the person I have been searching for all my adult life.

'Mum?' I gasp.

'Alexis,' she says, her hands shaking. 'I'm . . . I'm so sorry, I . . .'

'How did you know where to find me?' I say, staring at her face, drinking in every detail.

'Through the book,' she says tearfully. 'I've been in Goa these last few years, gardening, drifting. One day, I wandered into a little shop and the book was displayed on a table. I picked it up and was astonished to see my mother and father's names on the front. I bought it and took it down to the beach, reading it in one sitting. When I saw your name and your new publishing house mentioned in the acknowledgements I burst into tears. It was as though a circle had been completed – Maeve and William, reunited at last, by my brilliant daughter. That was what I always wanted. I saw the award nominations announced online and made a note of when and where the ceremony would be taking place. I knew I had to come and find you. Both of you.'

Maeve lets go of my arm then and grabs my mother's hands, pulls her towards us.

And as she holds her girls close, there are no words – for none are needed now. We have all, after a circuitous route, come home.

MAEVE

Les Deux Magots

Four years later, sunset

You think it will never happen, old age. And yet it comes creeping for you just as it did for your grandparents, your parents, your loved ones.

These are the thoughts that whirr around Maeve O'Malley's exhausted brain as she sits in Siberia, nursing a Pernod and watching as the Parisian skyline changes from gold to pink to violet.

It has been a long life, longer than she would ever have imagined, and though it's had its dark moments they have only served to humble her, to make her even more grateful when she got the chance to make a comeback right at the end of Act Three. I mean, who gets to do that?

As the sun dips, she hears a familiar melody and looks up to see a lone violinist playing in the square just as on the first day she came here. With a smile, she reaches into her pocket and pulls out a tattered old notebook, its embossed gold star almost faded now, and places it on the rickety table in front of her. Closing her eyes she remembers a warm April evening, music in the air, and the whole of life laid out before her like an unbroken chain.

She feels time slowing, her body shutting down, and in her final moments she closes her eyes.

'Excuse me, is anyone sitting here?'

Opening her eyes she looks up and sees a figure standing before her, though his face is obscured by a dazzling light.

'William?' she whispers, rising to her feet, her body strangely weightless.

'Who else,' he says, extending his hand to her. 'Now, what took you so long? It's been years.'

'Oh, my darling,' she sighs, taking his hand as they walk together into the brilliant white light. 'Surely you know by now that some things are worth waiting a lifetime for.'

Acknowledgements

I would like to thank the following people for their encouragement and support as I wrote *The Paris Bookshop Secret*.

Vikki Moynes and Lydia Fried for their editorial magic. It has been such a joy to work with you.

My agent, Liv Maidment, and all the team at the Madeleine Milburn Literary, TV & Film Agency – the best support team an author could wish for.

Ellie Hudson, Rosie Safaty, Leah Boulton and everyone at Viking Penguin.

Thanks also to Mary Chamberlain for the meticulous copy-editing.

Heartfelt thanks to Trudy Nicholls and Dido for the generous insights into life on the road in a VW camper van.

The magical book palace of dreams that is Shakespeare and Company, and its late founder, George Whitman. Thank you for captivating me all those years ago and continuing to inspire and delight in equal measure.

I wrote this book in the aftermath of the deaths of my parents, Luke and Mavis Casey, and a period of profound and life-altering changes. As I navigated this strange new world of loss and grief, I knew the only way I would be able to make sense of it all was to write through it. And, as always, storytelling proved to be the life raft that I needed. *The Paris Bookshop Secret* is not only a tribute to my parents – who raised me on a diet of Behan, Hemingway and

Fitzgerald, while never doubting the existence of angels, kismet and true love – but also a testament to the importance of living life authentically, of taking a leap into the unknown, and, in this increasingly volatile world, the healing power of words.

Special thanks to my wonderful family and friends for their unstinting love and support.

Finally, to my son, Luke. Thank you for being my biggest inspiration. I love you all the world.

I found the following books and broadcasts incredibly helpful as I wrote and researched *The Paris Bookshop Secret*:

Brendan Behan in Paris, RTÉ documentary, produced by Deirdre McMahon and Tim Desmond. First broadcast on RTÉ Radio 1, 6 September 2019.

Shakespeare and Company by Sylvia Beach.

À Propos de Paris by Henri Cartier-Bresson.

Paris Journal: 1956–1964 by Janet Flanner.

Paris by Julien Green.

A Moveable Feast by Ernest Hemingway.

Books, Baguettes and Bedbugs: The Left Bank World of Shakespeare and Co. by Jeremy Mercer.

The Beat Hotel: Ginsberg, Burroughs, and Corso in Paris, 1957–1963 by Barry Miles.

On a station platform, with nothing to read,
and a four-hour train journey stretching ahead of him...

That's where the story began for Penguin founder Allen Lane.
With only 'shabby reprints of shoddy novels' on offer,
he resolved to make better books for readers everywhere.

By the time his train pulled into London, the idea was formed.
He would bring the best writing, in stylish and affordable
formats, to everyone. His books would be sold in bookstores,
stationers and tobacconists, for no more than the price
of a ten-pack of cigarettes.

And on every book would be a Penguin, a bird with a certain
'dignified flippancy', and a friendly invitation to anyone who
wished to spend their time reading.

In 1935, the first ten Penguin paperbacks were published.
Just a year later, three million Penguins had made their
way onto our shelves.

Reading was changed forever.

—

A lot has changed since 1935, including Penguin, but in the
most important ways we're still the same. We still believe that
books and reading are for everyone. And we still believe that
whether you're seeking an afternoon's escape, a vigorous debate
or a soothing bedtime story, all possibilities open with a book.

Whoever you are, whatever you're looking for,
you can find it with Penguin.